a pretty mouth

"*A Pretty Mouth* is a fine and stylish collection that pays homage to the tradition of the weird while blazing its own sinister mark. Tanzer's debut is as sharp and polished as any I've seen."
—**LAIRD BARRON**, author of *The Croning*

"If Hieronymus Bosch and William Hogarth had together designed a Fabergé egg, the final result could not be more beautifully and deliciously perverse than what awaits the readers in *A Pretty Mouth*. Molly Tanzer's first novel is a witty history of the centuries-long exploits of one joyfully corrupt (and somewhat moist) Calipash dynasty, a family both cursed and elevated by darkness of the most squamous sort. This is a sly and sparkling jewel of a book, and I can't recommend it enough—get *A Pretty Mouth* in your hands or tentacles, post-haste, and prepare to be shocked, charmed, and (somewhat moistly) entertained!"
—**LIVIA LLEWELLYN**, author of *Engines of Desire*

"Molly Tanzer is a prose Edward Gorey, decadent, delicious, and ever so slightly mad."
—**NATHAN LONG**, author of *Jane Carver of Waar*

"This is form and content and diction and tone and imagination all looking up at the exact same moment: when Molly Tanzer claps once at the front of the classroom."
—**STEPHEN GRAHAM JONES**, author of *The Last Final Girl*

"Had the nineteenth century really been like this—with the flounces and corsets and blood and tentacles and whatnot—we'd all be dead by now. Unlucky us, but lucky you, Dear Reader, as you are alive to read this book."
—**NICK MAMATAS**, author of *Bullettime*

"The stories and short novel in Molly Tanzer's impressive debut collection move steadily backwards through English history, from an Edwardian resort to a Roman encampment, stopping on the way for the nineteenth, eighteenth, and seventeenth centuries, all in the interest of tracing the main trunk of the notorious Calipash family tree all the way to its roots. It's a line

marked by its excesses of sensuality, cruelty, and sorcery, and in excerpting the exploits of its storied members, Tanzer demonstrates her facility with a variety of voices and styles, from Wodehousian farce to Victorian erotica to Restoration class comedy. Each of the narratives collected here stands and succeeds on its own terms, but taken together, they add to a whole greater than the sum of its parts, in which the recurrence of key motifs in a diversity of settings creates the sense of a family living out its doom generation after generation. Tanzer is an ambitious writer, and she is talented enough for her ambition to matter."
—**JOHN LANGAN**, author of *The Wide, Carnivorous Sky and Other Monstrous Geographies*

"*A Pretty Mouth* is many things; erudite, hilarious, profane, moving, learned, engaging, horrific, terrifying, and profound. Molly moves through the multi-forms of prose like a shark in wine-dark seas, rife with allusion, deep in emotion, and sometimes giving you a little salty-mouth. A fantastic collection and not one to be missed."
—**JOHN HORNOR JACOBS**, author of *This Dark Earth*

"Molly Tanzer's *A Pretty Mouth* is a spectacular book, rad and weird and fun. With winks to P. G. Wodehouse, Robert E. Howard and the Cthulhu Mythos of H. P. Lovecraft, it showcases the work of a woman who delights in writing. She writes very well indeed! This is a book I will return to, for to read it is such a naughty pleasure."
—**W. H. PUGMIRE**, author of *The Twisted Muse*

"I am a bit bashful about being titillated by Molly Tanzer's naughty debut, A PRETTY MOUTH, but I must admit it in order to write this blurb. While having segments that are hot and sexy, it is also a dark and disturbing tale with a wicked sense of humor and compelling chracaters. I blush just thinking about it and might have to go read it again!"
—**ALAN M. CLARK**, author of *A Parliament of Crows* and *Of Thimble and Threat: The Life of a Ripper Victim*

"It's been repeatedly said we're enjoying in a new golden age of weird and fantastic fiction. We are, and this lady is one the gifted magicians whose literary creations are keeping the bonfire burning brightly!"
—**JOSEPH S. PULVER, SR.**, author of *The Orphan Palace*

"Tanzer lifts the skirts of Victorian hypocrisy for a full Monty view of perverted hijinks and fun."
—**MARIO ACEVEDO**, author of *Werewolf Smackdown*

a pretty mouth

Wendy!!!
I ♡ you!
you're so awesome.

[signature] HPLFF 2013

A LAZY FASCIST ORIGINAL

Lazy Fascist Press
an imprint of Eraserhead Press
205 NE Bryant Street
Portland, Oregon 97211

www.lazyfascistpress.com
www.bizarrocentral.com

ISBN: 978-1-62105-050-6

a
pretty mouth

molly tanzer

lazy fascist press

table of contents

"The provision, then, which we have here made is no other than *Human Nature*. Nor do I fear that my sensible reader, though most luxurious in his taste, will start, cavil, or be offended, because I have named but one article. The tortoise—as the alderman of Bristol, well learned in eating, knows by much experience—besides the delicious calipash and calipee, contains many different kinds of food; nor can the learned reader be ignorant, that in human nature, though here collected under one general name, is such prodigious variety, that a cook will have sooner gone through all the several species of animal and vegetable food in the world, than an author will be able to exhaust so extensive a subject ..."

—Henry Fielding, from *Tom Jones*

a spotted trouble at dolor-on-the-downs

Though I am certain my fellow members of the Junior Ganymede Club for Gentlemen's Personal Gentlemen are well aware of the pleasures concomitant with our profession, it is, I believe, still worth noting that there are several substantial risks when one's chosen profession is that of valet, especially when contrasted with butling. Butlers serve households, and households, being inanimate entities, are therefore neither whimsical nor capricious; nor, as is perhaps more relevant to my point, are they able to lose wagers so spectacularly that it necessitates the loaning out of their employees to settle their debts.

Perhaps I stretch my metaphor too far; then again, perhaps not. I would do well at this juncture to cease speaking in generalities, and note that I am in fact referring to a recent, and specific incident.

Since the Junior Ganymede's rules specify that "every member must promptly, accurately, and unflinchingly record any compromising or embarrassing information about his employer in the Club Book," I should confess straightaway that the antecedent to my taking up the pen this afternoon was another instance of my employer's regrettable inability to successfully win a bet. One might think that a gentleman so well-known to himself and to others as particularly possessed of poor luck—or, if I might be forgiven for saying it, *insight*—would cease to gamble, but then again, one of Mr. Wooster's most endearing characteristics is his eternal optimism, and, it must be said, perpetual unwillingness to heed the Socratic advice "*gnothi seauton.*"

This particular loss was keenly felt by him I am sure, but, unusually, it affected me, as his failure brought about my temporarily leaving his service and remaining at a seedy seaside resort at Dolor-on-the-Downs in the service of a frightful heiress and her notorious brother, and participating in certain events so scandalous an account of them could, for a considerable time after the conclusion of the affair, be found in all the major papers, though those accounts were not at all complete. Therefore, perhaps my earlier analogy is an apt one.

***

The troubling incident to which I refer happened some weeks back, during Mr. Wooster's annual mid-summer seaside holidaying. This year was unusually vexing during the planning portions of the sojourn, for Mr. Wooster's formidable aunt, Mrs. Agatha Gregson, requested—which in her case means *required of him*—that he join her at Dolor-on-the-Downs, in the south.

Truth be told, my employer did not much want to attend Mrs. Gregson during his seaside holidaying, Dolor-on-the-Downs not being his usual haunt and Mrs. Gregson being the sort of lady who enjoys match-making and whist more than bracing sea air, but she impressed upon him that it was important to her. After the fifteenth telegram in three days demanding his presence, and the nigh-constant arrivals of mail-order holidaying necessities such as umbrellas, bathing costumes, and straw hats in both his and my sizes, he realized that to go down for a week or so would be far less of an inconvenience than continuing to refuse.

Dolor-on-the-Downs is, like so many seaside towns, a place of distinct seediness. There was one street of hotels acceptable for human habitation, and the rest of the place was a hotch-potch of inferior lodgings, taffy shops, ice cream parlors, boardwalks, performers busking on streetcorners, teashops where the very windows bore a light sheen of grease, and, of course, public houses. During the season, children with sticky faces and sunburns run hither and yon without heed for the eardrums of others, and the beaches are clogged with their adoring parents, also sunburned, but less often sticky-faced.

The hotel where we were to attend Mrs. Gregson was one of the acceptable ones, though barely. The Marine Vivarium, as the place was called, tended toward the ostentatious rather than the tastefully luxurious. It was once owned and managed by a man of Continental extraction, Mr. Gabriel Prideaux, who had a passion for aquariums; after he died, his daughter, a Miss Cirrina Prideaux, took over management—as well as her father's life's work: Collecting rare and unusual aquatic specimens for the greater glory of the hotel. Thus, everywhere one looked there were aquaria—some large, some small, some salt, some fresh, all lined with stones and filled with colorful, ornamental creatures and underwater plants. There were big square aquaria full of native sea-beasts (as Milton might call them) set about on pedestal tables and sideboards, there were vase-shaped ones containing Asian specimens that adorned shelves and sinks; in the hotel's restaurant there was even one entire wall that was an aquarium, full of fish one could, if one so chose, select and then consume. The memory of such a frightful gimmick in an establishment of alleged good reputation still troubles me.

At the time, I thought the garishness must be the reason there were so few other patrons, and also the strange lassitude of those who were out and about. Now I know it simply contributed to that situation, but I do not like to get ahead of myself.

One of the reasons Mr. Wooster was so reluctant to join his aunt at Dolor-on-the-Downs is that, as I previously noted, Mrs. Gregson has often attempted to marry him to this girl or that. 'Often' is, perhaps, an understatement. She has for several years pursued this aim with as much vigor as a Continental monarch eager to expand his nation's borders through wedding his son to an adjacent king's daughter. It frustrates Mrs. Gregson to no end when Mr. Wooster refuses her help, however, so after her third unsuccessful attempt to lure my employer into a matrimonial state with the young ladies she had discovered among the local families of good breeding—including, unsurprisingly, Miss Cirrina Prideaux— Mrs. Gregson took her leave of us, and in rather high dudgeon. I am sorry to report that it was then that my troubles began.

Here I should mention that also staying at the Vivarium at that time was an old school acquaintance of Mr. Wooster's ("chum" being perhaps too strong a word to use here), Alastair Fitzroy, the twenty-seventh Lord Calipash. I had never met the man before, but knew something of the Calipash family, of course—it is not for nothing that the good people at Burke's contacted me when compiling their most recent edition of the *Peerage*—and suffice it to say I possessed less enthusiasm about this turn of events than my employer. The Calipash line, as I am sure all the other members of this club well know, is … *tainted*. Members of that family tend to be eccentric if not totally insane, and from their origins to the present day there have been reports of Calipashes engaging in such behaviors as voluntary demonic possession, murder, necromancy in the classical and modern sense of the word, black magics of all kinds, sexual perversion, cannibalism, and, perhaps counterintuitively, militant veg-etarianism. I was therefore grateful we had not seen much of the Lord Calipash; only when he was eating alone in the dining room or drinking alone at the bar. He spoke to no one and looked, if I may be so bold, rather moth-eaten and out of spirits for someone of his rank. But as the rest of the noblesse who were staying at the Vivarium also appeared somewhat depressed, at the time I attributed it, as I said, to the décor.

Prior to Mrs. Gregson's departure Mr. Wooster had not much time to idle at the bar; once she departed he headed there directly. As a courtesy he invited me to come along, which is how I came to make the observations that began this account.

"What-ho, Fizzy," said Mr. Wooster, as I took a seat at the furthest end of the countertop, where I could observe both a tank full of exotic Caribbean fishes, and how my employer got on with the famously waspish Lord Calipash. "Care for some company? You look about as happy as a fox who's eaten the last chicken. Which is to say, not at all."

The Lord Calipash looked at my employer with some coolness.

"What?" he asked.

"You know," said Mr. Wooster, undaunted, "because foxes are hungry little coves, aren't they, and thus it seems likely they'd be prone to despondency when the bouillon's been slurped. Let me buy you a drink?"

"What about a Corpse Reviver #2?" suggested the bartender. He was polishing a glass at the time, of course. "Just learned that one. My friend just came back from London with the recipe. Learned it from Mr. Harry Craddock himself."

"Just the thing! Young Fizzy over here does have a rather *mortuary* look about him, what?"

As I idled over my glass of porter, the bartender mixed together Lillet, lemon juice, gin, and a few other ingredients, and the libation was consumed quickly by the two gentlemen. The drink did seem to revive the Lord Calipash, and he and Mr. Wooster consumed several more over the next hour.

"Well, Bertie. You certainly seem to be doing well for yourself," said the Lord Calipash. "Natty suit, smile on your face. Plenty of cash to throw around as you like."

"Can't complain," said my employer jovially. "Lots of days in a year and I live all of them more or less happily. But what about you, Fizzy? What's got you all long in the face? Everyone staying here seems down in the mouth, but *you*—you look, if I may say so, awful."

"Oh, it's nothing," said the Lord Calipash, running his finger around the rim of his glass. "Rum bit of business. Too bally complicated to bother you with."

Mr. Wooster smiled, and ordered another round from the bartender. "I forgive your coyness as we haven't had a wheeze since Oxford, but you should know I'm a bit of a whiz-bang with rum businesses, Fizzy. Tell me of your troubles, and if I can't aid you, then my valet will—the dark, tall fellow over there in the corner: Jeeves. He's the brainiest man I've ever met! Solves five unsolvable quandaries before breakfast, you know, just to keep in practice." Mr. Wooster, after relaying these flattering sentiments, leaned in to the Lord Calipash conspiratorially. "*It's the fish.* Eats it all the time—were I that French Fancy who runs this flophouse, I'd be watching the tanks!"

"Really," said the Lord Calipash, and though I am neither a whimsical man by nature, nor the heroine of a Gothic romance, I felt a chill as his eyes raked over me. "You know, come to think of it I've heard of this Jeeves of yours. Ran into young Tuppy Glossop last Christmas. Said Jeeves was the only reason he was still engaged to your cousin Angela."

"Very likely the case."

The Lord Calipash tipped the last of his drink down his throat. "Not a bad plan of yours, this. The drinks, I mean."

"We Woosters have a knack for bucking up comrades in need," agreed Mr. Wooster, who was listing slightly by then, his constitution having been depleted by several days of aunt-induced abstinence. "Pity you didn't come and see me in London about your woes. I'm a dashed good mixer of cocktails myself."

"Are you?"

"I am."

An unpleasant light came into the Lord Calipash's eye.

"If I recall correctly, when we were at Oxford you were always just the bloke for a little sport, weren't you, Bertie?" he said. "How's about it? Think you're a better barman than our fine mister—what's your name again?"

"My name is Marincola, m'lord."

"So you think you're better at drink-making than Mr. Marincola here?"

My spirits sank as I saw Mr. Wooster perk up.

"Indeed," said he, slapping his hand on the countertop. "This Mr. Marincola's as good as they come for the old what-and-mixer—really Mr. Marincola, you are to be commended—but me? I'm the real Tabasco."

Now, I do not like to speak ill of any member of the aristocracy, but I suspect, given what transpired next, that the Lord Calipash proposed his wager out of interest rather than sportsmanship. I suspect this due entirely to the quickness with which the Lord Calipash proposed these very high stakes: If my employer won, it was decided the Lord Calipash would give him the use of his country seat in Devon, Calipash Manor, for a week-long retreat, expenses paid, guest list to be determined by

Mr. Wooster. But if the Lord Calipash won, then my employer would be compelled to give him the use of his valet—*me*—in order to help the Lord with a delicate endeavor that needed prompt and insightful attention.

Though Mr. Wooster is deservedly proud of his ability with bar spoon and shaker, that day, owing I suspect to his being first a drinker of cocktails before a mixer of the same, he flubbed the proportions of his "Rob Roy" and produced a drink unworthy of the Highland cowherd for which the liquid refreshment receives its appellation. The libation's reception by an impartial judge (Lord Tolbert of Holland Park, who was also staying at the Vivarium) was, unsurprisingly, not favorable. After shaking awake Lord Tolbert, who had fallen asleep in his chair, Mr. Wooster told him of the wager. Undeterred by the Lord Tolbert's protestations that he was too indisposed to do anything as rigorous as taste one drink much less two, Mr. Wooster handed him the glass, he sipped—and spat. Feeling as though to get Lord Tolbert to sample Mr. Marincola's cocktail would be adding insult to injury, the bet was peremptorily decided in the bartender's favor, and it was with a dour air that my employer joined me, after the Lord Calipash staggered off to dress for dinner.

"Well, Jeeves," said Mr. Wooster, "I've done you a mischief this day, I fear."

"Is that so, sir?"

"Promised your services to that cove Fizzy, to help him with some sort of trouble. Said he would only discuss it with you."

"I shall endeavor to assist him, sir."

"Well you'll be endeavoring by yourself. I'll still return to London tomorrow, need to get back to it, what? The daily grind, all the matters requiring my attention."

"I imagine your social club will have missed you sorely, sir."

"Do I detect a sour note in the dulcet chord of your voice, Jeeves?"

"Oh, I hope not, sir."

"Wouldn't show the proper feudal spirit at all."

"No, sir."

"You understand … things are a bit, well, *dull* here, is all."

I saw my employer looking out over the bar, where each and every patron dozed wanly in his chair, including Lord Tolbert, who had fallen back into his reverie the moment he was no longer needed as a judge; outside, on the deck, men and women alike napped in their lounge chairs, too.

"Things do seem strangely quiet at the Vivarium, sir."

"*Too* quiet, if you ask me. Just—well, mind yourself, Jeeves, with this weird snoozy crew at Dolor-on-the-Downs, and keep a sharp lookout for Fizzy, too. Strange chap." Mr. Wooster looked thoughtful for a moment. "Seem to recall something when we were at school, maybe about an alleged murder or two, nothing much. Oh, and some unpleasantness where he was found to be keeping a girl under his bed."

"Sir?"

"No girls allowed in the rooms."

"I should imagine not, sir."

"But that wasn't the real scandal. No, no. I saw the filly when the police came. Didn't look well. Bony thing, pale. Needed to get more sun. But what can you do? Lads will be lads, what? And you know, old school chum and all that. You'll be fine."

"As you say, sir."

"Just be happy his dreadful twin sister isn't here on holiday with him. She's a fright. We were thrown together a few times at mixers, she was at Girton and would come down from Cambridge sometimes. Never tried to get engaged to me, that's the most I can say for her. She was one of those brassy, brazen, loud-talking, short-haired, tweed-wearing girls you find all too often in this lax post-war era. Yes," said Mr. Wooster, shoving his hands into his pockets, "If Alethea were here, by Jove, you'd really have a problem."

I am sorry to report that Alethea Fitzroy actually *was* staying at the Vivarium. I had seen her arrive with her brother a few days after we did, but not since. All I knew from below-stairs gossip was that she used quite a lot of bath-water and took all her meals in her rooms.

"Fizzy said he wouldn't keep you for more than a few days. You should be back home in no time."

"Let us hope so, sir. Shall I help you dress for dinner and pack up your things?"

"Excellent notion. Oh, and I'll hop an early train tomorrow."

"How early, sir?"

"Not before noon, I'd say. Need to be full of beans for when I'm back in the old metrop., you know." Then Mr. Wooster lost all his color and began to twitch like a ferret.

"Sir, are you in need of—"

"Must run, Jeeves—there's Cirrina, the odious manageress. She's an *eel*, Jeeves—wrapped around me and began to squeeze the moment Aunt Agatha introduced us."

"The behavior you describe is more akin to a python than an eel, sir."

"Bother that, Jeeves. It was too close a shave—she's a menace. Let us fly!"

So it was after the luncheon hour the next day that I knocked on the Lord Calipash's door.

He flung it open, and for a moment we regarded one another in silence. I cannot say what the Lord Calipash was thinking, but I know for my part I was feeling ill at ease over the sartorial blindness of the Lord Calipash's valet. I simply could not account for it. The gentleman was sandy-haired and pale, thus the lightness of the suit he wore gave him a sallow appearance, and he was wearing his trousers too low. And the trousers themselves! They had not been brushed or pressed properly for some time, and the material, though initially of good quality, was beginning to look worn and unbefitting someone of his station.

"Come in, Jeeves," he said at last, "and tell me what you know about octopuses."

I stepped inside and put my valise down beside the hall table. As I looked around, I began to wonder if the Lord Calipash had brought a valet with him—or employed one at all. First his clothing, and now, these chambers! The rooms were similar to Mr. Wooster's, but with fewer windows and furnishings, and on a significantly lower floor. Though of an acceptable size the apartment seemed cramped, for it was strewn with shed clothing, cups with a quarter inch of wine in them, plates fouled with crumbs and bits of nibbled crust, and, I noted, several aquaria that I believe if I had enquired with the management, should have been elsewhere than the Lord Calipash's private rooms.

"I am not unacquainted with those unique characteristics of the cephalopodan mollusks of the order octopoda, m'lord," I said. "What in particular, may I ask, has piqued your curiosity?"

The Lord Calipash was smoking a cigarette, and before answering took a drag on it in a languid, idle manner that might have been pleasing in a gentleman with a more affable expression—but his contemptuous mien made his affections appear more dissolute than elegant.

"What I want to know is what the deuce is so fascinating about the little blighters," he said, exhaling twin blue plumes through his nostrils.

"I could not say, m'lord. I am sure to octopodean enthusiasts, the creatures are possessed of many interesting attributes. Take, for example, *amphioctopus marginatus,* sometimes called the 'coconut octopus.' This unusual specimen from the Pacific Ocean has been seen using shells or discarded coconut husks as a form of shelter. Additionally, it—"

"Never mind your ruddy coconut husks, Jeeves."

"No, m'lord."

"I don't care a jot for this or that sort and what they do with their time."

"Yes, m'lord."

"What I want to know is why anyone would travel to Dolor-on-the-Downs to see one, and then choose to remain here for the whole of the spring and summer months, declining any and all invitations to do anything other than laze about and be close to it."

"That *would* be curious behavior, m'lord."

The Lord Calipash looked peeved. "Was that supposed to be a joke?"

"No, m'lord."

"Good. For such a thing has happened, Jeeves. In fact, it's happening right now. Do you know, no less than *eighteen* chaps and fillies of my acquaintance have come here to this benighted hamlet to see the bally thing?"

"I have noted several members of the noblesse staying at this establishment, m'lord."

"And they're all jolly queer, aren't they? Got to get a pry bar to get them out of their deck chairs, or even eat proper meals, much less have a sociable drink. Like that rotter Tolbert, you know, they're all like that. Even Roger—Roger Winthrop—he who sent me a wire saying I simply had to come and see the thing. I should have known, I suppose. His telegram was rather ... odd. Full of strange weirdnesses."

"I was not aware Mr. Winthrop was staying at the Vivarium, m'lord."

"Roger? Oh yes."

This struck me as curious. Mr. Winthrop, as his valet will confirm I am sure, is a social gentleman; when he is out and about, one knows it. Yet something else concerned me more.

"May I enquire what you meant by 'strange weirdnesses,' m'lord?"

The Lord Calipash slunk over to his escritoire and pulled open the top drawer, then, after rifling through a messy stack of papers, withdrew a single piece of stationary.

"Well go on. See for yourself."

DEAR FIZZY YOU MUST COME TO STAY AT THE VIVARIUM HERE AT DOLOR-ON-THE-DOWNS STOP THERE IS A FELLOW YOU SIMPLY MUST MEET STOP

HE HAS EIGHT LEGS AND BLUE SPOTS STOP HAVE
YOU GUESSED THE SECRET STOP IF YOU HAVENT
HERES ANOTHER CLUE ITS BETTER THAN THOSE
BOTTLES OF TOOTHACHE REMEDY WE USED TO
GUZZLE AT SCHOOL STOP REALLY STOP

"Well?" asked the Lord Calipash, when I looked up at him.

"It is certainly perplexing, m'lord. You obviously guessed the octopus part of the riddle—but whatever do you think he means by *toothache remedy?*"

"Heroin," said the Lord Calipash shortly. "Bayer used to sell it, but it all got rather rum at Oxford when the lads started to really, I don't know, crave it at all hours. So old Boffo stopped importing it and now it's much harder to come by."

"I see. And have you ... seen this octopus? Or sampled its ..."

"Yes to the first, no to the second. Alethea took a suck—my sister—but not me."

"And what was the lady's opinion?" I asked, though I was more curious about the verbal action described by the Lord Calipash.

This question seemed to sour the Lord Calipash's mood significantly.

"It's hard to say," he snapped. "Well, I suppose you should come and see. It's part of my—our—conundrum."

Let me say that I know this next part of my narrative strains credulity, but it is wholly true. The Lord Calipash beckoned to me, bidding me follow him into the private bathroom off his suite. It was with some discomfort that I followed, saying that if the lady were occupied in some indiscreet manner I would not have intruded for all the world, but the Lord Calipash laughed unpleasantly and said that she certainly was, and that was the problem.

The Lady Alethea was ... in the bath. And when I say in the bath, I do not mean that she was laving herself in a tub full of frothy suds and rubber ducks. She was in the nude and fully submerged under the surface of the water, which trickled into the large basin out of the faucet, and though I did not like to look upon her so indisposed, when I noticed some, let us call them *physical peculiarities*, I could not help but stare.

"It's hereditary," said the Lord Calipash. "Happens sometimes to Calipash females. Dunno what ancestor's fault it is, but it's a damn nuisance. Worse than the monthlies if you know what I mean."

"M'lord, I—"

"No need to be polite about it, Jeeves, I know you can see the gills as well as I. To say nothing of the webbing between her fingers." He leaned in to me and said behind his hand, "She gets it between the toes, too, but don't tell her I told you."

I confess I was at a loss. I had no notion of what to say. I had never seen anything so strange during the whole of my life. Her condition baffled me—as did the Lord Calipash's insouciance about it. For her part, Lady Alethea wriggled under the surface of the water and blew bubbles at us.

Alastair lit another cigarette and blew a cloud of smoke back at his sister. "Well, what should we do about it?"

"M'lord?"

"How do we get her to change back?!" He seemed annoyed. "Bertie said you could solve any problem. Well?"

"I—I believe I require further insight into the situation, m'lord," I said. "Are you implying the, ah, octopus induced some sort of, ah …"

"Well, we don't know, do we?" The Lord Calipash sighed. "Usually it just happens during the dark of the moon. She goes all froggy for a night, so we bung her in a handy pond or tub or water-barrel and fish her out again in the morning and that's that. But the dark of the moon was *ages* ago. Sucking on that blasted tentacle, I dunno, caused it, and ever since then she's been like this. Is it permanent, do you think?"

"I could not say, m'lord. Certainly I could call a doctor if you—" The Lord Calipash backhanded me across the mouth.

"You will not speak of this to anyone," he said softly, cracking his knuckles one-handed. "If you do I shall personally see to it that the rest of your natural life is as unpleasant and painful as possible. Do you understand me?"

The Lord Calipash was several inches shorter than me and I had at least a stone on him, but it seemed ill-advised to champion myself in that moment. I decided to wait—little did he know he could not so easily bully Reginald Jeeves.

"My discretion is absolute, m'lord," I said, withdrawing a handkerchief from my pocket and dabbing at the side of my mouth, where I felt the blood trickling down. "I merely thought if Lady Alethea was in some discomfort, then perhaps some medicine might aid her."

There was a splash, and the lady sat up in her tub. She was attractive in a nervous, lean way, like an overbred whippet. Her wet hair, cut into a 'bob' as they call it, streamed water all over her face. I tried not to look anywhere else, but I am only human.

"If you don't know how to deal with my condition yet, you can think about it more later. The first thing we need you to do is figure out how best we can snatch and then smuggle that stupid octopus back with us to London," she said, in a gasping, breathy sort of voice. "I'm fine. I can even get up, but people notice, and my skin dries out terrible quick."

Most valets have, at some time or another, engaged in acts outside the guidelines of local law—it is part of our job, if our gentlemen require such, of course. I bowed to the lady.

"I did not realize you desired to possess the cephalopod that induced your unfortunate condition, Lady Alethea," I said. "I am sure it could be managed—but if I may, *why*? I only ask as your particular needs may affect my planning. Do you suspect a study of its venom would produce an antidote, perhaps?"

"Never thought a moment about it," said Lady Alethea. She swept her sodden hair out of her eyes with a webbed hand. I held back a shudder.

"Our grand scheme is to harvest whatever comes out of it and *sell* it, Jeeves. We'll make a mint!" The Lord Calipash rubbed his hands together in anticipation. "We can bottle it as a cure-all or tonic or whatever to idiots keen on health clubs and sanatoriums and things, and we can sell it on the black market to opium addicts, maybe promote it as a cure for morphine addiction, like they did with that heroin stuff."

"M'lord, I know a little of that scandal, and researchers discovered that heroin was metabolized as morphine, and, as it was faster acting, it was thusly more addictive than—"

"Jeeves—*Jeeves*. Silence," urged the Lord Calipash, withdrawing a small switchblade knife from his pocket and, after releasing the blade, fingering it in a manner I can only assume was meant to impress upon me that I should take him seriously. "You don't need to worry about the, I dunno, *ethics* or whatnot. I promise you, if you aid us, then we will telegraph you the name of the product so you need never worry about purchasing it. Of course, if you tell anyone about what it really is, my earlier threats stand. Neither Alethea nor I have any wish to end up like our American cousins, the Mortlows. Humiliated, shamed, imprisoned. Bally depressing."

"But be assured, as a reward for your assistance, we'll make sure you can look out for number one. That's what we're doing, after all," added Lady Alethea.

"My lady?"

"We're broke," said the Lord Calipash. "Bankrupt. Glad Bertie didn't win that little wager, Calipash Manor's been seized by our creditors.

A Swiss family lives there now, and much good may it do them. We made off with the most valuable things and have been hawking them at various jewelers and what have you. Infernal mess. Most of what we own is in this room, frankly."

"You're being hyperbolic," wheezed Lady Alethea. "We still have the flat in London, you know."

"For now."

"Anyways who is this fellow, Alastair?" asked Lady Alethea. "Never seen him before. Wherever did you find him?"

"He's Bertie Wooster's valet, if you can imagine. Supposed to be brainy."

"Good thing. We need someone with more than a few kippers in the jug. Lord knows you're not fit for thinking."

"And what are you fit for? Malt vinegar and brown paper?"

This aspersion seemed to agitate the Lady Alethea, and I feared I might be party to a row. Fortunately, I was there to intercede. I did not do this on their behalf, however—merely that I discerned that they were both rather flighty and given to intellectual wandering; I wished to aid them so I could get away from them as quickly as possible afterwards.

"Perhaps we would do best to plan this caper, m'lord, Lady Alethea," I said, nodding to each in turn. "Tell me of where the beast is kept, and your vision for how you would best like this to all work out. I shall make my recommendations directly."

I know this account is longer than many of my others in this book, but it does contain the foibles of not one, but two gentlemen who might at some point require a valet. The purpose of this tome is to educate and warn, so I feel being more specific rather than less is the right thing to do. But, out of consideration for my peers, I will try to be brief in my recounting the conclusion of this affair.

Lady Alethea and the Lord Calipash told me this tale about their initial encounter with the octopus: After receiving the telegram from Mr. Winthrop, they had sought him here only to be informed by Miss Cirrina Prideaux that he was not staying at the Vivarium. After they showed her the missive, however, she apparently conceded that he was indeed her guest, but was disinclined to see any visitors at this time. But would they like to see the reason for his summoning them?

They agreed, and the young lady somewhat unexpectedly escorted them down into the basement of her hotel. There, she kicked open a grate and had them descend a ladder, whereupon they walked for a time down a tunnel. According to them, it was quite dark and damp—one of the pair of the Lord Calipash's best brogues apparently suffered substantial water damage—but after persevering for a time, they perceived a dim light. Eventually they ascertained that it emanated from a strange, blue-spotted octopus kept in an elaborate tank that opened via grate or grill to the ocean proper, so the fellow's water-supply was always fresh and clean I suppose.

Though both Fitzroys expressed some curiosity over the iridescence of the creature, Cirrina Prideaux told them not to worry about it. She then began, according to the Fitzroys, to sing to the creature in a strange language. The octopus apparently responded with some enthusiasm, emitting a keening in a similar key, and then rose to the surface of the tank and extended an arm over the edge of the tank.

As the Lord Calipash had some reservations over Miss Prideaux's instruction to accept the tentacle orally and suckle at it, Lady Alethea stepped up and did so at Miss Prideaux's urging. According to the lady, the effect was as potent as it was instantaneous; whatever coated the tentacle, venom or ink I cannot say, caused pleasant sensations of euphoria, deep tranquility, mild dizziness, and fearfully powerful suggestibility. It was at that point, reportedly, that Lady Alethea began to experience symptoms of her lunar transformation, though it was not her customary time. She and her brother raced back up to their rooms, whereupon she had submerged herself quickly in the tub (the ocean being unacceptable; Lady Alethea must have fresh-water rather than salt during her indisposition), leaving her brother to try to puzzle out how best to steal the creature for their own purposes and—discreetly—reverse his sister's condition.

"And what have you considered, m'lord?" I asked.

"Best plan so far is kidnapping that bitch hotel-owner and forcing her at gun- or knifepoint or whatever to sing her ruddy song and get the blighter into a salt tank we would earlier poach from the hotel itself," said the Lord Calipash. "I've retrieved a few. Then we kill her and make a run for it. Corker of a notion, I think, eh?" He looked at me. "What? You don't think so?"

"Only—m'lord—if you were to disappear so quickly after the death of the proprietress, there might be some questions on the part of the police of whether you were motivated by interest or eagerness to be away from the Vivarium. Suspicion might fall upon you and your sister."

"Well, what do you suggest?"

"If I may, m'lord ..."

"Yes?"

"How desperate are you to obtain this octopus?"

"Totally committed."

"Would you be willing to commit acts of ... self-sacrifice, m'lord?"

"Steady on, Jeeves. How martyry are we talking? Hair shirt? Vulture at the liver every day?"

There are moments in every valet's career when he must decide whose happiness is more important, his or his employer's. I speak now of Mr. Wooster, not the Lord Calipash, who did not employ me so much as manage me for a time. All the same, I had to take a moment to contemplate exactly how Mr. Wooster would wish me to acquit myself. Would he wish me to follow my heart and do what I thought was right, or would he wish me to follow any and all instructions given to me by the Lord Calipash? I quickly tallied points in favor of both options, factored in my employer's temperament, moods, and inclinations, and made my decision.

"I believe you would find the sacrifices of an easy, pleasant nature," I said. "Both of you. If you leave the groundwork up to me, I think I can manage to successfully resolve everything in your favor."

"*Really?*" the Lord Calipash and Lady Alethea said, in unison.

"Absolutely," said I. "May I have m'lord's permission to begin?"

"Do it, then!" cried the Lord Calipash. Thus, I bowed, and left.

The first thing I did was to seek Miss Cirrina Prideaux in her office. I needed to ascertain some things about her character that would be necessary for me to proceed. I found the young woman busily calculating something, using an abacus and biting the end of her pencil, but at my knock she looked up and smiled at me pleasantly.

"Ah, Mr. Jeeves, is it? I thought you'd gone with Mr. Wooster."

"I stayed behind to settle a few matters for a friend of Mr. Wooster's. May I have a moment of your time, Miss?"

"How may I be of service, Mr. Jeeves? Please, sit."

I sat across from Miss Prideaux. She was an attractive young woman, with dark hair styled in a French fashion and a pleasant smile. Her eyes were widely set, with brilliant blue irises, and her complexion, while tanned by the sun, was smooth and bespoke health. While I may have expressed reservations over whether she would be a suitable partner for Mr. Wooster, I found her charming when my employer was trying to avoid getting engaged to her, and I found her charming in that moment, too.

"I was curious, Miss, if you might do me a very great favor."

"If it is within my power."

"I am currently in the employ of the Lord Calipash, and he mentioned in passing that you had a lovely specimen of the Greater Blue-Ringed Octopus here at the Vivarium. I am, I confess, something of an amateur teuthologist and would very much like to see the creature if it is possible?"

Miss Prideaux put down her pencil. "I'm afraid I must disappoint you, Mr. Jeeves. I do not have a Greater Blue-Ringed Octopus here at the Vivarium."

"What a pity. It sounded from the description the Lord Calipash gave that you had one, somewhere below the hotel, in a rather ingenious tank—one that allows the open sea to clean and maintain the creature's habitat naturally."

I perceived some discomfort in Miss Prideaux's expressions and actions, but she eventually ceased to fidget.

"I *do* have a species of octopus in such a tank ... but it is not a Greater Blue-Ringed Octopus. It is a different species, one not yet named by the Academy."

"I should be even keener to see it then, Miss Prideaux."

"Would you? Would you also swear to secrecy regarding its existence?"

"Of course, Miss Prideaux."

"Come, then, Mr. Jeeves."

In silence, Miss Prideaux took me through the hotel, down through the kitchens, into one of the root cellars, and then, just as described by the Lord Calipash, kicked open a drainage grate and descended into an abyssal pit. I followed with not a little trepidation, but, perhaps sensing this, she called up to me that it was quite all right.

"Are you a nervous man, Mr. Jeeves?" she asked, as we walked down the stone-walled tunnel. "I know the Lady Alethea said she was; I believe she found the remedy produced by my little friend ... helpful."

"She reported the experience was most beneficial to her spirits," said I. "But I confess I am not nervous by nature; merely curious about the natural world."

"A pity. Many of our wealthier clientele have come to treat this hotel as a ... sanatorium, perhaps, and stay here for extended periods of time when they feel stressed or anxious. My pet helps them forget their cares, drift for a time in pleasantness."

"An admirable service. Are all of your guests aware of this available remedy?"

"Surely not, only the wealthier ones. The ones who can afford the fee."

"*Fee*, Miss Prideaux?"

"I look upon this hotel as something more than just an establishment where holidaying ladies and gentlemen may enjoy themselves in peace. I see it as a ... zoological park, a valuable menagerie. A collection, for posterity. Did you know, Mr. Jeeves, that the recent advances in refrigeration have increased the demands on sea-fishermen to the point that they are allying themselves with one another and forming companies to supply inland diners? But often this leads to overfishing ... in ten, twenty, seventy years, what will the oceans look like, Mr. Jeeves? Will they still be troves of nigh-unlimited species diversity? Or barren wastelands, wet deserts if you will?" She sighed, and as we walked, I began to perceive that faint glow I had been told of. "I hope to keep safe the fishes of the world, and if I take in extra funds by providing a unique service to the very wealthy, why should I not?"

"I cannot see a reason, except, I wonder ..."

"What?"

"Have you had any men or women with medical training look at whatever it is that is produced by your octopus? Are you aware of what exactly it does to the human body? For example, is it ... addictive?"

"If it is, then so much the better, Mr. Jeeves. If they keep coming back for more, well, more money in the till."

We had come at last to the octopus—or at least, what the Lord Calipash and Lady Alethea *thought* was an octopus. Looking at the tentacled creature, I myself was not so sure it was a member of the family octopoda, though I am not, as I presented myself to Miss Prideaux, actually a scholar of malacology.

The animal had only six sucker-covered arms, and was covered in bright blue spots. Its eyes—all three of them—looked distinctly human, with blue irises much like Miss Prideaux's. It—I hesitate to write this, though if you, my fellow valets, have believed me thus far, I suppose you will continue to do so—was playing at something like marbles, using the small stones at the bottom of its open-sea cage at the bars that comprised the open-sea grate at the rear of its cage. I say something like, as it had, perhaps owing to the wave action's effect on sand, created a circle of larger stones and was tossing smaller stones at the circle, trying to get them inside the ring. I have heard, of course, that octopuses are quite intelligent, but it was playing this game not with its more tentacle-like arms, but with two nauseatingly human hands that emanated from where, in a usual specimen, the creature's 'beak' should be. The appendages had four fingers and a thumb and seemed quite dexterous, but, upsettingly, they adorned arms that looked far more like birds' legs than arms, human or cephalopodan.

"What do you think, Mr. Jeeves. Is my specimen as unusual as you believed?"

"Rather moreso, Miss Prideaux," I said, struggling to retain my composure. "Wherever did you find him?"

"Rock-diving with my parents off the coast of Australia," she replied. "If you hold his hands, he can speak right into your mind, and when we told him of our hotel, he said he should like nothing more than to come home with us and share his delicious secretions with the world. He has a very large family, you see, and hopes that through small, regular doses of his mild venom, we should all live in harmony with one another. He and his family are *very* smart."

This horrifying piece of intelligence from Miss Prideaux gave me pause. I considered whether or not to move forward with my plan, knowing what I did. In the end you all may judge me for it, but due to my forthcoming description of how it all played out, you will know not to take your gentlemen within fifty miles of Dolor-on-the-Downs or The Marine Vivarium, and thank me for it.

"Miss Prideaux," I said, after a moment, "you are a marvel. May I ask you a few questions of a bold, personal nature?"

"You may ask them, of course ..."

"Very fair. I was curious if you were still interested in, if I may be so bold, affairs matrimonial?"

"That *is* bold," said Miss Prideaux. "May I ask why? Have you come to offer me your hand, Mr. Jeeves?"

"Regrettably no, Miss," said I. "I ask on behalf of the curiosity of another."

"A pity," said Miss Prideaux, giving me a calculating look. "I rather think you'd do for a husband, Mr. Jeeves. Just the sort of mind that would be useful for running this hotel and managing things."

"If I may, Miss, what I perceive you need is not another mind," said I. "You are clearly a woman of intelligence and drive."

"Thank you, Jeeves."

"It is only the truth."

"Perhaps. What were your other questions?"

"If you felt yourself in need of further inducements to bring potential guests to your hotel."

"Always."

"Excellent. And thirdly, do you already have a method of bottling your friend's unique medicine?"

"Yes, after the first visit, patrons may pay a premium to have me bring it to them. They almost always do."

I smiled. "Please, if I may impose on your time for only a few more moments, then let me propose something to you, Miss Prideaux ..."

Thankfully, Mr. Wooster has taught me something of mixology, and so it was with confidence, later that night, that I presented a complicated potation to the Lord Calipash before he went down to dinner. He drank it, and we discussed his future for a time afterwards. He seemed pleased with my solutions to his pecuniary troubles and his sister's discomfort with her state and confinement, and thus I was able to return sooner than I thought to London—and to the side of my employer. Rather than boring you with further descriptions—and to save my poor hand, which is cramping after writing all this, I present to you two newspaper clippings of some interest to the general public, but perhaps of more interest to the private members of this Club, who shall appreciate what is not said in them even more than what is.

FITZROY—PRIDEAUX—June 24, at St. Michael's Church at Dolor-on-the-Downs, Dorset by the Rev. S. M. Grant, Alastair Fitzroy Lord Calipash of Devon to Cirrina Prideaux, only daughter of Mr. Gabriel Prideaux, proprietress of The Marine Vivarium, hotel and sanatorium.

REAL LIVE MERMAID DISPLAYED AT HOTEL AT DOLOR-ON-THE-DOWNS!

DORSET, August 12—After hearing gossip and rumor regarding such, this paper sent down our own Mr. B, investigative reporter on entertainment hoaxes, to Dorset to see if the "Real Live Mermaid" advertised by The Marine Vivarium, a seaside hotel at Dolor-on-the-Downs, was indeed real, live, and, well, a mermaid, or another carnivalesque deception. Shockingly, the creature seems *not* to be a hoax. Mr. B observed the creature in a freshwater tank labeled "Real English Mermaid" and there behind glass she floated, shockingly naked and ill-tempered. She makes rude gestures with thin, greenish webbed fingers at all those who pay sixpence to have the curtain lifted so they might observe her, and floats about, or sometimes sits cross-legged on a large rock inside her tank, or reads whatever book is set on a stand just outside her tank, ringing a bell whenever she wishes the page turned (NB: at the time this reporter saw her, she was reading Rafael Sabatini's recently-published *Scaramouche*). When asked where this marvel was found, the proprietress, the recently-married Lady Cirrina Calipash (*née* Prideaux) claimed her husband caught her on a fishing trip, whereupon she begged to be educated and allowed to socialize with the better element as much as she could. That the Lord Calipash began to tear up at the recollection bespeaks the love and attention given to this freak of nature by her caretakers. For our readership, the author wishes to note that those looking for a tranquil, relaxed seaside holidaying venue could go further and fare fouler than The Marine Vivarium: Very few screaming children or even chit-chatting adults could be found, the entire hotel was quiet, almost silent, and all patrons, when asked, said they had the loveliest time at the Vivarium, and would live there permanently if given the choice.

the hour of the tortoise

4 April 1887, early morning. Traveling.

I sat alone in my train-carriage watching the beech-copses and white sheep and mist-wreathed fields flashing by. I am sure this countryside could be anywhere in England, but these were the trees and fields of Devon, my home county! And I had not seen them from the time I was sent away to learn what I could at Miss Coote's Academy for Young Women of Breeding and Promise.

More than a decade has passed, but the native beauty of this place remains ever-first in my heart. How could it not be but so? My happiest days were spent in Devonshire, when I was but a lass running hither and yon, and always by the side of my cousin Laurent. Two years my junior, he had been my constant childhood companion—but what of now? What sort of man has he grown into?

'Twas a kiss that separated us, a kiss seen by his mother, Lady Fanchone. That woman, whom some would call great, mistook our embrace for the blossoming of love rather than the affection shared by near-siblings, and would brook no explanations. Laurent became but a memory, and Devon, too—until now! For I am coming home ...

***

Yes, that should do nicely, I think, for the introduction. A heroine at the end of her pupal stage, all grown up and ready to break through childhood's chrysalis.

Christ above, save me from choking upon my own vomit.

I must find a way to add some spice directly lest I bore myself into an early grave, to say nothing of losing us the whole of our readership. Perhaps she (need name, floral in nature: Violet? Camilla? Camilla is nice) shall lose her maidenhead on the train. But to whom: the conductor? A handsome fellow-traveler? I must think on it.

No, I should delay the jimmying open of Love's crimson gate slightly longer. She could be introduced to the art of prick-sucking by a

25

gallant stranger ... but then he leaves her unsatisfied?

Better better, and yet! While it's true my editrix has never once given me poor counsel regarding my pornographies, I find Gothic fiction so very tiresome. I really cannot account for its popularity, but I am sure that is the reason Susan is so beside herself with excitement over this project. "Dearest Chelone, you shall write me *Jane Eyre*—but with lots and lots of fucking! It shall be our new serial and make us ever so much money!" Not exactly the response I anticipated when I told her I must take an extended leave of absence from *Milady's Ruby Vase* so I might journey into the dreariest parish in Devon to sit by the side of my former guardian while he lies gasping out his last upon his deathbed.

To stay once again under the gabled roof of Calipash Manor, after being so unceremoniously chucked out a decade ago ... I have mixed feelings about this journey, to say the least. I am certain Susan believes I am going to encounter a country house full of secret passages, drafty towers, mysterious mysteries, and handsome cousins. Well, that will happen in the pornography, of course, and to be fair, Calipash Manor *does* have a tower. And, I suppose, its share of silly rumors about the family. But the reality is far more boring: An old man in his tidy house, wasting away with few to comfort him, having alienated himself during his life from those who might have loved him unto death.

I suppose there is something rather *Wuthering Heights* about that, but not like any of the better parts, like when So-and-So threatens to cut off the boy's ears or whatever it is that happens.

***

Later—Funny, how I had thought to include a handsome stranger-*cum*-deflowerer in my story; I just met a rather natty fellow that will do nicely as a model! I should liked to have had some sport with him myself, except, it was so queer. He apologized for approaching me without a proper introduction, but asked if I was by chance related to the Calipash family. I told him I wasn't—which isn't strictly true, of course, but we illegitimate children of the noblesse are trained to be discreet—but he would not let the matter go. He shook his head and apologized, with the excuse that he was a native of Ivybridge, so knew "the Calipash look," and said I had a serious case of it.

"The Calipash look!" I exclaimed, delighted. "Surely you must be referring to the Calipash Curse?"

"I suppose I am," said he. I was surprised by how alarmed he seemed by my amusement. "You know of the curse, miss?"

"Of course I do, but I have not heard anybody mention it for nigh ten years!"

"You may smile," he said, furrowing his brow at me as if his very life depended on it, "but we Ivybridge folk know nothing connected with that family is a laughing matter. Bad blood, they have—diabolists, deviants, and necromancers all!"

"I am acquainted with the Lord Calipash, and a better man I have rarely met." Well, it was a true enough statement. I let him take it as he would.

"He's a good sort, true enough, but they go bad easy. I'd be on the lookout, miss. You surely look like a Calipash, perhaps you were ... well, I won't curse you by suggesting you have a twin lurking somewhere—but best to stay out of the ponds, just the same!"

I told him I had every intention of staying out of ponds, lakes, rivers, streams, sloughs, and for that matter, lagoons. He seemed relieved, but the way such a dapper young man took notice of piffling country legends, well, it gave me pause.

Of course when I used to go into the village as a girl I heard tell of the Calipash family curse—when twins are born, the devil is their father, and something about taking to the sea, or to ponds, and something about frog people maybe, of all the outlandish claims! I may not be remembering it all correctly; as a girl once I came home enquiring about it, but Lizzie, the housekeeper, reprimanded me for repeating such twaddle and I never again mentioned it. I am glad I was taught at a young age to be skeptical of supernatural nonsense.

Really, what family that lives in a manor-house rather than a cottage doesn't have some sort of rumor or another hanging over them like the sword of Damocles?

Rum analogy to use when going to see a dying man, perhaps.

Ooh—but we are slowing, and there is the whistle! I must ready myself.

***

Evening. In my old room—The dolls I left behind are still here, and the white bedstead still has its rose-sprigged coverlet and pink frilly canopy. It is only how yellowed and worn everything appears that keeps me from thinking I have stepped back into another time. I feel fourteen years old in this room.

Ah well, why bother changing the décor? I was always made to maintain the illusion of juvenescence to please my guardian, so why not keep my chambers in a state of static girlishness, too?

But I should not speak ill of Lord Calipash, or rather, he who was Lord Calipash until his death—his death that I fear I may have caused not an hour ago! And already there is a new lord under the manor-roof tonight …

Things are far stranger here at Calipash Manor than I anticipated. Perhaps there is something to the idea of a family curse—no! Stop that, Chelone. You are simply tired from your journey, and overwrought.

Here is what happened, the facts, I mean: I arrived at the Ivybridge station on time, but no one was waiting for me, to my distress. The skies promised rain, and it was miles to walk to Calipash Manor.

After waiting at the station for some time, I begged the use of a little wheeled cart for my trunk and went into Ivybridge proper, thinking I would visit the post office. It was from thence I had received the letter from my guardian summoning me hither. I thought perhaps I could, rather than sending a message by courier, ride with said courier (if the horse would bear us both) and come back later for my luggage.

The town looked the same, snug stone houses and muddy streets, the occasional chicken scurrying across the main thoroughfare. The post office was in the same dilapidated cottage, I was happy to discover, with what could have been the same geraniums blooming in the window-box as when I was a girl. I went inside and explained my situation.

"Quite a lot of traffic to and from the manor-house of late," remarked the woman at the window, not answering my query of how I might get myself to Calipash Manor. "Telegraph yesterday, and was barely a week ago the prodigal son come in to send a letter. Queer fellow."

"Mr. Vincent has come home, then?"

"Aye, for his father is soon for the grave, they say."

"How is he queer?" I was madly curious about Orlando Vincent, the cousin I had never seen. I should remember later to ask him about Rotterdam, where he was educated. Might be able to write something for the *Vase* about Dutch schoolboys or something …

"Didn't say nothing when he came in." The woman's frown would have shamed the devil himself. "Grunted his yeses and noes as if he had no human power of speech in him. Gave me a turn, he did. At first I thought he was the Ghast o'the Hills, come to take my soul. Mr. Vincent is very like the apparition, though of course his clothing is different."

Her words made me laugh, which I could tell displeased her. As a child I heard tell of the 'Ghast o'the Hills,' some sort of spirit in a frock-coat that is said to haunt the parish of Ivybridge. Once I even thought I saw it … a childish fancy, of course. I am lucky that education—and, of course, living in London—has disabused me of such country superstitions.

"So you've seen the Ghast?" I asked, amused.

"You may laugh, miss, but around here, there's precious few who haven't seen the Ghast! He's as real as you or I, and wanders at night moanin and groanin. It's said he seeks a wife to keep him company."

"And Mr. Vincent looks like him?"

"Well, he's thin, tall, with that Calipash face. All thems what come from the Manor have a look, don't they? In fact, you have it too, my girl. Are you related?"

I didn't want to get into that. "I didn't realize the Ghast was part of the Calipash Curse?"

"Well, that family's queer, of course, so if this town had some sort of malign spirit, it'd come from thems what—"

"You hush your foolish old mouth, Hazel Smith! Telling ghost stories like a heathen. You ought to be ashamed!"

I turned 'round, surprised, and was pleased to see Old Bill, the groundskeeper and jack-of-all for Calipash Manor, standing behind me.

"Bill!" I cried, and embraced him. "How are you? Oh, just look at you!"

"Let us be gone, Miss Burchell," he said gruffly. "Waited for you at the station, but they said you'd traipsed hither for your own purposes. Hold your tongue, we can talk on the drive. Lord Calipash is not long for this world and I have no wish to follow him into the grave if this weather turns wet."

At first I attributed his poor spirits to his age, for he must be closer to seventy than sixty these days, white-haired and gaunt as a skeleton. But he got my trunk onto his skinny back and into the cart quickly enough; indeed, by the time he had scrambled onto the seat, ready to leave, I had hardly finished saying hello and asking after my guardian.

"Things are quite dire," was his reply. "'Tis good you've come now, though you might've sent more notice of your arriving. Lizzie is beside herself getting your old room ready, not to mention the cooking for an extra person."

"I telegraphed yesterday," I replied, rather taken aback by this admonition. "And really, Lord Calipash himself invited me—bid me come with all possible haste!"

"As you say," said Bill, looking at me askance as he chucked the reins.

"What do you mean by that?"

"Master's not been able to lift a quill in some time," he said with a shrug. "Before his son come home, I was writing all his letters for him."

"You, Bill!"

"Aye. I went to the village school as a youth and learned to read, write, and cipher—no need to look so surprised, Miss! I do tolerable justice to my lord's handwriting, he himself asked me to learn the trick of it when he was struck with arthritis. But now him that's to be the next Lord Calipash has taken over the duty, so he says, but unless he posts the letters himself, nothing's gone out in some time. Hasn't asked me to go into the village since his arrival anyways."

"But that woman said Mr. Vincent delivered the letter himself!"

"Did she now?"

"Yes … perhaps Mr. Vincent was the one who wrote to me. But, then, why disguise his writing? I should have come if he had extended the invitation to me, of course."

"Couldn't say, Miss. He's a strange creature, full of notions and temper. Perhaps he thinks you are like him. I had to write to him in the Lord Calipash's own hand, begging for his return, to get him to come! Ignored all the letters I wrote as myself."

"Rotterdam is a very far distance to travel on short notice …"

"Aye, and the road to hell is a short and easy path! Honor thy father says the Bible."

"Oh, Bill. I've missed you," said I, shocked to find it was the truth, as I had always remembered him as the bane of my childhood. Somehow he knew when I was up to mischief and would foil my plans if he could, with a Bible verse ready to shame me for my willfulness.

I opened my mouth to ask him another question, one about Mr. Vincent, but my power of speech left me entirely at that moment. We'd crested a hill, and Calipash Manor had come into view.

I looked upon the ivy-wreathed front doors and the ancient moldering stone of the house, pale in the weird light of the coming storm, and felt a strange flutter inside my chest. I could not help thinking that manor looked as if it had weathered a good deal more than ten years during my decade-long absence. The tower, where I had once held tea-parties with my dolls, or played at being Rapunzel, now looked so rickety it would not support a dove's nest; the plentiful windows, upon which I had painted frost-pictures in the winter and opened to feel the breeze during the mild country summers, looked smaller, and dark with the kind of soot and filth one sees in London but few other places.

"I have been away a very long time," I whispered hoarsely. "Drive 'round, Bill, so I may get inside and see the place."

"Go through the front doors, Miss Burchell," urged Bill.

This drew a laugh to my lips, and I wiped my eyes. "I am no lady, and certainly not the lady of the house. Drive 'round, the servants' door was always good enough for me."

"No, Miss. You're here as our guest now, after all."

I knew that tone, and it meant no arguing, so I thanked Bill and hopped down from the haywain. I was seized with a girlish fancy to take the steps two at a time as I had always used to do, but I only managed a few such leaps before my corset prevented further exertion. Thus I was sweaty-faced and breathing hard when I threw open the door—and saw the foyer for the first time in ten years.

The floorboards groaned under my shoes as I entered, and the high ceilings amplified the echoes of both footfall and wood-creak. The first thing I noticed was that the watery light spilling in from the door was hazy with little swirling motes of dust. My hasty entrance had stirred the air more than it had been in some time. Indeed, filth and grime lay thick on every surface, and I was overwhelmed by the smell of mold. When I looked up, I saw the chandelier was missing more than one pendalogue, and the candle-cups did not look like they had held tapers in recent memory.

I could not move for astonishment. I remembered this room as a bright and welcoming space; recalled the sound of my guardian's laughter as he would chase me, shrieking, through the hallways, much to the displeasure of the housekeeper, Lizzie, who said I should grow up wild.

Shouting and stomping startled me out of my reverie. It was a man's voice I heard coming from the interior of the house—and all of a sudden there was a tall, thin fellow with messy black hair and bulging eyes at the top of the front staircase, then galloping down it! He was too busy howling at the top of his lungs to notice me.

"Bill! Lizzie! Anyone! The old bastard is in need of something, but I cannot understand his infernal mumblings!"

It was such an excellent entrance that upon recollection, I cannot help but now contemplate how I will translate it into my narrative of Camilla's coming-of-age:

I have no words to express my surprise when I saw that Laurent was all grown up! Pale of skin and darkly handsome, his face held a haughty, cruel expression that checked my first impulse to rush into his arms and demand a longed-for kiss from my oldest, dearest friend in the world. How serious he looked! His black coat and trousers would have been better suited for a funeral in London than his ancestral country home. Still, I blushed to see him—and felt a blush where not three hours ago I had been brought to the golden threshold of love by the gamahuching of Mr. Reeves. I never thought I would see my cousin in such a light—and yet …

But of course, my Camilla has her memories of Laurent to *contrast* with the man she meets upon arriving at The Beeches, as I think I shall call her former home. ("A Camilla Among The Beeches" sounds like an excellent title to me—we shall see what Susan thinks.) I, however, had never before laid eyes upon Orlando Vincent. My first impression was of a flustered wretch of about my own age, clad in a wrinkled suit, and waving his arms about and carrying on in a dreadful manner. I could see how someone might mistake him for the Ghast o'the Hills—if one were inclined to see ghosts and spirits everywhere, that is.

"Why Mr. Vincent, I declare!" cried Lizzie, stepping into the dusty foyer, drying her hands with a dingy rag. How old must she be now, I wondered? Always slender and tall, she was now made all of angles, and her impressive mane of dark hair was now a lustrous gray—handsome, to be sure, but no longer youthful. "And here's our Chelone! Why, just look at you, grown! I'm surprised at you, Mr. Vincent. Let the young lady come in and rest herself before alarming her with your profuse ejaculations!"

I am aware those not in my profession use that word without heed for its alternative definition, but I confess I giggled—which caused Mr. Vincent to blush very pink indeed, and sneer at me down his long narrow nose.

"It is good to meet you at last," said I, to cover the awkwardness I had caused. "I used to read your letters to the Lord Calipash. How was your journey from Rotterdam?"

"Spare me this nonsense," he snapped. "You must come, Lizzie—now—he gurgles and sweats out his very life, I think. You can understand him better than I, come and discover what it is he wants!"

Lizzie looked appalled. "Mr. Vincent, you must not—"

"I shall make love to the chit later if it please you—only come now and see to my father! Are you so silly that the health of your lord does not take precedence over your sense of decorum?"

"Excuse me, Chelone," said Lizzie. "I shall get you settled directly, but if you like, please go now to your old room. I know you know the way."

"Let me come with you," I suggested. I had no wish to be left alone in this dreary, unremembered house! "Perhaps I can be of some help."

"You'll be the most help if you shut your mouth and stop distracting us all! Why you have come now, at the eleventh hour, is a mystery to me!" Mr. Vincent turned on his heel and fairly ran away from us, taking the steps two at a time.

I was, of course, concerned that he who had posted, and I had supposed, written the letter to me also had no notion of my coming, but I had no time to muse on this—Lizzie had followed after him, saying over her shoulder:

"Come along, then. You always had a certain rapport with the Lord Calipash, perhaps the unexpected sight of you will restore him."

"I cannot account for this," I said, as I followed her. "Why did he not tell anyone of his invitation to me, I wonder? And how did he get the letter into the post?" I laughed. "Perhaps it really was the Ghast!"

"I beg your pardon?"

"Oh, nothing—just, the woman at the post office said Mr. Vincent was very like the Ghast o'the Hills, you know, the ghost that—"

"There's no such thing as ghosts," interrupted Lizzie. "Let us see what the Lord Calipash requires, yes?"

During our trip upstairs to my guardian's chambers I had noticed the same disrepair and neglect throughout Calipash Manor as had been evident in the foyer. The banisters were unpolished and slick with moisture; the carpet felt damp beneath my feet. Even the portrait-frames looked strangely aged. The gold leaf had flaked away and, curiously, the people in the pictures appeared older than I remembered them. The Calipash family has always been an attractive one, though just as the gentleman on the train mentioned, bizarrely alike in aspect, and with frequent incidences of twins. Long did I study their thin, aristocratic faces as a girl, making up silly stories about their lives—but today, instead of looking like an ancient and noble line, all seemed to carry in their eyes a hateful and sinister expression I had never before noticed. It made me shiver.

Yet the dilapidation of the house was most evident when Lizzie turned the brass knob of the door into my lord's chambers and pushed through the decaying portal into the interior. The horrible smell of warm putrefaction hit me first, and then, through the gloom—for the thick window-dressings blocked most of the already-dim light—I could see more of the awful dust that coated every surface. Soiled garments were piled upon the floor, and his desk was messy with papers and spilled candle-wax.

This place had always been so fastidiously-kept when I was a child! Nauseated, shocked, I looked to my left and saw my guardian in his bed, the curtains of which were stained and the linens unclean. And then there was my lord himself ... I remembered him as a vigorous older man, with thick white hair swept back from his temples and a ruddy, narrow, pleasant face, but the person I saw gave me no hint as to his former appearance. He was swollen, bloated even; his hair was thinner, and his face drooped horribly on the left side from the palsy that struck him some weeks back. His skin was as brown as a walnut, and had a patchy, unwholesome appearance.

I was glad Bill had prepared me for the sight, I do not know if I could have kept from crying out had I gone to see him unaware.

Lizzie bustled into the room saying, "Well, well, my lord, what may I fetch you?"

The series of sounds that came from my guardian's mouth could not be called speech, yet Lizzie seemed to understand them well enough.

"Such a fuss and for what? Only the want of a cup of Darjeeling!" she exclaimed.

"My God, is that all?" cried Mr. Vincent, giving me quite a fright—I had not noticed him lurking like a spider on the other side of my lord's bed.

"I'll have it for you before you can say Jack Robinson," said Lizzie, "but while you wait, here's something for you, my lord—your guest is here!"

More wet grunting and smacking. Lizzie's face fell.

"Well, surely you will be pleased when you see who it is—come closer, my dear, don't hang in the doorway like some sort of apparition!"

With not a little trepidation I took a few faltering steps toward the bed. He really looked as miserable as the house itself; indeed, the only thing bright or beautiful about him was a curious jade pendant he wore on a chain upon his breast, just visible where his nightshirt was unbuttoned. Carved in the shape of a winged tortoise, it had a face more lupine than reptilian, and great clawed monkey-paw hands that gave the impression that the ornament was clinging to his skin. The craftsmanship looked almost Egyptian, and it glowed faintly in the gloaming. I thought I recognized the image ... but I know not where, for surely he never wore it while I lived in this house.

Something about it captivated me, made me long to look upon it further, to hold it in my hand and run my fingertips over the smoothness of the stone.

"What a lovely necklace," I blurted, unable to help myself.

A grunt that sounded like agreement came from him—and then his bleary eyes focused on my face.

"Whooo?" he said, like a tubercular owl.

"Your letter bid me come," said I, remembering myself at last. I took his hand in mine, but almost dropped it in surprise. It felt leathery and chitinous at once; I could not feel the bones beneath the skin. "It is I, Chelone Burchell, your ward. I had not expected to see you again. I am so glad—"

There was more I was going to say, but, unexpectedly, my greeting induced a sort of apoplexy in the Lord Calipash. He began to cry out and wheeze and make such a ruckus I let go his hand immediately.

"Never!" I managed to understand through it all, and also, "Begone!"

This cut me to the quick. It was not as though I had forgotten what was supposed to be my permanent banishment when I received his missive! How could I fail to recall the day I was turned out of the house and sent alone in a coach to attend Miss Redcombe's School for Girls of Quality? I was not even allowed to pack, my things were sent after me. All I had were the clothes on my back, a few shillings in my pocket, and a letter of explanation in my hand that stated, among other things, that payment would soon arrive to cover my education until I came of age; that I should stay at the school for all holidays unless invited to a friend's house, and that every effort must be taken to keep me away from young men!

And yet I had always hoped we would be reconciled, despite his returning every letter I ever sent him, unopened; that he would come to regret punishing me so severely for such a trifling youthful indiscretion.

"I'm—sorry, the letter, it must have, I don't know," I stammered, backing away from the bed. The old man had begun to twitch and froth at the mouth, looking wildly back and forth between myself and Mr. Vincent.

"Begone!" he cried again, and then he fell back on the pillows—stone dead!

Lizzie, Mr. Vincent, and I stood still for some minutes, all shocked by what had transpired.

I was the first to speak.

"I brought the letter," I heard myself saying, protesting this awful scene and my part in it. "You can see it for yourselves!"

Mr. Vincent—or rather, Lord Calipash, as I should start to call him, checked for the old man's pulse.

"Well," he sighed. "That's that. There is nothing to be done but prepare ourselves for the funeral and legal expenses. A damned nuisance, I'll warrant, but it shall be soon done with."

"My lord," said Lizzie, in her *how shameful* voice that I knew too well. "How can you say such things? And at a time like this?"

"I barely knew the man," said the new Lord Calipash with a dismissive wave of his pale hand. "He sent me away to live with strangers as soon as I could walk, and called me home only so he could instruct me as to the management of this estate. He cared nothing for me, nor I for him. Now get thee to the kitchen to make my supper, and have Bill dress the body and put it in the crypt to keep it cool until the official burial. Oh—and have him go into the village to send a telegram to our lawyer in London, too."

And he left the room, slamming the door behind him.

I jumped—and then jumped again. The skies had made good on the storm promised since I arrived at the station; thunder crashed, a sudden spatter of thick raindrops hit the glass window. The room lit up with lightning, then fell dark again.

"For goodness' sake, it's only rain," said Lizzie, reprimanding me for my jumpiness. I detected a note of bitterness in her voice. "You'd better go settle in. You will not want to try to return to London tonight."

"Of course," I heard myself say. "I—I am sorry ..."

"And what good does that do anybody?" she said, not looking at me. She looked wracked, grief-stricken, bereft even. "You've ruined so much this day, girl."

Then she said what I had been feeling since my arrival:

"You should never have come back to this house, Chelone Burchell. Not for love or money."

***

Night. In my room—I thought I should not to go down to supper, but hunger drove me from my chambers. Out of respect I dressed in my most somber gown—but I found the new Lord Calipash tipsy as a lord in his father's chair at the head of the table, cravat untied, his meal unfinished before him. A cold collation awaited me on the dirty sideboard; apparently Lizzie was too occupied to cook something hot. At least the platters looked clean.

"My lord," I said, entering the shabby dining room. "You must allow me to apologize—I had no notion my presence would so upset your late father. If I had known—"

"If *I* had known, I should have invited you myself, and weeks ago," he slurred, looking at me half-lidded. "Have some wine, cousin? And some salad, and meat? The cold boiled is particularly good."

I was surprised to hear him address me as *cousin*, for while that is certainly true, I was taught from a young age that my illegitimate origins prevented me from claiming such a connection with the Calipash family.

I could not bring myself to be so informal with him.

"Thank you, my lord. I am thirsty," I said, and he poured me a large glass out of the crystal decanter by his elbow. The claret was blood-red, and sparkled as it flowed. I knew just by looking at it that it was of a better vintage than I had ever before tasted.

"Allow me to apologize for the rude hello I gave you earlier," he said. "I was flustered and not myself."

"It has already been forgotten," I said, accepting the glass he handed me. I took nothing else, I found I did not wish to eat just then, during our first real encounter. "I understand. Meeting each other—now! It is a queer thing."

"What, that a strumpet's whelp should have lived here, in this house, while the son of the lord was exiled? Yes, that is a queer thing," he said. His eyes finally focused on me. "A queer thing indeed."

I knew not what to make of his mood, so I said nothing. I do not enjoy verbal fencing with mercurial gentlemen, that is for sharp-tongued spinsters with many cats and well-thumbed copies of *Emma*.

"Well, let bygones be bygones," he said at last. "'Twas not your fault, my situation, and it would make me unreasonable to blame you. Tell me about yourself, Miss Burchell. What do you do?"

"I am—a writer," I said. "I live in London, where I work for a ladies' periodical."

"Which?"

"You would not have heard of it," I said demurely. Experience has taught me not to divulge my status as pornographer too readily, I have found it is better to let people form an opinion of me before revealing how disreputable I am.

"You might be surprised," he said. "I read all sorts of things."

"Indeed?"

"Things that would make you blush, I'll warrant."

I thought this a sorry attempt at rakishness. "My lord?"

"I should show you my collection sometime ... even though you are but a distant, and to be truthful, unwanted relation, you have Calipash blood in you, and thus should appreciate certain genres considered *outré* by the masses. It is really too bad the Private Library was burned to ashes—"

A clap of thunder from outside, where the storm still raged, silenced him, but I did not mind. I needed a moment to recover myself: He had mentioned the Private Library! That was what had been written on each bookplate: *This Book Belongs to the Private Library of the Calipash Family.*

"Perhaps you are referring to the collection of infamous volumes that used to be housed on the leftmost bookcase of the library? The one that required spinning about to find what it *really* contained?"

It was my turn to surprise him! He sat up in his chair and looked at me keenly. I began to doubt he had drunk as much wine as I had first thought.

"Yes—yes I do! Ach, how can it be that such a lowly urchin has sampled the legendary delights of the Calipash Private Library, and yet I have never done so?"

"I could not say, my lord."

"Perhaps—do you then know why it was burned? I could not understand what my father said regarding the matter. His speech was too far gone when I asked."

I was happy to have something to hold over him, so instead of answering him directly, I stood and began to fill a plate from the contents of the sideboard—salmon salad, cold chicken, succulent orange-slices, tongue in aspic. I avoided the cold boiled.

As I selected the last elements of my repast, over my shoulder I said, "Your father did not share your opinions, my lord."

"Oh? How so?"

"He burned the collection after finding me perusing an illustrated copy of *Fanny Hill*—or, at least, what I know now was a ... let us say *variant* edition of that classic pornography, rewritten to emphasize more deviant black magics than matters carnal. He was so very horrified that he whipped me out the door and into his coach, to be taken directly to school, never permitted to return."

I did not add that he had discovered me with my hand under my own skirts, frigging myself furiously whilst looking at the naughty pictures, strange though some surely were.

It had been a humid summer day, and I had just that year discovered the delights of that revolving bookcase. Actually, I do not believe my guardian knew of the Private Library before that day, as when the old Lord Calipash walked in on me, he snatched the book away, and, eyes wide, had demanded to know where I found such a thing; after seeing what else the collection held he had shouted that he would burn the lot of it, that such titles could do nothing but induce evil in women and men alike.

Though I have never had any reason to doubt my lord's having followed through on the threat, it made me sad to hear he had really done so. It was, after all, an impressive collection of very rare, decadent, and often shockingly corrupt tomes. Those on the subject of fornication were my favorite, of course, but those were fewer and farther between than I liked. Far more of the collection was made up of rather moldy books on performing dark sorceries and profane rituals to honor a pack of heathen gods who sounded rather rum compared to Zeus or Thor. There was one I recall that had loads of filthy pictures—a translation of some sort of foreign sex and murder manual, it seemed to me. I can't recall the title but I know an Englishman named Dee saw fit to have the book available in our tongue, but I question his decision there. It was a far cry from Burton's *Kama Sutra*; I can't imagine anyone would find those positions or actions pleasurable, but there's no accounting for taste, I suppose. But that wasn't all: there were books on horrid-sounding cannibal cults of the ancient world—*Nameless Cults*, I think the title was—and I recall there was even a treatise on the delights of necromancy by a young woman of the family, Rosemary Vincent, whose portrait still hangs in the gallery! Though a stilted homage—or, funny, it must have been a precursor, for she lived during the eighteenth century—to Shelley's *Frankenstein*, my ancestor's manual, *Resurrecting the Dead for Work and Pleasure* was entertaining reading at the very least, as it detailed how one might create some sort of composite creature from dead bodies using common household items and magic spells, many drawn from some of the other books in the Private Library. I had even cross-referenced a few, bored creature that I was … I wonder if Shelley had a copy of her work? It seems the sort of thing Byron would have had lying about.

It occurs to me as I write this that it was in that strange sex-manual where I had once before seen the chimerical tortoise-image my guardian had been wearing. There had been two creatures hand-drawn upon the page, one very like my guardian's pendant, and another in the same style, of a winged, hound-faced sphinx. I saw the same image in a few books, come to think of it, though those had Latin titles and were indecipherable to me.

"Well well well, *Fanny Hill*," said Orlando Vincent, interrupting my thoughts as he poured himself another tipple from the decanter. "Variant or not, it seems the adage *is* true—what is bred in the bone will come out in the flesh. The slut's pup is a slut herself!"

"Then you must be as illegitimate as I, for you are no gentleman!" I said hotly.

"Mind that temper, cousin," he said, and slurped his wine at me lewdly.

"And you mind your manners!" said I. "I shall not be calumniated by a messy-haired stripling, drunk on his father's wine. Good night, sir!" Thus I rose, and took my leave of him.

I wasn't really that offended, I just wanted to make it clear to him that he could not speak to me like that. But upon reaching my rooms I regretted my decision; I was not yet tired. The strange day had enlivened me rather than the reverse.

Remembering that when I was a girl and wakeful in the night I used to sit at my window and brush my hair until I was sleepy, I changed into my night-clothes and blew out the candle. Yet while I thought the ritual would settle my mind, when I saw how ill-tended the storm-lit grounds of Calipash Manor were, instead of relaxing me, looking upon them brought back my earlier feelings of gloom, horror, and ruination.

Especially when I saw that the woods were not so overgrown as to prevent me from seeing the Calipash family crypt through the pine-boughs!

I felt a shock when I saw the crumbling Doric structure, quite as if I had been struck by a bolt of the lightning still occasionally illuminating the night sky—how had I forgotten the nightmarish sepulcher until that very moment? Not that there was anything actually frightening about the place, of course. I had merely scared myself nearly out of my wits in there as a child.

What it is about graveyards that so captivate children I know not, but I would venture there often as a girl. It was far from the house proper, which made it exciting, and overgrown, which put me in mind of fairy-circles or some such nonsense. The day I found enough bravery in myself to push open the door—and found it unlocked—I made my one and only exploration of its interior. There I had fancied I saw a ghost, or perhaps it was the Ghast, a puerile notion I know ... though I confess, looking out upon that temple in miniature again, the little hairs on the back of my neck rose quivering.

A sudden movement tore my eyes away from the loathsome mausoleum. A lone figure ran across the grounds. It was, of all people, Orlando Vincent! Pell-mell he pelted over the grass and through the dregs of the rainstorm, and he was headed toward the graveyard, curiously enough. I wondered on what errand he went; it must be something so urgent it could not wait until morning, so I watched him dash to the crypt and duck inside its carven doorway.

It could not have been five minutes later that he emerged, though with quite a different air about him. Instead of seeming like a man possessed of a desperate mission, he had the lackadaisical aspect of a gentleman very much at his leisure. He stood casually under the overhang of the crypt-entrance for a moment, hands in his pockets—and then he looked up at me!

How he knew I was at my casement I could not say, but I am sure he knew, and I felt another strange shock when his shadowed eyes met mine. I raised my hand in greeting, not knowing if he could see the gesture, but he mirrored it. When a final flash of lightning illuminated the grounds I saw he was smiling at me.

I felt a flush of passion worthy of my heroine Camilla and rose from my seat, alarmed at myself. It was then that I re-lit the candle and sat down here—to write—to try to settle my mind. I am not sure if it has worked ...

***

I was too disturbed by my newfound carnal thoughts about my cousin to sleep, so I crept from my room to the tower stairs, thinking I should like to see how altered was the place we had used to play together as children. Up and up I climbed, my candle casting strange shadows on the walls of the staircase, until I reached the door. Upon pushing it open, I found the room unchanged by time. There was even still a sheet strung from wall to wall, the roof of our play-castle in which we had pretended to be lords and ladies. I took a faltering step and my foot hit something—looking down, I saw it was the play-sword that Laurent once used to carve dragons and monsters to pieces. That sword was the only thing that had gotten me to come up to the tower, for the first time we braved the stairs, I had believed it haunted!

A sudden movement made me scream—perhaps there really was a ghost that haunted this room! But then my cousin emerged from the shadows, grinning at me.

"Why Camilla! Venturing up here—and in the dark!"

"Oh, Laurent! You gave me such a fright!" I cried. My legs were trembling beneath my night-dress; perceiving this, he offered me his arm and led me to a dusty sofa.

"Will you allow me to make it up to you?" said he. "I know a treatment that is said to cure nervousness in women, it is called *fucking.*"

"Oh, I know all about fucking," I laughed weakly. "I have never done it, but nearly everything but. The girls at school said I could lick a quim better than anybody, and a gentleman on the train said my cock-sucking was first rate!"

"Let us see about that," he said, putting my hand on his stiffening prick. It was quite a large affair, larger than anything I had yet encountered. "If you are as good as you say, then I shall introduce you to the very best pleasure of all!"

5 April 1887, Morning. In my room.

Oh, what a good night's sleep can do to improve one's spirits! Or at the very least, a good night's *something*. Susan was right, my visit home has yielded quite a lot of inspiration for my serial!

Not a quarter of an hour after I blew out my candle for the second time I heard a soft knock at my door. Somehow I knew who was outside—the new Lord Calipash—but unsure if I wanted to see him, I did not answer. He had been unpleasant, yes, but he was also rather attractive, at least in a squirrely sort of way, and I have enjoyed my share of casual romps with far more irksome men. Many and manifest are the advantages of having no inclination to marry and an excellent understanding of abortifacients.

A second knock, then the handle turned. Without lifting my head from my pillow I saw in the doorway the outline of Orlando, whom I think I may now safely call by his Christian name!

He stole into my chamber, closing the door softly behind him, and then shed his coat, throwing it upon the chair in which I had earlier sat scribbling on my latest story, which, if I do say so myself, is coming along nicely. After kicking off his shoes, to my surprise, he slid wordlessly into bed beside me.

"My God," I whispered, for he stank of death from his trip into the family crypt. "What is it you want so badly that you could not bathe before coming to me, I wonder?"

He said nothing—merely groaned in the most fetching, desperate manner, and put his hand on where my right breast swelled beneath my nightgown. I turned over, and his lips found mine.

I drew back, appalled by his stench. It emanated from every pore in his body; his mouth was foul with the reek of the grave.

"Go and wash," I said. I love an unexpected frolick, but the unclean human body is disgusting to me.

He groaned again, urgently, but due to his odor I was no longer inclined to engage in any amorous endeavors. I pushed him away, but he grabbed my wrist, and held up something in his other hand. It swung to and fro in the moonlight, for the fading storm had parted her clouds to reveal the last sliver of that waning sphere, and I could just see what he held out to me.

It was the jade tortoise I had earlier seen hanging 'round my guardian's neck!

"For me?" I asked him, surprised. He grunted his assent, and then fastened the clasp around my neck.

When I felt the weight of the cold stone on my skin (I am ashamed to write this, for I cannot account for it—not even to myself, here in my private diary) I was possessed of a passion stronger than any I have ever felt before. I was ever so desperate to be fucked, more than when I finally managed to sneak Lord Crim-Con away from his wife for a quick one in a servant's bed at their tenth anniversary party, more even than the time on the occasion of my twenty-third birthday when Susan surprised me by taking me on holiday to Winsor, and snuck me into her brother's dormitory so I could have some sport with five handsome youths of that year's senior class.

"Why, Lord Calipash," said I, snaking my hand down his chest and under the lip of his trousers. "You have inflamed—bewitched me! I simply must have you! Do let us make love!"

He kissed his answer upon my neck, and then lower, lower. I know I am in the habit of describing my encounters in detail here, for my personal enjoyment when I am in my dotage, but we sported for so long, and in so many ways, I fear I shall miss breakfast if I record everything. Suffice it to say, a more tender, compassionate lover I could never want, and he made full use of every place of pleasure I possess. It is sadly rare to find a man as able with bottom-hole as with cunt, but Orlando knew the unique needs, challenges, and delights to be had behind as well as in front. He also had no reservations allowing me to do what I would with him, even going so far as to allow me to work my favorite dildo (I always take it with me) up into his fundament to induce the truly copious spending which is nigh impossible for men to produce any other way.

Good Lord, but I am hungry! It's only natural after taking so much exercise in the night, I suppose.

***

Later—Orlando was not at breakfast. Lizzie says he will not come out of his room.

***

Later still—Feeling rather lonely, for neither Lizzie nor Bill seem to want much to do with me (they are holed up in the kitchen, apparently "doing what must be done" regarding the Lord Calipash's death, though I swear I saw Bill sweep away a trick of bezique when I came into the room … but I must have imagined it, for the sanctimonious old ferret never trucks with any games at all, and certainly not cards!) I went for a walk after my meal.

The grounds are still very lovely here, I think their being so overgrown actually adds to their savage charm. And yet … one would think such a wilderness would attract more wild creatures, but I saw no life within the twilit deeps except for a tiny, but bright red bird of a type I had never seen before. It landed on a tree and peered at me silently. I know it will sound strange, but I swear that once it was sure it held my attention, it fluttered to a close-by tree and did not move until I stepped toward it. Then it did the same thing again, and again, until it led me—by chance, surely—to the Calipash family crypt. There it landed on the pediment—and after a moment, flew inside the crypt itself. The door was ajar from Orlando's midnight sojourn.

The charnel smell that had clung to Orlando's flesh last night whilst we frolicked emanated from the black interior; I found it nauseating but strangely compelling, and reached out my hand to push open the door and further investigate what lay inside the sepulcher. In I went, and once again braved the stone steps down into the crypt proper.

It is a horrid place, the crypt, a burial-place worthy of the strange legends concocted by the locals. Grinning carven demons watch over the bodies of former Calipash lords, and from their mouths emanate awful orange and purple light, very like sunlight through filtered glass, but they shine even at night! My steps echoed on the granite floor as I peered about, revisiting that dead place where the dead dwell, thinking of the strange ghost I had thought I had seen as a child—but then I am ashamed to say my courage failed me. I fancied I heard the ghost groaning at me; looking up, I saw a shadow of a man, tall and thin—and screamed!

"It is surely the Ghast!" I cried, and fled, nearly falling back down the moisture-slick stairs several times in my haste, but by the time the handle of the garden-door of Calipash Manor was in my hand I was laughing at myself for being such a noodle. The wind often moans when it passes over stone, does it not, and I had left the door ajar—and why, I wondered, had it not occurred to me that Orlando could have walked in front of the crypt-door? That would have cast a shadow very like the "ghost" I saw.

If there is any *real* danger here at Calipash Manor, it is too much sunshine. I must be more careful of my skin—my complexion will be ruined if I continue taking morning walks. My skin is browner already, I am sure of it.

***

Afternoon—Orlando did not come down to dinner. I fear I must have done him a mischief. Perhaps attempting to induce a fourth occasion took more out of him than I anticipated?

I had a solitary, silent meal in the dining room; again, Lizzie and Bill would not allow me to dine with them. They were really rather stern with me about it.

"We would have notions of rank preserved in this house, Chelone," said Lizzie. "Anarchy results elseways."

"Yes indeed, a woman of your breeding mustn't break bread with those such as us," said Bill—which in anyone else I would think to be a crack about my lack of proper parentage, but not from Bill!

Ah well. I have eaten lonelier meals.

I wonder, though, if I didn't work myself into rather an agitated state, too—I could stomach only the vegetable courses.

***

Late Afternoon—Something strange is going on, I am sure of it. Orlando *must* be ill. Before going down to tea I knocked on the door of his room, and heard nothing. I raised my voice and told him it was tea-time, and I heard a faint moan from within. Who declines tea? Even invalids must have their refreshing cuppa and hot buttered toast, surely.

***

After Tea—I went to consult with Lizzie about Orlando, though I hated to disturb her again after her earlier sternness with me. It is funny, as I approached the kitchen-door, I am sure I misheard her, but before I knocked, I heard her conversing with Bill. He said, "that he will not stir is a good sign," and I thought I overheard her say "Soon will come the hour of the tortoise," which made Bill laugh, a harsh sound. Then I knocked; they fell silent as I entered.

"I fear the Lord Calipash may be ill," said I.

"As I said, he was up late last night," said Lizzie. "When I retired he had called Bill to bring him another bottle of wine. Have you never had a hangover?"

"Even if he was up late—"

"Likely he's a cold upon him," said Bill. He had obviously been doing something that required his high boots (come to think of it, he could have been the source of the shadow, as he is tall and thin, too). Mud plastered his feet and calves nearly to the knee, but he had not shed his footwear before coming to sit at the table. Lizzie, I was surprised to note, did not chide him for this; indeed, she seemed hardly to notice his mess. This was quite a change from the attitude she used to take when I came in from outside without a care!

"A cold!" I exclaimed.

"He went outside last night, in the storm," said Bill, and shrugged at me as he put his boots up on one of the kitchen chairs, fouling it horribly. "I tried to speak reason to him, but he would not listen. Said he wished to keep vigil by the side of his dead father. Heathen notion—perhaps it is as you say, and the Lord has punished him with an ailment."

"Then he must be in need of at least a cup of tea," I said, exasperated. "Let me bring it to him, you needn't trouble yourselves."

"Oh, go on then," said Lizzie, pouring some liquid the color of wash-water into a chipped cup. "Take him this, if you must be meddlesome."

It was in low spirits indeed that I went up to Orlando's room, tea in hand. I have rarely felt so depressed. This slapdash housekeeping and surly language would be understandable, of course, if Bill and Lizzie seemed distraught over my guardian's death, but neither seem to care tuppence about it—they have not even mentioned it to me! And come to think of it, the house was topsy-turvy when I arrived. From what I saw, taking care of the former Lord Calipash would not have occupied the whole of their waking hours, so how can they account for how decrepit Calipash Manor has become? It pains me to write this, but I feel as though the two of them have no emotion whatsoever as regards their former master; I get the strange feeling if no one would notice the irregularity of it, they would not even attend to the funereal arrangements. When I was a girl neither one of them seemed the sort of servant who would take a "when the cat's away" attitude toward their duties, but perhaps I was not a perceptive child?

Well, regardless, I went up to Orlando's room and entered without knocking, only to find him prostrate on the bed, sheets wound around him like a shroud. The curtains were drawn and I could barely see my way over to him.

"Lord Calipash?" I whispered. "It is I—Chelone, your cousin, come to see if you need anything?"

He groaned and stirred, and I took this as a good sign. Setting the cup of tea down beside him, I took the liberty of seating myself on his bed and patting his shoulder.

"It is after tea-time, please—won't you take a bite or sip of anything?"

"My head," he groaned. "Oh, Chelone—I was beastly to you last night, was I not?"

"Never mind that," I said. "I believe you have already apologized enough."

"Did I?" He flopped over onto his side and looked at me. "I must have had more wine than I thought."

"Not all apologies must be spoken," I said, and touched where my new lovely necklace hung below my blouse. Stroking the pendant, even through the fabric, gave me the most visceral shock! Plenty of times I have received trinkets from lovers, but this—it comforted me to have it about my neck, as if it were a warm extension of my very flesh.

"True enough, I suppose! Draw back the curtains, cousin, and hand me that tea—*ahh*," he said, sipping it. "Better. I should not have lingered in bed so long, but ach—my head! How it aches!"

"Well, you had a long night," I said over my shoulder.

"Indeed I did. Ventured out to that tomb—well, you must know that already. Dreadfully wet, and I fell—or hit my head—or something. Must have slipped." He took another long slurp of tea and fell back upon the pillows of his bed. "Well, no lasting harm done. Still feel miserable, though."

"Is there anything I can do?"

"I wonder …" He looked at me. "You seem in a maternal sort of mood, eh? Would you be so kind—no."

"Ask anything and it shall be yours, if it is within my power to give it."

"Just sit with me, talk to me. Keep me company. I never had a relative to look after me before."

Poor dear! "Let me read to you, then—and perhaps you will doze until supper-time."

"Smashing idea, Chelone. What would you like to read?"

"You claimed to have a collection that would make me blush," I suggested, having retained no small curiosity regarding his literary tastes. "Even if you no longer think me so easily shocked, I should like to see what you have."

Even in the dim light—for though I had drawn back the drapes, the hour was late, and the sunlight waning—I saw him blush pinker than a rose! I had no expectation of his showing any shyness after the events of last night, and felt such a rush of tenderness for the dear boy that I kissed him on the forehead.

"N—no," he stammered. "I was, ah, drinking last night, you see, and loose-tongued; I was not myself, and should not have mentioned such things about—about my family, myself, and …"

Such an endearing display! Charmed, I put my finger to his lips and shook my head. I was not to be dissuaded.

"Let me read something—I shall pick it. Just nod where you have stowed them. Coyness will only make me all the more eager!"

He looked miserable as a wet cat, but pointed with a trembling finger towards a valise not yet unpacked. Opening the top, I discovered to my delight that it was entirely full of pornography! He had a lovely old edition of *Juliette*, several volumes of *The Pearl* and *The Oyster* (I cannot fault him; though Lazenby has always been a competitor, his work is very fine), a chapbook of Swinburne's "Reginald's Flogging," *The Sins of the Cities of the Plain*, which perhaps would explain his ability with arses—and, I was happy to see, quite a few editions of *Milady's Ruby Vase*!

"I see you are quite an avid reader," said I, which caused him to choke on the dregs of his tea. "Here, I have selected something. Let me read to you—ah, yes! Here is a good-sounding yarn, 'What My Brother Learned in India' by a Rosa Birchbottom."

"Not that one," he said with such trepidation I felt rather wounded.

"Why ever not?"

"I ... please, Chelone. She is my very favorite author, and I fear I should—embarrass myself."

"Rosa Birchbottom is your favorite author?" How could I not laugh! "Let me read this story, then. I trust your taste, cousin."

"I—"

"*My brother studied a great many things whilst in India, and upon his return he was good enough to teach me some of what he learned about the voluptuous peculiarities of the human body,*" I read, or rather, recited half from memory. "*Given that I am soon to die of a wasting sickness that has claimed my beauty, rendering me unfit to engage in any amorous sport, I have decided to spend my remaining days writing down some of the most exotic techniques he taught me, techniques to induce to sensual erotic pleasure in man or woman ... *Orlando!"

He had begun to weep, and I set aside the volume, feeling rather rotten indeed.

"Whatever is the matter?" I asked him.

"I am a disgusting creature," said he, "to own such wicked books—and to ask a young lady to read them! Here I have you debasing yourself before me, and—"

"None of that," I said sternly. "It is no debasement to read these words, pornography is not a wicked art! Oh, Orlando, I apologize. I was only so very amused. You see, *I* am Rosa Birchbottom. It tickled me last night when you implied I should read pornography—I write it for my living!"

"You?" he sat up straight and looked at me with fresh, adoring eyes. "You wouldn't tease me, cousin?"

"Never, I assure you. I told you I worked for a periodical, did I not? I authored 'What My Brother Learned in India,' 'The Personal Papers of Lady Strokinpoke,' 'A Penny Spent,' and 'A Sporting Attitude Indeed.' I had to take a *nom de plume* or risk all sort of unpleasantness if our publication is ever shut down on obscenity charges. It is a bad pun, I know, but my very first story was a Mrs. Lechworthy tale, you see."

"I have it in my collection," said he, placing his hand upon my knee in an endearingly familiar manner. "I really think 'Le Vice Anglese' is one of the very best stories ever written."

"Flatterer," I said.

"Not at all—but …" He blushed again.

"What?"

"I am sorry, I was about to trouble you with an impertinence …"

"What could be impertinent between us, cousin?"

"Do you … ever … do you write from experience? Or is it all … imagination?"

The dear young man! "I know why you ask, Orlando, but fear not. Though I have in the past used my experiences to inform my writings, I never do so directly. And I never name names."

"I see … so you are not, oh, how did you put it so delightfully in 'A Penny Spent'? *Burdened by an exasperating virginity?*"

I laughed. "Is that a question you needed to ask me? Could you not tell?"

Orlando's lip twitched and then his face lit up in the most handsome smile I had ever seen on a man's face. "Oh, Chelone, I am feeling ever so much better now, you have raised my spirits to the point I think I could manage a bit of supper! Would you like to dress and come down with me?"

"Very much so, my dear Orlando," said I.

"I am ever so glad you came to Calipash Manor," he said. "Why—I feel as though I've known you my whole life. It is funny, before you arrived my father was speaking of twins, twins born into this family— do you not think we could be siblings? Look in the mirror, there—are not our faces quite alike?"

"I hope we are not twins," said I, though it gave me quite a start to see how alike we were. "Are not Calipash twins always supposed to be cursed? Evil?"

"That was what my father told me, at least. Well, well, it seems an unlikely coincidence, does it not? But we shall talk more about it over dinner, eh, cousin?"

And thus I must hurry—he will be awaiting me! Oh, I am ever so glad I came home again. It is rare, when one writes under a false name, to meet one's public in person! Very enjoyable, as is Orlando himself. I do think I shall have another go with him after our meal, if he is willing and able …

***

The dress I wore that night was not expensive, and though it had been turned once, I thought it looked well enough when I gazed at my reflection in the glass. My only regret was how high the neckline, for though I wore his gift none could see it. Still, its warm weight was a secret comfort to me, for he had given this present to me as a token of affection, and feeling it 'round my neck reminded me that I needed not fear disgracing myself in front of my nobler relation with my ignorant manners and common conversation.

When I heard the knock at my door I very nearly turned my ankle in my dash to answer the summons. It was Laurent, looking very dashing indeed, and he even took my hand and kissed it when he saw me!

"Dearest Camilla, how beautiful you look," he said, lasciviously licking his lips with his red tongue. "Why, my cock is half-standing just looking at you, remembering the rapturous sensation of Mr. John Thomas battering his way up inside of you, taking for my own your troublesome maidenhead! Careful, or I might make a mistake—and eat *you* instead of my supper."

"I am glad you have not had your fill of me. I have heard it said in town that you are indeed a rake and libertine."

"It is all in the past," he assured me. "I have never thought to marry, but you, my cousin, have won my heart, body, and soul."

Alas, for I was a fool to believe such words! I assure you, as I write this, locked up for crimes I did not commit, that no woman has ever suffered more than I on account of love!

We lingered over supper, which consisted of every food known to inspire amorous devotion: caviar, asparagus, oysters, champagne, artichokes in white wine, and finally, a tiny cup of potent chocolate. By the end of it I was swooning with passion and anxious to retire, but it was not to be. As a final course, Laurent's housekeeper surprised us by coming in with two chilled glasses of a French anisette liqueur as a digestif—but when I reached to take mine off the silver tray, the silver-filigreed cameo Laurent had given me spilled out from the neckline of my gown.

"Thief!" cried his housekeeper. "Why, it is Lady Fanchone's favorite ornament, long thought to be missing! How did it come to be concealed on your person, I wonder?"

"Laurent gave it to me last night," said I, shocked by her implication.

"How could he, when it has been gone these ten years? As I recall it, Lady Fanchone wished to bequeath it to her only son and heir—and could not, for it had vanished!"

I thought Laurent would come to my defense, but when I raised my tear-filled eyes to meet his, I saw only cruelty there.

"Indeed, it had long been my desire to have that ornament turned into a cravat-pin—and here you are, possessed of it! My, my ... Camilla! I never thought you would be the sort of girl around whom I should have to count the silver! To discover the woman I thought to make my bride is actually a low thief—and a thief so bold as to wear her ill-gotten possessions around those who might miss them!"

I know it does not speak to my honesty to confess here that I bolted from the table then, thinking to leave The Beeches on foot. But I ask you, dearest reader, what hope I had of protesting my innocence when Laurent—he whom I had thought devoted to me—was speaking such dreadful falsehoods? You, my friend, know that I am innocent, that I would never steal, but I was apprehended by the handyman before I had taken ten steps out the front door. I screamed and beat his breast with my fists, demanding he release me, but he was far stronger than I, and restrained me easily. Then a policeman was called, and the matter seemed more and more hopeless. My character is no longer known in these parts, after all, and so it was the easiest thing to conclude I was a thief!

To keep me from fleeing before my trial, I was locked into the tower with only a meager supply of candles to keep me from the grim darkness at night.

It seems a century past, but it was less than a fortnight ago that I was found guilty of the crime of stealing the cameo necklace, and tomorrow I shall be hanged for it. The town being so small I was locked back into the tower at The Beeches for safekeeping; they bring me my meals fairly regularly, but already my dress hangs off my body, so hungry, cold, and lonely am I. Woe is me! I asked my jailers for paper and pencil so I could write my story; this, as it is my last request, they have given me. Thus I have recorded all that transpired during my fateful journey to my home county, where, instead of love, I have found only death. My only conclusion is that Laurent always intended to cast me aside, and gave me the necklace to have a good reason to do so.

I have no regrets but one as to my actions in life, the things I have enjoyed and done—but trusting such a knave as Laurent and his hateful staff was a greater mistake than any of my amorous encounters. Would that I had taken Mr. Milliner up on his offer to elope with him! I am sure I should be happier than here, alone, in the darkness, awaiting my death.

***

That should do; I shall copy it out now.

Date unknown, time of day uncertain, languishing in the crypt

My plan has not worked, all hope has left me. I must conclude that either my dear editrix Susan did not perceive the cipher I painstakingly included in the handwritten conclusion I composed for "A Camilla Among the Beeches," or it has not been sent to her as was promised. I suspect the latter; given the extent of the treachery I have experienced, I cannot believe in human kindness any longer.

Here I shall record what actually befell me more than a fortnight ago, if my sense of time has not been too much disturbed by living as I have been, in the Calipash family crypt. (I have counted meals, but they have been thrown down to me at strange intervals with no difference between breakfast and dinner, as I can no longer stomach much.) It pains me to write about my misfortunes, for this honors a hideous request, but at the very least I know this document will live on in the Private Library—which I have found out was never burnt, and exists today, and is now one book richer. I suppose it is every writer's wish to compose something that others might enjoy, and though future Calipash heirs may take pleasure in the real account which inspired 'A Camilla Among the Beeches' more for my suffering than any greatness of prose, such is life.

I went down to dinner in my most modest gown, for when I was dressing for dinner I saw how brown and mottled my skin had become. I thought then it was from too much sun during my earlier walk; I know better now. Regardless, Orlando, sweet boy, remarked upon my dress favorably, and we enjoyed our meal.

But when Lizzie came in with our dessert, I reached for the decanter of wine upon the table—and the jade tortoise pendant fell from my décolletage. Then all was confusion!

"My God, it is my father's necklace!" cried Orlando, pointing at the glowing object dangling before my bosom. "How has it come into your possession, Chelone?"

"It is the potent thing itself!" cried Lizzie, dropping the tray of blancmange. "Bill!" she screeched at the top of her lungs. "Brother! Come! I have discovered it! It is *not* lost!"

"What?" said I, backing away quickly from the table. "Orlando! Tell them you gave it to me late last night!"

"I did not give it to you, nor did I see you after you left this room!" he exclaimed. "I drank and drank, then went down into the crypt after Bill came to me and told me he had forgotten to strip the pendant from my father's body. I went to get it—and there was my father's corpse, cold on the marble slab where Bill had put him, but the necklace was gone! And then there was a strange sound ... and I startled away from the body—and hit my head—and woke up in my own bed!"

"Indeed," said Bill, coming into the room, "I think I have an explanation for that, dearest Lizzie. I've just had a visit with Rosemary's golem."

"The golem!" exclaimed Lizzie. "Well, I never!"

"Explain yourselves," demanded Orlando. He was standing between myself and Lizzie and Bill. "Tell me what is happening here!"

At this, Bill slapped Orlando across the mouth, and the young Lord fell to the carpet, howling and clutching his mouth.

"Silence, churl," said Bill, and spat on his master. "You speak unto your rightful lord! I am William Fitzroy, Lord Calipash, and you are nothing but a lesser man's son, thou shameful usurper!"

It was such a strange scene—and my confusion so great—that I made to run away from the room; indeed, I wished to quit the house entirely, but Lizzie stuck out her foot and tripped me. After I fell to the ground with a cry, I tried to claw my way to the door with my hands, but she lifted up her skirts and sat upon my chest to hold me hostage. When I cried out she punched me in the side so hard I wept for the pain.

"Dearest William," said she, "why is it you suspect the golem?"

"He told me—or rather, I had him write it all down for me," said Bill. "When I saw how fit and healthy Orlando looked when he came down to dinner, I knew his earlier indisposition must be from some other source than the necklace's transformative properties. Looking upon Chelone, how dreadful her skin appears now, I suspected some trickery, and went to the crypt for insight. And look at this!"

He held up a scrap of paper before Lizzie's eyes, and I caught a glimpse of it—the note was in my guardian's own handwriting!

"It wrote to her," said Bill. "It apparently saw her as a girl and took a fancy to her, and in the confusion over our brother's decline it thought it could safely invite her back and have some sport with her. It's smarter than I ever realized, and it *does* look rather like Orlando—if one doesn't peer too closely. Thus it was able to sneak down to the village and send her the note that called her hither! It wants a *bride*, dear sister. Just like the legends about it! Imagine that—the peasants knew something we didn't!"

"It seems from this note that they had quite a wedding night," said Lizzie, looking up from the parchment to leer at me.

I could barely breathe for her sitting on me, and choked on my tears. What, I wondered, was a golem, to live in a crypt, and send false letters?

"Careful, sister, or you'll give her fits," said Bill. "We can't have another one die on us, after the failure with our brother."

"I shan't let her suffocate. If we keep her and allow her to pupate into the Guardian, then all we'll have to worry about is *that*," here she pointed to where Orlando whimpered on the ground, "We can't have him destroying the illusion that we are a happy family ..."

"Indeed," said Bill. "We can use him for all sorts of things, actually. I believe he's a virgin, which could prove ... useful."

"What is happening," I wept. "Oh, do get up, do let me go, please!"

"It's too late for you, stupid girl," said Lizzie, and kicked me in the side with her boot-heel. "Though it may please you to know you alone have been the agent of your undoing. Rather amusing! If you hadn't surprised the former Lord into death, then he would have completed his transmutation, and you should have gotten away from here safely."

"Sister, do think—if she had not been discovered perusing the Private Library, inducing the anger that made our loathsome brother wish to destroy it, then we never would have thought to create a Guardian to protect our family legacy from future well-meaning fools! Ha! It is very funny, how a young girl's curiosity can result in such tragedy." He smiled thinly. "Rather Gothic, really. Isn't the bitch some sort of petty writer? Too bad she'll never put it all into a story."

"Perhaps we should have her chronicle her transformation!" sniggered Lizzie. "It might be of great scientific interest one day."

"So it is *you* who are the twins of whom my father spoke," mumbled Orlando, his hand raised to where his cheek still bled. "I thought he had become completely insensible when he began to rant about how he had siblings—twins, yes, but not terrible he thought, though he said to be on the lookout for you, lest you show some sign of treachery! Alas—I have realized it too late!"

I know it sounds incredible, that in this modern time such things as curses are real, but as I languish in the crypt, surrounded by my mummified ancestors and these strange stone gargoyles that emit the weird light by which I can see to write this, gradually changing into the creature whose jade likeness I so unwittingly wore upon my breast, I have been forced to admit I should have heeded the warning given to me during my train-ride home to Ivybridge. Lizzie and Bill, two people whom I should never have suspected of evil, have been proven to be nothing but. Long did they plot their revenge on my former guardian for his decision to destroy the Private Library; long have they cursed fortune for having made he who I knew as the Lord Calipash the legitimate heir, and them the servitors of an estate they could claim no right to manage.

The worst part is, Bill was not being hyperbolic when he accused me of authoring my own undoing—indeed, it is the case, in so very many ways. When the former Lord Calipash found me so entranced by that strange, deviant copy of *Fanny Hill*, he resolved to burn the collection. Bill told me that, horrified by the idea of his family's Private Library destroyed, *he* offered to do it for his master and half-brother—but instead he stoked the bonfire with other books, all the while secreting the foul tomes of the Private Library in the family crypt, where I will now dwell until the end of my life, which I think will be for decades, if not centuries, if what I have been told is true.

It seems the very day I was sent away to school, Lizzie and Bill resolved to create for the Calipash family's possessions a Guardian, immortal and terrible, who would protect the satanic heirlooms of this degenerate family if again they were threatened. Such will be my fate. The golem—he with whom I am miserably and all-too-closely acquainted—would not do for the office, being constructed by his mistress, as I understand it, out of dead Calipash males for pleasure-purposes, and thus is more lover than fighter.

But the twins, like me, had gazed upon the fell contents of that strange, leather-bound book wherein I first saw the image of the winged tortoise, only they knew how to decipher its malignant text. Discovering that the pendant would transform its owner into rabid protectors of mortal treasure, long did they search for the idol that has changed me, and when they at last found it, they gave it unto my guardian—but I surprised him into death before he could fully transmute! Thus I was many times over my own executioner, and I use that word for I sense I shall be Miss Chelone Burchell for not too much more of my life. I can tell by the thickening of my skin and the swelling of my belly; the seizing of my hands into clawed monkey's paws, the growing of two strange protuberances upon my already insensate back.

The twins had wanted the old Lord Calipash for a guardian, to punish him for his attempt to destroy the Private Library; my heinous half-aunt and half-uncle, evil though they surely are, held no ill-will towards me, and to their credit have expressed some regret over the unfortunate circumstances that have led me to this very particular doom. Their next victim was to have been Orlando; indeed, Bill himself had sent my cousin out to the crypt that night, to suffer the transformation himself. Now they are holding him for purposes of their own, I know not what—and likely never shall. They have told me only that Bill, shaven, is very like the old Lord Calipash, and so plans on impersonating his old master until the end of his days, claiming to have had a miraculous recovery from the illness that, unexpectedly, claimed his own groundskeeper!

At least I shall not be lonely. There is the voiceless golem who tries in his way to comfort me, poor creature, and the massive Private Library to read, and demoniac treasures I have found, and spend many hours contemplating. Oh, but none of it is any comfort to me; how I wish I had never come home! Calipash Manor is a blasphemous, unthinkable place, and to visit here is to face not death, but the vast terror of selfish, unfathomable evil. So ends my tale—my hands stiffen, my eyes dull—and the world shall never know what became of me. Beware those who would seek to rob my family: Soon it shall come the hour of the tortoise!

the infernal history of the ivybridge twins

I.

Concerning the life and death of Clement Fitzroy Vincent, Lord Calipash—the suffering of the Lady Calipash—the unsavory endeavors of Lord Calipash's cousin Mr. Villein—as well as an account of the curious circumstances surrounding the birth of the future Lord Calipash and his twin sister

In the county of Devonshire, in the parish of Ivybridge, stood the ancestral home of the Lords Calipash. Calipash Manor was large, built sturdily of the local limestone, and had stood for many years without fire or other catastrophe marring its expanse. No one could impugn the size and antiquity of the house, yet often one or another of those among Lord Calipash's acquaintance might be heard to comment that the Manor had a rather rambling, hodgepodge look to it, and this could not be easily refuted without the peril of speaking a falsehood. The reason for this was that the Lords Calipash had always been the very essence of English patriotism, and rather than ever tearing down any part of the house and building anew, each Lord Calipash had chosen to make additions and improvements to older structures. Thus, though the prospect was somewhat sprawling, it served as a pleasant enough reminder of the various styles of Devonian architecture, and became something of a local attraction.

Clement Fitzroy Vincent, Lord Calipash, was a handsome man, tall, fair-haired, and blue-eyed. He had been bred up as any gentleman of rank and fortune might be, and therefore the manner of his death was more singular than any aspect of his life. Now, given that this is, indeed, an *Infernal* History, the sad circumstances surrounding this good man's unexpected and early demise demand attention by the author, and they are inextricably linked with the Lord Calipash's cousin, a young scholar called Mr. Villein, who will figure more prominently in this narrative than his nobler relation.

Mr. Villein came to stay at Calipash Manor during the Seven

Years' War, in order to prevent his being conscripted into the French army. Though indifference had previously characterized the relationship between Lord Calipash and Mr. Villein (Mr. Villein belonging to a significantly lower branch of the family tree), when Mr. Villein wrote to Lord Calipash to beg sanctuary, the good Lord would not deny his own flesh and blood. This was not to say, however, that Lord Calipash was above subtly encouraging his own flesh and blood to make his stay a short one, and to that end, he gave Mr. Villein the tower bedroom that had been built by one of the more eccentric Lords some generations prior to our tale, who so enjoyed pretending to be the Lady Jane Grey that he had the edifice constructed so his wife could dress up as member of the Privy Council and keep him locked up there for as long as nine days at a stretch. But that was not the reason Lord Calipash bade his cousin reside there—the tower was a drafty place, and given to damp, and thus seemed certain of securing Mr. Villein's speedy departure. As it turns out, however, the two men were so unlike one another, that what Lord Calipash thought was an insulting situation, Mr. Villein found entirely salubrious, and so, happily, out of a case of simple misunderstanding grew an affection, founded on deepest admiration for Mr. Villein's part, and for Lord Calipash's, enjoyment of toadying.

All the long years of the international conflict Mr. Villein remained at Calipash Manor, and with the passing of each and every day he came more into the confidence of Lord Calipash, until it was not an uncommon occurrence to hear members of Lord Calipash's circle using words like *inseparable* to describe their relationship. Then, only six months before the signing of the Treaty of Paris, the possibility of continued fellowship between Lord Calipash and Mr. Villein was quite suddenly extinguished. A Mr. Fellingworth moved into the neighborhood with his family, among them his daughter of fifteen years, Miss Alys Fellingworth. Dark of hair and eye but pale of cheek, her beauty did not go long unnoticed by the local swains. She had many suitors and many offers, but from among a nosegay of sparks she chose as her favorite blossom the Lord Calipash.

Mr. Villein had also been among Miss Fellingworth's admirers, and her decision wounded him—not so much that he refused to come to the wedding (he was very fond of cake), but certainly enough that all the love Mr. Villein had felt for Lord Calipash was instantly converted, as if by alchemy, to pure hatred. In his dolor, Mr. Villein managed to convince himself that Miss Fellingworth's father had pressured her to accept Lord Calipash's offer for the sake of his rank and income, against her true inclinations; that had she been allowed to pick her heart's choice, she certainly would have accepted Mr. Villein's suit rather than his cousin's. Such notions occupied Mr. Villein's thoughts whenever he saw the happy couple together, and every day his mind became more and more inhospitable to any pleasure he might have otherwise felt on account of his friend's newfound felicity.

A reader of this history might well wonder why Mr. Villein did not quit Calipash Manor, given that his situation, previously so agreeable, he now found intolerable. Mr. Villein was, however, loath to leave England. He had received a letter from his sister informing him that during his absence, his modest home had been commandeered by the army, and thus his furniture was in want of replacing, his lands trampled without hope of harvest, his stores pilfered, and, perhaps worst of all, his wretched sister was with child by an Austrian soldier who had, it seemed, lied about his interest in playing the rôle of father beyond the few minutes required to grant him that status. It seemed prudent to Mr. Villein to keep apart from such appalling circumstances for as long as possible.

Then one evening, from the window of his tower bedroom, Mr. Villein saw Lord Calipash partaking of certain marital pleasures with the new Lady Calipash against a tree in one of the gardens. Nauseated, Mr. Villein called for his servant and announced his determination to secretly leave Calipash Manor once and for all early the following morning. While the servant packed his bags and trunks, Mr. Villein penned a letter explaining his hasty departure to Lord Calipash, and left it, along with a token of remembrance, in the Lord Calipash's study.

Quite early the next morning, just as he was securing his cravat, Mr. Villein was treated to the unexpected but tantalizing sight of Lady Calipash in *deshabille*. She was beside herself with grief, but eventually Mr. Villein, entirely sympathetic and eager to understand the source of her woe, coaxed the story from her fevered mind:

"I woke early, quite cold," gibbered Lady Calipash. "Lord Calipash had never come to bed, though he promised me when I went up that he should follow me after settling a few accounts. When I discovered him absent I rose and sought him in his study only to find him—*dead*. Oh! It was too terrible! His eyes were open, wide and round and staring. At first I thought it looked very much like he had been badly frightened, but then I thought he had almost a look of ... of *ecstasy* about him. I believe—"

Here the Lady Calipash faltered, and it took some minutes for Mr.

Villein to get the rest of the story from her, for her agitated state required his fetching smelling salts from out of his valise. Eventually, she calmed enough to relate the following:

"I believe he might have done himself the injury that took him from me," she sobbed. "His wrists were slit, and next to him lay his letter-opener. He ... he had used his own blood to scrawl a message on the skirtingboards ... oh Mr. Villein!"

"What did the message say?" asked Mr. Villein.

"It said, *he is calling, he is calling, I hear him*," she said, and then she hesitated.

"What is it, Lady Calipash?" asked Mr. Villein.

"I cannot see its importance, but he had this in his other hand," said she, and handed to Mr. Villein a small object wrapped in a handkerchief.

He took it from her, and saw that it was an odd bit of ivory, wrought to look like a lad's head crowned with laurel. Mr. Villein put it in his pocket and smiled at the Lady Calipash.

"Likely it has nothing to do with your husband's tragic end," he said gently. "I purchased this whilst in Greece, and the late Lord Calipash had often admired it. I gave it to him as a parting gift, for I had meant to withdraw from Calipash Manor this very morning."

"Oh, but you mustn't," begged Lady Calipash. "Not now, not after ... Lord Calipash would wish you to be here. You mustn't go just now, please! For my sake ..."

Mr. Villein would have been happy to remain on those terms, had the Lady Calipash finished speaking, but alas, there was one piece of information she had yet to relate.

" ... and for our child's sake, as well," she concluded.

While the Lord Calipash's final message was being scrubbed from the skirtingboards, and his death was being declared *an accident* by the constable in order that the departed Lord might be buried in the churchyard, Mr. Villein violently interrogated Lady Calipash's serving-maid. The story was true—the Lady was indeed expecting—and this intelligence displeased Mr. Villein so immensely that even as he made himself pleasant and helpful with the hope that he might eventually win the Lady Calipash's affections, he sought to find a method of ridding her of her unborn child.

To Mr. Villein's mind, Lady Calipash could not but fall in love with her loyal confidant—believing as he did that she had always secretly admired him—but Mr. Villein knew that should she bear the late

Lord Calipash's son, the estate would one day be entirely lost to him. Thus he dosed the Lady with recipes born of his own researches, for while Mr. Villein's *current* profession was that of scholar, in his youth he had pursued lines of study related to all manner of black magics and sorceries. For many years he had put aside his wicked thaumaturgy, being too happy in the company of Lord Calipash to travel those paths that demand solitude and gloom and suffering, but, newly motivated, he returned to his former interests with a desperate passion.

Like the Wife of Bath, Mr. Villein knew all manner of remedies for love's mischances, and he put wicked spells on the decoctions and tisanes that he prepared to help his cause. Yet despite Mr. Villein's skill with infusion and incantation, Lady Calipash grew heavy with child; indeed, she had such a healthy maternal glow about her that the doctor exclaimed that for one so young to be brought to childbed, she was certain of a healthy *accouchement*. Mr. Villein, as canny and adept at lying as other arts, appeared to be thrilled by his Lady's prospects, and was every day by her side. Though privately discouraged by her salutary condition, he was cheered by all manner of odd portents that he observed as her lying-in drew ever closer. First, a murder of large, evil-looking ravens took up residence upon the roof of Calipash Manor, cackling and cawing day and night, and then the ivy growing on Calipash Manor's aged walls turned from green to scarlet, a circumstance no naturalist in the area could satisfactorily explain. Though the Lady Calipash's delivery was expected in midwinter, a she-goat was found to be unexpectedly in the same delicate condition as her mistress, and gave birth to a two-headed kid that was promptly beaten to death and buried far from the Manor.

Not long after that unhappy parturition, which had disturbed the residents of Calipash Manor so greatly that the news was kept from Lady Calipash for fear of doing her or her unborn child a mischief, the Lady began to feel the pangs of her own travail. At the very stroke of midnight, on the night of the dark of the moon, during a lighting storm that was as out of season as the she-goat's unusual kid, the Lady Calipash was happy to give birth to a healthy baby boy, the future Lord Calipash, and as surprised as the midwife when a second child followed, an equally plump and squalling girl. They were so alike that Lady Calipash named them Basil and Rosemary, and then promptly gave them over to the wet-nurse to be washed and fed.

The wet-nurse was a stout woman from the village, good-natured and well-intentioned, but a sounder sleeper than was wanted in that house. Though an infant's wail would rouse her in an instant, footfalls masked by thunder were too subtle for her country-bred ear, and thus she did not observe the solitary figure that stole silently into the nursery in the wee hours of that morning. For only a few moments did the individual linger, knowing well how restive infants can be in their first hours of life. By the eldritch glow of a lightning strike, Mr. Villein uncorked a phial containing the blood of the two-headed kid now buried, and he smeared upon both of those rosy foreheads an unholy mark, which, before the next burst of thunder, sank without a trace into their soft and delicate skin.

II.

A brief account of the infancy, childhood, education, and adolescence of Basil Vincent, the future Lord Calipash, and his sister Rosemary—as well as a discussion of the effect that reputation has on the prospect of obtaining satisfactory friends and lovers

While the author cannot offer an opinion as to whether any person deserves to suffer during his or her lifetime, the author *will* say with utter certainty that Lady Calipash endured more on account of her Twins than any good woman should expect when she finds herself in the happy condition of mother. Their easy birth and her quick recovery were the end of Lady Calipash's maternal bliss, for not long after she could sit up and cradle her infant son in her arms, she was informed that a new wet-nurse must be hired, as the old had quit the morning after the birth.

Lady Calipash was never told of the reason for the nurse's hasty departure, only that for a few days her newborns had been nourished with goat's milk, there being no suitable women in the neighborhood to feed the hungry young lord and his equally rapacious sister. The truth of the matter was that little Rosemary had bitten off the wet-nurse's nipple not an hour after witnessing her first sunrise. When the poor woman ran out of the nursery, clutching her bloody breast and screaming, the rest of the servants did not much credit her account of the injury; when it was discovered that the newborn was possessed of a set of thin, needle-sharp teeth behind her innocent mouth, they would have drowned the girl in the well if not for Mr. Villein, who scolded them for peasant superstition and told them to feed the babes on the milk of the nanny goat who had borne the two-headed kid until such a time when a new wet-nurse could be hired. That the wet-nurse's nipple was never found became a source of ominous legend in the household, theories swapped from servant to servant, until Mr. Villein heard two chambermaids chattering and beat them both dreadfully in order that they might serve as an example of the consequences of idle gossip.

This incident was only the first of its kind, but alas, the chronicles of the sufferings of those living in or employed at Calipash Manor after the birth of the Infernal Twins (as they were called by servant, tenant farmer, villager and gentleperson alike, well out of the hearing of either Lady Calipash or Mr. Villein, of course) could comprise their own lengthy volume, and thus must be abridged for the author's current purposes. Sufficient must be the following collection of vignettes:

From the first morning, Basil's cries sounded distinctly syllabic, and when the vicar came to baptize the Twins, he recognized the future Lord Calipash's wailing as an ancient language known only to the most disreputable sort of cultist.

On the first dark of the moon after their birth, it was discovered that Rosemary had sprouted pale greenish webbing between her toes and fingers, as well as a set of pulsing gills just below her shell-pink earlobes. The next morning the odd amphibious attributes were gone, but to the distress of all, their appearance seemed inexorably linked to the lunar cycle, for they appeared every month thereafter.

Before either could speak a word, whenever a person stumbled or belched in their presence, one would laugh like a hyena, then the other, and then they would be both fall silent, staring at the individual until he or she fled the room.

One day after Basil began to teethe, Rosemary was discovered to be missing. No one could find her for several hours, but eventually she reappeared in Basil's crib apparently of her own volition. She was asleep and curled against her brother, who was contentedly gnawing on a bone that had been neatly and inexplicably removed from the lamb roast that was to have been Lady Calipash and Mr. Villein's supper that night.

Yet such accounts are nothing to the constant uproar that ensued when at last Basil and Rosemary began to walk and speak. These accomplishments, usually met with celebration in most houses, were heralded by the staff formally petitioning for the Twins to be confined to certain areas of the house, but Mr. Villein, who had taken as much control of the business of Calipash Manor as he could, insisted that they be given as much freedom as they desired. This caused all manner of problems for the servants, but their complaints were met with cruel indifference by their new, if unofficial, master. It seemed to all that Mr. Villein actually delighted in making life difficult at Calipash Manor, and it may be safely assumed that part of his wicked tyranny stemmed from the unwillingness of Lady Calipash to put aside her mourning, and her being too constantly occupied with the unusual worries yielded by her motherhood to consider entering once again into a state of matrimony, despite his constant hints.

For the Twins, their newfound mobility was a source of constant joy. They were intelligent, inventive children, strong and active, and they managed to discover all manner of secret passageways and caches of treasure the Lady Calipash never knew of and Mr. Villein had not imagined existing, even in his wildest fancies of sustaining this period of living as a gentleman. The siblings were often found in all manner of places at odd times—after their being put to bed, it was not unusual to discover one or both in the library come midnight, claiming to be "looking at the pictures" in books that were only printed text; at cock-crow one might encounter them in the attic, drawing betentacled things on the floorboards with bits of charcoal or less pleasant substances. Though they always secured the windows and triple-locked the nursery door come the dark of the moon, there was never a month that passed without Rosemary escaping to do what she would in the lakes and ponds that were part of the Calipash estate, the only indication of her black frolics bits of fish-bones stuck between her teeth and pond-weed braided through her midnight tresses.

Still, it was often easy to forget the Twins' wickedness between incidents, for they appeared frequently to be mere children at play. They would bring their mother natural oddities from the gardens, like a pretty stone or a perfect pine cone, and beg to be allowed to help feed the hunting hounds in the old Lord Calipash's now-neglected kennels. All the same, even when they were sweet, it saddened Lady Calipash that Basil was from the first a dark and sniveling creature, and pretty Rosemary more likely to bite with her sharp teeth than return an affectionate kiss. Even on good days they had to be prevented from entering the greenhouse or the kitchen—their presence withered vegetation, and should one of them reach a hand into a cookie jar or steal a nibble of carrot or potato from the night's dinner, the remaining food would be found fouled with mold or ash upon their withdrawing.

Given the universal truth that servants will gossip, when stories like these began to circulate throughout the neighborhood, the once-steady stream of visitors who had used to come to tour Calipash Manor decreased to a trickle, and no tutor could be hired at any salary. Lady Calipash thanked God that Mr. Villein was there to conduct her children's education, but others were not so sure this was such a boon. Surely, had Lady Calipash realized that Mr. Villein viewed the Lady's request as an opportunity to teach the Twins not only Latin and Greek and English and Geography and Maths, but also his sorcerous arts, she might have heeded the voices of dissent, instead of dismissing their concerns as utter nonsense.

Though often cursed for their vileness, Basil and Rosemary grew up quite happily in the company of Mr. Villein, their mother, and the servants, until they reached that age when children often begin to want for society. The spring after they celebrated their eighth birthday they pleaded with their mother to be allowed to attend the May Day celebration in town. Against her better judgment, Lady Calipash begged the favor of her father (who was hosting the event); against *his* better judgment, Mr. Fellingworth, who suffered perpetual and extraordinary dyspepsia as a result of worrying about his decidedly odd grandchildren, said the Infernal Twins might come—if, and *only* if they promised to behave themselves. After the incident the previous month, at the birthday party of a young country gentleman, where the Twins were accused to no resolution of somehow having put dead frogs under the icing of the celebrant's towering cake, all were exceedingly cautious of allowing them to attend.

This caution was, regrettably, more deserved than the invitation. Rosemary arrived at the event in a costume of her own making, that of the nymph Flora; when Mr. Villein was interrogated as to his reasoning for such grotesque and ill-advised indulgence of childish fancy, he replied that she had earlier proved her understanding that May Day had once been the Roman festival of Floralia, and it seemed a just reward for her attentiveness in the schoolroom. This bit of pagan heresy might have been overlooked by the other families had not Mr. Villein later used the exact same justification for Basil's behavior when the boy appeared at the celebration later-on, clad only in a bit of blue cloth wrapped about his slender body, and then staged a reenactment for the children of Favonius' rape of Flora, Rosemary playing her part with unbridled enthusiasm. Mr. Villein could not account for the resentment of the other parents, nor the ban placed on the Twins' presence at any future public observances, for, as he told Lady Calipash, the pantomime was accurate, and thus a rare educational moment during a day given over to otherwise pointless frivolity.

Unfortunately for the Twins, the result of that display was total social isolation—quite the opposite of their intention. From that day forward they saw no other children except for those of the staff, and the sense of rank instilled in the future Lord Calipash and his sister from an early age forbade them from playing with those humble urchins. Instead, they began to amuse themselves by trying out a few of the easier invocations taught to them by Mr. Villein, and in this manner summoned two fiends, one an amorphous spirit who would follow them about if it wasn't too windy a day, the other an eel with a donkey's head who lived, much to the gardener's distress, in the pond at the center of the rose garden. Rosemary also successfully re-animated an incredibly nasty, incredibly ancient goose when it died of choking on a strawberry, and the fell creature went about its former business of hissing at everyone and shitting everywhere until the stable boy hacked off its head with the edge of a shovel, and buried the remains at opposite ends of the estate.

Unfortunately, these childish amusements could not long entertain the Twins once they reached an age when they should, by all accounts, have been interfering with common girls (in Lord Calipash's case) or being courted by the local boys (in Rosemary's). For his part, Basil could not be bothered with the fairer sex, so absorbed was he in mastering languages more *recherché* than his indwelling R'lyehian or native English, or even the Latin, Hebrew, and Assyrian he had mastered before his tenth birthday (Greek he never took to—that was Rosemary's province, and the only foreign tongue she ever mastered). Truth be told, even had Basil been interested in women, his slouching posture, slight physique, and petulant mouth would have likely ensured a series of speedy rejections. Contrariwise, Rosemary was a remarkably appealing creature, but there was something so frightening about her sharp-toothed smile and wicked gaze that no boy in the county could imagine comparing her lips to cherubs' or her eyes to the night sky, and thus she, too, wanted for a lover.

Nature will, however, induce the most enlightened of us to act according to our animal inclinations, and to that end, one night, just before their sixteenth birthday, Rosemary slipped into her brother's chambers after everyone else had gone to bed. She found Basil studying by himself. He did not look up at her to greet her, merely said *fhtagn-e* and ignored her. He had taught her a bit of his blood-tongue, and their understanding of one another was so profound that she did not mind heeding the imperative, and knelt patiently at his feet for him to come to the end of his work. Before the candle had burned too low, he looked down at her with a fond frown.

"What?" he asked.

"Brother," said she, with a serious expression, "I have no wish to die an old maid."

"What have I to do with that?" said he, wiping his eternally-drippy nose on his sleeve.

"No one will do it to me if you won't."

Basil considered this, realizing she spoke, not of matrimony, but of the act of love.

"Why should you want to?" asked he, at last. "From everything I've read, intercourse yields nothing but trouble for those who engage in libidinous sport."

Rosemary laughed.

"Would you like to come out with me, two nights hence?"

"On our birthday?"

"It's the dark of the moon," said she.

Basil straightened up and looked at her keenly. He nodded once, briskly, and that was enough for her. As she left him, she kissed his smooth cheek, and at her touch, he blushed for the first time in his life.

Before progressing to the following scene of depravity that the author finds it her sad duty to relate, let several things be said about this History. First, this is as true and accurate an account of the Infernal Twins of Ivybridge as anyone has yet attempted. Second, it is the duty of all historians to recount events with as much veracity as possible, never eliding over unpleasantness for propriety's sake. Had Suetonius shied away from his subject, we might never have known the true degeneracy of Caligula, and no one could argue that Suetonius' dedication to his work has not allowed mankind to learn from the mistakes made by the Twelve Caesars. Thus the author moves on to her third point, that her own humble chronicle of the Ivybridge Twins is intended to be morally instructive rather than titillating. With this understanding, we must, unfortunately, press on.

The future Lord Calipash had never once attended his sister on her monthly jaunts, and so it must be said that, to his credit, it was curiosity rather than lust that comprised the bulk of his motivation that night. He dressed himself warmly, tiptoed to her door, and knocked very softly, only to find his sister standing beside him in a thin silk sheath, though her door had not yet been unlocked. He looked her up and down—there was snow on the ground outside, what was she about, dressing in such a nymphean manner?—but when she saw his alarm, given his own winter ensemble, she merely smiled. Basil was in that moment struck by how appealing were his sister's kitten-teeth, how her ebon tresses looked as soft as raven-down in the guttering candle-light. He swallowed nervously. Holding a single slender finger to her lips, with gestures Rosemary bid him follow her, and they made their way down the hallway without a light. She knew the way, and her moist palm gripped his dry one as they slipped downstairs, out the servant's door, and into the cold, midwinter night.

Rosemary led her brother to one of the gardens—the pleasure-garden, full of little private grottoes—and there, against a tree already familiar with love's pleasures, she kissed him on the mouth. It was a clumsy kiss. The Twins had been well-tutored by the Greeks and Romans in the theory of love, but theory can take one only so far. To their observer—for indeed they were observed—it seemed that both possessed an overabundance of carnal knowledge, and thus it was a longer encounter than most young people's inaugural attempts at amatory relations. Rosemary was eager and Basil shy, though when he kissed her neck and encountered her delicate sea-green gill pulsating against her ivory skin, gasping for something more substantial than air, he felt himself completely inflamed, and pressed himself into the webbed hand that fumbled with his breeches buttons in the gloaming.

The Twins thought themselves invisible; that the location which they chose to celebrate their induction into Hymen's temple was completely obscure, and thus they were too completely occupied with their personal concerns to notice something very interesting—that Calipash Manor was *not* completely dark, even at that early hour of the morning. A light shone dimly from the tower bedroom, where a lone figure, wracked with anger and jealousy and hatred, watched the Twins from the same window where he had observed two other individuals fornicate, perhaps somewhat less wantonly, almost sixteen years earlier.

III.

Containing more of the terrible wickedness of Mr. Villein—a record of the circumstances surrounding the unhappy separation of the Ivybridge Twins—how Rosemary became Mrs. Villein—concluding with the arrival of a curious visitor to Calipash Manor and the results of his unexpected intrusion

Mr. Villein's pursuit of the Lady Calipash had lasted for as many years as Rosemary remained a child, but when the blood in her girl's veins began to quicken and wrought those womanly changes upon her youthful body so pleasing to the male eye, Mr. Villein found his lascivious dreams to be newly occupied with daughter rather than mother. Since the time, earlier in the year, when Rosemary had finally been allowed to dress her hair and wear long skirts, Mr. Villein started paying her the sort of little compliments that he assumed a young lady might find pleasing. Little did he imagine that Rosemary thought him elderly, something less than handsome, a dreary conversationalist, and one whose manners were not those of a true gentleman; thus, when he watched the virginal object of his affection sullied enthusiastically by her ithyphallic brother, the indecent tableau came as a substantial shock to Mr. Villein's mind.

The following day found Mr. Villein in a state of unwellness, plagued by a fever and chills, but he appeared again the morning after that. The Infernal Twins enquired kindly of his health, and Mr. Villein gave them a warm smile and assured them as to his feeling much better. He was, indeed, so very hale that he should like to give them their birthday presents (a day or so late, but no matter) if they might be compelled to attend him after breakfast? The Twins agreed eagerly—both *loved* presents—and midmorning found the threesome in Mr. Villein's private study, formerly that of Clement Fitzroy, Lord Calipash.

"Children," said he, "I bequeath unto you two priceless antiques, but unlike most of the gifts I have given you over the years, what is for one is not to be used by the other. Rosemary, to you I give these—a set of tortoiseshell combs carved into the likeness of Boubastos. To Basil, this bit of ivory. Careful with it, my dearest boy. It was the instrument of your father's undoing."

Basil, surprised, took the handkerchief-swaddled object, and saw it was the carven head of a young man, crowned with a wreath of laurel-leaves. As Rosemary cooed over her gift and vowed to wear the combs in her hair every day thereafter, Basil looked up at his tutor inquisitively.

"How—what?" he asked, too surprised to speak more intelligently.

"The idol's head was given to me by a youth of remarkable beauty whilst I was abroad in Greece," said Mr. Villein. "I have never touched it.

The young man said that one day I should encounter the one for whom it was truly intended, the new earthly manifestation of the ancient god which it represents, and that I must give it to him and him alone. Given your abilities, Basil, I believe *you* are that manifestation. I made the mistake of showing it to your father, and he coveted it from the moment he saw it—but when he touched the effigy, I believe the god drove him mad to punish him. I have never told you this, but your father took his own life, likely for the heinous crime of—of *besmirching* that which was always intended for other, wiser hands."

Basil clutched the fetish and nodded his deep thanks, too moved by Mr. Villein's words to notice the agitated tone in which the last sentiment was expressed. That he was the embodiment of a deity came as little surprise to Basil—from an early age, he had sensed he was destined for greatness—but he found it curious that Mr. Villein should have failed to tell him this until now.

The ivory figurine occupied his thoughts all during the day, and late that same night, after a few hours spent in his sister's chambers, during which time they successfully collaborated on a matter of urgent business, Basil unwrapped the icon and touched it with his fingertips. To his great frustration, nothing at all happened, not even after he held it in his palm for a full quarter of an hour. Bitterly disappointed, Basil went unhappily to bed, only to experience strange dreams during the night.

He saw a city of grand marble edifices, fathoms below the surface of the sea and immemorially ancient, and he saw that it was peopled by a shining dolphin-headed race, whose only profession seemed to be conducting the hierophantic rites of a radiant god. He walked unseen among those people, and touched with his hands the columns of the temple which housed the god, carved richly with scenes of worship. A voice called to him over and over in the language he had known since his birth, and he walked into the interior of the fane to see the god for himself, only to realize the face was already known to him, for it was the exact likeness of the ivory idol! Then the eyes of the god, though wrought of a glowing stone, seemed to turn in their sockets and meet his gaze, and with that look Basil understood many things beyond human comprehension that both terrified and delighted him.

The future Lord Calipash awoke the next morning bleary-eyed and stupid, to the alarm of both his sister and mother. He was irritable and shrewish when interrogated as to the nature of his indisposition, and his condition did not improve the following day, nor the following, for his sleep was every night disturbed by his seeking that which called to him. He would not speak to any body of his troubles, and when his ill humor still persisted after a week, Rosemary and Lady Calipash agreed on the prudence of summoning the doctor to attend the future Lord. Basil, however, turned away the physician, claiming that he was merely tired, and, annoyed, left to take a long walk in the woods that comprised a large part of the Calipash estate.

Let it be noted here that it was Mr. Villein who suggested that Basil's room be searched in his absence. There, to the family's collective horror, a ball of opium and a pipe were discovered among Basil's personal effects. The doctor was quite alarmed by this, for, he said, while tincture of opium is a well-regarded remedy, smoking it in its raw state was a foul practice only undertaken by degenerates and Orientals, and so it was decided that Basil should be confined to his room for as long as it took to rid him of the habit. Upon the lad's return there was a sort of ambush, comprised of stern words from the doctor, disappointed head-shakes from Mr. Villein, tears from Lady Calipash, and, for Rosemary's part, anger (she was, frankly, rather hurt that he hadn't invited her to partake of the drug). Basil insisted he had no knowledge of how the paraphernalia came to be in his room, but no rational person would much heed the ravings of an opium-addict, and so he was locked in and all his meals were sent up to his room.

A week later Basil was not to be found within his chambers, and a note in his own hand lay upon his unmade bed. His maid found it, but, being illiterate, she gave it over to Lady Calipash while the lady and her daughter were just sitting down to table. Scanning the missive brought on such a fit of histrionics in Lady Calipash that Mr. Villein came down to see what was the matter. He could not get any sense out of the Lady, and Rosemary had quit the breakfasting room before he even arrived, too private a creature to show anyone the depth of her distress, so Mr. Villein snatched the letter away from the wailing Lady Calipash and read it himself. He was as alarmed by its contents as she, for it said only that Basil had found his confinement intolerable, and had left home to seek his fortune apart from those who would keep him imprisoned.

The author has heard it said that certain birds, like the canary or the nightingale, cannot sing without their mate, and suffer a decline when isolated. Similarly, upon Basil's unexpected flight from Calipash Manor, did Rosemary enter a period of great melancholy, where no one and nothing could lift her spirits. She could not account for Basil's behavior—not his moodiness, nor his failure to take her with him—and so she believed him cross with her for her part in his quarantine, or, worse still, indifferent to her entirely. Seasons passed without her smiling over the misfortunes of others or raising up a single spirit of the damned to haunt the living, and so, upon the year's anniversary of Basil's absence, Mr. Villein sat down with Lady Calipash and made a proposal.

"My lady," he said, "Rosemary has grown to a pretty age, and I believe her state of mind would be much improved by matrimony and, God willing, motherhood. To this end, I appeal to you to allow me to marry her, whereupon I shall endeavor to provide for her as the most doting of husbands."

Lady Calipash was at first disturbed by this request, as she had long assumed that Mr. Villein's affections were settled upon her and not her daughter, but when Mr. Villein mentioned offhandedly that, with Basil absent, he was the only known male heir to the Calipash estate, and should he marry outside the family, neither Lady Calipash nor Rosemary would have any claim to the land or money beyond their annuities, the Lady found it prudent to accept Mr. Villein's suit on Rosemary's behalf.

Mr. Villein expected, and, (it must be admitted) rather ghoulishly anticipated Rosemary's disinclination to form such an alliance, but to the surprise of all, she accepted her fate with a degree of insouciance that might have worried a mother less invested in her own continued state of affluence. Without a single flicker of interest Rosemary agreed to the union, took the requisite journey into town to buy her wedding clothes, said her vows, and laid down upon the marriage bed in order that Mr. Villein could defile her body with all manner of terrible perversions, a description of which will not be found in these pages, lest it inspire others to sink to such depths. The author will only say that Rosemary found herself subjected to iterations of Mr. Villein's profane attentions every night thereafter. If any good came out of these acts of wickedness performed upon her person, it was that it roused her out of her dysthymia and inspired her to once again care about her situation.

Not unexpectedly, Rosemary's emotional rejuvenation compelled her to journey down paths more corrupt than any the Twins had yet trod. Her nightly, nightmarish trysts with Mr. Villein had driven her slightly mad, as well as made her violently aware that not all lovers are interested in their partner's pleasure. Remembering with fondness those occasions when her brother had conjured up from the depths of her body all manner of rapturous sensations, in her deep misery Rosemary concocted a theory drawn as much from her own experience as from the works of the ancient physician Galen of Pergamon. As she accurately recalled, Galen had claimed that male and female reproductive systems are perfect inversions of one another, and thus, she deduced, the ecstasy she felt whilst coupling with her brother was likely due to their being twins and the mirror-image of one another.

To once again achieve satisfactory companionship Rosemary therefore resolved upon creating a companion for herself out of the remains housed in the Calipash family crypt. By means of the necromancies learned in her youth, she stitched together a pleasure-golem made of the best-preserved parts of her ancestors, thanking whatever foul gods she was accustomed to petitioning for the unusually gelid temperature of that tomb. Taking a nose that looked like Basil's from this corpse, a pair of hands from that one, and her father's genitalia, she neatly managed the feat, and, dressing the creature in Basil's clothing, slipped often into that frigid darkness to lie with it. Sadly, her newfound happiness with her ersatz brother was, for two reasons, imperfect. The first was that none of the vocal chords she could obtain were capable of reproducing Basil's distinctively nasal snarl, and thus the *doppelgänger* remained mute, lest an unfamiliar moan ruin Rosemary's obscene delights. The second trouble was more pernicious: she realized too late she had been unable to entirely excise the putrefaction wrought by death upon the limbs of her relations, and thus she contracted a form of gangrene that began to slowly rot her once-pristine limbs.

For another year did this unhappy *status quo* persist, until one dreary afternoon when Rosemary, returning from a long walk about the grounds, noticed a disreputable, slouching individual taking in the fine prospect offered by the approach to Calipash Manor. Rosemary advanced on him, unafraid, though she noticed the burliness of the man's figure, the darkness of his skin, and the shabby state of his long overcoat.

"Are you in want of something?" she called to the stranger, and he looked up at her, his face shaded by a mildewing tricorn. "There is scant comfort to be found here at Calipash Manor, but if you require any thing, it will be given to you."

"To whom do I have the pleasure of speaking?" queried he in the rasping accent of a white Creole, all the while stealing polite glances of her slightly moldy countenance.

"I am the daughter of the lady of this house," answered Rosemary.

"Then thank you, my lady," said the man. "My name is Valentine, and I have only just returned from Jamaica to find my family dead and my house occupied by those with no obligation to provide for me."

"Have you no friends?"

"None, not being the sort of man who either makes or keeps them easily."

"Come with me, then," said Rosemary, admiring his honesty. She led Valentine up to the house and settled them in her private parlor, whereupon she bid the servants bring him meat and drink. As he ate, he seemed to revive. Rosemary saw a nasty flicker in his eyes that she quite liked, and bid him tell her more of himself. He laughed dryly, and Rosemary had his tale:

"I'm afraid, my Lady, that I owe you an apology, for I know one so fine as yourself would never let me into such a house knowing my true history. I was born into the world nothing more than the seventh son of a drunk cottar, and we were always in want as there was never enough work to be had for all of us. I killed my own brother over a bite of mutton, but given that we were all starving, the magistrate saw it fitting that I should not be hanged, but impressed to work as a common hand aboard a naval ship bound for the West Indies. I won't distress you by relating the conditions I endured, suffice it to say I survived.

"When I arrived at our destination, however, I found that it was not my fate to remain in the navy, for my sea-captain promptly clapped me in irons and sold me as a white slave, likely due to my being an indifferent sailor and more likely to start riots among the men than help to settle them. I was bought by a plantation-owner who went by the name of Thistlewood, and this man got what labor he could out of me for several years, until I managed to escape to Port Royal with only the clothes on my back and a bit of food I'd stolen. There I lived in a manner I shan't alarm you by describing, and only say that having done one murder, it was easy to repeat the crime for hire until I had enough coin to buy passage back to England—but as I said earlier, when I returned home, I found every living person known to me dead or gone, except those with long memories who recalled enough of my character to kick me away from their doorsteps like a dog."

Rosemary could not but be profoundly moved by such a tale, and she felt her dormant heart begin to warm anew with sympathy for this stranger. She assured him that he should have some work on her estate, and Valentine was so overcome that he took Rosemary's hand in his— but their mutual felicity was interrupted by Mr. Villein, who chose that inopportune moment to enter Rosemary's chambers uninvited.

"What is the meaning of this treachery?" cried Mr. Villein, for though he often engaged in infidelities, the notion that his bride might do the same did not sit well with him, being that he was a jealous man by nature. "Release my wife, foul vagabond!"

"Wife!" exclaimed Valentine, his yellowish complexion turning grey. "How is it that I return home, only to find myself betrayed by one whom I thought harbored love for me?"

It would be impossible to guess whether Rosemary or Mr. Villein was more confused by this ejaculation, but neither had time to linger in a state of wonder for very long. The man withdrew a veritable cannon of a flintlock, and cast off his wretched, threadbare overcoat to reveal that beneath it, he wore a rich emerald-green brocade vest threaded through with designs wrought in gold and silver, and his breeches were of the finest satin. When he looked down his nose at them like a lord instead of lowering his eyes like a cottar's son, they saw he had all the bearing of a gentleman of high rank. Recognizing him at last, Rosemary shrieked, and Mr. Villein paled and took a step back. Though strangely altered by time, the man was unmistakably Basil Vincent, Lord Calipash, returned at last to reclaim by force what should have been his by right of birth!

IV.

The conclusion, detailing the reunion of the Ivybridge Twins—an account of the singular manner in which Rosemary defeated the gangrene that threatened her continued good health—what the author hopes the reader will take away from this Infernal History

"You!" cried Mr. Villein in alarm. "How *dare* you? How *can* you? They said the navy would keep you at least a decade in the service of this country!"

"*They?*" demanded Rosemary. "Who?"

"The press gang!" blustered Mr. Villein. "For the sum I paid them, I'll have them—"

But the Infernal Twins never discovered what Mr. Villein's intentions were regarding the unsatisfactory press gang, for Rosemary, overcome with grief and rage, snatched the flintlock pistol out of Basil's grasp and shot Mr. Villein through the throat. A fountain of blood gushed forth from just above Mr. Villein's cravat-pin, soaking his waistcoat and then the carpet as he gasped his surprise and fell down dead upon the ground.

"Basil," she said. "Basil, I'm so—I didn't—"

"You *married* him?"

"It was all Mother's doing," said Rosemary, rather hurt by his tone. "But—"

"You were gone," she snapped, "and lest Mr. Villein marry some common slut and turn Mother and myself out of our house …"

Even with such reasonable excuses, it was some time before Rosemary could adequately cajole Basil out of his peevish humor; indeed, only when Rosemary asked if Basil had lived as a monk during the years of their estrangement did he glower at her as he had used to do and embraced her. They sat companionably together then, and Basil gave her a truer account of his absence from Calipash Manor:

"The carven ivory head which our loathsome former tutor bequeathed unto me on the sixteenth anniversary of my birth was the instrument, strangely, of both my undoing and my salvation," said Basil. "Mr. Villein lied to me that I was the manifestation of the old god which it represents—indeed, I believe now that his intention was take me away from you so that he might have you for his own; that I, like my father before me, would be driven to suicide by the whispered secrets of that divine entity. Little did he know that while I am not some sort of fleshly incarnation of that deity, I was born with the capacity to understand His whispered will, and walk along the sacred paths that were more often trod when His worship was better known to our race.

"I believe once Mr. Villein saw that I was only mildly troubled by these new visions, he concocted a plot to be rid of me in a less arcane manner. The night before you discovered my absence, he let himself into my chambers and put a spell upon me while I slept that made me subject to his diabolical will. I awoke a prisoner of his desire, and he bade me rise and do as he wished. Dearest sister, I tell you now that you did not detect a forgery in my note, for it was written by none other than myself. After I had penned the false missive, Mr. Villein bade me follow him down to Ivybridge, whereupon he put a pint of ale before me and compelled me, via his fell hold upon me, to act in the manner of a drunken commoner, brawling with the local boys until the constable was called and I was thrown in jail. Not recognizing me, due to my long isolation, my sentence was as I told you—that of forced conscription into the navy.

"To a certain point, my tale as I told it to you whilst in the character of the scoundrel Valentine was true—I suffered much on my voyage to Jamaica, and was subsequently sold as a slave. What I did not tell you was the astonishing manner of my escape from that abominable plantation. My master hated me, likely because he instinctively sensed his inferiority to my person. My manners mark me as a noble individual, even when clad in rags, and being that he was a low sort who was considered a gentleman due to his profession rather than his birth, my master gave to me the most dangerous and disgusting tasks. One of his favorite degradations was to station me at the small dock where the little coracles were tied up, so that I could be given the catches of fish to clean them, constantly subjected to wasp stings and cuts and other indignities of that sort.

"Yet it was this task that liberated me, for one afternoon I arrived at the dock to see the fishermen in a tizzy, as one had the good fortune of catching a dolphin. The creature was still alive, incredibly, and I heard its voice in my mind as clearly as I heard their celebration. *Save me, and I shall save you*, it said unto me in that language that has always marked me as bacchant to the god of which I earlier spoke. I picked up a large stick to use as a cudgel and beat the fisherfolk away from their catch, telling them to get back to work as the cetacean was of no use to our master, he should want snapper or jackfish for his dinner rather than oily porpoise-flesh. They heeded me, for they were a little afraid of me—often, as you might imagine, dear sister, bad things would happen to those who chose to cross me in some way—and I heaved the dolphin back into the sea. At first I thought it swam away and that it had merely been sun-madness that had earlier made me hear its voice, but then, after the fishermen had paddled out of sight, the dolphin surfaced with a bulging leather satchel clutched in its beak. It contained gold and jewels that my new friend told me were gathered from shipwrecks on the ocean floor, and that I should use this wealth to outfit myself as a gentleman and buy passage back to England. The creature's only caveat was that upon my arrival I must once again visit the sea, and return to one of its kin the ivory head, as our tutor had not, as it turns out, been given the object. Rather, it seems that Mr. Villein defiled an ancient holy place near Delphi during his travels in Greece by stealing the artifact away from its proper alcove.

"I agreed to these terms and, after waiting at the docks for a little longer so I might poison the fish it was my duty to clean, and thus enact a paltry revenge upon my tyrannical master, hastened back to Devonshire, as I knew nothing of your situation, but feared much.

Upon returning home I assumed the persona of Valentine as a way of ascertaining if, in my absence, your sentiments had changed toward your long-absent brother and the manner in which we were accustomed to living with one another. Seeing your heart go out to such a picaroon assured me of your constancy, and I regret very much that I earlier so impugned your honor. But sister, now that you know of my distresses, you must tell me of yours—pray, how did you come to be married to Mr. Villein and so afflicted by the disease that I see nibbles away at your perfect flesh?"

Rosemary then recounted what has already been recorded here, and she and Basil resolved upon a course of action that shall comprise the *denoument* of this chronicle. Both were determined that the gangrenous affliction should not claim Rosemary, but until Lady Calipash, wondering why her daughter did not come down to dinner, intruded into the parlor where the siblings colluded, they could not see how. The idea occurred to the Twins when Lady Calipash's alarm at seeing Mr. Villein's corpse upon the carpet was so tremendous that she began to scream. Basil, fearing they should be overheard and the murder discovered before they had concocted an adequate reason for his unfortunate death, caught Lady Calipash by the neck when she would not calm herself. As he wrapped his fingers about her throat, Basil noticed the softness of his mother's skin, and, looking deeply into her fearful eyes, saw that she was still a handsome creature of not five-and-thirty.

"Sister," he began, but Rosemary had already anticipated his mind, and agreed that she should immediately switch her consciousness with Lady Calipash's by means of witchcraft she and Basil had long ago learned (and once utilized in their youthful lovemaking) from the donkey-headed eel-creature they had conjured, and henceforth inhabit her own mother's skin. This was done directly, and after securely locking Rosemary's former body (now occupied by their terrified mother) into the family crypt, along with Mr. Villein's corpse, mother and prodigal son, rather than brother and sister, had the carriage made ready, and they drove to the head of the River Plym, whereupon Basil summoned one of the aquatic priests of his god, and handed over the relic that has figured so prominently in their narrative.

To conclude, the author hopes that readers of this History will find this account entirely mortifying and disgusting, and seek to avoid modeling any part of their behavior upon that of the Infernal Ivybridge Twins—though to be fair, it must be recorded that, for all the duration of their cacodemoniacal lives, the Twins preserved the tenderest affection for each other. Still, there has never been found anywhere in the world a less-worthy man or woman than they, and, until the moonless night when the Twins decided to join the ranks of the cetaceous worshipers of their unholy deity—Lord Calipash being called thence, his sister long-missing her former amphibious wanderings—there was not a neighbor, a tenant, or a servant who did not rue the day they came into the company of Basil and Rosemary.

a pretty mouth

CHAPTER ONE:
AGAINST DEVOTION

"They found another one this morning, did you hear?"

"You don't say!"

"Yes, in the bins behind the buttery, in the unclean garbage. Buried—well, I don't think you could really say *alive*, but ..."

"Christ's mercy. How did you hear?"

"Perkins' study-chamber has a view of the yard. He heard the shouting and poked out his head. Thought it might be some news of what King Charles has been up to in Dover, but then—"

"Shhh—*ow!*" said a third boy, from behind the first two.

Henry Milliner scooted his ample bottom to the edge of the bench as the victim of his sharp kick sideways to the shins rubbed his leg. Sweeter than the scent of dinner was catching a whiff of juicy canard— and Henry smelled a feast in the younger boys' whispers. Or at the very least, a substantial snack to get him through Master Fulkerson's lecture on Plato's *Symposium*. Given how exceptionally boring the lesson had been it was difficult to believe that the topic of the day was sexual intercourse, but what the Master was saying about it was—as was damn near everything the Master lectured on—rather beyond Henry's ken. Ah, well. The information, Henry reasoned, would continue to waft hither and yon somewhere a few feet over his head whether he attempted to pay attention or not, so why bother?

From the whispers, Henry figured someone must have discovered another queer dog on campus, a topic much more relevant to his life than anything Plato or his friends had to say about lads buggering each other, which seemed to be what the *Symposium* was about. Those blighters had been dead for over a thousand years and were likely to stay so until the seventh trumpet sounded—which, Henry thought ruefully, would likely not happen before his next examination. Thus, for now, it would be more to his advantage to hearken to the youths in front of him. Once he got the measure of the gossip, Henry reckoned there would be just enough time after class to sidle up to the clique of popular natural philosophy majors—the Blithe Company, as they called themselves—and relate what he'd heard. Such an anomalous happening should interest them, being as it was some sort of unnatural occurrence in the natural world. What*ever*. The important thing was, if he played his cards right, Henry figured he might be asked to attend the by-invitation-only gathering rumored to be happening tonight at The Horse and Hat ...

Henry glanced over to his left at the pack of handsome, immaculately-groomed Fellow Commoners, and he shivered a little when his eyes lighted upon the Blithe Company's unofficial leader: St John Clement, the current Lord Calipash. In the center of the throng like a spider in her web, his long white quill pen was bobbing gracefully as he scribbled away, taking pages of notes on Master Fulkerson's lecture. His unwavering interest was beautiful to behold; how he managed to use so much ink without ever getting a drop on himself, even his slender fingers ... *that* was the most mesmerizing academic mystery Henry had yet encountered at Wadham College.

As he surreptitiously gazed at St John, Henry felt the familiar warm flutterings of what he deemed his "deep admiration" for the young lord in his guts, and a bit lower down, too. Hopefully this bit of tittle-tattle would provide Henry the opportunity he needed to get closer to St John, but that meant he'd do well to pay better attention to the gossiping boys!

"... surgery. Even when they beat it, it never made a sound." The boy shuddered. "They smothered it out of mercy."

Damnation! He'd let himself get distracted and had missed some crucial information. Well, he could fill in the details himself easily enough. Probably. All of this recent weirdness with dead-eyed, strangely lethargic dogs sounded awfully similar to the Wadham legend from a few years back, when that bloke Christopher Wren had injected opium and wine directly into a dog's arteries to test the theory of circulation. The story went that he and a few of his chums had been forced to flog the poor creature all through the Grove garden until the drugs wore off to keep it from falling into a coma.

Dabbling in natural philosophy was considered quite fashionable these days; perhaps someone was trying to duplicate his results. Wren was lecturing in Oxford still, so it seemed entirely possible.

One of the two boys in front of Henry glanced down at the front of the auditorium, but Master Fulkerson had either failed to notice their inattention, or he didn't care.

"Spooky, isn't it?" he whispered to his companion. "Seems less like, you know, a philosophical experiment, and more like ..."

"Black magic," murmured the second boy, with a sage nod of his head. "The devil's left hand."

"What do you make of it all, Rochester?" Henry hissed to the youth seated next to him, but his neighbor did not reply. Henry cast him a sidelong look to see if his friend's silence was interest in the master's lecture or wounded feelings over the earlier kick to his shin. "Do you think it's the *devil?*"

Rochester didn't smile, but his nostrils narrowed slightly and his lips pressed together as he tried not to. Encouraged, Henry began to search for a folded piece of parchment he'd that morning hidden among his notes. As the boys in front of them had segued into a discussion of whether Satan would concern himself with dogs, and he was still disinclined to pay attention to the lecture, Henry felt this was a good time to unveil his recent masterpiece. Then he noticed that the rustling was eliciting dirty looks from several other students sitting near him.

He flashed them his most winning smile and they all turned away quickly. *That*, he congratulated himself, was the way to popularity. Be affable, and quick to admit your wrongs to your fellow men. Anyways, he'd found what he'd been looking for.

Henry waited for Master Fulkerson to look away; when the moment came, he slid the paper proudly along the table to Rochester. But upon receiving the document, the boy's shoulders slumped.

Henry's irked *tchah* came out a bit too loud, so he looked away quickly and feigned interest in the lecture. When had he ever expressed dismay over having to read one of Rochester's shabby efforts? Never, not once! Rochester was a rotten, ungentlemanlike little bully-fop. If he wanted Henry to read his moldy old poems, he should at least be willing to return the favor with grace. But that was how they all were, the Fellow Commoners. Even those of them who didn't have a title were still pretty goddamn entitled.

Except St John. At least that was Henry's 'hypothesis,' as the natural philosophers would say. He hadn't been able to actually verify his conclusion. Not yet.

"You promised you'd have a look when I'd finished," hissed Henry out of the corner of his mouth, for when he glanced back, he saw the parchment still lay where he had left it. "You said you'd *help*."

"Yes, but—"

"Come on, then! Tell me what you think!" he urged, as Rochester reluctantly accepted the note. "I think it's my best effort yet."

"That it may be," murmured Rochester, his eyes rapidly scanning left to right and back again as he read. "But I … don't you think …"

"What?" Henry, anxious, leaned forward and craned his neck to see his friend's expression better. He was not encouraged by what he saw: Rochester's slender eyebrows were cocked up nearly at his hairline and his full cupid's-bow mouth twitched as if it were dancing a jig. These were not the signifiers of a young man profoundly moved by the depth of feeling expressed in an artistic endeavor, and Henry stiffened in his seat as his friend, now quivering like an autumn leaf, placed his elbows on the table to support himself through the final lines.

"This is …" said Rochester, not looking at Henry.

"Brilliant?"

"Really dirty? I knew you fancied him, but—"

"I do not *fancy* him!" huffed Henry. "I simply admire him for his, his devotion to academics, and his—"

"Creamy offerings?" supplied Rochester.

"I say! You have a nasty turn of mind!"

"Do you really think he'll appreciate the punning on his title?" Rochester canted his head to the right, considering. "I dunno if someone wrote me an ode to the glory of, ummmm, 'Rochestnuts' or somesuch, if I'd particularly appreciate it."

"You might if it was said with *feeling*!" Henry, offended, snatched back his parchment. "I should never have shown it to you; should've known you'd be a jealous—"

"Jealous?" Rochester looked genuinely surprised. "Jealous of what?"

"Yes, I too am quite curious," said Master Fulkerson, snatching the scrap of parchment out of Henry's plump hand with his withered, clawlike fingers.

Henry gasped in surprise. Busted, big time! How had he not heard the master's footfalls on the rickety wooden stairs up to where he and Rochester sat?

"What have we here? Not notes on the *Symposium*, no indeed. This is …" Master Fulkerson's eyes widened. "Well, Mr. Milliner, I can see why you've been doing so pitifully in my class—and others, I hear—if *this* is how you spend your time. I'd assumed that like the rest of this college you were neglecting your studies to swap rumors of the King's plans to once again rule England from English soil, but it seems your interests lie ... elsewhere."

"What is it?" someone called. Henry swallowed; he felt himself blushing.

"It's a *poem*, Mr. Neville," drawled Master Fulkerson. "Written in honor of a respected member of the peerage—and one of our Fellow Commoners here at Wadham, as it turns out."

"May I have it back?" croaked Henry.

"No, read it!" called another boy, to general cheering. Henry felt he might faint, and, offering up a quick prayer, begged God in His wisdom to intervene on his behalf. An earthquake or a fire would work, if Master Fulkerson were in too foul a mood for even the Lord to move him to Christian pity ...

The Master did seem to be weighing his options as he scanned the page; Henry did not dare to hope, but St John *was* one of the Master's favorites. Perhaps Master Fulkerson sensed if he read the poem to the class, the Lord Calipash would suffer, too?

The Master laughed. It was not a nice laugh.

"With work this ... *remarkable* ... I think it would be a crime *not* to share it with an audience," said the Master, looking down at Henry with a thin smile. "And, I suppose, the subject—or object, perhaps—of the composition does possess a deep and abiding appreciation of, a*hem*, modern poetry."

For the first time since the scene had begun, St John looked interested instead of annoyed by the distraction. Henry contemplated running out of the room, but to do so would be to admit guilt, or perhaps some feeling other than respect for the poem's object. Better to sit up tall and accept his fate with bravery.

"Please do," said Henry, willing his voice not to quaver. "It would be my honor to have my work judged by my colleagues."

"Indeed? Well, then. Let us oblige Mr. Milliner." Master Fulkerson cleared his throat and spat something yellowish on the floor. "This, ah, poem is entitled 'The Hour of the Tortoise.' Quiet, quiet," he said in reedy tones, as sniggers, like hot fat in a pan, bubbled and popped throughout the classroom. Then he began in earnest:

> "Send away this feast, it tastes of ash!
> Fie on your jellies, mince, and pies.
> If you see me fasting, *this* it belies:
> Forevermore shall I sup upon *CALIPASH*.

Oh *CALIPASH!* This humble tongue yearns to lick and suck
A creamy offering of jellied delights testudinarious.
To claim it inferior or unwelcome is truly nefarious.
Gobs shall slide down my throat have I any luck!

Write your paeans to men or dogs or ladies named Eloise,
CALIPASH possesses many virtues, not just one.
Alas! I have said it all. Too quickly have I come
My heart hears the chime calling the hour of the tortoise!"

By the time Master Fulkerson read, "Composed in honor of the Lord Calipash, May, 1660," he was shouting to be heard over the laughter and cat-calling. Henry was pained to see how comically his effort was regarded; nearly all were howling, and several students had pretended to fall out of their chairs from mirth and were rolling about on the floor, clutching their sides. The foofaraw was so loud that several other masters and students had stuck their heads in the doorway to see what on earth could have caused such a riot.

Henry accepted the taunting with poise befitting a Stoic, sitting tall in his chair though his face burned like a fire, but once his classmates got the bright idea of pelting him with balled-up scraps of parchment and then, painfully, an apple-core, he hastily scooped up his belongings and decided it was time to make his exit. Not before pocketing a few of the parchment-wads, though—he'd seen many of the missiles were notes on the day's lecture. If they were going to hand him the information, he might as well take it.

The volume of the heckling increased as Henry rose with as much dignity as he could muster, but as he descended the stairs of the auditorium, he chanced looking over at St John. The Lord Calipash, unlike the rest of the Blithe Company, was *not* cackling at him; neither did he seem to be upset or angry. Instead, catching Henry's eye, the curly-haired, pretty-faced lad smiled … and blew him a kiss!

Distracted, confused, Henry looked away only to see a foot jut out in front of him. *Bugger*, he thought as he tripped, and half-tumbled, half-slid down the rest of the stairs.

"*Oof*," he grunted, and his eyes went all black and starry for a moment. When his vision cleared he found he'd landed on his back, which was nice as he hadn't broken his nose, but his position afforded him the unfortunate sight of his notes and papers fluttering down around him as several of the boys from the Blithe Company fell upon him like the wolf-pack they were. He saw the savage cruelty in their faces; he knew he was really in for it now. Pathetically, he tried to scoot away from them using his feet, but one of them stepped on his stomach, immobilizing him. Worse even than the pain in his guts, he farted loudly.

Mortified and on the verge of tears, Henry was hauled to his feet as the rest of the class, the shitwigs, chanted "Stink-Pig, Pink-Pig, Oink Oink Oink!" He heard Master Fulkerson's voice above the din but could not make out the words, and so had no idea if his assailants were disobeying or carrying out the Master's orders when they deposited him on his knees at the base of the stairs leading to where St John yet lounged, surveying the hubbub with amused detachment.

"What shall we do with him, Calipash?" asked one of the Blithe Company, a tall, black-haired boy called Nicholas Jay. "You decide! He's yours—*by right of conquest.*"

This drew another round of laughter and cheering, but the din quieted when St John raised his pale hand. Henry looked up through weary, defeated eyes to see St John smiling down at him. He felt the stirrings of hope in his breast. The Company all looked up to St John. Perhaps he would curb the cruelty of his fellows.

"Let him go," said St John softly. Henry had never heard him speak much above a murmur, and why should he? The whole room went silent whenever he spoke. "I thought it was a sweet little poem. Why should I punish someone who has shown such appreciation for our noble person?"

There was booing at this. St John waved them away.

"You asked me what to do with him, I say turn him loose. That is what I want; I was curious to learn more about Aristophanes' speech in the *Symposium.* Master Fulkerson, I'm intrigued—why have Aristophanes, the great *comic* playwright, make a speech that is so very *tragic*? His remark that some humans—I believe he was speaking of homosexuals, the children of the sun—though split asunder like everyone else, are forced by social convention to marry those who are not their other half, and beget children with them, despite their inclinations. That seems rather distressing; I'd like to hear more, and our class time is not yet over for the day ..."

Henry felt the hands that held him loosen their death-grip at St John's reprieve; he sank to the floor, wobbly-legged. Of course the Lord Calipash would be the essence of *noblesse oblige*, he was so perfect in every way, so generous, so—

"Mr. Milliner, if you will not remove your fat backside from my classroom floor, I will remove it for you," said Master Fulkerson.

"Do it!" hooted someone.

"I—y-yes, of course, my apologies," stammered Henry, getting to his knees and dazedly collecting his scattered papers as Master Fulkerson resumed his lecture. So occupied, Henry failed to realize that he had presented the master with a generous opportunity for more mischief-making; just as he regained his feet and reached down one final time to retrieve a quill that had skittered away from him across the floor, he felt something hard collide with his posterior. Off-balance, he rolled arse over teakettle towards the door, which had thankfully been left ajar, his papers fluttering out of his grasp once again as if he had let go the neck of a sack stuffed with live pigeons.

The students broke into applause as Master Fulkerson thoughtfully rubbed his knee.

"I was a champion footballer in my youth," remarked the Master. "Why—your bottom has scuffed my shoe, Mr. Milliner. I shall summon you later to attend to the mark."

"I'll make sure he does so," said a sonorous, disapproving voice from somewhere above Henry's head. He looked up—and saw the last person at Wadham College he wanted to encounter at that moment.

It was his academic advisor, Phineas Berry.

CHAPTER TWO:
UPON RECEIVING A WARNING

Henry's backside throbbed awfully where Master Fulkerson had punted him out of the classroom, but he did not complain about the cushionless wooden chair that amplified the ache. Instead, he sat as quietly as possible, eyes fixed upon his folded hands, while Phineas Berry sighed and fretted at him.

"You really must apply yourself more," said Mr. Berry, leaning forward over his desk and peering at Henry with watery grey eyes partially obscured by greasy silver-rimmed spectacles. "Even before I heard from another student about the—ah—*incident* in Fulkerson's class today, I was going to come and speak to you about your academic performance here at Wadham College."

Henry looked up, his interest in the conversation rekindled. He'd petitioned to be admitted to the Natural Philosophy class in the fall—perhaps he had been approved?

"Yes, sir? What about my performance, sir?"

"That it's shameful of course. Your marks in Mathematics are poor—and before you waggle your waddle saying that mathematics don't matter as you're intending to become a lawyer like your father, let me remind you that your performance in Logic is disgraceful, and your languages make me wonder how it is you are able to speak passable *English*."

Mr. Berry fell silent. Henry presumed his advisor was giving him an opportunity to defend himself.

"I try—I really do. And my Latin isn't so very bad—"

"No, it isn't," began Mr. Berry, his tone easing somewhat, "but only your written work," he finished, Henry's spirits sinking further as his advisor's voice hardened again, like a pond re-freezing after an all too brief thaw. "Your oral examinations are *terrible*, and frankly, looking upon your Greek translations strikes the eyes like a blow. Overall your work is abysmal—no, that is insulting to abysses, for they are deep by nature, and you are merely deep in the soup." Mr. Berry polished his spectacles and re-settled them on his nose. "To summarize my complaints, you are not doing well here, and that could mean bad things for you if you can't find a way to turn your performance *substantially* around."

Henry nodded, now staring at the tips of his shoes just visible beyond the hem of his black robe.

"You told me you wished to take Natural Philosophy next semester."

"Yes, sir." Henry figured showing some enthusiasm might go a long way. "I do, sir. Very much, sir."

"Well, it's only for advanced students—the best of the best here at Wadham. I don't need to tell you that you are not the best of the best. You are not even *good* at anything, as far as I can tell." Mr. Berry sighed. "I'm sorry, Henry, but I cannot recommend you."

Henry despaired. St John and the rest of the Company all had Natural Philosophy together, and his plan for months now had been to get in with them via that class. There were so few students in Natural Philosophy they all had to work together during their laboratory experiments; to be thrown together with them would give him ample opportunity to show he was worthy enough—witty enough—*smart* enough to be part of the Blithe Company. If he couldn't even qualify for the class he was destined to get their attention only through unintentionally becoming the class jackanapes.

"I know you're disappointed, but—"

"Please, sir ... I ... I want it so very much, Mr. Berry."

"Wanting is not enough, Henry. Really, your priorities are as nightmarish as your marks. If you don't pull up your marks you'll have a lot more to worry about than not being in Natural Philosophy in the fall."

"Yes, sir."

"Well, well," said Mr. Berry, not unkindly. "That's enough of that. Tell me of your plan, then."

Henry looked up. "My what?"

"Your plan. To improve your performance. You've been nodding at me like a performing donkey, it's time to show me you've absorbed some of my wisdom! Tell me what you intend to do to keep yourself here."

"Oh," said Henry. He thought wildly for a moment, then settled on, "I'll ... find a tutor?"

"A Greek tutor?"

"Oh no, an English one, I should think."

Mr. Berry pressed his fingertips to his eyebrows. "Yes. Well. That does seem like a good idea, good show. Of whom were you thinking?"

St John's winsome countenance blazed across Henry's mind like an avenging angel in a saint's vision, but he decided against mentioning the Lord Calipash, just in case his tutor had heard the antecedent to his being booted—quite literally—out of the classroom. "Lord … Rochester?"

"Are you asking me or telling me?"

"Well, sir, if I could get your take on the matter, that might help me pick someone most able to help me."

"Haven't had enough of boots today, so you come a-licking at them?" Mr. Berry rolled his eyes. "Well, Henry, in that case *no*—I *don't* think the Lord Rochester would be a good tutor for you. His Greek is good only in comparison to yours, and I know you two are friends and thus would likely get up to freaks and high jinks rather than anything useful."

"The Lord Rochester is quite studious, really; he's a serious lad, academically inclined—"

"No, he's a stick in the mud, there's a difference—and I don't want you turning what he has for a mind toward dissipation and indolence. He's a good lad, while *you*, Henry, are … I cannot even find the words. It seems unfair to call you stupid, for I believe you have a mind somewhere inside that skull of yours, but you waste yourself. I've seen how eager you are to ingratiate yourself with as pernicious a crowd of ne'er-do-wells as we've ever had at Wadham. Yes, I do speak of the Lord Calipash and his dreadful posse of badgers, and your tendency to pursue them like a bulling cow. What advantage do you see in it, Henry?"

Henry thought of St John: His easy manners, academic ability, his lordly, lean face free of spots or flaws, the way he was able to make even the rotten college-issue student robes look like a new suit of clothing from a high-end tailor on St. James' Street; he contemplated the Blithe Company as a whole, the fancy parties they threw for their peers, their wittiness, camaraderie, and popularity, the tales—those told by them and those that were mere rumor among the lesser students of the college—of sneaking out after hours to drink and to seduce women, the way no one challenged them when they always snagged the best seats (those by the brazier in winter; by the windows in summer), how their dinners always looked so much more ample and carefully-prepared, and most of all, how all the Masters and advisors and everyone else turned a blind eye to their faults and disobediences—and sighed. Eventually, Mr. Berry did the same.

"It occurs to me your desire to get into Natural Philosophy has less to do with your desire to learn the scientific method, and more with St John and his boys, does it not?"

Henry could not deny it, so he said nothing.

"All right, all right. Perhaps we can use this as a motivating force, eh? Listen to me, Henry: *If* you promptly find yourself a tutor, and *if*, afterwards, your grades improve—substantially—I shall recommend you for the class next year. Do we have a deal?"

Henry, thrilled, opened his mouth to agree, but Mr. Berry interrupted him.

"Yes, yes, you're delighted, you'll surely follow through, and all that. We'll see. For now, leave me," he said, shooing Henry out of his office with a flicker of his fingers. "Go, begone! I can see by your vapid expression that save for my dubious notion to bribe you everything I have said has gone in one of your ears and fallen out of the other. No wonder you're such a menace in the classroom, I'm sure all the other students must take care not to slip on the bits of knowledge that must seep out of you and puddle on the floor. There's the bell anyhow. Go. You must be longing for your dinner."

Insulting, but not untrue. Henry rose and slunk toward the door, only to hear a knock. He looked back at Mr. Berry, who nodded, and Henry opened it, revealing a freckle-faced boy of about fourteen years old.

"M-Mr. Berry," he said apologetically, "Master Fulkerson, he sent me on to escort Hen—uh, I mean, Mr. Milliner to his office. He says he can't go to dinner with his boots in such a state, and Mr. Milliner is to—"

"I'm to polish them, yes," said Henry dully. "Lead on."

"Don't sound so distressed, Henry! It's only one pair, I'm sure you'll get your slice of meat-pie," chuckled Mr. Berry as Henry followed his escort out the door. "And if not, well, it'll only help your studying. Don't they underfeed watchdogs to keep them keen? Perhaps we should apply that theory to our kitchens, I'm sure our foundress would be most pleased to see the reduction in our annual expenses—and the Warden, too."

As it turned out, it wasn't only the one pair of boots Henry had to polish. *Of course* it wasn't only one pair, he thought bitterly as he plodded back to his chambers in the gloaming. Master Fulkerson had insisted Henry clean every pair in his closet, and it had apparently been some time since he had meted out this task to anyone, servant or student.

Henry's stomach rumbled from emptiness, his knees ached from kneeling on the wooden floor of Master Fulkerson's chambers, and his hands were blacker than the night sky with filth and polish. But it was the unfairness of it all that chaffed worse than anything! Really, who *didn't* write poetry these days—and yet he alone was punished for the crime of artistic expression! How could he have anticipated that, at Wadham, admiring one's betters through verse would be viewed as some gross sin, akin to shitting on the Bible or poisoning an especially cherubic child?

Like most of the common students, Henry shared a room with two other boys. It was a decent enough situation; Henry had heard tell of the terrible overcrowding at many of the other universities in Oxford, and Maximilian Dee and Bruce Travers weren't bad sorts. But they *were* stupid and frivolous, so Henry was not entirely surprised when he pushed open the door of the dormitory and was greeted by the sight of them and several other boys bent over, mooning him, with one of his bed-sheets hung like a banner above their pale bottom-cheeks, the words *Congratulations Henry, Best Poet at Wadham* scrawled across the linen in charcoal.

"Did you keep watch for me, or have you been hanging about with your trousers down for hours?" he said wearily, shutting the door behind him.

"Oh, hello there, Henry—we didn't hear you come in!" giggled Maximilian, getting to his feet and hiking up his breeches. The rest of the lads followed suit. "Didn't see you at dinner—where were you? Out gazing at the stars, committing more verses to parchment?"

"Oh, of course. Wrote an entire saga on my way up the stairs," said Henry. He tugged on the edge of his sheet to try to pull it down from where they'd tacked it. "You bastards, I haven't got a spare, and it's a week 'till laundry-day."

"It was filthy already. What are all those *stains*, eh?" said Bruce, poking him in the side.

"You know we're not supposed to have *girls* in our rooms—not even Miss Rosie Palmer and her five daughters," hooted a boy called Richmond Blakemore.

"Hilarious." Henry wadded up the sheet and threw it on his bed. "Didn't snag me anything at dinner, did you?"

The boys' giggling was all the answer he needed. Entirely defeated, Henry sat down on his bedstead and took off his square cap; tossing it on his pillow, he ran his hands through his mouse-brown hair.

"Ho there, anyone at home?"

Henry looked up at the familiar voice and saw Lord Rochester there, holding—could it be true, could it be real?—a plate with a hunk of bread and a wedge of pie oozing gravy.

"Welcome, my lord," said Bruce, with a bow. Though Henry and his roommates were all about sixteen and Rochester had barely thirteen winters to his name, the Earl's rank could not be ignored. "You honor us with your presence."

"Do I? How nice," said Rochester, stepping inside with such an aristocratic air that even Henry felt the urge to bow and scrape. "Hungry, Henry? It's a nice evening, care you to dine out in the Grove?"

Nodding and grabbing his hat, Henry followed his friend into the cool quiet of the hallway and out into the twilit garden. Rochester handed over the plate as they ambled, and Henry, too hungry for dignity, immediately grabbed the bread with his dirty hand and gobbled it in two bites.

"How did you know?" he said, through a mouthful.

"Fellow Commoners dine with the Masters, don't we?" said Rochester, with a shrug. "I heard Master Fulkerson comment that you'd be polishing his shoes all night."

"Thank you, my friend," said Henry, feeling a little overwhelmed by this show of kindness after the day he'd had. He hoped his misty eyes wouldn't drip.

Rochester smiled, his beautiful, almost girlish mouth turning upwards, the lips parting to show pearly teeth. "You're a good friend to me, too, you know."

"But to give up your dinner!"

"Oh, that's not mine." Rochester shook his head. "It's Robert's. I asked them for a second helping, but they wouldn't. He said he didn't mind."

Robert was Rochester's manservant. Henry felt a brief flash of guilt, but then shrugged it off. "Well, thank you. It's more than appreciated."

"My pleasure. You can't know how nice it is to have someone I can, I dunno … be myself around. The rest of the Fellow Commoners … well, I'd rather be here with you in the garden than out at that beano at the Hors—ah."

"You were invited?" Henry paused, pie-slice halfway to his mouth. "You didn't tell me!"

"I—well, I didn't, well …" Rochester looked as miserable as a cat in the rain. "Henry, I couldn't bring you, and I didn't want, you know, to—"

"Nonsense!" Henry bit into his pie and yamed the slice noisily. At last, the opportunity he'd been waiting for! Today was finally looking up, at last—if he could but convince Rochester to take him hence to the Horse and Hat, he could use it as an opportunity to thank St John for his benevolence—and tell him, in turn, of his recent academic woes. He was sure, if St John knew how badly he struggled in Greek, he would agree to tutor him. Why else would he have shown him such mercy today if he did not care for him a little?

"Henry—"

Henry spoke through a mouthful of pie. "Let me just finish this and we'll be off. I haven't anything better to change into anyway."

"But we're not allowed to leave the campus except in the company of an older student—"

"I'm older than you."

Rochester's lip trembled, he looked as though he might burst into tears at any moment. "I don't think it's a good idea, Henry. What if we're caught?"

"We won't be caught," scoffed Henry. "We'll slip out the back gate and be home before anyone notices!"

"But if they see you! They'll know you weren't invited ..."

"You saw the Lord Calipash's kindness to me in class, did you not? You think he, after such treatment, would kick me in the whirlegigs and cast me out into the street like a dog?"

Rochester was shaking his head so vehemently Henry thought his cap was in danger of flying off. "It's not a good idea, you don't understand what they're like away from school—"

Henry frowned. "And you do?"

"Oh. Well ..."

"So you've gone off to these parties before, without me?" Henry huffed. "I should've known."

"Yes, I went once," snapped Rochester. "I need not give *you* an account of all my activities, you know. But before you ask—yes, there was drink, and there was music, and there were women, too. Lots of them, breasts everywhere, their skirts hiked up to show their dark hairy cunnies." Rochester snuffled and wiped his nose on his sleeve. "Edwin Harris stuck his tongue into one and wiggled it about for the—I don't know, edification of us all, he said, as well as for her pleasure. He kept at it for so very long that your precious, kindly, benevolent Lord Calipash, exclaiming how boring it was to watch such a display, snuck up behind them and poured claret down her belly."

"I say!"

"Edwin nearly drowned. And afterwards, your St John announced he would use them all in a line, so the ladies—women, rather—bent over the tables while the rest of the Company cheered him on." Rochester sighed. "A few other lads did it, too. I wouldn't, and they mocked me for it—as if chastity wasn't *respectable*."

Henry thought back to Phineas Berry's allegation that Rochester was 'a stick in the mud.' He was such a soggy merkin, what was wrong with him? Could he be allergic to fun? His nose was certainly running enough while he described a scenario Henry thought sounded jolly good. "How did I never hear tell of this? Surely there must have been a scandal …"

"They wear disguises," sniffled Rochester. "If you go like that, in your robes, there'll be a scene."

"Then lend me a coat!"

"But I don't even want to go!"

Henry looked away, disgusted. How like a lord to despair of an invitation; to scorn what he'd been handed by right of birth. It was so very unjust. Here he was, sitting in this clammy garden, alone except for a prudish little boy, while others drank and sang and—

"You really want to go, don't you," said Rochester softly. "You'd rather be there with them, than here with me."

Henry felt a pang. "I—well." He coughed. "I wouldn't put it like *that*."

"Fine then." Rochester stood, his slender figure silhouetted against the candle- and torchlight of Wadham College. "We'll go, and you'll see how *miserable* it is. But you'll have to wear Robert's coat." Rochester turned on his heel and said over his shoulder, "You won't fit into any of mine, you great pudding."

CHAPTER THREE:
HERE THE DEITIES DISAPPROVE

"*Shh*," cautioned Rochester. Henry had uttered a prodigious groan as he heaved the Earl up onto the ledge of the wall surrounding the college. "Come on, before someone sees you!"

Henry mopped his brow with a handkerchief and stuffed it back into a pocket of the coat Robert had—rather grudgingly, Henry thought—given him the use of for the night. With a sigh he dug his fingers in among the bricks and managed to scramble up after his friend. He heard a rending sound and, panicking, risked reaching around to feel his behind; it wasn't his trousers that had split, thank God. Just a rip in the coat where a button had torn free from its moorings. Too bad for Robert.

"Come down!" cried Rochester, when Henry crested the wall. "*Hurry!*"

With another grunt, Henry jumped, nearly twisting his ankle as he landed on the hard earth of the street. He readjusted the hideous cap he'd also borrowed, checked his pocket to make sure his mask was still there, and nodded. "All right, I'm ready. Dunno how we'll get back in, though."

"They always have a plan," said Rochester, trotting down the street away from the college. "St John has a manservant, too, and he usually stays behind to prepare some sort of discreet ingress after-hours. Now, come on, we must go quickly. They'll have been there some time already."

Henry was very nervous. He had trouble catching his breath as he took off after Rochester; the urge to urinate came upon him strong every few seconds. He'd never snuck out of the college, and after Mr. Berry's lecture that afternoon, he knew that should he be caught he might very well be thrown out, having no academic record to balance the scales against this indiscretion.

But to hell with all of that—he was going to a party!

The Horse and Hat was not particularly far from Wadham; given that the tavern's politics were as flexible as the college's, Henry knew the professors with Royalist sympathies, oblique or otherwise, went there to drink and get a bite to eat on Saturday nights. Henry, however, had never been there, and was glad Rochester knew the way, for he was lost within five minutes, Oxford after dark being much, well, darker and more confusing than he had anticipated.

Down alleyways they tramped, and scampered across thoroughfares, until, perhaps a quarter of an hour later, a sign-board, swinging in the light spring breeze, came into sight: A rearing stallion and, behind it, a plumed hat. Lights blazed inside, and through the windows Henry saw many figures moving about within. He mopped his forehead again, and hoped against hope he wasn't sweating too badly, like he usually did when he was anxious.

"Here we go," said Rochester. "Put your mask on, and someone at the Horse will direct us accordingly. They have an understanding with the management."

"Who's they?"

"The Blithe Company, nodgecombe!"

"Oh," said Henry, and tied the black mask over his eyes, knotting it behind his head. "Let me do yours—you won't be able to manage with that awful wig."

"I like this wig." Rochester was pouting.

"Pick up that lip or you're liable to trip over it," said Henry, clapping his friend on the back. "Come—I have dreamed of this for so very long. Let us have some fun!"

"You may be surprised," said Rochester, but he pushed open the door of the inn and bowed Henry inside.

It was very crowded, and smelled strongly of middling beer and body odor. Men and women of all sorts bumped shoulders as they tried to make it to the bar and back again; the three sweaty-faced barmaids could not serve the throng quickly enough. A sign of the changing times, a bearded fellow in a weathered leather jacket was singing "When the King Enjoys His Own Again" from atop a table to much general raising of tankards and exclamations of "Long live the King!"

Henry thought it a splendid scene, and drank it all in eagerly. Now *this* was what he'd been missing! He was all smiles until a yeoman lurched into him and then swore at him for the outrage; Henry panicked and began to blather apologies—but the man moved on without further aggression, and he relaxed.

He was concerned, however, that he could see no one else wearing masks—or for that matter, anything remotely fine. Desperate, he looked around for Rochester, but it seemed he had been pushed or pulled away from Henry by one of the currents in that ocean of humanity. Seeing a flash of the dark purple of the boy's coat in the rear left corner, Henry tried his best to wind his way quickly over.

Rochester had his ear pressed to a wooden door.

"What's the rumpus?" Henry asked. "What are we to do?"

"They're in the private room behind this door. It's begun already. I'm waiting for them to finish whatever they're doing so we don't interrupt."

"Interrupt them at what? A party? I thought—"

"Shut *up*, will you? Ah—here's our moment," said Rochester. He knocked in a pattern Henry didn't fully catch, then ducked inside. Henry followed after.

There were perhaps nine masked gentlemen and a handful of "ladies"—also disguised—in the private chamber, but it seemed far more crowded than it was, being a small space and better-furnished than the common room. All present were bedecked in the kind of finery that might get one arrested for anti-Puritan sympathies in mixed company. Mother-of pearl buttons gleamed on coats of hunter green, slate grey, wine red, and deep purple. Long wigs trailed everywhere; ladies' wide skirts endangered cups of claret.

Now *this* was the party Henry had been expecting!

"Stop gawping," hissed Rochester, bringing Henry back to himself. "Try to look natural. I'd suggest sitting, and keep in mind if you speak to anyone they'll know you don't belong."

That the little weasel should lecture him about looking natural—why, Rochester looked about as comfortable as a Roundhead at an Anglican mass. But Henry took his point, and, pouring himself a glass of wine, sat on a crimson-velvet upholstered chaise not too near the stage he'd spied at the back of the room. All seats and benches pointed toward it, and after Rochester's remark about "interrupting" he assumed some entertainment would happen upon it presently.

He was correct. Just as he was growing weary of crowd-watching—enough so to get up and attempt to mingle, as Rochester had been doing—the very person he had been trying to catch a glimpse of all night appeared on the stage.

Henry had been able to recognize most of his masked colleagues as they milled about, eating things and chatting. There was Nicholas Jay, kissing the left breast of a similarly masked woman, and beside him, Anthony Neville, who said something that made everyone giggle. There was Edwin Harris, and Rowan Zwarteslang, and Richard Smith, placing wagers on something. Some of the other lads resisted identification— but there was no mistaking St John Clement.

His appearance caused the din to momentarily rise and then recede, like a wave crashing upon the seashore and quickly withdrawing. He was, to Henry's eyes, magnificent: dressed in a coat of pearlescent sea-foam green embroidered with silver thread, he stood out among the darker raiment of his comrades, and his wig was white, rather than black. He was wearing white stockings, too, and his slender calves seemed to shine against the red curtain that obscured the makeshift backstage.

"What do you think will be the final act tonight?"

Some masked young man plunked down beside Henry on the chaise, smelling of wine and some sort of perfume. It was Aldous Clark, he thought—they had several classes together, so Henry shrugged, not trusting himself to speak. He didn't want to be recognized. Not yet.

"Last time was rather entertaining, if—not to sound unapprecia- tive—a little more outré than usual, don't you think? Never watched a fellow go at it with a blower before." Clark giggled. "Interesting, that. Can't say I didn't learn a few things, that St John can really give it to the ladies. But here we go anyhow, no need to wonder further."

Henry was glad his companion hadn't noticed anything strange, and was now wholly occupied by what was happening on stage. St John had summoned two beautiful youths to stand beside him, red-haired and freckle-faced, one female, one male, and they were so very alike they must be siblings, Henry decided, if not twins. The girl wore only her shift; the boy, his shirt, which was slightly too big for him, and hung down well past his knees. Even in the candlelight, Henry saw them both blushing to be so bare in front of all the fine gentlemen and ladies.

St John bowed to the settling crowd. The curls of his white wig fell forward over his shoulders, and when he stood, he swept them back dramatically.

"Good evening, colleagues!" he said, not raising his voice but extending his arms in a gesture of welcome. When the room went completely still, he dropped his hands, placing one on each of the heads of the siblings. They flinched slightly at his touch. Applause followed this; after it subsided, St John cleared his throat and began anew.

"Thank you all for coming tonight," he said. "I trust the earlier entertainments were to your liking?"

Mutterings of assent from everyone. St John looked pleased—but then waggled a finger at the gathering like a nurse scolding a disobedient child.

"Such a host of naughty boys—and girls—to sneak away so late just to see a parade of performing dogs, bawdy songs sung by those of small talent, and the—*ahem*—unusual abilities of Mistress Lavinia! We must have some intellectual purpose to our gathering, methinks. To that end, I propose to conclude this evening not with another common production, but with a *philosophical experiment*."

Henry leaned forward a little, as did the rest of the company. This was, judging by their reactions, a rather unusual announcement.

"Tonight, my two companions—Irish twins, orphans I paid ten shillings to appear before you—will help resolve a theological conundrum. Fear not, we will not be debating how many angels may sit on the head of a pin! I think, rather, that all of you will be quite riveted by our question … as well as our method of inquiry."

"I say, this *is* a strange sort of party," whispered Henry to Rochester, who'd taken a seat on a stool next to him.

"*Shh!*" hissed Rochester, for Henry thought maybe the hundredth time that night. Prig.

"I propose," continued St John, "that tonight, we, the Blithe Company, determine whether the act of love," here St John, to Henry's surprise, dismay—and excitement—waggled his hips in a lewd manner, "is a *spiritual* thing, or a *physical* one. We are told it is spiritual—God joins us together, and let no man put that asunder, *et cetera*—but may man join together what God wills asunder? If such is possible, we can, I think, conclude that intercourse is a *physical* act—and thus may, with clean consciences, indulge in it without fear of anything worse than the pox."

General laughter; more applause. Henry joined in half-heartedly, looking at the twins. The lad was crying a little, his nose was dripping and he kept wiping it on the back of his hand, where the slimy slug-trails of snot sparkled in the candlelight. Surely … *surely nothing*, Henry told himself—and for good measure, he also told himself to suck it up and be the man he wanted to be. This is what he'd desired to be a party to, after all. He couldn't back out now.

"My hypothesis," St John said when the applause died down, "is that Christ—God—the Holy Ghost—all of the angles—they have nothing to do with it. With fucking, I mean. Though I claim to have been *divinely inspired* during pursuit," here he moved away from the twins and drew a young woman out of the audience, kissing her deeply on the mouth only to push her away once her very visible bosom began to heave, "and, truth be told, *consummation*," he took a young man by the hand this time, and kissed him on the mouth whilst fondling what he found just below where the stripling's coat split and fanned out, "I have heard time again in church and in the classroom that to do what I like best is an offense—a spiritual crime, if you will, against myself, against my future wife, and against God. Well, if intercourse is a spiritual act, then it could not, to my mind, be performed by those without spiritual *desire*. Take, for example, these twins."

Henry felt queasy, but kept his seat. He couldn't have left the company if he wanted to. St John's overtures toward the audience members had excited him too much for him to rise without humiliation.

"Brothers and sisters do not look at one another with the eyes of lust. Such a thing is impossible. It is wrong—it is an *abomination*. And these twins are not abominations—are you?"

Neither of the siblings replied, so St John knocked the boy on the head as if rapping his knuckles on a door.

"Are you an abomination, sir?"

"No," he managed.

"And you, Madam?"

"No m'lord," she whispered, not looking up.

"So neither of you have ever desired the other in a sexual fashion?"

They looked up at St John with identical wild, wide eyes filled with terror. He smiled down at them beatifically.

"Let a couch be placed upon the stage!" he said. "Some of you must stand, a pity, but it cannot be helped. A couch!"

The only couch appropriate for what Henry feared was about to ensue was under his own bottom, so he stood quickly and slunk into the corner behind it, trying his best to melt into the shadows. St John caught his eye—and smiled slightly. Henry's heart began to pound when St John bid two of the bigger members of the Company to move the chaise to the front of the room. He then sat in the center of it, and then patted the thigh of his leg as though encouraging a kitten to jump up there.

"Sit, Madam," he said to the girl. She did, reluctantly. "And you, sir—sit here," he said, thumping the cushion beside him.

Henry crouched beside Rochester. "Is he really going to make them …"

"You said you wanted to come, so wait and watch," hissed Rochester.

"Your brother is very handsome," said St John, to the girl. "Have you ever thought about that?"

"Nay, sir," said the girl.

"You're very pretty—do you think your brother has ever looked at you and thought so?"

"He brought me a flower once, sir, after our aunt had cuffed me bad on the ear for breaking one of the eggs I gathered from the coop."

"You didn't do that out of *lust* for your sister, though," enquired St John, turning to the lad. He blushed crimson, and shook his head.

"Well! I think we have established these twins are neither perverts nor sinners—quite normal, yes?" The audience nodded its approval. St John smiled, and lifted the girl by her narrow waist, then plunked her down beside her brother. "Finally," he said to the company, "I say to you that we must agree, for this experiment to go forward, that ten shillings is not a spiritual matter. Does the Bible, or Aquinas, or anyone ever say that ten shillings is spiritual, rather than physical, in nature?"

"Get on with it!" cried someone.

"Patience, patience," admonished St John, but he seemed to sense he was losing his audience. "All right you two—boy, I want you to kiss your sister. On the lips, like a man kisses a woman."

He refused; St John slapped him. Weeping, the lad acquiesced to the Lord Calipash's demand. Henry's legs felt shaky, wobbly—he saw colored blackness flashing behind his eyes. Never had he thought—dear God, the lad was a quick study, and had commenced fondling his sister's breast!

The chit seemed shyer than her brother, and when his assault on her chastity became increasingly one-sided, St John apparently felt it was time to intervene. He snuck up behind her, pantomiming for the giggling crowd, and then with firm but gentle pressure, pushed her head down to the part of her brother that was beginning to show signs of excitement: His shirt was tenting over his groin, and there was a small wet stain obvious against the white linen.

"Unleash the beast," encouraged St John. "So far it seems as though my hypothesis has been confirmed, but if you, Madam, are not sufficiently moved by the flesh alone, then I fear we may have to declare a draw rather than draw a conclusion!"

When the girl uncovered her brother's cockstand, Henry felt as though it were a toss-up if he would vomit or ejaculate in his breeches; when she pushed the lad back onto the couch and took his affair into herself with a catlike yowl of pain and then rode him with short jerking motions of her hips until both shouted their climax to the company, Henry was sure he would never again think about touching another person in lust.

A triumphant St John was smoothing their sweaty hair away from their foreheads, kissing their exhausted brows, and claiming loudly that his experiment was a success—but Henry could not help but disagree. He had felt aroused watching the display, to be sure, but he also felt sick at heart.

"You look like you need a drink," Rochester was saying in his ear. Henry started and stared at him, uncomprehending. "I've seen peacocks less green than you."

"He made them—"

"You wanted to come. Are you happy now?" Rochester's voice was as bitter as horehound. Henry looked up in surprise.

"I ..."

"Come on, then. Now you know, and we may safely be friends without this between us, I think." Rochester, nearly three years his junior, was leading him by the hand to a flagon of wine. Though already tipsy, Henry took the goblet and drank it with great gulps. He felt positively parched.

Snippets of conversation hit him as the rest of the party mingled and took some refreshment. "Strange," "different," "interesting," were words that stood out to him. Henry was taken aback—while the reaction from the Company seemed more thoughtful than enthusiastic, it shocked him that no one thought to protest such an outrage ...

"And what did *you* think, sir?"

Henry turned—St John was there, smiling at him. His eyes sparkled behind his mask.

"I—"

"Did you find my methods convincing? And what of my conclusion?"

"I ..."

"Were you entertained by the show?"

Henry considered this. He had been disgusted, appalled—but some part of him *had* enjoyed the spectacle. He couldn't lie to St John ...

"I think so, my lord—"

St John took a step back. "My Lord? Who do you think I am?" He looked really annoyed. "Dare you presume anything among this company? We are all anonymous, sir!"

"Oh, yes sir, I am sorry sir, it's my first time, and—"

"First time?" St John frowned. "Boys! This one says its his first time—did we invite anyone new?"

Henry's heart sank, and he began to sweat into the borrowed coat. He caught Rochester's eye; the boy shook his head and shrugged, doing nothing to aid him. Henry began to sweat as cries of "no!" and "not me!" filled the room.

Busted. Big-time.

"I don't know who you are, or what you're doing here, but you are most unwelcome," said St John in a low, violent tone that alarmed Henry more than anything he'd seen that night. "If you tell anyone of this, I will personally see to it that you are flogged for leaving school, destroyed socially, beaten within an inch of—"

"I wouldn't, I swear it," Henry protested. Masked faces framed by luxurious wigs were closing in all around them. "My lord, it is I, Henry Milliner. After your kindness to me today in Master Fulkerson's class, I wanted to come, to thank you for showing such mercy. I—it's that I admire you so very much, you see," Henry risked putting a hand out to touch St John's wrist, "and my advisor told me to find a Greek tutor, so—"

"He says he came for tutoring!" said St John, pulling away from Henry. "Let's give him a lesson, shall we?"

Henry would never forget the conclusion of that night, how hands fell upon him and hoisted him aloft above the mob; how they complained loudly of his weight as they paraded him through the tavern; how they tossed him by the coat into the street, where he landed face-first in a pile of turds that had decomposed to the point that he could not tell if they'd been left there by pig, horse, dog, or man.

"And stay out!" shouted someone after him.

Henry felt the words a kick to the kidneys. How could he? Why would he? What had changed since that afternoon? Tears started in Henry's eyes, hot, stinging, angry tears. He could not help his common heritage; he hadn't chosen it any more than St John had chosen to be born a fine lord. It was fate—luck of the draw!

So St John was just like the rest of them, the rotten aristocratic shitwigs. Even Rochester! Talking to him like that at the party, leaving him to be tossed out into the street like a drunken cottar. The indignity of it all!

A few moments later, he felt a hand on him—a gentle hand.

"I told you we shouldn't come," said Rochester. "Let's get you home. Oh, Henry," he said, shaking his head, "please, after tonight, consider leaving the sheep-chasing to the shepherds?"

The sound that came out of Henry's mouth was indeed rather like a bleat, but he had no intention of taking Rochester's advice. He sat up and spat out a mouthful of filth, resolving to keep hope alive in his heart. St John had been showing off, was all. He was simply acting the consummate host for the Blithe Company's secret meeting. So Henry had violated the rules—well, he knew better now. What he really needed was to catch St John alone. *Then* he might get to the bottom of why the lord had blown such a tender kiss at him in class, only to treat him in so shabby a fashion later. Henry had no hypothesis about that, not yet—but in that moment, he vowed not even the celebrated philosopher Christopher Wren would investigate the mystery with more diligence.

CHAPTER FOUR:
MY LORD ALL-SHAME

Henry knew he was being petulant when he said *tchah* in a dismissive manner to Rochester after the latter's protest that he had stayed behind for a few moments only to enquire of the "official plan" for getting back into Wadham, but that didn't stop him from saying *tchah* in a dismissive manner with all his heart. That Rochester, who hadn't even wanted to go to the party, had done better socially than him—it was too insulting to contemplate. At least Rochester seemed to realize this, and was apologetic. Sort of.

"Please don't be cross with me," he said plaintively as they padded back to the college. "I told you, didn't I? Didn't I? We could have had a nice night chatting in the garden, just the two of us ... alone ... but you just had to go! Well, I knew, and I told you, and, and ..."

Good Christ, Rochester was weeping! This turn of events took Henry rather aback. Whatever could be the matter with the boy? If *he* wasn't crying, after everything, whatever could Rochester be on about?

"Buck up, John." Henry awkwardly clapped his friend on the back. Wadham was in sight: It wouldn't do to be seen returning from somewhere while wearing a borrowed coat covered in excrement, to say nothing of being accompanied by a teary-faced Lord Rochester. Rochester looked at him, clearly surprised. Henry but rarely used his Christian name. "It's not so bad?" said Henry. "You're not up to your eyebrows in shit, are you? And you weren't shamed before your friends?"

"Friends? Pray tell, who back there is your friend?"

It stung like a switch, but it was true—and Henry, in that moment, hated Rochester for saying it, hated him more than anyone he'd ever met before in his entire life. The little bitch! It wasn't enough, apparently, that he was richer, smarter, better-bred, as well as being Henry's superior in beauty, grace, and talent. He also had to get the upper hand when it came to society, too.

"Do forgive me, my lord," said Henry, pausing to bow to Rochester as low as he could, so low he swept the ground with his cap. "I am but an ignorant lawyer's son, and have experienced no real friendship since coming to Wadham and mixing with the noblesse. Twice now I seem to have mistaken impersonal courtesy from my betters for real camaraderie, to my shame. I shan't make such an error again, I assure you."

Rochester stared at him, lower lip trembling—and smacked Henry across the face.

"You—you *ninny!*" said Rochester; Henry, shocked, was thwarted in his attempt to raise his hand to where his cheek smarted when Rochester, standing on his tip-toes, kissed Henry wantonly on the mouth.

Henry had kissed a girl just once in his life. When he had lived in London, before attending Wadham, his cousin Abigail, two years his elder, had come to town with her mother to see the sights. Smitten, Henry had purchased her a costly pomander he'd seen her eyeing at the market, and, catching her alone, had dangled it before her, telling her it was hers forever if she would pay for it with one single kiss. Henry had been perfectly aware the lust he'd seen in her eyes was for the souvenir she could show her friends back in Norfolk, but so what to that—the feeling of her face so close to his; the way her mouth had tasted of small beer, garlic, and beef-and-barley stew when he'd briefly parted her lips with his tongue—well, it had gotten him through the lonely nights on more than one occasion.

Kissing Rochester was surprisingly similar except he was much shorter than Abigail, and he tasted better, too. Henry's heart fluttered a little in his chest when it occurred to him that he was kissing a *boy.* He didn't like boys ... well, except St John, of course, and it *was* true that one of the things he'd liked so much about Abigail was the faint mustache that adorned her upper lip. It made her look rakish and daring, like a cavalier. Contrary to fashion, they sometimes wore a little facial hair.

Rochester pulled away, and for a moment, Henry could see a thin dotted strand of saliva connecting them, but it snapped, and Rochester wiped his face, looking even younger than his thirteen years.

"You're a silly ass," he said, his mouth turning upward at the corners. "I've, Henry ... I confess, since I met you ..." Rochester canted his head to the right. "What's wrong, Henry?"

Henry felt as though his feet had grown roots; could not ascertain if his heart was still beating.

They were being watched.

Eyes glinted in the darkness just beyond the locked front gate of Wadham College. Henry opened his mouth and closed it again, unable to speak, unable to move, unable to think of what the fucking fuck he would do if his father learned he'd been out of bed after curfew, kissing noblemen in the dead of night.

"Henry?"

"*Shuttup!*" He hissed at Rochester through his teeth, not moving his lips. "*Someone's watching us.*"

"What?"

Christ, Rochester was such an idiot! The little fool was now casting about, looking for the spy like a housewife hunting for the best radishes to be had on market-day. Things could not get any worse.

"Stop that!"

"Where did you see him?" asked Rochester. "Oh!"

The boy's backbone had suddenly straightened, and he'd stopped his worthless head-waggling. Then he turned around with a big stupid grin on his face.

"It's just a dog, Henry!"

"What?" Henry felt a sudden deep lassitude in his limbs after taking a few steps forward and realizing that Rochester was right—the eyes belonged to a smallish poodlehound that was ...

It was just *staring* at them. Utterly motionless, the dog sat behind the gate, looking at them keenly. Its tail was swishing back and forth lackadaisically, but it made no noise at all. It gave Henry the creeps, big-time.

"Why isn't it barking?" he whispered.

"What?"

"Look at it. Why doesn't it care we're here?"

Rochester took a step forward. The dog got up, rubbed its great square head against the metal grate, then fell over onto its back and began to roll around, looking at them plaintively.

"You're right. Never seen a dog act like that before. How odd."

"It's more than odd. It's unnatural." Henry thought back to that morning—well, yesterday morning, at this point—listening to the boys gossiping in class, and shivered. "Do you think ..."

"It's not bloodied, or dead-eyed," said Rochester firmly. "The others were, you know."

"No, I don't." Rochester knew more about the queer dogs, too?

"The one yesterday—the day before—whatever, its heart had," Rochester swallowed. "There was a hole in its chest, plugged with a bit of cork. When they finally put it down, they noticed. And the one before that, the whole back of its *head* was missing. Its brain had been … violated."

Henry knelt down in the street, feeling faint, but Rochester tugged him up to his feet again.

"We've got to get back," he said. "We've got to get you cleaned up, and you know. Dispose of the evidence and all that."

"To the devil with your evidence." Henry felt more nauseated than he had at the Blithe Company gathering. The dog continued to roll about, silent and weird. "I just want to go to bed."

"You can't go to bed until we're back inside the gate." How Henry hated it when Rochester used that oh-so-reasonable voice! "Come on, the plan was to head through the Fellows' Garden, Thomas apparently set out a ladder!"

"Who's Thomas?"

"The Lord Calipash's man." Rochester shook his head. "Don't you ever pay attention to anything?"

"Honestly? Not really."

They left the dog, scurrying along the side until they had to cut down the side street to reach the wall that guarded the Fellows' Garden.

"Should we tell someone?" Henry swallowed. "About the dog?"

"Why?"

"Just, that it's there, and … mad, perhaps."

"And confess we were out of bed?" Rochester was the one to say *tchah* now. "See you first."

"All right, all right."

"There's the ladder." Rochester pointed.

Henry heard a creak from back the way they'd come, as of a gate swinging open.

Sounds of a brief struggle, then a feeble cry.

"Did you hear that?"

"I don't care," said Rochester. He was very pale. Henry would not have gone to investigate the matter by himself for love or money, so he nodded, and followed the boy up the ladder, over the wall, and down a second ladder onto the green lawn.

"Nothing to be done about the mess you've made of poor Robert's coat, he'll just have to wash it tomorrow," said Rochester. "You, however, we must clean." He took off at a canter toward the shadowy fountain at the center of the garden.

Henry, a less able runner even when not sleep-deprived and sore from misuse, nearly stumbled when a sudden motion and then a *clang* caught his attention. Glancing over his left shoulder, he saw ... he didn't know *what* he saw, but it looked like someone in school robes—maybe Wadham's, maybe another university's, he couldn't tell in the starlight— carrying a squirming creature away from the shut gate, back towards town.

The weird thing was, it looked like ... ah, but it couldn't be! He would still be at the Horse, with his friends. And anyways, this person had dark hair, and St John tawny ...

"Will you come *on!*"

"You sound like a goose when you hiss like that," said Henry, but he obeyed Rochester's command and headed away from the gate.

The water was freezing cold, what with the dismal, wet spring they'd had, and Henry had to make sure to get as clean as possible. After this late of a night, he doubted he'd be able to get up in time to wash before class tomorrow.

"I know this was hard for you," said Rochester, after using his handkerchief to wipe behind Henry's ears. "But I'm—well. I, ah, I'm glad we went tonight ... if not for the reasons I should be, I mean to say ..."

Henry shook the water from his hair, looked into Rochester's limpid, adoring eyes—and took a brief moment to consider his situation. He could, to his mind, embrace the lad, and see where such a romance might take them. Fun places, no doubt. The lordling, though a goody-goody, could be a way to get into more of the right kinds of gatherings, gatherings like the one they'd attended that night ... well, better ones than that, in content if not company. And once Henry had his degree, well, presumably Rochester would be in the position to need a lawyer one day, would he not? As a lover, or—better—*former* lover, Henry could put the idea of engaging him in the boy's head without much trouble at all. With such a patron, surely Henry would be set up for life, and with minimal effort, too ...

"John," he said, moving a curl of the boy's wig away from where it clung to his smooth cheek, "if the tale of our night together becomes common knowledge, it will not be from *my* lips."

It took Rochester a moment, but comprehension eventually dawned. Henry almost felt bad to see the look of transcendent joy that slowly crept over the boy's face like warm sunlight inching across the stone wall of a manor-house—but he purposefully recalled to mind the way Rochester had looked whilst sniggering at him along with the rest of Master Fulkerson's rotten class.

And yet he also understood that sniggering a little better in that moment: The taste of power was, apparently, sweeter even than a lime-tree's blossom ...

"Goodnight," he said, and, taking Rochester's head in his hands, he bent down and kissed the boy on his forehead. "Thank you—for *everything.*"

"Oh—I, I am glad you, well." Rochester smiled at him. "We shall have even better nights in the future, I am sure. Henry, if only I had known—that I risked, dared—oh, I am so very, very happy."

Rochester scampered toward the stairs to the Fellow Commoners' rooms on the upper storey, clutching Robert's shit-stained coat in his little hands, and Henry, feeling quite pleased with himself, tiptoed toward his room. There were no lights in the windows; it was very late indeed, and dark—which is why, perhaps, Henry was able to detect the pale glow of a folded piece of parchment sticking out from under his shoe after he stepped inside. Surprised, as quietly as he could he bent down and held the object to the faint light that came in through the doorway. His heart swelled: There, barely visible on the wine-dark wax sealing the letter shut, Henry could just make out the embossed image of a tortoise.

CHAPTER FIVE:
I WILL NOT CHANGE, AS OTHERS MIGHT

Henry could not risk lighting a candle, so it was not until very early the next morning, under the pretense of visiting the jakes before prayers, that he was able, with fingers all a-tremble, to crack the wax sealing the missive and finally—finally!—peruse its contents with his sleep-bleared eyes.

He tried not to be disappointed, but all it said was:

> *Do not speak or even look at me at all today. Instead, meet me after dusk in the Grove, at the Doric Temple. Come alone. Tell no one.*
> *'Till then,*
> *I remain,*
> *St John Clement*

Even after reading it for a fourth time, squinting in the pre-dawn light, Henry could not make heads nor tails of the letter. Why should St John wish to meet with him if he didn't want to speak with him? Why in the garden? And "after dusk?" After dusk could mean practically any time—right after dusk? Just before prayers, at eight in the evening? Midnight, technically speaking, was "after dusk."

The bell calling all students to morning prayers tolled as Henry sat alone in the outhouse, the wood of the seat cutting into the flesh of his bottom. He swore, stuffed the parchment down the front of his robes, and scurried off to chapel. He slunk in the back door just in time, and safely took a seat in the back before anyone noticed him.

Christ was not the lord on Henry's mind as the priest led them through the usual prayers. He kept glancing up, trying to locate St John's lion's mane of curls among the sea of bowed heads—and once he did so, he tried with his eyes and willpower to bore a hole into that well-formed skull in order to discern its contents. Such a strange young man, a chimera in more ways than one … what interest could he possibly have in Henry? Did he want to apologize for his actions? Humiliate him further?

That thought sent a chill down Henry's spine, and he shivered on his pew. The thought of coming, innocent, to the Temple—only to discover the Blithe Company there, wild and womble-ty-cropt, ready to tear him to pieces like the horde of howling maenads they were …

Henry smiled to himself as he took his feet—Master Fulkerson and Mr. Berry would like that rather classical analogy, would they not? Well, they could expect that sort of intelligence from him from here on out. He'd show them all. Whatever happened that evening—even if St John wouldn't be his tutor, even if the meeting was an ambush—he had finally found a reason to care about academics: Rochester.

Well, more specifically, eventually obtaining Rochester's patronage.

But even with his newfound academic motivation and the promise of secret meetings, the day was a rough one for Henry. Never at his best after a sleepless night, the three or so hours he had managed to snatch after returning—and spending not a little time blinking at the darkness in his dormitory, wondering about the contents of St John's letter—did not exactly increase Henry's mental acuity. He was called on several times during Logic only to flub his answers entirely, much to the delight of the rest of the students; Geometry was an unmitigated disaster, Moral Philosophy humiliating, and, after dinner, Classics … Classics was the worst of all.

He had, after all, given Master Fulkerson all the ammunition he needed to make those hours of his life a living hell. Henry was forced to endure not only the Master's opening remarks on how, despite having made a recent—if impromptu—study of "modern English poetry," they would continue with studying Aristophanes' speech in *Symposium* that day, but Master Fulkerson's questions pertaining to material he had but dimly understood—and, truth be told, barely skimmed.

"Mr. Milliner!" called Master Fulkerson, not looking up from his podium at the bottom of the auditorium. "As you seem lately much occupied with matters of *love*," he drawled the word to much hooting and howling from the appreciative class, the shitwigs, "let us hear your thoughts concerning the *Symposium*. Yesterday, after you took your leave of us, we ended with a spirited debate as to whether Aristophanes' allegory was comic or tragic. Our Lord Calipash, tender soul that he is, seemed to think the plight of homosexuals rather sad. But what do *you* think, Mr. Milliner? Is it sad when one loves someone with whom he may never truly be, due to God's laws, or society's laws, or some other factor ... such as, oh, I don't know—*social class?*"

It was a nasty thing to say, even for Master Fulkerson. Henry could not help but flush—many of his classmates did, as well. Christ, if he had held his hands in front of Rochester's face he would have burned them! But he had to answer, so he thought for a moment, then cleared his throat.

"Master Fulkerson, I would say that, ah, since we, because of the gods and all, are now all born separately—well, ah, most of us," he stammered, thinking of the twins he had seen last night, "it must be really difficult to find one's other half—and, I guess, to know what to do once you do find him? Or her? Especially since we're all so confused if love is a physical thing. Rather than spiritual." He was blushing terribly now. "I mean, Plato—or Aristophanes, rather—seems to think love is spiritual a lot of the time, right, but he's talking about sex, too ... you know, like we were discussing yesterday, before I left," *Good show Henry*, thought Henry, *nicely done indeed, show you were listening*, "it's still the convention that you've got to, you know, marry and sire heirs and have a family and everything, even if you don't want to. That seems a trifle unfortunate, I think, even if God in His wisdom has decreed that homosexuals are abominations and all that. As for social class, well, you're really hard-up if you fancy someone higher than you, but if some rich lady or lord takes an interest, they can sometimes do what they like, like if she's a widow for example. And a gentleman may refresh the old family stock with some wild blood, right? But a lot of the time it's no good at all for unfortunate, star-crossed souls."

He'd done it—by God, he had *actually* acquitted himself decently! Master Fulkerson was staring at him, obviously struck dumb by the sheer brilliance of his answer. Henry shot Rochester a smug look, but Rochester didn't seem to be interested in meeting his eyes.

"Mr. Milliner," said Master Fulkerson at last, "that was, I think, the single worst response to a question I have ever personally heard uttered here at Wadham, even these days, when merry-making seems to have replaced scholarship as the predominant goal of our student body. That you would express such nonsense under the roof of this hallowed place of learning shames me. Yes, *me*—for if you for one minute think that was an educated opinion, worthy of giving voice to in the English tongue, I have failed completely in my—"

"But it *is* sad when anyone is denied a perfect union with his true other half!"

The students, who had begun to whisper and jeer, fell silent at the pronouncement that rang out in a low, clear, musical tenor. Henry felt as though all the wind had been pulled out of his lungs with a bellows. St John had spoken out of turn—and on his behalf?

"My Lord Calipash," wheezed Master Fulkerson. "I didn't realize you had some wisdom to bestow upon us this day. Had I but known, I should have called on you. My apologies."

Henry was amazed—St John was the only boy who didn't flinch at the Master's acid tone. Had he ... had he gone mad? He seemed oblivious to his danger; when Master Fulkerson spoke like that, everyone knew heads would soon roll.

"Perhaps not *wisdom*," said St John, heatedly if not loudly, "I could not be the judge of that. But *agreement*, there is no doubt! Mr. Milliner's phrasing was perhaps rudimentary, but his reasoning shows ... a compassionate heart. I know well enough, Master Fulkerson, that your intention was to mock our person for our theory on the matter, and mock Mr. Milliner too, for his admittedly questionable decision to write poetry during your class, but wise men—men I personally admire—have thought long and hard on the subject, and come up with no better solution! Why, when I think of 'Platonick Love' by the master-poet Abraham Cowley, I—"

"Calm yourself, Lord Calipash," said Master Fulkerson, banging his palm on the podium. "You speak from your guts and not your mind. To begin with, contemporary poets, especially those as inferior and frivolous as Cowley, have no place in this classroom." The Master mopped his forehead with a handkerchief. "You are also failing to take into account that Aristophanes' encomium is not meant to be read as seriously as the rest. Any Christian would recognize it is an impossible origin myth. 'Male and female He created them,' and in His image, yes? And answer me, too—if Aristophanes' theory is to be taken seriously, heaven help me, when these big round prehistoric humans were split in two, what would have happened to their *souls*?"

"Perhaps the soul can be split," said St John, with vigor. "Perhaps it can be further manipulated than that, even! Christopher Wren believed perfect blood transfusion was possible; why, if the soul were to be isolated, or even captured, could it not—"

"Save it for Master Deutsch's Natural Philosophy class, though he will likely find your theories as nonsensical as I do," interrupted Master Fulkerson. "Well, well. I see I have been far too lax in my management of this class. Even my students with some mean bit of academic promise are shouting silly theories and day-dreams when we should be *learning*. I must have committed some grave pedagogical error indeed. Now, to remedy that …"

It was all his fault, thought Henry wretchedly. How awful, to see St John humiliated so! Miserable, during the rest of the class Henry diligently took notes, refusing even to lift his eyes from his parchment; walking to dinner, though Rochester tried to talk to him about this-and-that as they headed to the dining hall, he only grunted his replies, too consumed by thoughts of what he might encounter at the Doric Temple to pay attention. His mind was so thoroughly occupied that when Rochester stomped away from him like an infuriated little girl he genuinely had no idea what offense he could have committed against the lad.

But time passes, though it may seem slower or quicker depending on one's circumstances. Though Henry despaired of it ever doing so, the sun did indeed sink that day, and he did indeed manage to wait until it did so before approaching the Temple.

To his surprise, St John was already there, smoking sweet-smelling tobacco out of a long clay pipe and peering at a book in the fading light. His servant Thomas, a black-haired young man with a rakish moustache, stood beside him, arms clasped behind his back, leg turned out, revealing a well-shaped calf.

Henry saw them from behind at first, for St John sat with his back to the college, leaning against one of the columns. The sight of his straight, sprawling limbs and naked head took Henry's breath away. He had never seen his idol in such an unconscious moment, and sitting there, hat tossed aside, legs crossed at the ankles where they rested on the second step of the temple's stylobate, arm hefting his book aloft and moving his lips as he read—he was certainly not aware he was observed.

Henry coughed politely to announce himself, not wanting it to seem like he was eavesdropping, or whatever one might call watching someone who thinks he is alone.

St John exhaled a blue plume of smoke. "I think our visitor has arrived. Leave us, Thomas," he said and handed over the pipe.

Thomas bowed, accepted it with a flourish.

"Does my lord require anything else?" he said. "Should I remain close-by, in case of—"

"I said leave us, Thomas."

Thomas bowed again and strode away into the gloaming, pipe cradled in his hands.

After he had retreated from view, St John sighed, and read:

"In thy immortal part,
Man, as well as I, thou art;
But something 'tis that differs thee and me;
And we must one even in that difference be.
I thee, both man and woman prize,
For a perfect love implies
Love in all capacities."

Henry waited for more, but that seemed to be the last of it.

"Very pretty," he said, wishing he could think of more to say, but being in a garden—at twilight—with St John—who was reading, he was reasonably certain, love poetry ... it was overwhelming.

"You wouldn't consider it *inferior*? Or *frivolous*?" St John turned 'round and looked up at Henry with anxious eyes. "Master Fulkerson and I are not always of a mind, of course, but to hear him casting such— such *vile aspersions* upon my dear Mr. Cowley! How could he expect me to bear it?"

"I ... I suppose I couldn't really say," said Henry. "Master Fulkerson and I have never been of a mind on anything, so perhaps I am more used to disagreeing with him."

St John laughed, a beautiful high laugh belonging more to a boy than a young man, and patted the stone beside him three times, two short, and one long.

"I propose you sit beside me," he said. "And I propose that after you sit, we talk."

Henry tried not to make himself ridiculous as he awkwardly lowered himself beside the Lord Calipash, and almost managed it. He only grunted a little.

"Last night," said St John, "was unfortunate."

Henry said nothing. The image of two red-headed twins eagerly fornicating floated across his mind like a cloud across the moon, as did the memory of the feeling of dung coating his face.

"There are rules, Mr. Milliner, to our little symposia, you know. You would not have been tossed out in such a way had you learned them before attending."

"And how might I have achieved that?"

"Your little friend, did he tell you nothing? I was surprised to see him. I believe his first time among our company gave him indigestion."

"He told me it was anonymous, but I didn't think—"

"Well, next time you'll know."

Henry twitched. "Next ..."

"Did last night give you indigestion, too? How surprising; I thought you made of sterner stuff than little Johnny Wilmot, the half-pint Earl. He is *such* a dildo!"

Henry laughed, delighted. "No, no! I was quite intrigued—and curious to know more." He took care not to blurt out this last like a yeoman's son proposing to a dairymaid. "I simply had no reason to suspect that—"

"We desire you to become a part of our entourage," said St John, and Henry hoped against hope he was speaking in the nobleman's third, rather than on behalf of the Blithe Company as a whole. "We desire it most ardently. But you must tell us a little more about yourself, Mr. Milliner. What are your plans? For your life?"

Henry decided to be honest. "Nothing particularly noble, my lord," he said with a shrug. "I wish only to earn enough to be comfortable eating and drinking my fill every day, and to marry a woman who will keep my house tolerably well. My father achieved this via lawyering, and as he had his heart set on me following his trade, I decided to do what he wished, believing it could help me achieve my goals. I have tried to please him in the following, but I fear I have not done so well at that. I am not ... academically gifted."

"What are you gifted at?"

"Taste, my lord."

St John seemed surprised at this. "Taste?"

"Yes my lord. I have always had an ability to identify which is the finest blossom of the bouquet—even if, being only the son of a lawyer, I have never had the pleasure of plucking the bloom."

St John laughed again. "You have a gift for language, Mr. Milliner, which after hearing your poem, I confess I had no expectation of. What a delightful surprise, that your conversation should be so entertaining."

Ouch. "Thank you, my lord."

St John said no more. They sat in silence as twilight yielded to dusk, bird-song to bat-squeak, and Henry felt a chimera himself, all made up of strange parts. That St John had complimented his person gave him joy, while he was wounded at the blackguarding of his poetry. He was pleased to hear he should be invited to future meetings of the Blithe Company while feeling their notion of entertainment was a little stranger than he had anticipated. And he was thrilled that St John was "taking an interest" in his life, though confused as to why, exactly.

"Would you be open to a proposition?"

Startled, Henry nodded. "Yes!"

"Before even knowing what it is?"

"Oh. I, well—if you think it's a good idea ..."

"Think *what* is a good idea?"

Henry adored and despised the look on St John's sweet face, the joy one sees in the eyes of a cat who has a bird pinned and beating against her paw.

"I shouldn't tease you, Mr. Milliner. I simply delight in making you uncomfortable. Would you deny me my delights?"

"Never, my lord."

"Well, then, what I propose is that you rent the cockloft above our private room. It is not much done, for chumming is the preference of the Dean for those of your class—social and academic—but today I spoke to him, and to your advisor, Mr. Berry. I think Mr. Berry was uneasy about me influencing you, but when I pressed him, he confessed he did not know of another who could help you with your Greek *and* with your goal of adding natural philosophy to your accomplishments." St John laughed. "There was some worry about the increase in your rent, but I proposed that if I began to tutor you, they would reduce *my* rent by the same sum, so we'll call it a wash. What do you say?"

Henry threw up his hands. "What can I say? You have defeated me, having anticipated all possible objections. I will, with great thanks to your noble person, accept your generosity—though I am bemused why you should want to offer it to me. I know what I am, and I know what you are."

"What do you mean?"

"I mean, my lord, that I will not be an ornament to your chambers— you cannot want me for that—and I fear with such a hopeless student as myself, despite your skill, you will never earn your laurels as a teacher. As for anything else, well, I have little money to pay out for freaks, much less regular ones."

"Henry," said St John, and Henry's heart thrilled—he didn't know St John even knew his name. To hear him use it! "Dear, dear Henry. Why—you're shivering! Is it the chill of the early spring evening, or something else? You cannot be ill ... well, we must get you inside and warm you up, just the same. And then, tomorrow, you shall move in to my cockloft. Is that not a wondrous thing?" St John leaned back away from Henry and looked at him appraisingly. "I think you judge yourself too harshly. I think you *will* be an ornament to our chambers. I tire of these lean, long Wadham boys with their pinched faces and angular lines. I cannot believe you are not sixteen, you have such a … *mature* look to you. Your flesh gives you an advantage, Henry, you already look the successful lawyer—I dare say, once we train you up a bit, you will be impressing everyone, ladies and gentlemen alike."

"Do you really think so?" Something occurred to him. "Train me?"

St John smiled, and pressed his finger to Henry's lips. "Close your pretty mouth, my handsome protégé. If you are patient, all will be made clear to you. I *will* get your grades up so that you can join the Natural Philosophy class in the fall, and I *will* teach you how to act so that others do you the honor you deserve. I promise."

CHAPTER SIX:
THIS WILL THE SUBSTANCE; HE THE SHADOW BE

Maximilian and young master Bruce were surprised when, the next day during their after-dinner study hour, Henry did not settle down with his books, but instead began to pack up his belongings; they both looked as if they'd unexpectedly bitten into lemons when Henry said, so casually even *he* was impressed, that the Lord Calipash had invited him to rent the garret above his private room, and he had taken him up on the offer.

"*You?*" Bruce wrinkled his nose. "But you're absurd—not to mention that you lumber about like a drugged bear. He should have asked you to walk around up there before offering it to you. You'll shake his inkwells off his desk!"

"Oh, well, you know how it is Brucie, when you distinguish yourself in some way, people will take an interest," Henry said loftily. "I'm sure one day you'll find someone who will recognize whatever good qualities I'm sure you must possess."

"How very charitable of you," said Bruce, and turned back to his notes with a sulky expression.

Henry tossed the last of his possessions into the center of his bed-linens and tied the ends, making a lumpy parcel, then tightened the leather strap around his books. "Well," he grunted as he slung each over a shoulder, "I'm off. I'll see you in class! Oh, don't look so wet about it, lads. Try to be happy for me?"

"I hope they don't raise our rent now that there's only two of us in here," said Maximilian, crossing his arms over his chest. He stood in front of the window, a shadow made darker by bright sunlight and disapproval.

"Oh, surely they'll find *someone* to bunk with you!" Henry was enjoying how his cheeriness was perceptibly blackening the moods of his former dorm-mates. "Buck up! I'm sure, in time, you'll learn not to miss me."

One of the two boys shouted something after Henry as he shut the door behind him, but he couldn't make out exactly what it was. Probably for the best. Such jealousy from his former comrades! He hadn't expected his departure to so unsettle them, though he had, admittedly, hoped it would.

It was with a spring in his step and a smile on his face that he approached St John's door—no, *their* door—and knocked with a flourish. By Jove, things were really looking up for Henry Milliner! He imagined himself after a year or two of St John's tutelage, how nobly he would be able to present himself, the kinds of connections he would have made ...

St John poked his head out of the door, startling Henry out of his reverie. He was squinting at him through a pair of large gold-rimmed spectacles. The glass in them was so dark and shimmery it looked like quicksilver.

"What?" he snapped.

"What?" said Henry, flustered.

"What?"

"What?"

St John looked really annoyed. "What is it that you *want?*"

"To—to ..." Henry hefted his books. "You told me to come today ..."

"Oh!" St John frowned. "Wait a mo'." And after pulling his head back inside, he slammed the door.

As Henry stood alone in the corridor for several long minutes his spirits fell like a murderer from a gibbet. If St John had changed his mind—to go back to Maximilian and Bruce—he'd rather quit school!

Thankfully, that didn't seem to be a necessary course. Soon enough the door flew open and there was St John. He looked a tad rattled, and was no longer wearing his spectacles.

"Sorry about that," he said, holding the door for Henry. "Got wrapped up in something, lost track of time. Welcome, welcome, and all that."

Henry stepped inside and looked around. He was surprised—the room was fully as large as he anticipated, having had the so-called privilege of attending Lord Rochester in his chambers more than once, but it was far neater than any student's room he had ever seen, despite the fact that it was cluttered with ... for lack of a better way to describe it, "strange things."

There were apparatuses Henry assumed were philosophical or

alchemical in nature sitting out on an enormous wooden work-table that took up most of the front room: Glass phials and pipettes and decanters covered the surface, some with odd-colored fires blazing underneath. Fumes wafted from their tops as the contents bubbled and fizzed. There was a large crank-powered tub with more philosophic glassware inside; Henry had no idea what its function might be. Against the tub lay a bellows made of gold and glass and rich buttery russet-colored leather of higher quality than Henry had ever had for his shoes.

Across the room, in front of the window stood a table covered in green growing things. Henry started to see a rose-plant blooming—he had seen roses before, of course, but none that had blossoms so very like a tulip. There was a philodendron, too, that had been trained around a miniature pomegranate tree, and he was hard-pressed to ascertain where one began and the other left off, Baucis and Philemon in miniature. Both seemed to sprout the other's leaves, though that was of course impossible—and yet, it did seem that the vine was producing tiny red trumpet-bell blooms upon it, and provided more support to the tree than the reverse. Shaking his head in wonder, Henry noticed a little nozzle hung above the table. It was connected to a tube that dipped into something that looked like a cross between a bellows and a barrel. As he stared at the contraption, there was a rattle that sounded like clockwork, a clicking sound, and then the nozzle released a mist that rained down upon the plants.

The sudden spray was followed by a sharp yipping bark. Henry jumped at the sound.

"That's just Lady Franco, my cat," said St John, with a quiet laugh. "She's just about to birth her kittens, so she's rather excitable."

Henry looked where St John pointed, and saw a calico face poking out from behind a screen. The cat looked at him with dull curiosity, then withdrew again.

Wadham students were not allowed to keep pets.

"I trust you'll say nothing to anyone about my pussy?"

Henry almost choked. "What?"

"My cat."

"Oh. No, of course not."

Yet all this was not the half of the weirdness. There was a mirror that did not show a reflection for either Henry or St John when they walked in front of it, a cauldron set up on a tripod with some sort of bubbling, shining, mercury-like substance inside, and sundry awful-looking medical devices too, including a vacuum pump. The walls were covered in tacked-up posters of famous natural philosophers—Henry did not recognize them all, but noted Aristotle, Francis Bacon, Robert Boyle (looking especially winsome), and William Harvey among their numbers. There was a shelf of jars that were completely empty, yet all were meticulously labeled in a clear, even script. Henry did not inspect them to see what they said. Instead, he turned back to the work-table. Scattered among the glassware were a lined book filled with handwritten notes, a Galilean "micro-scope," the spectacles St John had earlier worn, and a phial of some dark substance that looked uncomfortably like blood.

"What are you doing here?" asked Henry.

"An experiment," said St John. "I was looking at Lady Franco's blood with my micro-scope."

Henry laughed, but St John didn't. He was serious.

"Really?" said Henry. "Whatever for?"

"To see her blood, of course."

"Yes ... but why should you want to do that?"

"To make a study of it." St John hesitated, then shrugged and said, "I took a sample of her blood a week ago, and I am comparing the two. To see if there were any changes."

"What changes should there be?"

St John canted his head to the side and looked at Henry keenly. "Things aren't always as they should be, are they? Lady Franco is pregnant, for example. That could account for changes, could it not?"

"Er ... I suppose?"

"Take nothing as given, Henry. If you want to be a natural philosopher, you'll have to start being curious about the natural world." St John poked him in the stomach. "Perhaps you are full of cat's blood. How can you be sure, if you never check?"

"I don't meow."

"Is it cat's blood that makes cats meow?" St John smiled. "I suppose it's possible. The Hebrews believed the soul resided in the blood, and I believe they were closer to the truth than Galen—who thought the soul lived in the liver—or later Christian philosophers who believed the soul resides in the brain. I think the brain theory became popular only because so much blood circulates through the brain constantly. The brain uses nearly twenty percent of our blood, did you know that? So if the soul resided in the blood, if those Christian philosophers were using a psychoscope—a soul-viewer—that might account for their mistake. A much more advanced theory than that idiot Descartes put forward, don't you think, though it's centuries older?"

"What?" Henry was still on 'psychoscope.' Did such a device exist? Was what St John suggested so casually even possible? It seemed vaguely heretical, but then again, much natural philosophy did. Dissecting corpses, blood transfusions, other nasty things like that—Henry wasn't particularly devout, but he had his limits.

"Descartes believed animals were soulless, that they could not feel pain or pleasure, which is nonsense, of course," said St John patiently. "Then again, he believed the human soul used the pineal gland as a resonator to communicate with the body."

"And—it doesn't?"

St John laughed. "I don't think so, no. Animals have pineal glands."

"And no souls?"

"Aristotle believed they had 'sensitive souls' that allowed them to have emotions and feelings and experience sensations."

Henry's head was beginning to spin. "If Aristotle has so much to do with modern natural philosophy, I suppose I really must get better at Greek."

This delighted St John. "Indeed," he said. "Well, enough of that. You are here! Are you happy with your new lodgings so far?"

"Oh, yes," said Henry. "I see you are tidy. I hope I won't bother you, I am not as—"

"Tidiness is a habit you must cultivate," said St John. "You must be neat if you wish to live with me. I must occasionally utilize my garret for my philosophic researches— you won't be disturbed by my overflow up there, I trust?"

Henry wasn't exactly thrilled by this new information, but he nodded. "I shall endeavor to be as unobtrusive as possible."

"I assumed as much. I have a lot of personal avenues of study which I explore during my free hours, you must understand."

"Free hours?" Henry laughed. "You must be the busiest man alive! Between homework and studying, your ... whatever it is you do here ... and the Blithe Company! And now you will be tutoring me in, well, in all sorts of things, too. Do you ever sleep?"

St John shrugged and half-smiled. "When I can. There is always so much that seems to require my attention."

Henry opened his mouth, intending to remark that while he was grateful to be one of St John's projects he hoped he wouldn't be a burden, when he was suddenly overcome with the sensation that he was being watched. He looked about and quickly dismissed the thought. He could see nowhere in such a crowded space for anyone to hide.

As he cast about, his gaze fell upon what must be St John's desk. Another simple wooden table, it was distinguished from its fellows in two ways: It had mostly papers upon it, rather than anything bizarre or at the very least breakable, and it also had upon it twin gilt-framed portraits, held together in the center with a hinge.

Henry saw one of the paintings was of St John and stepped over to look at it. It was a tolerable likeness, though Henry thought it didn't quite do the Lord Calipash justice. The other visage was a woman's. Though she was darker of hair, the two were much alike, and they had been painted, Henry noticed, in such a way that they appeared to be looking into one another's eyes.

"That is my sister," said St John, noticing Henry's interest.

"What—er, may I enquire after her name?"

"Honor. Miss Honor Clement. She is my twin. More than that, I should say—we are very similar in appearance, to be sure, but also in … other ways." St John lifted the portrait and stroked his sister's face with an elegant finger. "When we were children, we were very close. It is my one unhappiness here at Wadham that she cannot attend with me. She has a fine mind—finer than mine, truth be told, though there are many who think such a thing is impossible in a woman." St John looked over at Henry. "Do you think so?"

"I could not say, my lord. I suppose that I have never met a woman with as fine a mind as yours does not mean that she cannot exist. And truth be told, I have not met many women."

St John laughed and laughed. "That tongue of yours, Henry! I wonder if it is honest as well as elegant. Go, and put away your things—we will be wanted in class soon."

"Thank you, my lord."

"But mind you don't stomp up the steps—Thomas's room is below them."

"Yes, my lord."

St John did not follow Henry up the stairs, but Henry was not unhappy to be alone the first time seeing his new lodgings. He was feeling slightly anxious about having agreed to the move without inspecting the room, especially after St John's remark about "overflow," but in the end, he had no complaints. The garret was a simple space, true, and crowded with furniture and equipment, but it was more than he'd had with Bruce and Maximilian, and it was private, too. There was only one small window, but it faced east and let in a decent amount of light, and the room had clearly been recently cleaned and readied for a boarder.

A chest had been pushed against the far wall, opposite the window; an old, though serviceable desk lurked in the corner, clean save for a few more of the empty, labeled jars with cork stoppers. Henry picked one up, and the legend read "17 April 1660, 5th attempt. Partial Success." Henry replaced it. He also noted an astrolabe, a collection of tuning forks, a hand-drawn herbal full of plants that looked to have been written by St John—it was in his handwriting—and of all things, a hurdy-gurdy on a stand. Everything had either been tucked out of the way or stacked neatly, so Henry decided to say nothing about their presence for now.

He quickly stowed what he had brought with him, and descended into the chamber below. St John was not around, but Henry heard rustling from his bedroom.

Not wishing to disturb his new chum, he looked around and tried not to break anything. Idly he looked at the plants again, marveling at their strangeness, and at the device that watered them. The equipment he did not touch, but he picked up St John's spectacles that he'd left out on the table. Putting them on, he was surprised that his vision did not seem at all enhanced nor even dimmed by the hazy glass. Baffled, he looked around—and gasped.

The empty jars were filled with ... *something!*

He walked closer, and noted they seemed to all contain some sort of gas, but not the same kind. Though the substances within them swirled like London fog churned up by carriage-horses, every jar held a slightly different color, gold and green and blue and pink and purple and even a burgundy-flecked one, though they were all variations on the same phosphorescent theme.

"What the ..." he muttered. A little discomfited, Henry reached up to take off his glasses, and gasped again.

His hand was glowing, too! He could see his veins, they were silver-green, and flecked with off-white particles the color of fresh cream. On a whim, he decided to peek into St John's room and see what he looked like.

Peering around the corner, he saw St John was filled with a swirling tempest of black and gold. Henry, now more than a little creeped out, took off the spectacles, pocketed them, and coughed discreetly.

St John paused in his straightening of his robes and his cap in front of a mirror. He looked perfect—like he was a part of the elegantly-furnished chamber. Henry, for his part, felt even more like a flabby malkintrash than he usually did—a disgrace; absurd, as Bruce had said. An impostor.

"Yes?" St John looked Henry up and down. "Are you pleased with— I'm sorry, are you planning on attending class like that?"

Henry looked down. His robes were dusty and wrinkled from moving, true, but did it really make a difference?

"You do not look like someone with whom we would associate," said St John matter-of-factly. "If you are going to chum with us, you must be as beautiful as we know you can be."

A sound escaped Henry, something in between a snort and a bark. "My lord, I hate to contradict you, but I fear I shall be a disappointment if you ever want me to be *beautiful*. I may learn to dress myself better, or act more elegant—or even get better at Greek—but even you cannot make me handsome. I am too fat, for one, and—"

"You are *not* too fat," interrupted St John. "Go you and lay down upon my bed."

"My lord, I—"

"Do it." St John's tone was adamant.

Henry meekly complied, and discovered another poster tacked to the ceiling above the mattress. It was of a young man's face in profile, looking romantically into the middle distance. He wore no wig, and his shoulder-length golden hair fell in curls about his face, which Henry felt could charitably be called plump; uncharitably, porky.

"My dear Mr. Cowley," said St John soupily. "I think him *very* handsome. I feel positively inspired sleeping underneath him, though I am no poet myself, of course."

"I confess I am not much acquainted with his works," said Henry.

St John sighed happily, then reverently chanted:

"She *Loves*, and she *confesses* too;
There's then at last, no more to do.
The happy *work's* entirely done;
Enter the *Town* which thou'st *won*;
The *Fruits* of *Conquest* now begin;
Iô Triumph! Enter in."

Henry was musing on how if Rochester had thought *his* poem was dirty, then just wait until he heard this one, when a voice harsh as new spirits came from the bedroom doorway.

"My lord."

Henry started up from where he lay, but relaxed when he saw it was only St John's manservant.

St John looked at the intruder evenly. "What is it?"

"I believe it is near time for my lord's afternoon class."

St John flushed. "We are well aware of that, Thomas, and shall be leaving soon."

Thomas remained in the doorway, his arms crossed over his chest. Between his frown, dark, long hair, and thin moustache, he looked the spitting image of the cartoons of those wanted by the police on suspicion of being Cavaliers one still saw tacked to buildings occasionally, even now that Richard Cromwell was under house arrest and the Declaration of Breda had effectively pardoned the Royalists. All he needed was a lace ruffle at his throat and a long sword at his waist.

St John mirrored his posture, crossing his arms over his robes. "Why are you still here? Have you nothing to occupy yourself? I am sure I could find something for you to do if you are bored."

"When my lord has gone to class I shall attend to repairing his evening dress, and washing his robes."

"Mr. Milliner." St John's tone curdled Henry's blood; it was the quietness with which he perpetually spoke that made his angry intensity so goddamn spooky. "Thomas is conveniently doing laundry today. Go and change into clean robes, and bring the dirty set down. He will have them cleaned and pressed for you."

"My lord?" Thomas did not look particularly pleased by this. Henry rose but didn't know what to do—to push past Thomas would be unspeakably rude; to stay would be to disobey St John's order …

Thomas, thank God, stepped aside. Henry scurried past and pelted upstairs; as he hastily changed he heard raised voices, and took a few extra moments to arrange himself to the best of his abilities before descending.

"We must go, Mr. Milliner." St John was standing in the main room when Henry's foot touched the floorboards. Thomas was nowhere to be seen. "Have you your books?"

"Yes, my lord." Henry held up his two required tomes.

"And your robe?"

Shit. "I … left it on my bed, my lord. Shall I go and fetch it—"

"Thomas will get it. Thomas, did you hear that?" St John raised his voice. The servant was nowhere to be seen, but either from the bedroom or the chamber under the stairs, a grunt of assent could be distinguished.

"Let us away, then," said St John, and came as close to breaking into a trot as Henry had ever seen a nobleman get in his haste to be out the door and down the stairs. Henry had to trot to catch up, and once he did, he puffed in an undignified manner as St John strode across the gravel quadrangle towards the classrooms.

"Now that you have come to stay with us, we shall instruct you in many things," St John said, when the color had returned to his cheeks. "I shall, of course, tutor you in Greek and prepare you for entering the natural philosophy seminar, but also in proper dress, manners, deportment, eating habits, cleanliness, and how, how to *manage* one's *servants.*"

This last came out in a sort of low snarl, and Henry made a mental note to try never to piss St John off. He was maybe being a little scary.

"And you shall sit with us in class."

"What?" The day was cool and misty, even this late in the afternoon; to sit near the brazier would be wonderful. "I mean, *yes*, my lord, if it pleases you. Thank you, my lord."

"Good. For a moment I thought you would not like to."

Henry protested this with the comeliest language he could muster, but he did not confess what made him happiest about this new arrangement.

Rochester, he guessed, would turn positively green at the sight of him, deep in the bosom of the Blithe Company.

CHAPTER SEVEN:
AN UNHEROIC EXCHANGE

Henry tried not to act as if he noticed—and enjoyed—the palpable surprise in the classroom when he entered beside St John, but when the Lord Calipash took him by the hand and introduced him to the assembled Blithe Company as "young Henry Milliner, who shall be one of *us* now," he was hard-pressed not to grin like a Merry-Andrew. Simply everyone noticed; he saw an extraordinary number of elbows digging into sides and heads inclining in his direction. Being popular must be wonderful, he concluded, but to rise in a blaze of glory, phoenix-like, from the ashes of disgrace—that was *awesome*.

It did bother him how distraught Rochester looked when the boy glanced over and saw Henry making small talk with the Company. The young lord had, of course, taken up their customary position far off to the upper right of the Master's podium, and though Henry motioned him over, he refused, looking dejected. Henry had anticipated envy rather than dismay from that quarter, but honestly, if Rochester couldn't be happy for his newfound social success, then bugger him. Bugger him right up the bottom-hole. Of course it would annoy a member of the noblesse to see an upstart middling sort enjoying the same advantages that had been handed him all his life. Bugger bugger *bugger* him.

"I say, what's this?" A young man of about seventeen with a shock of dark hair was looking down at Henry with an ugly sneer. "You're in my seat, piggy. Move."

"*You* may find another seat, Mr. Jones," said St John. He was getting out his parchment and quills, arranging them meticulously, and did not look up as he spoke. "Mr. Milliner's presence is at our request. We would not have you treat him shabbily."

"But I've sat here for *years*." Jones looked disproportionally annoyed.

"Give it a rest, Lucas," said Anthony Neville, who was clearly enjoying the scene. He was finishing off an apple—Henry wondered if Neville had been the one who'd pelted him with that apple-core—and spat out a seed just at Jones's feet. "Milliner's all right, let him be."

The worm, Henry mused, had truly turned.

"I will not give it a rest! This is my seat!"

Henry, not wanting to cause strife among the Company so soon after his inclusion, half-rose from his seat, an apology hovering on his lips, when St John finally looked up. He gave Lucas Jones such a withering glare Henry wondered why the boy didn't run away and skip class entirely.

"Sit *down*, Mr. Jones."

"Give him Neville's seat, he's Scots." Jones spat back at Neville. "They're used to being colonized by now, I should think."

Neville was instantly on his feet, his dark eyes blazing, and he backhanded Jones across the mouth. Jones squealed when he was struck, and kept whimpering after Neville had been pushed back down into his chair by Aldous Clark and soothed into stillness by the rest of the boys.

"Mr. Jones, you are making a scene," murmured St John, who hadn't gotten up at any point. "If you cannot *control* yourself, then you must, I think, *excuse* yourself." He smiled. "If you prefer the former, I think there is a seat beside Lord Rochester."

"You can't kick me out, St John," hissed Jones. "I know everything, I could ruin you—break up your whole little party here. So you just keep that in mind before you cross me again, all right?" And then he flounced off across the room, kicking the chair beside Rochester out from under the table and sitting in it with a loud huff.

Rochester looked even more pained at this turn of events, but Henry couldn't spare him much thought. The Blithe Company boys were all deep in conference about what was to be done about Lucas Jones.

"Do you think he'll really squeal?" asked Henry nervously.

"Nay," said Neville, obviously still a little hot under the collar. His face was flushed and though his eyes had dimmed to a shine much less violent than their earlier inferno, his expression was still rather frightening. "He knows what we'd do to him. Wounded pride isn't worth that."

Huh. This sent a chill down Henry's spine, but he didn't have long to think about it.

"We will remind him of his duty to the Company," whispered St John, lowering his voice. Master Fulkerson had just entered the room. "Tonight. We were intending to get up to some high jinks anyways, were we not? I'll give instructions later; for now, act normally and say *nothing*. If he sits with you at supper, be kind and conciliatory, keep him thinking he's still one of us. Even you, Mr. Neville," said St John, and Henry was surprised when Neville inclined his head in acquiescence— but then St John smiled, and said, "I understand fully the wrong done to you this day. I promise you shall have your revenge, but you must trust me."

"I do, my lord," said Neville, but then Master Fulkerson cleared his throat, and class began.

Henry found it easier and harder to concentrate from within the merry band of gentlemen. Feeling more confident than he ever had before, he managed to correctly answer one of the Master's questions— he hadn't studied or anything, it was just that they had moved on to Plato's *Republic*, and Henry's father had read that to him as a child—and yet his thoughts were largely elsewhere. It was clear the Blithe Company had its own set of rules, and he had not been taught any of them. Perhaps he was supposed to learn through experience? It was already obvious to him that St John was completely in charge. Challenging his authority would lead to punishment; following him would lead to rewards. Mr. Neville's attitude toward the incident with Lucas Jones was enough to pick up on *that*, at the very least.

"You'll sit with us at supper, of course?"

Master Fulkerson was collecting his effects—class had ended while Henry had been contemplating these topics, and Neville was looking at him expectantly.

"Oh," said Henry. "I'd love to!"

"Do it, then." Neville smiled warmly, and it was like a ray of sunshine had fallen across Henry's face. He was extraordinarily handsome, and in quite a different way than St John. His black eyes snapped and sparkled, his wavy hair was a deep cocoa-brown, and there was a cheeky devilishness to his smile. Standing between him and St John was like being caught—pleasantly—between Dionysus and Apollo. "Happy to have you. But mind you guard your tongue—here comes Lucas now, the totty-headed mincer."

"Easily done," murmured Henry, as Jones slunk over to try to apologize to St John, "as I've nothing to say."

"No?"

"You are all the masters, and I the student." Henry smiled. "Though these might be the nicest lessons I've had, they are lessons still."

Neville's smile made the last one seem retroactively cold. "Good lad. Welcome, say we all." This last he pronounced with a much louder voice, which elicited nods from all the Company save Jones, who scowled. Regardless, it was a tremendous feeling to leave the classroom as part of a chattering, high-spirited throng.

Upon reaching the yard, it occurred to Henry that he'd left Rochester behind. When he looked back he saw the boy just leaving the classroom, books clutched to his chest, looking as wretched as a hen in a hailstorm.

"Save me a seat," he said to Neville, and cocked his thumb back at Rochester. Neville nodded amiably, and Henry backtracked.

"What-ho," he said. "Did you hear Master Fulkerson comment that my response was 'surprisingly adequate'? Not bad for young Henry Milliner, eh?"

Rochester sniffed at him. "Nice to see you're still talking to me."

Oh, good Christ. "Don't be sore. I invited you over! Not my fault if you declined."

"I don't want to be part of the Blithe Company," said Rochester in the snittiest voice Henry had ever heard. "They're not very nice, I don't think their frolics are funny, and I think *you*, Henry, will end up worse off than you were before you managed to get in with them."

"You're cheerful, aren't you? I wish you could be happy for me."

This seemed to wound Rochester. "I'd be happy for you if I thought there was reason to be so."

"And getting something I've wanted for so long isn't reason?"

"I had just thought—you know, after the other night ..." Rochester looked on the verge of tears. Henry felt conflicted. On one hand, he wanted to comfort his friend, but on the other, sticking it to the spoiled little brat right now, after all of his two-faced betrayals, would be the best of possible paybacks.

"After the other night *what*?"

"I thought ... after the other night ... what you wanted might have, you know. *Changed*."

Henry laughed. "During those brief, tender moments, you mean?" Henry shook his head. "If you think I'd trade the world for a kiss, you're sorely mistaken."

"What?" Rochester stopped walking toward the dining hall and stared at Henry, wide-eyed and hurt as a puppy who'd been cuffed for greeting his master. "What do you mean?"

"I mean that, for example, after one brief conference, the Lord Calipash has rented me his cockloft, invited me to sit with him in class, and promised to tutor me not only in Greek but in the refined arts of society." Henry looked down his nose at Rochester. "*You*, by contrast, have professed friendship since I came, but really, what have you done but ridicule and betray me? You laughed at me when Master Fulkerson humiliated me in class, and before that, you mocked my poetry!"

"I—"

"Did you offer me the rent of your garret at any point? Did you invite me to any of the Company's meetups, or did you hoard that pleasure for yourself?" Henry shrugged. "I know what I should have done were I the lord and you someone like me, but such is life."

"So you're saying you like him more because he gives you all the things you want." Henry could not help being impressed by Rochester's *tchah*, it held more contempt than Henry could have managed, he was sure of it. "Well. I'm not sure your admission casts you in the best light, but if you really are happy, so be it."

Henry's mind whirled. "If that's the way you want to think of it, then whatever makes *you* happy. Just keep in mind that I have never been so lucky in my friends as you; those in my situation are forced to earn them rather than the alternative."

"And what, exactly, is the alternative?"

Henry couldn't think of anything appropriately cutting. "What I mean is that not all of us are able to rely on our title to make friends. We have to distinguish ourselves in some way."

"And you've distinguished yourself through, what? Lickspittlery? Flattering?"

"Tut, tut, Lord Rochester. Just because you were never able to see my quality doesn't mean others are so blind." Henry looked over his shoulder where the rest of the boys had gone in to eat. "I must fly—I'm needed in the dining hall. Are you coming?"

Rochester's face was so purple it looked like he'd fallen into a vat of dye. "I—*I'm not hungry!*" he cried, and ran off toward the dormitories, tears streaming down his face.

CHAPTER EIGHT:
NOT ALL SOULS BEAUTY KNOW

Henry watched Rochester go with mixed feelings. Showing up the little rat hadn't felt as good as he'd anticipated; he was surprised to find that he felt kind of rotten about it. Annoyed—at himself, and at Rochester—Henry shoved his hands inside his pockets, whereupon he discovered he still had St John's curious spectacles. Putting them on, he saw Rochester was apparently filled up with an eggplant-purple mist.

So weird. He needed to ask St John about what the deuce he was up to with his philosophical researches. But that was for later—the Company awaited him, and upon entering the dining hall he forgot all of his troubles. Anthony Neville and Nicholas Jay waved him over, and he took his seat between them with enthusiastic dignity.

Meals were generally quiet affairs at Wadham. According to the statutes of the college, unless it were a feast day or some other special occasion, there was a strict rule against conversation during dinner or supper—unless it could be managed in a "useful" language like Latin. Given that it was difficult to spread gossip or discuss modern politics in such, the most that could usually be heard at table were the sounds of chewing and the occasional clipped whisper.

Henry was used to eating in silence, given his general lack of friends and poor language skills, but he was happy to be quiet that day. The mood among the Company boys was a thing to be savored. Most of them, upon catching his eye, smiled at him or raised their eyebrows conspiratorially; Lucas Jones, however, was sitting at the end, looking unhappy. For Henry, simply not to be an object of ridicule was a pleasure, and he gobbled his stew with more than his usual gusto.

"*Psst*," hissed Fitzroy Lowell into his armpit closest to Henry. "We'll mill about the lawn after, of course, but later—there's going to be a fête, all right? Just don't tell Jones."

"I'm game," whispered Henry, but that was all they could manage to communicate.

It was easier to chat after the meal's conclusion. When the weather was fine, most students typically milled about the gravel quad for half an hour or so before withdrawing to study, and the weather was indeed fine that night. The torches had been lit, and everyone was out and about discussing whether or not the King was really on his way home and whether he would retake the throne on his birthday, the 29th of May, or not. With General Monck's support and the Convention Parliament's declaration that Charles had been king since his father's execution, it seemed, for those students with Royalist sympathies at any rate, a happy inevitability, but there was no way of predicting the timing.

The members of the Blithe Company kept to these topics exclusively, which frustrated Henry even though he understood the reason. Of course he wished for Charles II's restoration as much as the next good Anglican, but he was not much in the mood for political discourse—he wanted to know the plan, and he could tell the rest of the Company were anxious to discuss it, too. But Jones, perhaps suspecting this, hung around them like a cat haunting a fishmonger's—until a boy came running up to him with news of some urgent matter requiring his attention.

Not a minute after Jones had reluctantly departed, St John shimmered into their midst.

"Goodness me," he said, smiling at them all, "if I could so easily bribe everyone with three shillings and a crumb of ginger-bread, I would rule all England, would I not?"

"Thought he might be acting on your orders," giggled Rowan Zwarteslang. "Poor Jones."

"What's the plan, Calipash?" demanded Lowell.

"Yes, how shall we entertain ourselves tonight?" said Neville, keener than a scent-hound who's sniffed a fox.

"Later tonight—eleven, say—let us convene in the Fellow's Common Room and Library," said St John, "and I will tell you all the details. Oh, and bring your cricketing bats—no, that's all I shall say on the matter." St John shook his head, raising his hand in a gesture that instantly dismissed all protests. "I have not had time to contemplate all which I wish to do to Lucas Jones, but I am in the mood for some *sport*."

Henry laughed along with everyone else, a new experience for him, but as the party broke up to go about their respective businesses, St John held him back.

"Here is the key to my—our rooms," he said. All of a sudden,

Henry thought he looked out of spirits, but it might have just been a trick of the light. "I shall not return with you. There is ... a matter which demands my attention."

Henry was deeply disappointed. "Of course, my lord."

St John cocked an eyebrow at him. "Is there something else?"

"Er, earlier ... you had intimated we might study together this evening ..."

"Oh, I *am* sorry, Henry," said St John. "Here—I promise, if you read the text and make notes on what you find difficult or confusing, I'll go over them with you early tomorrow, before our classes. And, for additional practice—" he smiled when Henry groaned, "I want you to translate the first ten lines of Plato's *Apology*. Find the original Greek on my rear left bookshelf, it's a slender, blue-bound edition."

"All right. But before you go ..."

"Yes?"

Henry withdrew the spectacles from his pocket. St John startled at the sight of them, and snatched them away rudely.

"Do *not* take my things!" he said, his voice higher and louder than Henry had yet heard.

"I didn't mean to. I put them on, I'm sorry, I ... what on earth are they?"

St John looked like he might strike Henry, but then he relaxed. "They ... are a device of my own invention."

"Oh?"

St John nodded. "Earlier I mentioned the psychoscope ..."

"Yes?"

St John grinned. "I managed to construct my own from a set of diagrams designed by the philosopher Leonardo da Vinci, from materials, let us say *borrowed* from this university ... and another. Psychology— the study of souls—is more advanced at Christ Church, given that the discipline originated from within the clergy."

"And so those jars are full of ... souls." Where, Henry wondered, had he gotten all of them?

As if anticipating this question, St John said, "The jars are full of plant souls, vegetative essences, as Aristotle would say. Do not worry."

"I'm not, my lord. But—"

"Eh?"

"What do you *do* with them?"

St John looked frustrated. He blew his breath out through the side of his mouth, then quoted:

"Indeed I must confess,
When souls mix 'tis an happiness;
        But not complete till bodies too do combine,
        And closely as our minds together join:
        But half of heaven the souls in glory taste,
Till by love in heaven, at last,
Their bodies too are plac'd."

Henry was unimpressed by St John's love of quoting poetry instead of answering questions. "So you're … combining essences?"

"Not … exactly, but—"

"Then what?"

"Whatever I am doing, I assure you, is my business alone," said St John shortly. Henry took a step back, and St John relented. "I'm sorry, Henry—I have a lot on my mind. I promise I shall explain everything to you in time, but I must run—and you must, too. Your work will take several hours, I think, but shouldn't be too difficult for you."

Henry wasn't so sure about that when he actually began on the task. Perhaps it was his curiosity over St John's strange quotes and stranger jars full of 'souls' or 'essences' or whatever (he'd thrown a cloth over those on his desk; they gave him the heebie-jeebies now that he knew what they held), perhaps it was St John's demand that he take notes on what he could not understand, but his homework took him far longer than he'd anticipated. He felt mentally exhausted when he opened the leather-bound *Apologia*. He yawned, the clock struck ten—

CHAPTER NINE:
THE LEARNED ARE THE LEAST DEVOUT

—and Henry heard it in the middle of striking quarter-till the hour when someone shook him awake.

"Come *on*, Henry," St John was saying, as Henry groggily opened his eyes and hastily wiped a puddle of cold drool from his cheek.

"Mwhaa?"

"Oh, Henry. You are *such* a mess. We're to meet in the Common Room at eleven, and here you are, napping." St John looked mightily annoyed. "And *where* is your bat?"

"Haven't got one," said Henry, that fact having slipped his mind earlier.

St John sighed. "You'll have to borrow Thomas's. Thomas—go and get your cricketing bat. Mr. Milliner must have the use of it tonight."

Thomas was hovering behind St John and with such an anxious, hangdog look on his face that Henry almost felt bad for the servant, even after his rudeness earlier that afternoon; with a bow, Thomas acknowledged his master's request and scampered down the stairs. Sounds of thumping and scraping drifted up to the second story, as if someone were searching frantically for something.

"Thomas is an excellent cricketer," commented St John, as Henry went over to his mirror, weaving in among the bulky instruments, and attempted to make himself more presentable. The hair on the left side of his head had flattened during his nap. When he was satisfied—and St John did not sneer when Henry turned round to face him, as he had the first two times—they descended and found Thomas awaiting them, cricket bat in hand.

"Let us away, then," said St John grandly. "Mr. Jones is in need of a visit."

"My Lord—" Thomas's voice was halting, apologetic.

"What is it?"

"You told Mr. Fitzroy to meet you here, my lord."

St John swore creatively. "I did, and Godfrey is *always* late—well, why don't you go ahead, Thomas, and tell the boys we are delayed?"

Thomas bowed, but when he opened the door to obey, there was a person standing there, his hand raised, knuckles poised as if to rap them upon wood.

"Godfrey!" cried St John. "Welcome to our humble abode once again."

"*Hush,*" said the stranger, tipping his hat at Thomas as he stepped inside. "Don't shout my name so, I just made it over the wall. Had a deuce of a time coming up here without being seen. Everyone's running hither and yon with wild rumors about the king."

Henry was impressed—who was this man to speak to St John so? And St John seemed not to mind his teasing. Perhaps they had been childhood friends, or even relatives—Godfrey was of a similar height to St John, and he looked as though he had been built from the same plans. He was also slender, and had a narrow, almost effeminate face with lovely features, but there was a mischief about his eyes and mouth where St John usually seemed melancholic—or disturbingly feral, as was the case now.

"We were just leaving anyhow. Ready to have some fun?"

"Always." Godfrey finally noticed Henry—and a look came into his eye that made Henry tremble, though he did not know why. "Ooh, who is *this*? You didn't tell me you were opening a bakery, yet here you have as pretty a *petit four* as I've ever seen in my life."

"This is our cousin, Godfrey Fitzroy," said St John, stepping between Henry and Godfrey. "He is at school in Oxford, at Christ Church. Godfrey, meet Mr. Milliner, who has rented our garret."

"A pleasure to meet you," said Godfrey, taking off his cap to bow; upon rising, he eyed Henry up and down. "I live for this sort of thing, don't you?"

"Well, I—"

"Education was all Father's idea, he sent me hither after catching me doing good works with a footman and two of the stable-lads back at home in Devon. Perhaps he thought I should be well-suited to ministering to the masses." Godfrey stuck out his very red tongue and licked his upper lip. "I had no objection. Far easier to do the Lord's work among the better element when you're all in such close quarters, don't you think?"

Henry did not know what to say, and so just stood there, mouth slightly ajar. Not only was Godfrey alarming in his manners, Henry realized he might very possibly be the person he had seen taking that queer dog away from Wadham the night he and Rochester had come back from the meeting at the Horse and Hat. Henry remembered thinking the man had looked much like St John, and here was someone with dark hair and the same general appearance ...

"The plump pretty one doesn't speak much, does he?" giggled Godfrey. "Mr. Milliner, you're silent as a glazed ham—and just as appetizing. Cat got your tongue? *Ooh*, that reminds me—how is Lady Franco?"

"She's fine," said St John, waving toward the screen behind which the calico cat perpetually lurked.

"May I—"

"You mustn't disturb her, Mr. Fitzroy," said Thomas anxiously. "She's nesting, and possessed of a delicate temperament, but the happy event should be any day now. Do you still want one of the litter as a companion for Pietra Poodle, sir?"

So Godfrey had a poodle!

"I suppose we'll see. Don't want her to get, er, territorial."

"As you say, sir."

"Enough," said St John. "Shall we adjourn and meet our brethren?"

Thomas coughed, and after St John acknowledged him, he handed his master a glass phial. "You had promised your friends, my lord."

"Yes, of course. Thank you, Thomas. Well, hold down the fort—and wait up for us. I shall need your help when I am finished tonight, I daresay."

"*Hmmmm*," said Godfrey, putting a fingertip to his lower lip and then lewdly sucking on it with a loud slurp. "And I daresay—"

"Hush," said St John.

There was no more talk among the three of them as they went quietly over the gravel quad and through the hallways of the college towards the library. Henry was excited—more excited, even, than the night he had snuck out to the Horse. He had never before seen the Fellow's Common Room, but had desperately wished to have the use of it as the wealthier students did. For the status of it, of course—not, he admitted readily enough, for the access to the books and quiet working spaces it allegedly provided. Rumor had it that the Common Room saw more silliness than study, and was, late at night, used as a bazaar for black-market goods.

"Here we are," murmured St John, and knocked in a pattern before opening the door.

The room inside was handsomely furnished with comfortable chairs and heavy oaken tables, lined with bookcases on all sides, and well-lit with several lanterns and candles. Looking around, it seemed to Henry that most of the Blithe Company were already assembled. Anthony Neville and Aldous Clark were playing a hand of cards at a study-table; Nicholas Jay, Edwin Harris, Rowan Zwarteslang, and Matthew Fletcher were passing around a clay tavern pipe whose smoke had a strange odor to it. As Godfrey went over to take a puff, hailing the assembled throng, Richard Smith and Fitzroy Lowell knocked and entered behind Henry and St John, red-cheeked, and with the aroma of a distillery on their breath.

"Hail, hail," said Lowell, looking about. "Are we assembled?"

"What's to be the rumpus tonight?" Neville, distracted from his game, swore when Clark set down a card with a triumphant 'Ha!'

"Peace," said St John, and his quiet voice, as always, immediately captured the attention of the room. "Does everyone have their bats?" After everyone nodded, he smiled a cruel smile that chilled Henry to the bone. "Excellent. Jones will *know* what hit him, I'll warrant, but such a drubbing he will not have had before, when we're done with him."

"I say!"

Everyone turned to look at Henry after his outburst. He blushed.

"Mr. Milliner has an objection?" St John said derisively.

"No, not really," said Henry quickly—with all eyes upon him and one hand of every pair holding a cricket bat, he wasn't going to stick his neck out *too* far. "I just didn't realize that was, you know. The plan."

"What did you think we were going to do, invite him out on the pitch to bowl a few overs? For honor's sake?" Neville was looking at him with a skeptical, if friendly expression. "Oh yes," he said, in a high, fruity voice, "I'm *thoroughly* satisfied now that Jones has been dismissed from the game!"

Godfrey laughed. "Nay indeed! I aim to give him such a case of Wadham-bottom he won't be able to sit for a week."

"Focus on your favorite part all you want," said St John, blowing a kiss at his cousin. "Personally I'm going to work him over. *All* over." Henry felt a hand come down on his shoulder, and he looked up into St John's face. The lord's expression was unreadable. "Only one caveat tonight, boys: Henry must start things off for us. And I hope he will not disappoint us, being so new to our Company. What do you say, Henry? Do you think you will disappoint us?"

Henry shook his head and said *no* with as much casual ease as he could muster, hoping they wouldn't notice that he'd begun to sweat. He hated to admit it, but maybe Rochester—and even Mr. Berry—had been right about these lads. Beating someone mercilessly with a cricket bat was a bit beyond anything he'd expected to be a party to in his daydreams of being a member of the Blithe Company. He'd thought they'd be more about wenching it up in style, drinking fine wine laced with Turkish poppy-juice. That sort of thing.

"Good," said St John, patting him on the back. "Well. Shall we get a bit lubricated before we set out? Don't want to sprain an elbow being too tight and nervous, eh Henry?"

"Did you bring us something from your laboratory?" asked Nicholas Jay.

"No," said St John, and produced the phial Thomas had earlier handed him. "Oh, don't look so glum, my comrades. I have something, of course, but I didn't manufacture these. They're *natural*. Coca leaves from the Americas. I could only afford three, we'll have to divvy them up. You chew them."

Jay led the group in a series of cheers that panicked Henry—what if they were heard, the crazy assholes—but the passing 'round of the shredded leaves and subsequent gnawing quieted the Company quickly. Henry accepted his roughage, but took only a few small nibbles before spitting the remainder into his palm and putting it into his pocket. He wasn't sure what coca was, but another treat from the Americas, cacao, had given him the trots the few times he'd tried it, so better safe than sorry.

"Come with me, in the front," said St John, as they made ready to leave. "I want you close. No welshing, right Henry? You're brave enough?"

Henry clutched his hands around the handle of the curved bat. His heart was pounding unusually fast, his hands were slick with sweat and linseed oil, and he felt nature calling to him, as she always did when he was nervous—but then, all of a sudden, he felt a rush of confidence and smiled at St John.

"Don't you worry, my lord." He hefted the bat. "I may be a rotten cricketer, but Jones's arse is a larger target than any ball."

If only such wit would come to him always! Henry was hailed to the rafters by the Blithe Company, and then they sallied forth in silence, running across the quad and up the steps to the upper-floor dormitory, robes billowing, *shh*ing one another when volleys of giggling burst out. Henry had never felt so good. This was the greatest night of his life he was pretty sure. He could do this!

No, holy shit, what was he thinking? He couldn't do this! Henry began to tremble and perspire again. Good Christ in heaven, he didn't want to beat poor Lucas Jones with a cricket bat! What if—what if he *hurt* him? Who would do such a thing? Who would think it was a good idea?

But it was far too late to back out now. They had reached Jones' door, and St John pushed Henry to the front.

"Here's your chance to prove yourself," he breathed down Henry's neck. "When I left you earlier this night I visited him, and when he wasn't watching, I drizzled some glue into the latch. It should have stuck by the time he went to bed, but he won't have gotten it fixed yet, of course. So you can just push on the door and run at him, all right? Make some noise, yell or something. Scare him."

"I—"

"You welshing?"

Henry looked into St John's eyes and found nothing there that let him think that running off would be all right, even just this once. Quite the reverse, actually. Henry took a deep breath, promised himself to strike Jones no more than twice—well, maybe three times—and swallowed.

With a nod to his new friends, Henry pushed open the door with a battle cry, cricket bat raised like a Turkish scimitar. He was ready for this. He was ready for *anything* ... except for Lucas Jones being awake when he barged into his room.

Henry's first thought was that St John had set him up, but the look on Jones' face when the Blithe Company charged his room *en masse*, Henry howling at the forefront and all wielding bats ... well, if Jones was acting, he was the best actor in the universe.

The boy lying on his bed, a candle burning beside him on his nightstand, which gave all of them perfect clarity of vision. What they saw was Lucas Jones in just his shirt. He shrieked as he tried to cover himself, one hand grabbing for his bunched-up blanket, the other ineffectively cupped to shield his exposed, swollen prick.

Lucas Jones was jerking off!

"Lucas Jones is jerking off!" cried Godfrey, pointing at Jones' crotch with the tip of his bat. Every other member of the Blithe Company was struck still and dumb by the sight—whether due to a sense of propriety or good fortune, however, was anyone's guess. "Look at him, lads! We can't beat a man in the middle of beating off, it's *rude*!"

"Get the *fuck* out of here!" Jones had found his voice, and screeched this like a London laundress as he sat up and got the blanket over his lap, where it utterly failed to obscure the source of the general hilarity.

Henry looked over at St John, who seemed dumbfounded—delighted—and breathed a heavy sigh of relief. It seemed he was off the proverbial hook ... until St John stepped forward, his eyes glinting like diamonds.

"We shall not, as you request, get 'the fuck' out of your room." Henry again felt sort of terrified by the Lord Calipash. He had already learned to recognize certain of St John's mercurial moods, and he sensed a shift towards the nasty. "We shall remain as long as we like, and do whatsoever to your person that pleases us."

"Why are you all carrying cricketing bats?" Jones was beginning to sense his peril. Godfrey and a few of the other boys sniggered. "What's so funny? I swear, St John, if you—"

"Did you just call me by my Christian name?" St John interrupted. If he had spoken any more quietly it would have been impossible to understand him.

The room went silent. Jones looked momentarily alarmed, then decided to try to bluster through it.

"I did," he scoffed. "What, am I supposed to 'm'lord' every burglar? Rise and bow to you and your, your band of criminals? You *shame* me in front of our class, you *ridicule* me while I'm enjoying a private moment—"

"You will rise and bow to me. Now." St John's face was contorted like a tragedian's mask. Henry wouldn't have refused him his last morsel of food during famine-time if he'd looked at him like that.

"I shall not!" Jones was getting angry now. "I shall not do that! You cannot make me!" Jones shook his head. "We are both students, both Fellow Commoners. After we graduate I will treat you like the lord you are, but for now, you're just a prank-pulling school boy with an inflated opinion of his own power."

The rest of the Company had gone very still. Even Godfrey was no longer tittering. What had started as a simple revenge-jape was becoming a very serious, very volatile situation. All of the boys looked uncomfortable; Neville jumped when Lowell shut the door of the dormitory behind them.

St John's face relaxed, and he smiled. It was not a nice smile.

"You will."

Jones snorted. "Or *what?*"

St John handed his bat to Henry, who accepted it meekly.

"You will rise and bow to me, or you will face the consequences."

Jones's hard-on had deflated, if the blankets were any indication. He shifted his bottom slightly and sat up a little straighter on the bed.

"Make me."

St John darted forward and grabbed Jones by the roots of his hair. Jones cried out in pain but choked on his wind when St John wrenched him forward off of the bed, causing Jones to fall onto his shoulder and hip. His bones knocked against the wooden floor of the room with an unsettling *thunk*. Jones righted himself quickly, but his attempt to rise was thwarted by St John rapping him hard on the head with his knuckles. Jones clutched at his skull and remained kneeling.

"You're on your knees now, aren't you?"

"And yet I still haven't *bowed*," said Jones through his teeth. He looked defiantly up at St John. "You cannot force me to do you honor, my Lord Calipash. And tomorrow, mark my words, everyone shall know about this Company, and what you've been up to of late at the Horse and Hat, and even *they*, with their Royalist sympathies, will be none too pleased to hear how you've abused their trust and ill-used their property!"

It does not take very long to withdraw a pistol from a coat-pocket, and yet it seemed to Henry to take a thousand years as he watched St John do so. The Lord Calipash's hand left pale trails in the air as he reached inside the lapel of his jacket and brought out an ivory-handled pistol. It was a beautiful piece, Henry thought—he had never seen a gun so close and thus could not really judge—but its presence was deeply alarming. Someone actually gasped.

Jones went white as St John trained the muzzle on his forehead.

"Do you bow to me *now*, Lucas Jones?"

"My Lord Calipash," began Jones, but St John cut him off.

"Do you bow to me or not?"

"I do, I do, you crazy bastard," said Jones, knocking his forehead against the floor. "I bow to you, are you satisfied?"

St John rotated the cock from half to full.

"Cousin, don't you—"

"Shut up, Godfrey," snapped St John, without taking his eyes from Jones. "You do me honor, Jones. I acknowledge this. But you have not apologized to our Company, whom you have now *twice* blackguarded as criminals and threatened with exposure. Do you apologize, Jones?"

"I do, I do, I apologize, I shan't say anything to anyone, I swear it!"

cried Jones, looking up and eyeing the weapon. "Stand down, Calipash! Please! For God's sake, man!"

St John smiled and tilted the muzzle of the pistol upwards so it faced the ceiling. The Blithe Company sighed as one, and Jones slumped, relieved.

"Christ in heaven, St John, that was a—" Jones began.

St John again leveled the gun at Jones and time once more seemed to slow as Henry saw the Lord Calipash tighten his finger on the trigger. It was too late to do anything—St John was murdering Lucas Jones, right here in front of everyone, and all for a minor slight! Henry's hands went over his eyes and both bats clattered to the floor. There was a click as the trigger was pulled—

The sound of gasping—

The smell of fresh excrement—

And St John laughing.

"You killed him!" cried Henry, his hands still over his eyes. "Oh God, I—"

"You're mad!" Jones screamed. "I'd already said I'd not tell!"

"I needed you to know what would happen if you considered going back on your word," said St John smoothly.

Henry looked up. The room was not full of smoke; Jones yet breathed. His brains were not splattered across the floor. Something else was.

"I think our work here is done," said St John, tucking the pistol back inside his coat. "Shall we leave Mr. Jones to clean himself and his chambers?" St John pinched his nose and pulled a face. "I feel rather overcome, don't you all? Let us be away, and conclude the night's amusements elsewhere."

But none among the Company seemed particularly amused by the events of the night; indeed, Henry could not detect even the ghost of a smile upon any face, even Godfrey's. Blithe was not a word Henry could easily apply to them. *Thoughtful*, perhaps, even *meditative*—and in Neville's case in particular, *furious*—but not blithe. Not blithe at all.

"It wasn't always like this, you know," said Neville, falling in beside Henry. "It used to be just a bit of a lark. Wenching it up in style, drinking fine wine laced with Turkish poppy juice, that sort of thing. But lately …" he shook his head.

"I'm sorry," said Henry.

"For what?" Neville seemed genuinely surprised. "It isn't your fault, Milliner. The beginning of the end came some time ago. I'm not sure when St John's entertainments took a turn for the dark, but it was certainly before you joined us." He shrugged. "I'm leaving Wadham soon anyhow. I've proven to be an indifferent scholar, and wish to return to the apprenticeship I abandoned in pursuit of bettering myself. It was a mistake, I know that now. But as for you—you're really in for it."

"You think so?"

"Yes," said Neville grimly, as St John threw open the door to the Common Room and began to usher the dejected Company inside like they'd all just had a lovely time. "You're living with him now, aren't you?"

CHAPTER TEN:
THE WANTON SHEPHERD

The Company broke up quickly that night, which soured St John's mood. He turned gloomy as they began to trickle out, and when Godfrey, the last of them, said he would also take his leave and return to Christ Church, St John sighed and began to blow out the candles and lanterns, reserving only one for their journey back to his rooms.

"My dear cousin," said Godfrey, hesitating with his hand on the doorknob.

"Hmm?"

"I—I must tell you something."

"What?"

"Well, that this will likely be the last time I'll be around for one of these little wingdings …"

"What? Why?"

"It's obvious to everyone at Christ Church I'll never graduate, including myself," said Godfrey, with a nonchalant shrug Henry couldn't wait to one day emulate at an appropriate moment, "so I've agreed to accompany a friend on his continental tour. We leave for London in a fortnight, to shop for clothes and other things."

"Oh," said St John dully. "Well, yes, it does sound like a good opportunity."

"You're not cross?"

St John shrugged. "You'll be missed." He looked up, eyes suddenly keen. "You do … plan to return, don't you?"

"Of course," said Godfrey, with the first display of sincerity Henry had seen from him. "I would never—will not—abandon you and your sister. I swear to you, I shall do nothing abroad that would interfere with our plans." Godfrey turned to Henry. "Miss Clement and I are betrothed."

"Oh," said Henry. "I mean, congratulations."

"Thank you. I am certain if St John's father yet lived he would protest the union, but last year passed from a—what was it?"

"An apoplectic attack."

"I'm sure it seems ghastly to call such a thing fortunate, and yet it has allowed Honor and I to pursue our happiness, since my father could have no rational objection to reuniting our families." Godfrey looked over at St John. "I assume you do not mind me discussing this with our new acquaintance?"

"Why should I? He'll be our lawyer one day."

Henry almost choked, and tried to play it off with a strained smile. "It seems we are all very fortunate of late."

Godfrey raised an eyebrow. "Indeed. Well, I must bid you both good evening," he said. "And St John—I don't think I need to tell you that tonight was a complete disaster."

"I know it."

"Well, *do* try to keep it together from here on out? There are those who are depending on you to not fuck up, you know."

St John acknowledged this with a depressed wave of his hand. Godfrey bowed to them both, then left. St John sunk deeper into his seat, emanating melancholy. Henry stood for a few awkward moments, then sat in a convenient chair with a sigh.

St John looked up. "Do you wish to leave as well, Mr. Milliner?"

"No, my lord."

"No?" St John pressed the fingertips of his right hand to his temple. He looked so woebegone Henry almost felt bad for him.

"My lord, are you in need of anything?"

St John laughed, and looked up at Henry with renewed interest. "And if I was, would you bring it to me? Like a servant?" St John shook his head. "You are more than that, Mr. Milliner. Much more."

"Am I? I find myself unsure of that. All I wanted since I came to Wadham was to be a part of your gang and lord it over the rest of the students. Now that I have it, I find myself bemused—unsure," he thought of Rochester's face that afternoon. "Regretful, perhaps. It has, I confess, not been quite what I expected."

"That is my fault, for planning this evening so poorly." St John straightened up. "I have myself longed for greatness, Henry, but every attempt I make seems to fail miserably."

"You are a good scholar, my lord, and a kind friend—at least, you have been to me."

St John shook his head. "A good scholar … well, perhaps. But the rest, it is smoke and mirrors. Everything I do is illusion."

"My lord, when I crashed your party at the Horse, that was not illusion."

"Was it not? Those orphans weren't orphans, nor twins. They weren't even siblings, or even that young, really. Merely actors I made up to look that way. His hair was a wig, and her shyness paid for with coin."

Henry was totally at a loss. He had no notion of what to say or do to combat St John's cafard. How to reassure him, restore his confidence? Henry did not possess any self-assurance, how was he supposed to lend to others what he could not manage for himself?

"Everyone enjoyed that night at the Horse," was what he settled upon, though it was a half-truth and they both knew it. St John was looking at him with narrowed eyes. "What I mean to say is that it did not matter to your friends whether those twins were really twins. I mean to say … it was titillating because of *your* doing, my lord. You created the illusion, you shaped our interpretation of the event. We were not entertained by watching two wantons; we were entertained by *you*."

"The act was preferable to the reality, then." St John would not relinquish his misery. "This I knew already without your confirming it. It is my lot to know such—to live such." He leaped from his chair and threw up his arms. "And here *you* are, telling me that to my face! How dare you—*you* of all people!"

Henry scrambled out of his chair when St John seized one of the cricket bats and brandished it at him. Henry began to panic. The Lord Calipash seemed like one possessed, and he could not fathom what he might have said to provoke him so. Henry got up, hoping he could make a run for it if necessary, and every step St John took toward him he answered with a step back, until his bottom collided with a bookshelf. Heart pounding, he raised his hands in supplication.

"My lord," he said, cowering as St John continued to advance on him, bat raised. "Please, I do not know how I have offended you, but—"

"You offend me with yourself, your presence—nay, your very existence! I shall not suffer you to usurp what is mine!"

"I—"

There came a knock at the door, in the pattern used as code by the Company. Henry and St John froze as they were, St John looming, Henry cringing. The knock came again, and the door opened. Thomas stepped inside, and raised his eyebrows when he saw the tableau before him. Henry hoped against hope his servant's presence would deter rather than encourage St John.

"My lord, you didn't return," he said mildly. "I came to see how everything went tonight."

"Oh *Thomas*," cried St John, and to Henry's surprise, he dropped the bat with a clatter and stumbled toward his servant, collapsing upon the boy's neck and sobbing. "It went all wrong, and I think, I think I ruined everything, I'm sorry, I'm so very sorry, I—I—"

Awkward. Henry looked away, ashamed to behold this spectacle, but after Thomas allowed St John to cry and snot all over him for a while, he helped his master into a chair.

"He gets like this sometimes, sir," whispered Thomas, after giving St John a handkerchief to honk on. "We must get him back to the room, and after—well. There's only one thing for it. You don't object to ... I should, rather, enquire if you are a light or heavy sleeper?"

"Neither," answered Henry, bewildered. "Why?"

Thomas half-smiled. "My lord has found that his blacker moods become easier to shake when he distracts himself with hard exercise. And the exercise he enjoys most is riding."

"At *this* hour?"

"There are ... certain fillies best suited to nighttime sport."

Henry blushed, finally understanding. "Of course. I shan't be a bother ... only ..."

"Hmm?"

With a sheepish grin, Henry said, "How ever do you smuggle them in?"

"The same way you snuck out, or Mr. Fitzroy snuck in. There is an establishment close to the college, I shall fly thither and return quickly." He glanced back at St. John. "Perhaps you should go on ahead, and make yourself ready for sleep. I shall attend to my lord."

"Yes—yes, of course. Thank you, Thomas. I—" He swallowed. "I do not know what I should have done without your intervention."

Thomas shook his head. "You are very new to all of this. You'll learn, in time."

"Hope so." Henry smiled at Thomas, he was finding that he rather liked the servant. "I shall go, then. And—*happy hunting*, should I say?"

"Take with you the lantern. I know the way well enough."

Henry nodded, and then did so; after closing the door behind him, he ran all the way back to their rooms. By the time he got up the stairs and inside, he was panting. What a night!

His intention had been to go directly to bed, for he did not wish to intrude upon the Lord Calipash's privacy—but as he put his foot on the first stair, it occurred to him that the room smelled strange. Earthy would be a good word for the odor, and so would metallic. Henry sniffed, and realized the scent was coming from the corner where Lady Franco had made her nest. Of course! Henry smiled, and navigated his way across the cluttered chamber to see whether the expecting mother had delivered.

She had indeed. Four wriggling, blind kittens of various colors pawed and suckled at her teats, as she licked a fifth clean of mess. When Henry cooed at her, she looked up at him with a bland but friendly expression, whined, thumped her tail several times against the blanket-covered floor, and went back to her work.

"Must be hungry," murmured Henry, but he did not want to poke through St John's belongings to see if he kept a store of snacks. If only he hadn't depleted his own cache through late-night munching! Surely Lady Franco would not eat the few dried apples he had upstairs—but perhaps she would take a biscuit? He'd seen cats rooting through trash before, and sometimes they would eat an old roll when there was nothing better …

Racing upstairs, he grabbed his sack of treats and found a handful of stale, crumbly crackers. Gathering what he could into the palm of his hand, he went back down and offered the largest piece to Lady Franco. She considered it for only a moment before gobbling it. Henry left the rest with her, and then went to refill her dish with water from the cistern that hosed down St John's weird plants. After doing so, he ambled back over toward the plant table.

Jars full of plant essences, he thought. And these strange plants. A rose that bloomed tulips; a cactus that loved wet soil. Did stripping an essence lead to … bizarre growth patterns? And how had St John managed the feat?

Henry inspected the plant table. Pulling out the top drawer—and feeling like the snoop he was—he discovered nothing more sinister than a book of poetry—Abraham Cowley's *The Mistress*. Henry opened it to a page, and it was "Platonick Love," which, he realized after scanning the verses, was the poem St John had earlier quoted at him.

Next to the poem was a note, in St John's clear script:

"A rose by any other name." The house of Tudor looks painted by Rembrandt, but is proof of what? Retaining some but not all of orig. body? What, really, is the soul of a flower? Of an animal? Of a man?

St John's interests certainly veered toward the strange!

Henry heard voices, approaching footsteps. He replaced the book, shut the drawer, and scooted up the stairs lest it be St John, Thomas, and whatever creature Thomas had procured for St John's "hard exercise."

It turned out his hunch had been correct. As he undressed, Henry heard the door open, then low voices. A woman spoke; a man laughed, and then there was silence.

Henry relaxed, blew out the lantern, and got into bed. He had very nearly fallen asleep when sounds began to drift up through the floorboards: a rhythmic thumping, and muffled groans. Instantly awake, he tried not to listen, but failed completely. He had not heard the sounds of coupling since his mother died when he was eight years old—his father had not remarried—and it was intensely exciting. Envisioning St John enthusiastically ploughing a rented field, as it were, Henry's cock quivered, and without his touching it once, lengthened and throbbed under the blankets of his bed.

He turned over onto his stomach and pressed his erection into the mattress, almost ejaculating from the luscious sensation. He held entirely still after that; he felt an intense desire to spend, but Henry refused himself the pleasure. It seemed weird and wrong to abuse himself whilst listening to his roommate fucking, to say nothing of the night's unpleasant events being still quite fresh in his mind. To his relief the sounds rapidly reached a crescendo and then subsided—as did he, after a few moments.

Henry congratulated himself on his self-control, but when it became apparent St John was getting his money's worth and enjoying a second occasion, Henry gave up, grabbed a stocking, and, spitting into his hand, began to gently stroke his shaft and balls. He took his time with himself, imagining St John's white buttocks tensing and releasing as he worked his lady-love; imagining, too, the rapturous sounds and heaving, jiggling flesh of his partner. Since coming to Wadham, Henry had been denied the opportunity to have a truly luxurious frig, his former roommates being night owls as well as given to teasing, so he went at it gently but enthusiastically until, well before St John finished up, he had spent copiously all over himself. After cleaning up the mess with the stocking, Henry Milliner fell deeply, contentedly asleep.

CHAPTER ELEVEN:
ART CAN INDEED SEEM MUCH LIKE LOVE

John Wilmot, the 2nd Earl of Rochester, sipped his ale in a smoky corner of the crowded public house and tried not to look like the person he knew he was: A jilted thirteen-year-old schoolboy who'd snuck out so he could cry into his beer instead of into his pillow. Unfortunately, the effort made him so self-conscious that hot stinging tears once again began to flow down his cheeks. The delicate skin around his eyes and under his nose was sore from wiping at his face, so he let them drip and puddle onto the greasy wood of the table.

Maybe it was a good thing he looked like a pathetic, snot-nosed little kid, though. People were certainly avoiding him, and that was what he wanted.

Before coming to Wadham, John would never have believed a crowded tavern could be more solitary than a private room, but here he was simply one among many and thus invisible. At school he ran the risk of people knocking on his door or hollering up at his window if he lit a candle, or just teasing him through the walls if they heard him sniffling.

Leaving Wadham had been damn scary, though—as was being out on the town all on his own! He had sneaked out of school exactly twice since he'd entered college in January, both times for Blithe Company events: The first folderol at the Horse where he'd seen cunt for the first time, and the second, where that slouch, that, that utter *Judas* Henry had made such an arse of himself. Whatever sangfroid he'd evinced had been entirely in the service of trying to impress Henry; the reality was that he'd been too nervous to fart during those moments getting over the gate, to say nothing of getting back in again—and both times there had been, you know, a plan, provided by St John who, whatever else he might be, was a bit brilliant at mischief. John wasn't so sure he could manage a similar caper on his own, but he'd missed supper due to being too red-faced to risk the dining hall, and he'd decided that if his heart was going to break, he'd rather it do so on a full stomach.

So to the Bear, a small, handsome coaching inn where he'd stayed for a fortnight before moving into the Wadham dormitories. He wasn't sure he'd made the right choice of where to go, though. When he'd gotten within sight he'd felt suddenly, powerfully homesick—but also too hungry to seek out somewhere else.

And really, what he was homesick for wasn't really the Bear, nor his childhood home, but his old tutor and governor, the Reverend Francis Giffard. Giffard had stayed with him during that fortnight but left the very day John started at Wadham, and John had not heard from him since. John had received a letter from his mother reporting that Giffard was now an ordained deacon at Lincoln Cathedral, and he wouldn't begrudge him that honor for anything in the world ... and yet. Giffard had come into his life when he was seven years old, and until a few months back, had been a constant presence. Why, until coming to Wadham, John had rarely passed a night without the Reverend sleeping alongside him in his bed ...

Upon hearing Giffard had been dismissed by his mother, who had decided John would live in private chambers like the other Fellow Commoners, he had experienced some anxiety over it: Would he be cold in the winter months without another body wrapped around his? Would the darkness come alive and consume him, as he had worried about since he was a babe in swaddling clothes? But when he had expressed these worries to Reverend Giffard the man had slapped John across the mouth and told him not to cry over nothing like a little girl.

"Guard yourself against sin and believe you in the Lord and His power," Giffard had said sternly. "You are an Earl and, more importantly, a fine scholar. There is nothing you need fear except temptation."

That was Giffard through and through. Words hard as flint and confusing messages that John must either puzzle out for himself or risk a beating if he dared ask for clarification. He preferred, therefore, to try on his own, but in the six years of his being tutored by Giffard he had yet to understand what the man considered 'sin,' or for that matter, 'temptation.' John knew the meanings of the words, of course, but not what *Giffard* meant by them, as the reverend's definitions sometimes seemed ... discrete.

But as they'd been discussing in Master Fulkerson's class, the Ancient Greeks had certainly seemed to think that the special relationship between a boy and his teacher contributed to a young man's intellectual and moral growth. Perhaps Giffard had been right about certain matters. Best not to dwell on the past. That chapter in his life was over forever, for better or for worse. Worse, it seemed. John had really thought Henry's friendship would fill the hole in his heart, only to discover the older boy was a badger, a liar, and a—

"Beer for you, m'lord!"

Startled, John jumped when the broad-faced, prettyish girl who worked at the Bear shouted at him over the din as she slammed down a tankard of ale. Some of the foam sloshed over of the lip, lacing the side of the mug as it dripped onto the table.

John looked from the beer up at her, confused. It didn't surprise him that she knew he was a lord—she had served him his food and drink the whole time he had stayed there. He had no idea of what her name was, of course, but the real mystery was that he hadn't ordered another drink. He opened his mouth to reply, but she cut him off.

"Gen'leman at the bar bought it for you. Said it looked like you needed it." She winked at him. "Pardon me for saying so, but I agree!"

"Perhaps," said John, nodding in agreement just in case she didn't catch what he said, and surrendered his old mug to accept the new.

As he sipped, he looked over the men sitting at the bar. None were looking at him—but then one of them, a fleshy fellow of perhaps five-and-thirty with butter-yellow hair and a ruddy, sunburned complexion glanced over his shoulder. He smiled when they made eye contact, and John lifted his glass as a gesture of thanks.

The man seemed to take this as an invitation and slid off his stool to elbow his way over to where John sat. John didn't know how he felt about the possibility of company; he certainly wasn't going to disclose the truth about why he was so miserable if the man asked.

As he drew nearer, John saw the stranger wasn't sunburned. His nose and cheeks were florid as a beet and dappled everywhere with tiny blue veins. John had an inkling of what that might betray about the man's habits, and when the fellow's aroma of sour beer announced his presence before he introduced himself, it served to confirm John's suspicions.

"Good evening, my Lord Rochester," he said, sitting down on the bench next to John and leaning in close. "Please forgive the forwardness of my buying your lordship a drink, but you seemed, if I may be so bold, in need of comfort."

John tried to make his scooting-away from this flatterer as surreptitious as possible; he was vaguely uncomfortable having a stranger sit so near to him at all, much less this one. He reminded John of Henry—though that might just be the girth and the obsequiousness.

"Thank you, sir. It is appreciated," said John, politely but without any indication he was in want of further conversation.

"We haven't met," said the man. He must be unaware of social cues, too drunk to heed them—or disinclined to respect them. "Alice, the girl, she knew who you were when I asked. I saw you come in, you see. You ... *attract the eye*, m'lord."

"It is kind of you to say so," said John. He was getting a weird feeling from this man. Who in the world was he, to speak to him with such confidence and familiarity? But to ask would be to further engage, so John did not.

"My name is Robert Whitehall," said the man. "I am many things—a fellow at Merton College, a drinker of fine ales, spirits, and wines, a man of the world—but most of all a poet. Yet I am a poet who seeks inspiration in such low places as these rather than sitting in meadows or praying at the Church, I'm afraid." He smiled at John hopefully. "Are you still inclined to speak to me? I hope so."

John didn't know quite how to reply, having been profoundly disinclined to speak with this Robert Whitehall to begin with—and yet he *was* distracting John from his woes. That counted for something.

"I enjoy poetry very much," said John, "but I'm afraid I don't know your work, Mr. Whitehall. Is it possible you write under an alias?"

John thought Whitehall looked annoyed for a moment, but it passed so quickly it might have been a trick of the light, or a brief repression of gas, for his next words were jovial enough.

"I have indeed written under aliases, and had some work published under my own name too, my lord." He sighed. "I am not famous, though some—Lord Clarendon and Catherine of Braganza, to mention two distinguished patrons of the arts, have said some kind things about my efforts."

John was impressed. Perhaps this Whitehall was all right; there was something in the man's manners that made John reconsider his first impression. No need to see users and losers like Henry in every face that smiled at him, he reminded himself. "You must be very wonderful, then." John hesitated, then said, blushing, "I confess I have tried my hand at verse-writing, but to no great success."

Whitehall closed the gap that John earlier had put between them, and cast his arm around John's slender shoulders. "My lord, I knew you for a savant when I saw you walk in, you have that ... ineffable sensitivity in your features and bearing that marks the true intellectual, the real lover of the arts."

"Really?"

"Why, my Lord Rochester! Surely you must have heard that before? From some admirer?"

John laughed. "I have had none."

"Ah!" cried Whitehall. "None that you know of, you mean! Surely you have broken hearts—who could not love that sweet face, those full lips!" He released John's shoulders to gently elbow him in the side. "You're telling me you've never made a girl cry? I'm certain you must have a sweetheart back home, that you kissed and left to pine away for you while you filled your head with education?"

"No, sir." John was surprised to find he was enjoying himself. "No to all of what you say."

"Well, if you've kissed a girl, then she's in love with you, whether you know it or not."

"I've never kissed a girl," said John, and then blushed crimson.

This seemed to delight Whitehall, who laughed and laughed and, still laughing, hailed the barmaid, demanding more drink be brought to them. Rochester laughed too, though he felt a bit queer and dizzy. He'd ordered small beer with his supper, and after, but given the state of his head Whitehall must have ordered him something strong. And he'd asked the girl for "another of the same." Ah, well ...

"I'll buy this round," said John, reaching into his purse and throwing a few coins on the table when the girl returned with the ale. Surely, as a poet, Whitehall wouldn't have the money to buy lords drinks all night—nor should he have to! John could distribute some largesse for once in his life.

"My lord is all kindness," said Whitehall, "even if he is cruel to deny the ladies his attentions."

"It's not that I *deny* them," giggled John, "I just, you know, I am busy. School has been the whole of my life."

"Has been? Is it not now?"

When he'd come to the Bear, John had felt like if he never saw Wadham again it would be to soon, but after this many pints he was feeling somewhat more reasonable. He shrugged.

"My studies are important to me," he said, and then more boldly, "but so is life."

Whitehall gulped his beer in great swallows that made his Adam's apple bob. "Ahh," he said. "That's better. Hard to talk with a dry throat, eh? And I am *so* enjoying talking to you, my lord. Are you enjoying talking to me?"

"I am."

"Ah! I am glad. To find an enthusiast for the arts among the nobility is rare—and composing verses is thirsty work."

"Is it?"

"Indeed it is."

"What exactly," said John archly, raising his eyebrow, "makes it so thirsty?"

With sudden and surprising agility Whitehall sprang to his feet and then, using the bench for a boost, leaped atop the table. He hoisted his beer aloft.

"My fellow men, hearken to me for only a moment," he cried, his voice carrying over the ruckus with impressive ease. "I have need of your attention, for there is something I must tell you all."

"Shut up!" shouted one wag, after the tavern quieted as everyone looked up to see what was happening, but Whitehall only bowed to the heckler.

"I shall, I shall," he said. "Only let me entertain you for a moment with some spontaneous verse. Only a few lines," he said, when the groaning began and the volume of conversation increased again. "Only a few short, sweet lines on the subject of a new friend of mine. If I may!"

And then he cleared his throat.

"My love is first in beauty, but in kindness too,
And though young, knows more than I ever learned at Wadham.
My love is perfection through and through,
For also knows my love the joys of Sodo—"

John watched, horrified, but before Whitehall could finish the verse he was hit in the face with a gravy-smeared potato. John, though amused, was glad Whitehall had not been able to finish his impromptu poem. Witty he might be, but so indecorous!

And John had to give credit where credit was due: Whitehall could take it like a champ. He seemed entirely unconcerned by the tavern's reception of his poetic efforts as he wiped gravy and mash off his nose.

"*That* is why being a poet is thirsty work," said Whitehall, as he settled down again beside John.

"At least it does not seem to be *hungry* work," said John, getting out his own handkerchief to catch a smear Whitehall had missed. "One cannot starve if food is literally thrown into one's mouth."

"My lord is a wit as well? I am so glad I came tonight. And yet ..."

"What?"

"It appears this audience is disinclined to treat artists like ourselves charitably." Whitehall drained his beer as John's heart soared. Whitehall thought him an artist! "Would you like to go somewhere else? Or perhaps back to my rooms?"

John wanted to, but he shook his head. "It is late, and I must get back to Wadham. I ... am not supposed to be out."

"I thought as much! They had rules like that at Christ Church, when I was a schoolboy." The man's tongue raked over his pink lips after saying this last, leaving them moist and shining. "May I at least escort you back?"

"Oh, that won't be necessary," said John to be polite, though he did like the idea of company on his way back. Dangerous times and all that.

Whitehall put his large hand over John's small, slender one. "Do me the honor of being your escort, it would be my pleasure." He smiled, and John felt his resolve melt away as Whitehall said, "It's dangerous out there for a beautiful boy, all alone, and so late at night ..."

CHAPTER TWELVE:
THE ABLE DEBAUCHEE

The tolling of the bell woke Henry the next morning, but upon dressing in the dark and clattering down the stairs, he found the room below Stygian as his loft, with no indication of St John's rising.

He idled in the shadows, watching the light coming in from the window gradually brighten, but when time came to pass that he would be late if he did not soon depart, he risked a knock at St John's bedroom door. He heard a groan from within.

"My lord?" Henry knocked again. "It is nearly time for prayers …"

Another groan.

"My lord? Are you ill?"

"*Go away*," came the plaintive wail.

Henry hesitated.

"Are you—in need of any assistance?"

Henry was able to discern the words "Thomas" and, again, "go away." Uneasy, Henry checked on Lady Franco, who looked at him with the same friendly, tired expression. Satisfied she was doing fine for the time being, he closed the door softly behind him, and pelted over the quad to the chapel.

He sat among the Company during church, and after, in Logic class, too. It wasn't as comfortable an experience as the previous day; St John did not appear, and the other boys were as subdued as Henry had ever seen them. They spoke but little, and seemed unsure what to do without St John to guide them. It wasn't so obvious during prayers, but when Lucas Jones approached them, before Logic commenced, there was an awkward moment. Neville stood up. Jones bowed to him.

"I was an utter shit to you yesterday, Anthony," he said calmly. "Please, accept my apologies. I should never have said what I did, and that I even thought it speaks to my poor character. Can we be friends again? Will you shake hands with me?"

"Absolutely," said Neville, and did so. Jones smiled, and the mood among the Blithe Company palpably improved. "Now, come and sit down. Look—Master Ward approacheth."

St John did not come to dinner, either. His absence was noted, though not much commented upon due to the college's rules. Then, just as Henry began sopping up the gravy from his pie with a hunk of bread, something occurred that drove the Lord Calipash entirely from his mind.

The door of the dining hall flew open with a bang, and a servant ran inside, waving a sheet of parchment over his head like a flag of truce.

"Charles has returned!" he cried. "King Charles celebrates his birthday at Whitehall today! We've just had word from London—the king rode into the city this morning! Three cheers for England—and *long live the King!*"

A moment of profound silence, and then such a roar of shouting, stamping, clapping, yelling, singing as Henry had never before heard. The Masters did not even try to silence the happy throng; they, too, were given over to jubilation. Wadham had more than its share of Royalists among the students as well as teachers, and it was obvious that none among their number felt the need to hide their emotions. Henry observed joyful weeping as well as merriment, and joined in the *huzzah*ing with enthusiasm. He wasn't so very political, but even he could not but feel a sense of joy that England was once again whole, and ruled by her rightful lord and master.

The rest of the afternoon was declared a holiday: Classes were cancelled, the campus was opened, and boys ran hither and yon, doing whatsoever they liked without supervision—or danger of chastisement. Most fled to the taverns, brothels, and coffee-houses for hope of more news, but some elected to make merry within Wadham's walls. Henry hung back, plucking dinner-scraps off of the abandoned plates, and as he did he heard a pack of boys discussing whether they should go and join the gathering mob of Oxford academics who had resolved to throw a sheep's rump through the window of Vice-Chancellor Greenwood, who had once invited the Roundhead troops to march on Oxford to awe the Royalists among his scholars.

Henry longed to join in the revels, but he was worried about St John—and Lady Franco. He liked cats, and she seemed a good sort; without her master to care for her, Henry worried she might starve. To that end, after he had gathered a nice selection of meaty morsels into a napkin, he returned to his room.

It was still quiet; St John's door was still closed. Henry tiptoed over to the corner and presented Lady Franco with her feast. Shedding her mewling brood she staggered to her feet and stuck her nose in the center of the scraps and began to gobble. Henry watched, happy to have helped. He would never have guessed St John would neglect his pets, but perhaps he had indulged in more vices than one last night. A hangover would account for his absence.

Henry thought his suspicions confirmed when St John staggered out of his room and out the door, murmuring about the privy. He returned half an hour later looking much better, and came over to see what Henry was doing.

"Lady Franco!" he said, crouching down beside where Henry sat cross-legged. "Why, you slut! Just look at all those kittens. Did you offer your fanny to all the toms in Oxford?"

"I think cats usually give birth in litters," said Henry.

St John laughed. "Are you defending her honor? Well, with such a gallant taking your side, Veronica, I shan't risk a duel by further impugning your morals." He scratched her behind the ear, and she thumped her tail on the ground a little. St John smiled one of his serious smiles. "They all seem very healthy and normal. Excellent."

"She's so calm, too. I've never seen a cat so mellow—almost like a dog."

"Maybe she is a dog."

"You'd know, wouldn't you?"

"Hmm?"

"You were checking her blood to make sure it was cat's blood, weren't you?"

"Oh. Yes, I was, wasn't I."

"And I've never heard her meow."

"I don't think we ever reached a conclusion on whether cat's blood makes cats meow."

"Perhaps not."

It occurred to Henry that St John smelled wonderful. He inhaled his scent, and, looking at him sidelong, Henry saw his hair was damp. He must have gone to the bathhouse.

"I do thank you for taking care of her while I was ... indisposed," said St John. "You probably saved her life, poor wretch."

"It was my pleasure. Are you ... feeling better?"

"A little." St John smiled wryly. "I overindulged even after ruining everyone's night. I do apologize Henry—to act so during your first escapade, it was inexcusable."

Henry opened his mouth to say it was all right, that things would be fine, when there came a loud knocking on the door. St John hesitated—he was wearing only his shirt and breeches—then rose and answered it.

It was Lucas Jones.

"Hello there," he said.

"Mr. Jones." St John bowed, but did not step aside. "What do you want?"

"Why, that's hardly friendly." Jones seemed to think something was very funny, Henry could tell even from where he remained, in the back of the room, in the shadows. "Aren't you going to invite me in?"

"No," said St John. "I'm not well."

"Too bad," said Jones. "Given what I know of your political opinions, you should be out in the streets with the rest of the rabble, hailing the return of the king."

St John straightened up. "What's this?"

"Haven't you heard? He rode into London this morning. England's monarchy has been restored."

"Wonderful." St John crossed his arms. "Did you come by to tell me the news? Or for some other purpose?"

"Let me come in, Calipash. I have much to say to you."

"I—"

"I'm of a mind to ruin you, St John. If you're cordial, I may not." He shrugged. "You decide."

Henry expected some sort of wittiness from St John, or at least some response beyond sighing and capitulating. He was disappointed when St John nodded and waved Jones inside. Jones entered like a lord and looked about with amused detachment.

"Ah, 'the laboratory,' as your friends call it," he drawled. "Plenty here to darken your character to the Masters should there be an investigation, eh?"

"Perhaps."

"Oh hello there, Milliner," said Jones, coming over. "What on earth are you—my my my," he said, catching sight of Lady Franco. "A pet! You're not allowed to keep a pet. None of us are."

"Is there a point to all of this, Lucas?" St John's tone was clipped.

"Yes," said Jones. "To be blunt, you embarrassed me last night. Terribly. And don't claim it was on Neville's behalf; he and I have already made up—and agree that you went too far. The rest of the Company concur."

"I am happy your friendship with Mr. Neville is reestablished," said St John. "What has that to do with me?"

"Well, that's the funny thing," said Jones. He was really starting to enjoy himself. "My friendship with *all* the Company is reestablished—well, save for some recent trash you let in. And we've been talking—classes were cancelled, you see—and it is our opinion that the Company is in need of some reorganization. Your recent leadership has been ... wanting, as have your frolics. None of us want to watch Irish orphans doing it, nor do we wish to suffer the mad rages of an unstable leader."

"You're a liar!" Henry stood.

"What?" St John and Jones in unison.

"Well, I can't say about the latter, but I was there—there at the Horse and Hat, that night—and all of you seemed entertained by what happened there, even if you found it ... challenging."

Jones regarded Henry with distaste, then laughed. "Well, St John, it looks like your Blithe Company has been reduced to one bulchin nincompoop who was until lately a total pariah. How droll."

"So be it," said St John. "I have more to my life than the Company—I was busy before I founded it, and I shall be busy after."

"Will you? What if you were expelled?"

"Expelled? For what?"

"And here I thought your Latin was supposed to be *good*," tittered Jones. "Or do little lordlings not take the same oath as the rest of us? I personally recall vowing not to disturb the peace of the college with distractions, evil speeches, or abusive language ... nor cast odious aspersions upon any member of the college. That sort of thing. Did you not make that same vow, my lord?"

"I did."

"And have you honored it?"

"As well as you have!" St John's voice was high with anger.

"Hmm, *is* that true?" Jones sneered happily. "If it is, then at the very least I've done a better job hiding my indiscretions than you. This room full of arcane nonsense and nesting vermin—piglets as well as cats, apparently." He stuck out his tongue at Henry. "Did you *really* go to the Masters to advocate for Milliner to move his sty to your garret?"

"I did, not that it's any of your business."

"Well, that's one thing you won't be punished for, then." Jones shrugged. "As for the rest, I suppose we'll just have to see, won't we?"

St John rolled his eyes. "What is it you want, Lucas?"

"What do I want? Why should you think I want anything?"

"You're trying to blackmail me, aren't you? Get on with it. What do you want—money?"

"You *would* think that," scoffed Jones. "But no. What I want is simply everything you have. Not money, not clothing—I'd take the looks, but that's impossible—what are you smirking at?"

"Nothing, go on."

"I want your power. I want your status here. I want the Blithe Company."

"Have it, then—and much good may it do you!"

This brought Jones up short. "You're done with it?"

"Whether or not I am, I give it freely to you this instant. May you enjoy your new *rôle*, I shan't say a word but in support of your regime."

Jones looked annoyed. "I ... bugger you, St John Clement!"

St John raised an eyebrow.

"No—not—God *damn* you!" Jones spat on the ground. "There is what I think of you and your devil-may-care attitude! I know it's killing you to give me what I want!"

"Is it?"

Henry said nothing, enjoying seeing St John reclaim the upper hand. He might be scary and a bit mad, but Lucas Jones was a total shitwig.

Jones seemed to sense the shift in power, too. Displeased, he shrugged and sniffed at St John.

"You're playing a dangerous game, Calipash. I could ruin you, and it's only by my goodwill that I don't." Jones's voice was even quieter than St John's now, and sounded more dangerous. "So just remember that as you sit in class with all the college looking to me, and as you watch the Company hail me for providing brilliant distractions, and as you eat your supper at the Master's table while I'm down with the rest of the lowly commoners. I may not have your privilege, or your wealth, or your airs and graces—but I have you by the whirlegigs, and you know it."

And he stormed out.

St John leaned back against his desk for support, and exhaled through his mouth. He looked very tired.

"There's nothing for it. I shall have to leave—return home, to Devon, to Calipash Manor."

Henry came over and dared to put an arm around St John's shoulders. "Cheer up! You might not."

"No, it is finished. My *indiscretions*, as Lucas called them, have caught up with me at last." He smiled at Henry. "Do not mourn, Henry. Calipash Manor is not such a terrible place. You shall come there one day, I think."

"You mentioned something last night."

"Well, even if you desire a different patron, you shall come as a friend."

More than anything in the world Henry wanted to embrace St John, to kiss his beautiful lips, to make him happy. He was so very pretty ... and perhaps he sensed something in Henry, for he reached up and moved one of Henry's lank locks away from his forehead.

"Henry ..."

"Yes, my lord?" He almost choked on the words, so moved was he by the touch.

"Henry, I wonder, do you love me?"

Henry took a deep breath. "I ... have been presumptuous, perhaps— impertinent—but ... yes, my lord. I do."

"I thought so. That poem you wrote me ... and I think you did not even know then how I love poetry, am I correct? You wrote it out of passion, not interest."

"Yes, my lord."

"Well," said St John. He stood and latched the door, "would you like to love me? It is a sin, but so is much I have already asked of you."

The next thing Henry knew St John was leaning over him, looking anxious. He was lying on something very soft—St John's mattress!—and there was a cool cloth on his forehead. St John was sitting on a chair beside his own bed, his shirt untied at the neck; his hair, now dry, was curling winsomely.

"You fainted," said St John. "Oh my dear Henry ... I don't know if I can ask this of you, to be so wicked on my behalf—"

Henry sat and swung his legs over the edge of the bed. Taking St John's face between his hands, Henry kissed the Lord Calipash like he had always wanted to kiss him. The taste of his mouth was almost painfully erotic, and when St John began to kiss him back, Henry had to break away or risk embarrassing himself.

"I apologize, my lord. I was overcome."

"Don't ... apologize."

His tone gave Henry pause—did St John look nervous?

"Henry, I have not been entirely honest with you."

"My lord?"

St John pulled off his shirt and stood there in the dim light of his bedroom. He was slender and pale, lean but strong. He also had a strange bandage wrapped many times around his chest.

"Are you injured, my lord?"

St John chuckled. "No. I am not injured. But I am also not St John." He began to tug at the bandage and unwound it, revealing, eventually, a small but feminine bosom. "St John is at home in Devon. I hope you are not disappointed, Henry, but ... my name is Honor. I am St John's twin, and have been playing him here at Wadham. It was the only way." She seemed to be pleading with Henry now. "Have you never noticed there are no women on campus? None of the servants, even—just the laundress, who comes to the gate, and never inside. I had to pretend I was a boy if I wanted to get an education. Not embroidery and penmanship, I mean—a *real* education. Oh Henry, you're not cross with me, are you? Do you only like boys?"

"Only you, St John—I mean, Miss Clement!"

"I think you may call me Honor now that you've beheld me in my nakedness," teased Honor. "Will you still make love to me?"

"I would do *anything* for you!" Henry leaped to his feet, his heart felt like it might pound its way out of his chest. He had never dreamed of such a turn of events, not St John loving him, nor him being a girl, but no matter, all was right with the world. St John—Honor—whoever! She loved him—and *wanted* him!

Honor untied the waist of her britches and shed them, revealing long slim legs and a gilded pudenda. She sat down upon the bed and reclined against the cushions.

"Then enter the town which thou hast won," she said, with a glance up at the poster of Abraham Cowley. Henry, disrobing with all possible haste, fell upon her like a jackal on a carcass.

CHAPTER THIRTEEN:
AN EMPTY SOURCE OF SOLID HARMS

Fucking Honor was tremendously exciting. She suggested all kinds of dirty things, including swallowing his prick to the balls and showing him, in turn, how to lick and suck at her slit, which seemed to delight her even though Henry despaired of deciphering her anatomy upon first glance. She even begged him to poke his tongue inside her bottom-hole, which he thought *outré* but ended up enjoying. She let him do whatever he liked with her, too, so he played with her tits and never thought he should have enough of them as he kissed and gently nibbled the shell-pink nipples. When he twined his fingers through her pubic hair she moaned and bucked against him wantonly.

When she broached the subject of intercourse, Henry would not believe she really wanted him to penetrate her, and initially refused for fear of injuring her—in the moment, to say nothing of nine months hence—but Honor was strong and agile. She flipped him onto his back and pinned him fast, begged him to, as she put it, 'roger her properly.'

"But I don't—how can you—it is—"

"Henry Milliner," she said, tossing her short tawny mane defiantly, "do you think I am the sort of person who doesn't know what she wants?"

He was hard-pressed to deny this, and so, trembling like a spent horse, he allowed her to straddle him and lower herself down upon his cockstand.

She was very slick, and moaned as she took him into herself, grinding her hips against his.

He immediately came inside her in great gushing bursts.

"Oh God, oh God, I'm so sorry," Henry babbled as the last spasms shook him, hiding his face with his hands. He did not know much about lovemaking, but he certainly knew to spend so quickly was considered impolite.

"Why are you apologizing?" Honor climbed off his wilting, dripping penis and snuggled up next to him on the bed. "Don't tell me you can only manage one go-round?"

"I have never managed even one go-round before today," said Henry, running his hand over her body from moist neck to moist thatch. "How can I know if more is possible?"

"Have you never frigged yourself more than once?"

Henry blushed. "Mayhap, once or twice." He hesitated, then whispered in her ear, "I stopped at one last night, listening to you."

"You heard?"

"Yes … at least, I think I did. I thought, of course, that Thomas had brought you a … and you were a …"

Honor nuzzled his neck. "Thomas is a good servant."

"Will he be …"

"Jealous? Cross? I suppose so, yes." She smiled sadly. "He loves me dearly."

"How could he not? All who behold you must."

"Sweet creature." She kissed him, sticking her tongue inside his mouth and cradling his balls with her left hand. He jumped, they were feeling rather sensitive, but soon her attentions to his vitals had him yearning to once again explore her charms.

He enjoyed her for much longer the second time. More confident, he thrust and thrust into her, trying to make it last as long as possible. He nearly lost it when she suggested he try it with her dog-fashion, but he controlled himself and discovered that way was very nice indeed. Something about the angle of it. When he came it was so intense he cried out from the pain and pleasure of it.

"Keep thrusting, Henry, please—I'm so nearly—nearly—*ohh*!"

He did his best to please her, and felt her cunt begin to pinch and pull at his cock; the spastic, nipping contractions stimulated him so intensely that he spent a *third* time, and so copiously it ran out of her and over his shaft, dripping down his scrotum and thighs. Incapable of moving more, he sat back on his ankles, gasping and still joined to her.

"Honor," he sighed. "Oh, Honor, I love you. Did you—did I …"

"I enjoyed myself completely," she said softly, sliding off him and collapsing onto the bed. "Very impressive."

"Really?"

"Yes, really."

Henry climbed down beside her and sighed happily. "I never hoped it would be so … wonderful."

"*Rather.*"

Henry dozed off for a time, and when he awoke, it was dusk. Honor was still asleep; naked and breathing quietly, she sighed. He ground his hips against her bottom as they spooned. Gazing at her pale, slender body with its boyish hips and firm high breasts, Henry thought himself the luckiest man in the world. She was a tremendous thing, Miss Honor Clement. To have hoodwinked him so extremely—why, to have hoodwinked an entire college of learnéd men! She had kept up with the best of the class, nay, *outstripped* them, and with her woman's mind and weaknesses, too! To think that she had attended classes, and probably turned in pages of perfect homework while dealing with her monthly curse! Tremendous was a word without the proper scope! She was ... a goddess. He knew they could never marry, but to have even dallied with such a creature was a privilege he would cherish forever.

Marry.

The word stuck in his mind. Honor was to marry Godfrey one day, after his continental tour. They were betrothed, he had learned that last night—they had spoken of it in front of him! Good Christ. But Honor couldn't have been a virgin before her decision to take Henry as a lover. Perhaps Godfrey had done the deed.

This seemed unlikely to Henry; Godfrey had also spoken proudly of having been caught with two stable-boys and a footman. That certainly seemed more up Godfrey's alley than him claiming the virtue of his cousin, no matter how boyish she might look—but there was no way of knowing if Godfrey's interest in lads was a strict preference. Perhaps he would make do with Thomas.

Where *was* Thomas?

"You seem preoccupied."

Honor rolled over and stroked the end of Henry's nose with her fingertips. Her eyes gleamed in the shadows.

"To be honest, I was contemplating Godfrey," said Henry.

"Really?" Honor looked surprised. "I thought you said you weren't a bugger?"

"I'm not—but he is?"

"Thoroughbred, as far as I can tell."

"What are you going to do, then?"

"Hmm?"

"If he won't—you know."

She slid her finger under the head of his cock and lifted it. Henry winced as some of his dried spendings tugged on the downy hairs on his thighs, and she chuckled. "I can feel the heat of your blushes from here, Mr. Milliner. Trust me, I shall make do. There is Thomas, after all—and you."

"Madame, I am honored you would consider making this an, ah … ongoing affair."

"Speaking of ongoing, I'm curious—can you manage again, do you think?"

She was insatiable! Henry's prick was sore from crown to root, but her hand had been teasing and tickling him, and the stimulation had yielded a passable cockstand. Perhaps if she would lick it a bit, as she had done earlier …

He worked up the nerve to ask, and she obliged, slurping on it like she couldn't get enough of the taste. This produced the desired result, and they wantonly fucked in the twilight, giggling about all the spirited screaming and hollering still happening outside, on the quad. She came twice, but the unusual amount of stimulation had numbed Henry somewhat.

"I'm sorry," he gasped, thrusting up into her as she rode a St. George upon him. "I'm very nearly there!"

"Try with me below you," she said. He heeded her council, but still he could not manage to finish, even with her calves encircling his neck. She was beginning to grimace with each thrust and her moans had changed in timbre. He must be making her sore; he certainly was—his cock felt more like a skinned knee than an object of pleasure. Still, he was eager, desperate to come, so out of politeness he gasped,

"What if you let me—in your mouth—"

"Oh no," she said, with a shake of her head. "No, it affords me too much pleasure to have my vitals bathed from within." She arched her back, and he felt her hand snake around behind him. "Let's try …"

To his bewilderment and alarm she worked her finger into his bottom-hole as he continued to fuck her, but the unexpected stimulation surprised him into a prodigious spending. She cried out as the first jet struck her insides, and he collapsed on top of her with the last burst, exhausted.

"Very nicely managed," she murmured, squirming out from underneath him. "Brilliantly done. You are *such* a sport, Henry. I like you."

"Oh," he said. After her earlier talk of love, this rather wounded him. "I … love you, I think." He saw sympathy in her expression, so he amended, "I know I must always do so from afar, but I don't mind!"

"Sweet boy," she said, and climbed over him to rise. Naked as the day she was born she walked across the room, lit a candle, then opened her wardrobe, and shrugged into a parrot-green *robe de chambre*. Clothes transformed her back into St John, but Henry still thought her mighty handsome.

His stomach grumbled, and it occurred to him that she might need some refreshment after all that, too.

"Honor—are you hungry?"

"Famished!"

"You know, when I came back with scraps for Lady Franco, the whole of the college was topsy-turvy. The gates were open … could I … would you let me …"

"Hmm?"

"Let me buy you dinner, Honor? We could go out to a tavern—the Horse, if you like, they'll certainly be busy what with King Charles's triumph and all that, but we could get a bite and a pint."

"If we do, you must let *me* treat *you*, Henry. I have taken your virtue today, after all. You must let me give you something back."

Henry blushed. "No, please. Let me do this for you—you have done so much for me. It would be very exciting for me, I've never taken a girl out to dinner before."

"You shan't start now. If we go, you shall be escorting St John. I am not here, remember? Regardless, I must take care of something first. Go and dress, as shall I."

Henry was so happy; he couldn't ever recall being so very happy. Head propped on his hand, he looked at Honor in the candlelight, her chiaroscuro figure, the way the light played over her cheekbones.

"Are you going to go?" she asked. "I really am very much in need. If you want to watch me make my pee then that's fine with me, but …"

Henry blushed. "All—all right, I'm sorry, I … I didn't realize." And, wrapping her bedsheet around his still-leaking nakedness, he scurried upstairs to dress in his best.

He wasn't too keen on his only real suit of clothes. The black cloth of the coat, the plain falling-collar, and conservatively-cut shirt made him look more like a Dutch spinet-tutor than an up-and-coming English lawyer, but it was clean and unwrinkled, and he knew he would not embarrass Honor in it. He gave his hat a quick brush, checked to make sure his stockings were straight, and headed down the stairs with his purse banging on his hip—and found Honor in her laboratory, still in her *robe de chambre*, holding a glass tube that appeared to be full of golden liquid over a candle-flame.

As he watched, she took a long glass rod and dipped the end into some sort of fluid in a glass jar, then shook a drop into the yellow-tinted tube. It turned a brilliant pansy-purple and began to smoke.

"Wonderful," exclaimed Honor—and then looked up and saw Henry standing there, staring at her. She sobered quickly. "I—ah, I had to conclude this experiment before getting ready. Please, excuse my tardiness."

"Was that …" It seemed absurd, but Henry asked anyways, the original color of the fluid in the tube having been rather distinct, "your pee?"

"Yes," she replied, tidying her workspace and retreating into her bedroom. "Why?"

"What were you doing with it?"

"Testing it."

"For what?"

Henry followed her into her bedroom, excited by the idea of watching her change clothes. She stripped, heedless of his gaze, and shimmied into a pair of stockings.

"Help me into this?"

She was holding a strip of cloth, the one Henry had earlier seen tied 'round her bosom. He helped her wrap it tightly, and she continued dressing without responding.

"Honor?"

"My family is given to kidney stones," she said, not looking at him. "I test my urine regularly to see what is safe for me to eat. If the acidity is off, I must stay away from such things as beans and peas, is all."

"Oh." Henry wasn't sure she was being honest, but then again, it was her piss, and thus her business. He instead focused on witnessing her remarkable transformation. Honor not only altered the line of her bosom, but wore a sort of special undergarment that simultaneously compressed the curve of her bottom and gave her a bulge in front. Her shirt was so ruffled she needn't have bothered binding her tits, he thought, and the same went for her petticoat breeches, but when he mentioned this she came down hard on the side of verisimilitude.

"It's an art form," she said, powdering her face lightly and then darkening under her cheekbones with some tinted paste. "I always use a bit of this to make my face look more masculine, though I'm so very manly-faced I needn't really bother."

"I don't think so!"

"Yes, but you're at least part bugger," she teased, as she donned her white wig. "All right, shall we dine? I'm famished."

"To the Horse?"

"Yes, that sounds lovely." She kissed him on the cheek. "You're such a dear, Henry. Everything has worked out so wonderfully."

Indeed, it seemed so. Henry had never felt so light of foot as he did during their walk to the Horse: Not only had he become a man that day, but he was taking his girl out to dinner, and that girl was St John Clement Lord Calipash! And not as part of a group or anything, just the two of them.

It was a good thing, too, he saw when the Horse and Hat came into view. The place was mobbed. Throngs of people were sitting and standing in the street, drinking flagons of ale and cups of wine, cheering and getting enthusiastically drunk; inside, there were no seats at all to be had, and most of the standing room was taken up with students, merchants, and farmers alike.

Henry felt a bit overwhelmed, and was just about to suggest they look elsewhere when Honor elbowed him in the ribs and nodded to a dark corner, where two figures sat deep in conversation.

"I say, isn't that your friend Lord Rochester?" she shouted over the din. "Whoever is he with?"

Henry squinted, peering into the dimness, and did not recognize the other man. He was corpulent and red-faced, with yellow hair and a simpering smile. Henry watched him take a deep draught of wine and then, of all things, he kissed Rochester on the mouth, and not in a strictly friendly fashion, either. He had his fat, hammy hand behind Rochester's small head and kissed him for a long time—and with tongue, Henry noted, mildly grossed out.

"Looks like you won't be the only chicken plucked this night," remarked Honor. Henry laughed. He was more comfortable with Honor when she was playing at being St John, things were so much easier.

"I should dearly love to go over there and see what's happening," cried Henry.

"Why don't we?" shouted Honor, looking mischievous. "What's stopping us?"

Henry saw her point, so they elbowed their way through the crowd, eliciting curses when they accidentally knocked into tipsy, lurching revelers.

"Hallo, Rochester!" Henry hailed his friend, who looked immediately annoyed, his companion even more so. "Nice to see you—we were just trying to find a place to sit! May we join you?"

"Do let us," said Honor, with a bow to the assembled pair. "You've no idea how hungry we are."

"All … right," said Rochester, looking sidelong at his benchmate. "If you're happy with it, Robert?"

"I don't think we've met," said Henry, plunking himself down on a stool before this 'Robert' had a chance to gainsay Rochester. "I'm Henry Milliner, our Lord Rochester's oldest and dearest friend at Wadham. And this," he said, indicating Honor, "is St John Clement, the current Lord Calipash, and the brightest star in our college's firmament."

The fat man seemed rather taken with St John and not at all interested in Henry. "My lord, it is a *pleasure*," he said unctuously. "I am Robert Whitehall, a humble composer of verses. I am a fellow at Merton, but lately come back to Oxford and looking to … make new friends."

"Robert Whitehall," said St John thoughtfully. "Didn't you get into a spot of trouble with the Roundheads over some poem—"

"Ah ha ha," Whitehall laughed unconvincingly; there was no mirth in his eyes.

"—and then got into trouble with the Royalists for writing turncoat doggerel?"

"Ah ha ha *ha*," he said, turning redder, if that was possible. "You are well informed, my lord."

"I follow poetry."

"Indeed, my lord? How *wonderful*," Whitehall said, his fleshy cheeks wobbling as he smiled. "Well then, I must compose some verses in your honor, for a poetically-inclined gentleman has no need for food, drink, or love—for he has found the greatest happiness of all. Would you not agree?"

When Whitehall spoke, Rochester got a sloppy sort of worshipful look in his eyes that Henry didn't like at all. Could the boy not see through the toady?

"I could not say," replied Honor. "I suppose it depends on the poetry. If such is true, however, I'd advise those trying such a thing to be careful—insipid verses would likely cause anemia as easily as an inadequate diet."

"Will you not shake hands, Rochester?" asked Henry, leaning over to converse with his friend. "You've not said a word to me."

"Why are you here, ruining my night?" snipped Rochester, tossing back his wig-curls. "Go and join the rest of the Blithe Company, I saw some of them earlier—look, there's Neville and Jones, they're having a private chat, and you seem to enjoy breaking up that sort of thing."

Oh, yes—there they were indeed, but Henry didn't care.

"You're sour as Belgian beer," he said. "Whatever's the matter with you?"

"Robert and I were having a lovely time before you barged in here."

"I saw. Watch yourself, John, or you'll end up spitted between the kidneys before this night's out."

Rochester's eyes widened. "You're vulgar common trash, Henry Milliner."

He had said it so loudly that Honor and Whitehall both fell silent and looked at the two of them. Henry flushed, angry and hurt, but then he saw something and went cold as the Thames in winter.

"St John," he hissed. "St John, *behind you.*"

Honor turned—and stiffened.

St John Clement Lord Calipash and his cousin Mr. Godfrey Fitzroy had just come in through the door of the Horse and Hat.

CHAPTER FOURTEEN:
A HISTORY OF THE UNFORTUNATE

"Shit," said Honor.

Rochester had noticed why their attentions had suddenly been diverted; Henry knew it because the young Earl's brow furrowed in consternation as he tried to puzzle out how there could be two St Johns at the Horse, identical but for the color of their coats. Henry was also curious, but Honor looked so panicked he didn't want to bother her.

"Arrrround firthehrourse!" shouted the other St John, waving his arms to gesture at the crowded tavern. He almost fell over but Godfrey caught him mid-sway. "Drink up!"

Godfrey, Henry saw, looked mildly perturbed by St John's behavior. Neither had yet seen Honor. Those in the bar didn't seem to have noticed the doppelgängers, they were too busy hailing their unexpected luck and claiming tankards filled and passed out by the staff.

Then the other St John climbed up on a table, hoisting his mug, which foamed and spilled over his hand and long, ruffled cuff.

"Toats," he slurred, "A toats to my breloved *sisterrrr*."

"God *damn* St John," swore Honor, looking increasingly cross. "I must leave—out the back—is there a way? I, I must ..."

"I don't understand what's going on," said Henry. "St John? But you said he was at your ancestral home, did you not?"

"I did," said Honor shortly, casting about for an exit and finding none. "Henry, do not speak to me about this now, I shall explain presently. Oh, we should never have come here!"

"Troday, I saw my sisterr joins inlussst—with an *asshole*," shouted St John, and then he took a long pull on his beer. Revived, he began anew. "Not *my* asshole neither, mush t'my constipation." He frowned. "Consertation. *Con*-ster-*na*-tion."

Henry felt a yawning in his stomach, as if he had been climbing stairs in the dark and at the top felt his foot sink lower than expected, having thought he had one more to go.

"Honor," he hissed. "Honor, is there something I should—"

"Oh *do* shut up!" she hissed back. She seemed frozen, unsure of what to do. To leave would mean walking past her double, past the Blithe Company members near the front, so she sat still and tall in her seat, eyes glued to the other St John, her brow growing increasingly damper. "I never thought he would—"

"You!"

"Huzzah," said Honor, "he's spotted us. Tonight just keeps getting better and better."

St John, still atop the table, pointed at Henry with his beer-hand— sloshing ale all over some very unhappy patrons—and shouted.

"You!" he cried again.

Godfrey looked amused for the first time since entering the Horse and Hat; St John did not seem to find any humor in the situation. He jumped down more nimbly than he had any right to and commenced making a beeline for them, elbowing annoyed yeoman aside.

Honor stood and went forth to meet her twin. Godfrey kept up and when St John stopped, he stepped in between the two St Johns, obviously trying to make the best of things.

"Why, look, here we are assembled!" he tittered nervously. "Hello all—nice to meet you," he said at Robert Whitehall, who looked more confused than anyone. "Cousin, you left a suit of clothes over at Christ Church, I gave them to Thomas to wear. He was quite upset when you wouldn't spend any time with him on this happy day, the birthday of our sovereign Charles the Second. You don't mind?"

Henry felt a momentary sense of relief—of course, it was just Thomas in a borrowed suit—but no, it couldn't be. Godfrey was attempting damage control: The other St John had been speaking of his sister, not his mistress.

Of course. Christ, he'd been such an idiot! Henry congratulated himself for finally figuring it all out. "Thomas" was St John Clement in disguise, masquerading as his own manservant, so his sister could masquerade as himself!

Or perhaps they switched off—what had Rochester said, and Aldous Clark confirmed? That St John had made love to a whore in the back room of the Horse while the whole Company looked on—quite the feat without a pizzle. He should have realized it sooner. And Godfrey, when he had spoken of marrying St John's sister—it had been St John-St John leading the Blithe Company the night they tormented Lucas Jones.

When Thomas had come to them it had been Honor, saving him from her wilder brother, speaking of black moods and hard exercise! Yes, yes.

Feeling rather smug, Henry stood, but before he could speak, someone else did.

"Ho now, what's this?"

Neville and Jones had joined them, looking as confused as everyone else. When no one spoke, Neville snorted.

"How funny," he said. "Is this a prank in honor of the restoration of the monarchy? Good one even for you, St John, this other really is your very double. So close I can't—I say, which of you is really St John?"

"I am," they both answered.

Jones laughed uncomfortably. Neville frowned.

Henry decided to take control of the situation.

"Thomas," he said sternly, "you must stop making a spectacle of yourself here in public. You shame yourself, but more than that, you shame my lord, and—"

Something collided with the side of Henry's face. When he came back to himself he was lying on the floor of the tavern, and realized it had been a fist—St John was rubbing his knuckles. Henry spit out a tooth and drew himself up unsteadily onto his elbows.

"We talked about this," Honor was saying, looking about at all the people staring at them. She seemed far calmer than before, as if she had accepted the situation and given up on trying to control it. "It was the only way."

"*You* talk'd'bout it." St John was far more drunk than he was articulate. "You tol'me—"

"Let us talk about what I may have told you back at the college, away from everyone." Honor's voice was stern.

Henry got to his feet. "Gentlemen," he said, "*I* propose—"

St John swung again. Henry, distracted by Rochester calling his name in alarm, failed to duck—and knew no more.

***

"I don't like it. You said I wouldn't mind, that I would learn to like it, but …"

"You must give it time, dearest. Just you wait—when my natural temperance has worked some changes to this flesh I'll be more to your taste, I'll warrant."

"But you were perfectly to my taste *before*."

"Life makes fools of us all." A sigh. "I hope you will learn to adjust. I do love you very much. That is why I did it, you know."

"I know. I just—I shall never see myself looking out of my own eyes again."

"A narcissistic wish."

"I mean—"

"I know what you meant, but do not despair. I am still, as I have been, wholly yours."

The voice was so familiar, but Henry could not place it. Still, he felt very queer, so he chose to not yet open his eyes. He had come back to himself with no notion of how long he had been out; all he knew was that he was lying on his back on a mattress.

"And you're ... certain?"

"Perfectly. Last night the hue was unmistakable."

"Well then. I suppose I must offer you my congratulations on the happy event."

A laugh. Henry couldn't place it. The last speaker had been St John, but as for the other ...

"It will have to be a quick wedding, which always has the hint of scandal—but I suppose it can't be helped." A sigh. "Godfrey, you *would* fly the coop just as St John ruined everything. Oh, brother mine. I know you were never very happy about the plan, but really. Such outbursts, such intemperance ... to say nothing of your putting yourself at risk for the clap, or worse. You forced my hand."

"Surely you knew enough." St John sounded sour.

"I knew *enough*, perhaps, but not all. I wanted to breed Lady Franco again, now that she is possessed of Pietra's sensitive essence, to see if her offspring were still normal." A laugh. "If the first is wanting, we may have to try again. Poor Henry. I wonder how he'll feel about *that*."

Henry opened his eyes upon hearing his name. His vision was strange, sharper than usual. The ceiling of the room was incredibly detailed in the candlelight. Looking to where the voices came from, the first thing he saw was ... himself. With a black eye and a bruise on his cheek. He closed his eyes again. The two blows to his head must have done something to his brain.

"Why did you wake up faster? He's certainly taking his sweet time."

"Oh, he's awake," said Godfrey, from somewhere behind Henry's head.

"Really?"

Henry opened his eyes again to find his vision remained queer. Still feeling rather peculiar, he sat up slowly—and again, was tormented by seeing himself standing off to the side, looking at him keenly. Good Christ, he looked gross and uncouth next to St John! When he was better, he would have to start cutting back at mealtimes. And stop getting himself punched repeatedly in the face.

"Weird not seeing you in you," said St John critically, canting his head to the left. "I still don't know about this, Honor."

"I confess even I retain mixed feelings on the matter." Henry watched his own mouth move, though he was not speaking. "I liked my body, to be sure, but now we may always enjoy ourselves, without worrying about my monthlies, or how to get ourselves an heir."

"What is going on?"

Henry jumped at the sound of his own voice—it was higher than it had been since his balls were smooth as eggs. He looked down, and instead of his person, he saw a thin cotton *robe de chambre* covering a small but elegant bosom.

"Good morning, Henry," said Henry.

Henry felt dizzy; he went to put his hands over his eyes and realized his left arm hurt. Looking at it, the crook of his elbow was wrapped with some sort of dressing, and a pinkish dot was evident on the cloth. He covered his overly-sharp eyes with his delicate right hand. "This is a nightmare, I will wake up, I will wake up soon."

"You are not asleep, Henry," said Henry. "I know this must come as a shock, but it's nothing to worry about. I have transferred your soul to a different body, by transfusion of the blood—along with a few other processes, of course."

"I don't think he's happy to hear it," commented Godfrey. "Poor duckling. Perhaps when he sees himself in his pretty wedding clothes he'll buck up."

Someone sat beside Henry on the mattress. He lowered his hand, and looked into his own, concerned face.

"I am sorry to have cozened you so awfully," said Henry. "You were far nicer than I realized when I decided on you."

"What is happening?" Henry cried. "Where am I? Who *are* you?"

"You're in my body," said Henry. "You were in it enough yesterday, do you not recognize it?"

Honor.

Henry looked down at himself again, and pulling open the neck of the *robe de chambre*, he realized he did indeed recognize those small, high breasts and pink nipples. Good Christ, he was a woman. Honor had somehow stolen his body. The bitch!

"How?" he managed. "Why?"

"As for your first question, my philosophical researches, of course," said Honor, with his voice, his tongue, his mouth. "Do you not recall what I said about the Hebrew theory of the soul residing in the blood? For the past year I have made a study of souls here at Wadham, and transfusion, too. My researches were long and arduous, but once I managed to create my psychoscopic spectacles it was simple enough to determine the soul does indeed reside in the blood. Basing my methods on Christopher Wren's, I theorized that since blood may be extracted, so might the soul. I even developed a method for removing the soul entirely from the blood, using spinning force—my crank-tub. Sometimes bloods do not agree with one another, for some reason I cannot determine, so it is necessary to extract and then re-introduce the soul."

"What?"

"Do you not recall my looking at Lady Franco's blood? I had switched her essence with Pietra Poodle's—Godfrey's dog—and wanted to make sure her essential biology went unchanged, since my dear plants, being vegetative, had demonstrated some ... unusual reactions. A rose producing a tulip's blossom, for example."

"Tudors and the Rembrandt," said Henry, finally understanding at least *that*.

"Yes, yes! But as it turns out, a flower's blossom is a bit like ... like our soul, I suppose. A beautiful thought, isn't it?"

"Quite," said Henry dryly.

Honor didn't seem to notice his irony. She patted Henry's newly-slender knee. "After I successfully exchanged Lady Franco and Pietra Poodle's souls—their sensitive essences, as Aristotle would say—well, it was time to find an appropriate vessel for *my* soul. Which leads me to your second question, the why."

"Honor, I—" St John looked uncomfortable.

"St John will not like me to tell you that he is infertile," said Honor, "But he is. Sterile as a stone. We tested him quite thoroughly to make sure it wasn't me who was the problem, and he couldn't get so much as a country milkmaid with child. But we had to have an heir, you see."

"You can't marry your sister," said Henry weakly.

"No, but you can marry your cousin," supplied Godfrey.

"It would not have been easy to find a man willing to marry a woman in love with her own twin brother," Honor said wistfully. "Do you recall Master Fulkerson's lecture on Plato's *Symposium*? I confirmed everything Aristophanes believed, looking through my spectacles. My brother and I, our souls look the same, we are … we are, as I said, more than twins." She smiled at her brother with Henry's lips.

"No longer," said St John.

"*Still.*" Honor's tone was irresistibly firm. "Godfrey was kind enough to propose to me, given that our interests could be mutually satisfied. I would not care who he took to bed, nor he me. But that did not help us with our need for an heir."

"If I could have gotten one on St John, that would have been different," said Godfrey, smirking.

"Not that I was ever averse to *trying*," said St John. He sighed, and shook his head. "You can see how biology thwarted us there, too."

"So the only thing for it was to find someone to, ah, *donate* an heir," said Honor. "Godfrey could have done that easily enough, but then I should still be sacrificed on the altar of womanhood, and I enjoy my freedom far too much for that. Who on earth would want to be a woman? Not objectively—all things being equal and all that—but in *this* world? I had to play dress-up, live a lie, just to go to school! And there's always the risk of death when a woman is brought to childbed, and how could I leave St John alone, should such a thing transpire?" She looked lovingly at her brother. "You are such a dear, but so helpless."

St John shook his head. "I cannot think I could survive without my … other half."

Henry's head was swimming, his heart—Honor's heart—was pounding. "So you—you stole my body?"

"No, of course not! I gave you more than an equal exchange for it, I'd say."

"But I didn't want to exchange it!"

"You said you'd do anything for me," said Honor. "And it won't be so bad. Once we pack up, we shall need to soon, I think the bell for prayers shall toll soon, you shall elope to London, with Godfrey—your future husband—and there you shall buy, with Calipash coin, the finest wardrobe a married woman could want. Then to the church, and after that, Godfrey has agreed to escort you to our home in Devon before he goes abroad. There you shall live like the noblewoman you are, and be given all possible honors when you bear our heir. *Your* heir, actually, come to think of it. How lovely."

"We, however, shall stay here," said St John. "Now that Honor's a boy, there won't be any trouble with her going to classes. I'll stay on as Thomas, and claim the Lord Calipash abandoned me when he ran away with Godfrey over the scandal of Lucas Jones' humiliation."

"And since you were already taking the proper classes, I can learn lawyering, and after I graduate come to live at Calipash Manor with you, and with St John, and with Godfrey. And our child, too, I suppose. Do you see now, Henry, how all has worked out?"

Henry blinked at her.

"Henry?"

"Worked out?!" he leaped to his feet, feeling strangely light and weak. "*What* has worked out? You speak of me possibly dying in the act of bearing your heir—my own child—after subjecting me to arcane torments and nefarious schemes? You won't get away with this!"

"We will," said St John.

Everyone looked at him.

"Tell anyone outside this room what's been done to you and you'll be sent to Bedlam." St John shrugged. "Far less comfortable accommodations than at Calipash Manor, I daresay."

"You're ... you're all *monsters!*" Henry began to cry, and even the tears felt alien on his face.

Honor looked surprised. "Henry, don't weep! You've gotten everything you wanted!"

"When did I want a cunt?" snuffled Henry, hating how petulant he sounded.

"You certainly wanted mine," she said reasonably. "Now it's yours forever, I gave it to you. And did I or did I not promise you that I'd help you get your grades up enough that you could join the Natural Philosophy class in the fall?"

St John laughed.

Honor shot him a look, then turned back to Henry. "All joking aside, I promise you your teachers will see an immense improvement in your schoolwork. See you now how you've gotten everything you wanted? Better grades, an easy life untroubled by social class or difficult academics, and, as you'll discover once you arrive at Calipash Manor, you'll finally have everyone at your beck and call, paying you respect, *et cetera.*" She smiled at him. "Oh, Henry. I'm sure you'll come to see everything in the right light—in time."

EPILOGUE:
JUST LIKE HENRY

John Wilmot sidled into Logic like it was no big deal, hoping no one would remark on how he hadn't been at the Chapel for prayers that morning. He had briefly waked upon hearing the bells calling him to worship, but he'd had such a splitting headache from all the wine he'd drunk with Robert that he just couldn't get out of bed. Five in the morning was simply too early to rise after getting in at two. He would need to be more temperate in the future.

Or less religious, one or the other.

He slid onto his accustomed bench with a groan. He still felt rotten as French cheese and like he might need to make a run for the jakes before class was finished. He rubbed his chin, feeling the sparse stubble of his beard; shaving had been beyond him. He knew he looked rough, but still, things could be worse. Idly, John wondered what had become of Henry after he'd taken that drubbing from one of the St Johns that had come to the Horse last night.

One of the St Johns. My, it *had* been a bizarre night, hadn't it! First he'd agreed to Robert's proposition that John pay for the use of a private room one night a week at some public house so they could meet *sub rosa* for "poetry lessons" and then that second St John had shown up and beat the daylights out of Henry. Robert's suggestion that they have another bottle of claret—apiece—after the unconscious Henry had been borne out of the tavern by that giggling fellow and the identical boys had seemed sound at the time, but now John wasn't so sure … he couldn't remember much after that. Robert had been on about something about school or—

The door to the auditorium banged open; John winced from the racket but quickly schooled his face into impassivity. It was the Blithe Company—and there was Henry, trailing behind on his fat little legs. How dare he have called Robert a toady! *He* was the toad, a squat, fat, ridiculous, warty, croaking little toad of a boy.

John shot him a nasty look, but was surprised, upon further inspection, to see that Henry looked … good. Tired, but good: For once in his life he looked like he'd gotten up in time to damp and comb his hair, his face looked clean, his robes were ironed, shoes were brushed and shined, and he was leaning against the wall of the auditorium in a casually confident manner, laughing with the rest of the boys. Maybe joining the Blithe Company really was proving to be a good influence on him?

Ah! *That* was what Robert had been saying, that John should 'get in' with the Company; that he would be surprised how old school ties came in useful in later life. When John had protested that the Blithe Company were rotters all, Robert had told John to trust him, and suggested that it was due to a lack of truly refined, artistic influences among them, and they were likely wanting for someone to bring that tone to their chord. Or something like.

Looking at Henry, John thought meanly that indeed the Company might want for more refined influences if *that* was the sort of trash they were allowing in these days. However Henry might have improved, he still had acne, and frankly, he looked ridiculous with that black eye. Not at all cool or roguish or dangerous or wicked, really. John congratulated himself for getting over his former crush so quickly. He simply wasn't worth it. Not like Robert.

But a soft voice inside John teased at him, made him to look at Henry a second time—and admit that, actually, Henry did look pretty cool and roguish and dangerous and wicked with that black eye. And … wait, was he coming over to sit beside him?

"Hallo, Rochester," said Henry, sliding onto the bench beside John and forcing him sideways across the wood with a thump from his liberal bottom. "How goes it? Have a good time with that fellow last night after I left?"

"Yes, though I wish you wouldn't shout so," said John acidly.

"Are you embarrassed? Or—is it that, mayhap, you had a few too many drinks?" Henry grinned, tapping the side of his nose. "I had a few in before I got to the Horse, but not many after the walloping to the face. Should never have gotten between the twins. Lesson learned—not that I'm too concerned about a repeat of that nonsense. St John's flown the coop, along with his sibling, and given everything, I don't think they shall ever return."

"What? Really?" John was surprised by this information. "Why?"

"Well they'd been seen together, hadn't they—cat's out of the bag and whatnot about them being twins, plus Lucas Jones has some *serious* dirt on the Lord Calipash after the incident. Can't tell you more though. Secret Blithe Company business."

John's head was spinning. "St John ... had ... a twin?"

"Yes, a *girl*. She was dressing in his clothes to go to classes for him. They'd switch off. Seems like we never knew which of them it was at any given moment, boy or girl, since they came! Well, except when St John would show his pizzle in public. Ha! But really, think of it—silly thing, to think she could hide in amongst us manly men forever, eh?" Henry chortled softly, *ho ho ho*. "Got what was coming to her, don't you think? Run out of Oxford in the dead of night for her crimes against the order of things!"

"St John was a girl?"

"Christ, you're a slow one, Rochester," said Henry. "But no matter, it seems you've got the measure of the situation at last. Sort of."

"That's shocking," said John. Mostly he was amazed St John and his sister had carried it off for so long. He wished he'd known—he had never before heard tell of such mastery of the art of going incognito. Robert had mentioned the necessity of teaching John how best to play at being someone other than himself—a skill he'd need to hone in order to discreetly crash the parties and receptions Robert wanted him to attend as his protégé, apparently—but John doubted Robert could teach him how to masquerade successfully as a woman! Perhaps he'd one day write to these Calipash twins for some advice ...

"But no matter, John—look, I'm very sorry about everything," Henry was saying. Surprised, John tried not to show it. "I've been a real shit to you of late, I think getting in with the Company went a little to my head."

"Really? How perceptive of you," said John coldly, and felt briefly triumphant when Henry looked wounded. After a moment John relented, feeling as though he'd gotten enough of his own back to be kindly to his oldest friend here at Wadham—and that this was just the way to get into the Company, as Robert had advised. "Well, I'll forgive you ... if ..."

"If?"

"If, after class, you let me come along with you lads? And sit with you during Classics?"

Henry looked rather surprised.

"I had no idea you wanted to ... I was thinking, now that St John's gone, you'd want things to go back the way they were?"

John did, oh how he did—but if he'd made the decision to trust Robert on these matters, he was going to trust Robert absolutely. What was it he always said? 'We have but one life to live, my dear Johnny, so really *live* it!' Good advice ...

"The way things were?" John smiled, and hoped it didn't look fake. "What, being Wadham's leper colony of two? No, I think I've finally realized life is for living, not wasting."

"John ... I don't know what to say," Henry said warmly, "other than I'm glad, so glad. I was ready to give them up for you, but I ... well, I like them, and I like you, and I'm thrilled the twain shall meet! I need an ally—Jones is sort of in charge for now, which is rotten, he's a ponce and a whip-jack as well as having all the imagination of a shoe, but they've promised to give me a chance with a lark at some point soon. I shall show them what Henry Milliner's made of then! Anyways the plan is that we'll rotate until we find the proper leader for our little company. It might even be *you*, Rochester."

They were momentarily distracted when a lad from their class came running into the room, panting like a racehorse. "No! Logic! Today!" he managed in between breaths, and John realized that indeed it was past time to start class. "Master's! A-bed! With stomach flu! And! There's no one! To take the lecture! For him!"

"*Flu!*" cried someone. "I saw him out last night playing darts at the Spotted Cow with Master Fulkerson, deep in his cups!"

"Things are all topsy-turvy these days, aren't they?" said Henry wistfully. "Looks like we have our morning free—let's go over now and see what the Company says about how best to spend our time, shall we?"

John had neglected his Latin homework, as well as his Logic and Classics readings, to go out with Robert the previous night; he knew, to keep up on things for whenever classes got back to normal, he should study ... and yet here, as Robert had put it, was an opportunity to live life.

"It'll be fun!" said Henry. "Come on, Rochester, what do you say?"

"I say ..."

"Say yes!"

John shrugged. "All right, yes!"

"Good," said Henry, nimbly hopping to his feet after throwing his legs over the edge of the bench. "I say, shall we try to convince Jones to let the two of us decide what we'll get up to?" He rubbed his pudgy hands together in anticipation.

"Let's," said John, feeling, if not happy, then at least as though he was putting his life on the right path for greatness. "You know, you might be on to something, Henry. If we outdo Jones with our suggestions, we could get some serious cred with the rest of the Company. Now that St John's gone they'll be waiting for someone to step into his shoes, eh? I think we could *really* show them a good time …"

damnatio memoriae

Petronius hauled himself onto the shore and vomited all over the rocky sand. He had not eaten for he did not know how long, so first he heaved up acid bile that stung his lips, then nothing at all except foamy mucus until he feared he would die. When at last his stomach settled he thanked the gods aloud for their mercy, but privately he felt divine attention at this point was too little too late.

His arms shook and his legs would not bear his weight when he tried to crawl away from the smell of the sick, so he clawed his way along the beach with his fingers. He did not get far. The driving rain blinded him, and brackish tide lapped at his feet and ankles, agonizingly cold. He knew he would freeze to death if he did not get warm but even this could not spur him to move again.

He thought dizzily of his homeland, sunny Syracuse. How warm the rains, how clear the ocean! Here, all the water was treacherously black and icy. During the storm it had chilled him from above and below, raining down upon him as it crashed over the bow of the bireme; he had nearly blacked out from shock when he jumped into the roiling sea after the ship had been dashed to pieces upon the jagged rocks of this unknown, godsforsaken coast. Petronius emitted a sound halfway between a laugh and a groan as he let the darkness take him, his last thought being that perhaps dying quietly of exposure would be better than encountering whatever horrors dwelt here in barbarian Britannia.

***

Groggy, Petronius opened his eyes. Starlight! The storm had broken while he lay insensate on the sand. He sat up, but the nightmare landscape yawed and he lay back down again, weeping for his misfortune. Oh gods, how could he ever survive this ordeal? *Of course* this would be his fate, just when everything was going so well! His *History of Sicily* had sold better than anyone—especially his publishers—had expected, his wife Caelina had just successfully delivered his twin boys, Hortensius Gemellus and Julius Gemellus—and where was he? Some awful, uninhabited coastline, with no one else around for miles. Maybe hundreds of miles. He was profoundly, utterly alone, and would die so. He would never see Caelina's face—or her fortune—ever again, would never feel a father's pride watching his twins growing up and donning their *toga virilis*. Sick at heart, Petronius could almost smell the fire in his hearth for longing …

A riot in his guts brought Petronius out of his misery and reminded him that his chances of survival would be even narrower if he didn't get something to eat—and more importantly, to drink. Cautiously he rolled onto his stomach and then got to his knees—there! What was that—could it be firelight in the distance? He'd thought he'd scented pine logs burning … and if he really listened, he could just discern the sound of voices. Still unable to stand, he cried out for help, his dry lips cracking.

A few moments later he saw several figures coming towards him, their faces obscure. Petronius felt a moment of doubt until he realized they were speaking Latin.

"Hail, Roman! Whoever you be, we shall—why, it's Petronius!"

Petronius' eyes filled with tears. He had not expected the sweet sound of a friend's voice!

"Manlius!" he croaked, "Can it really be you?"

"It is! Gods, it's good to see you. We thought you were dead!"

"I nearly am."

"Not so near as all that. You look fine!"

Petronius doubted this, if Manlius was any indication. The man was in bad shape. He looked gaunt, nearly skeletal, and bruised all over; his cheeks were dirty and dusted with fine reddish hairs, more of a beard than Petronius had ever seen him wear.

"Help me get to the fire, Manlius, lest I freeze."

"All right, then. Help him, boys!"

With several shoulders to lean on, Petronius was able to get up and begin stumbling over to where twelve, maybe fifteen Romans sat around a campfire just outside the treeline. Petronius despaired.

"Is this all?"

"No," said Manlius. "They're not able to tell us much of our comrades, but look down the beach—see the lights? They helped get several other campfires going for other groups before they came to help us with ours."

"Who's *they*?"

"The natives."

Petronius shivered. "Wild Britons, here? Are they hostile?" He'd heard tales of barbarian savagery from those who'd served during Julius Caesar's campaign, and indeed, little else had been discussed during the voyage before the storm began.

"Manlius?"

"We ... don't think they're Britons."

"You don't think? Shouldn't you *know*? I thought you were our translator!"

Manlius shrugged. "These people don't seem to understand much we say to them. Also ... we sent out a party before it was full dark."

"So?"

"There's been no sign of the white cliffs of Dubris."

Things were even worse than he'd thought. Not only were they shipwrecked, they were apparently shipwrecked nowhere near where they were supposed to be. An illustrious beginning for this mad plan of Caligula's, to build a sister-tower across the channel from Portus Itius. And yet Petronius sensed he would still be called upon when the emperor demanded an account of the voyage. If he survived.

"What are they like?" he asked.

"You'll see," said Manlius.

Petronius said nothing, feeling weak and horrible enough without contemplating unknowns. He focused instead on clumsily walking toward where the fire crackled cheerily in a night black as Pluto's left nostril. Then a strange sound reached his ears through the sound of the wind in the trees. It was a strange sound, like laughter, but also like speech. Squinting, he saw that a handful of those whom he had thought were Romans were not Romans at all, but outlandishly dressed barbarians who squatted around the campfire warming their hands and jabbering nonsense. He nearly pissed himself in fear.

"Manlius, I—"

"It's fine. Come on!"

Petronius was going to say that *no*, it was *not* fine, when something occurred to him, and he found the courage to take the few, final steps that would bring him within the ring of firelight. He might never get to Dubris, he might never be able to write an account of building a lighted tower to guide Roman ships through stormy seas (a project that seemed much more sensible now, come to think of it) but if he kept it together, he just might be able to use this wretched voyage to earn a name for himself. The very first ethnography of whatever blighted group of savages lived here would sell *sensationally* well back in Rome, he was sure of it.

***

Petronius was quickly passed a shallow wooden bowl full of some heinous-looking gruel that he ate so quickly he didn't taste it—probably for the best—and then some sort of liquor in a stone jug that reeked of rotten fruit. Petronius sipped it gingerly and afterwards felt both better and worse, but invigorated enough at least to sit for a time with his fellow Romans … and the natives.

They seemed nice enough, he supposed, what with the gifts of precious provisions and not stabbing them to death, but they smelled bad and were dreadful to look upon, and he also couldn't tell who among them were men and who were women. All had long black hair bound back with bits of rope or leather, and all wore similar garments, sleeveless tunics of rough wool and animal-fur capes with deep hoods that kept their features in shadow. Each of them—even the two of the five who Petronius suspected might be female—carried an assortment of brutal, inelegant weapons: hatchets, knives, short maces. All carried swords, and one had a rudimentary bow, as well.

"So they've no Brythonic at all?" Petronius asked Manlius, who squatted next to him.

"I've managed to communicate a little," he said, snatching the booze. "Well, I think we have. Lucius pointed out that really, what shipwreck survivors *wouldn't* be asking for dry wood, food, and drink— but hopefully their language is some thick dialect of the Briton tongue, and we can get by on cognates for a little while."

Petronius nodded, and chanced another look at the savages. What a find—a culture unknown to civilization! Upon his return he would be the only person in the whole world to have the authority to publish such a ground-breaking study …

As he pondered, the savage he felt least certain was female of the two possible candidates caught his eye and scowled at him. He realized he'd been staring at 'her' and immediately looked away lest these people be like wolves and take his gaze for a challenge—but this action, he saw out of the corner of his eye, only caused one of the other barbarians to elbow her in the ribs and, Petronius presumed from his tone, set to teasing her. Petronius was *appalled*. Even if she was female, she was a brute, a grotesque. A thing. Ha, thought Petronius. *Thing*.

The Thing's arms, brown as a nut, were covered in scrapes and bruises, and nearly as brawny as a man's. She could not be thirty, but he could see that two of her teeth were already missing. Her nose had been broken, and her eyes, though bright, were small. Yet at the teasing from her comrades The Thing tossed her black hair in such an elegant, Patrician manner that Petronius was intrigued—but when she caught him looking at her again she hurled a knife through the fire at him. It sank into the earth between his feet.

The camp went quiet.

Then several things happened at once: The barbarians leaped to their feet—along with Manlius and all the Romans save Petronius, who had frozen in fear—and all began to shout and gesture at one another. While a flustered Manlius tried to ascertain what in the world had happened, the soldiers began to cast about for objects that could serve as weapon or shield. When nothing came to hand, one of the troops, a tall, mighty blond-haired fellow picked up a log upon which three Romans had been seated and brandished it like a club.

This actually seemed to impress most of the barbarians and they quieted—except for The Thing, who began to cackle like a witch at the sight.

Everyone looked at her, and she opened her maw to speak.

"Barbar bar, barbarbar-bar, *bar*," she said, or something like.

The savages paused, then all started laughing and slapping The Thing on the back, as if she had told a tremendously entertaining joke. Manlius paused, confused—so did the rest of the Romans—but everyone quickly relaxed upon seeing the barbarians' obvious mirth. The big Roman with the log looked bemused but gave the seat back to his companions, and, running his hands through his blonde locks, began to grin like an imbecile and laugh along with the rest.

It seemed to Petronius he was the only one who didn't find the whole incident hilarious. These people were clearly insane and dangerous, so when The Thing came over to him to pluck her knife out of the ground he stood, not wanting to offend her. He was surprised to find she was far shorter than him.

He bowed; she made a slicing motion across her neck with the blade. Petronius's heart sank down between his kidneys, but her pantomime simply caused the wild people to say *ooooOOOooooh* as one, which then in turn caused The Thing to sheathe her knife and leap over the fire at them, fists balled. She struck one in the face, another in the balls, and soon there was a proper brawl on the opposite side of the fire.

"I think she likes you," said Manlius, sitting back down.

"I wish I'd drowned," said Petronius.

***

Morning-time was beautiful in Britannia, Petronius had to admit it. The dawn was *actually* rosy-fingered, big cloud bands of coral-pink and yellowish orange, and the racket the birds made! The sparrows and whatnot in the forest seemed to drip like dew from the branches of the looming black wood, twittering their joy into the gentle breeze; their cousins the sea-birds dove into the water for their breakfast, crying like lost children. The wild glory of the landscape did much to stay Petronius' irritation at having been awakened so early on a morning when he needed far more sleep to feel human.

But Petronius' appreciation was not long-lived. Daylight had revealed how dire the Romans' situation really was: They were not actually on the coast. Instead, they had somehow managed to navigate up a wide, winding river and wreck on the rocky bank. The ocean proper, shockingly, was nowhere in sight, but what remained of the bireme was. Great boards, bits of sackcloth, and damaged cargo lay about everywhere. Several soldiers were already gathering debris and sorting it into piles.

"Ugh," said Manlius, coming up behind him. "Where the hell are we, do you think?"

"Britannia." Petronius shrugged. "Maybe."

"Cheerful, aren't you."

Petronius turned slowly and raised an eyebrow at his friend. Manlius shrugged and pulled a "what can you do" face, his not-unhandsome features contorting comically. Petronius sneered.

"I wonder if any of my writing materials will be salvaged," he said. "Or do you think the Caesar will be pleased with an account scratched on leaves with charcoal?"

"What, you don't think the locals have a stockpile of ink and parchment?" Manlius poked Petronius in the gut. "You never know! Maybe that woman from last night will surprise you with a love-letter."

Petronius already had a mild headache, and Manlius' remark made the pain far worse.

"If she comes near me, I can't be held responsible," he said. "Better to snap a tendon in retreat than suffer *that* embrace. Ugh! I cannot wait to be home with my wife, balls deep in good white Roman womanflesh."

"I think you'd be missing out," said Manlius thoughtfully. "Just think of the stories you could tell."

"Horses have vaginas, too," said Petronius, "but that doesn't mean I'd brag if I fucked one."

An agonized, blaring sound, like a herd of sick cows giving birth in unison, distracted the pair from watching the salvage operation. It wasn't a trumpet, though—Petronius didn't know how to describe the vaguely musical tootling.

Then the big blonde fellow from the night before jogged up to them from the shoreline, wearing only a piece of tattered cloth wrapped around his trim waist and massive, muscular thighs. He was even more impressive in the daylight: Not a scrap of fat clung to him, his muscles were on display as if he'd been flensed. In the bright sunshine his sweat shimmered like gilding, and his tousled locks were blazing like Helios' own. His cheekbones could have been used to slice cheese, his chin for a battering ram, and he was smiling like he'd just been awarded a quaestorship instead of having spent his morning hauling waterlogged supplies out of an icy river.

"*Salvēte*, Romans!" he cried, as he jogged in place beside them. "We are summoned! See you not our standard upon yonder rock? Hail Caesar!"

Petronius snorted. "Oh, is he here? I didn't see him."

"We had heard some sort of noise, but did not realize what it was," said Manlius quickly, when the giant looked confused.

"Oh!" said the golden man. "You see, they've actually made themselves *trumpets* by taking a big shell and boring a hole in the narrow end!" He was still jogging. "These people are absolutely *ingenious*! And beautiful." This he said breathlessly.

"In*deed*," said Petronius. "Well, you'd better get over there. We'll be right behind you."

"Come! Run with me!"

"Er," said Manlius, eyeing the man's mighty, glistening thews.

"I ... am not feeling well enough to jog," Petronius made excuse.

The Roman turned his back to the pair and squatted down on his heels. For a brief moment Petronius thought the giant might take a shit right there to show his opinion of such weakness, but then he looked over his shoulder and gestured to Petronius.

"If you are in need, friend, then I shall carry you!" he said, when Petronius stared at him dumbly.

"That—that won't be necessary," said Petronius. "I think a walk would be good for me. Salubrious. Don't want the legs to atrophy and all that."

"Mind you walk quickly," said the man, straightening up. "You are wanted, Manlius, but I shall try to help while you are on your way." He grinned at them with teeth whiter than a *toga candida*. "I stayed up late trying to learn a few words of their language. Things like meat, drink, earth, water ... love ..."

"Then you'd better get over there," advised Petronius. "We'll be right behind you."

"Hail Caesar!" he agreed—and was gone, his big bare feet making dents in the sand as he ran swiftly along the shore.

"Who in the world is *that*?" asked Petronius, as they ambled after. "He knew your name."

"Do you really not know?"

"Should I?"

"Gods above! That's—that's Spurius Calipash, the greatest warrior in the Roman army! He's famous! I know it's treasonous to think so, but I reckon that long after people have forgotten the name Caligula, they'll still be talking about Spurius. He's fantastically strong and brave, he's been awarded honors for courage many times over. They say he's been offered the command of his own century thrice, but each time he says he's better as a follower of orders than a giver of the same." Manlius shrugged. "Supposed to be terrifically nice too, if a bit daft."

"A bit, you say?" Petronius sniffed. "Imagine, being impressed by a barbarian with a shell for a horn. Seems rather un-Roman, if you ask me."

"That's Spurius. Never spoken a mean word to his fellow man."

"Why, Manlius! You almost sound *impressed*."

Manlius shrugged. "I am. Maybe for the same reason Spurius liked those shell-trumpets."

"Eh?"

"Difference is always fascinating," said Manlius, and picked up his pace as he headed toward the gathering Roman army.

***

As he tramped upland with a pack strapped to his scrawny shoulders, Petronius decided his life could—officially—get no worse. The borrowed *caligae* on his feet were already giving him blisters, his helmet was slightly too large, and the stupid heavy short-sword at his side slapped his thigh annoyingly. Why the general had required him carry one was beyond him—he'd never fought with a sword, and had doubts as to whether he could even swing the stupid thing, much less hit a target. At least they hadn't given him one of those fancy new-fangled long swords, the *spathae*, that were even bigger and stupider and heavier.

But the worst part was he had no idea how long he would have to endure this torment. He and the rest of his party had been sent to scout out whether the white cliffs of Dubris were still mobbed with savage Britons (and if they were, to head north to Rutupiae, to beg some aid), so it could be weeks—nay, months, of constant danger, making haste through the wilds of Britannia. Angry natives were probably the least of their worries. What monsters lurked in these black forests, what horrors would he encounter on these blasted heaths?

Spurius slowed his pace and fell back beside Petronius, who briefly mused that he had been wrong—if the giant was going to talk to him the whole time, then his life *could* get worse.

"Are you excited, Roman? I am excited," he said, grinning. "Think of it!"

"Think of *what?*" gasped Petronius, out of breath from his exertions.

"Why, exploring this place!" Spurius looked ecstatic, as though he was actively having a religious experience. "This fresh new country, the wildernesses, the sights! I have been a military man my whole life," he said happily, "but never have I been assigned to this sort of mission! We'll be the first Romans to see this realm!"

By Jove, the man was tearing up! Had he no shame? Winded, Petronius couldn't sigh, but he really wanted to.

"Funny, isn't it, how we just met—and now, look, we're traveling companions!" Petronius had a sudden vision of Spurius running in circles and peeing himself like an excited puppy. "It's just you, me, and Manlius out here—and of course," here he uttered something guttural and incomprehensible.

"Oh, is that her name?" said Petronius, looking over at The Thing, who had a pack twice the size of any of theirs and yet seemed far less fatigued by the arduous pace of their journey. Like so much else associated with this voyage, she appeared even more sobering in the light of day.

"She is a vision," said Spurius, and even Manlius, who'd been moody and silent since they set out, laughed. The staccato sound caused The Thing's head to snap around, and she stopped and bared her teeth at them.

"Barbar," she said. "Bar?"

Petronius and Spurius turned to Manlius.

"Danger?" asked Spurius.

"Are we lost?" asked Petronius.

The Thing unslung her pack and began to root around in it, finally withdrawing a strip of smoked meat. She started to chew on it. At them. Open-mouthed.

"Oh, a break," said Manlius.

"You're really an *excellent* translator, do you know that?" said Petronius, as he stripped off his gear and sat down with a grunt. "How you parsed that grammar is beyond me, it was so very complex. You are to be commended."

"Shut up," said Manlius. "Save your breath for when we start walking again."

And save his breath he did, during an extended debate wherein Manlius and Spurius tried to ascertain why their guide was taking them due north, when the river they'd wrecked along had flowed south, and according to what they'd understood from the barbarians during the council, the coastline went vaguely east.

Dubris and Rutupiae were both on the coast.

"Bar, bar*bar*," insisted The Thing, pointing northward, looking frustrated. She turned to Petronius, as if expecting him to agree with him. "Bar?"

Spurius looked unhappy. "She's saying ... *yes*," he said uncertainly.

"She's definitely saying yes," retorted Manlius, "the issue is, what is she saying yes about?"

Inevitable, thought Petronius, turning away from them. He'd known something like this would happen, the previous day's council had been a total mess. The barbarians, to their credit, had gone hunting and brought them a reasonable amount of food—a surprising show of hospitality—but beyond their understanding that the Romans would be hungry, Petronius had his doubts how much had been made clear to them.

"Well, 'stones' is 'bar,' I think," Manlius had said, as they sat around after the feast with a group of savages, all wearing their outlandish garb and facepaint, weapons clacking against each other whenever they shifted. He'd lifted a rock and pointed to it. "Bar?"

The barbarians had nodded enthusiastically, laughing and poking one another.

"All right. So what if we try ... *many piled stones?*" he had said to Nerva, the legion's general.

"You are the translator, not me," Nerva had replied. He hadn't snapped, but his tone had been rather brusque.

"Well, I mean, that's what the fort would look like to them, right? They build with wattle, daub, and thatch, far as I can tell. And 'people' is 'bar' so I'll … here we go."

Manlius had then turned and bowed to the man with the nicest sword and the crown on his head, a great barrel-chested personage with a penetrating gaze and a black beard streaked white. He was scarier than any person Petronius had ever seen, save for The Thing—who seemed deep in the man's council. She sat on his right side, idly scratching behind the ears of a ferocious-looking mongrel with keen, yellow eyes and a shaggy grey coat that lay panting at her feet.

Manlius cleared his throat. "Er, barbar bar, bar-*bar*?" He gestured to the assembled Romans. "Barbar."

"Barbarbarbarbar," the man with the crown on his head had replied, looking very perturbed. "Bar? Barbarbar, bar, bar-bar, barbarbarbar."

"Barbar," murmured the rest of the savages.

"Barbar," said The Thing, shaking her head. "*Bar*."

"Well?" Nerva had asked.

"I think he said there was such a place, far from here, but his people do not like to go there," Manlius had said uncertainly.

"You *think*?" Nerva crossed his arms over his chest. "Thinking is less useful than knowing."

Manlius had deflated somewhat at this reprimand, but nodded and turned back to the assembled savages.

"Barbar?" Manlius then said to the king or chief or whatever he was. "Barbar, bar, *bar*bar?"

"Bar," The Thing had shouted, leaping to her feet. Her dog had done the same, howling like a wolf.

"Barbarbar," the king had said to The Thing, and she'd sat back down again, looking mutinous. Then he'd said "Barbar, barbarbarbarbarbar, bar," to Manlius.

"He says that yes, he's sure there is a great place of piled stones, and that his people avoid it because it is, ah, dangerous." Manlius had laughed nervously. "He says that many great terrible battles were fought there by his people and that the enemy was legion and skilled. They wore armor and were 'like us' apparently."

"It does sound as if they'd been thrashed by the Roman army," Nerva had said.

"He says we should not go there, but he will assign us a guide if we will not be dissuaded." Manlius sounded unhappy.

"Well, even if they're leading us on some wild goose chase you'll have time enough to learn more of their language," mused Nerva. "We can try again when you get back."

"Yes," Manlius had agreed, not looking too pleased about the prospect of traveling with the party. "So … you intend to send me along?"

"Of course. You're the only one who can speak their language," Nerva had said. Then he'd pointed at Spurius. "You, Roman, shall lead the endeavor, by your own request. Manlius shall translate. I want you to travel light, and with great haste, so only one other in your party. Whom do you choose?"

Manlius had piped right up. "If Petronius came with us, he could keep a record of the mission."

Petronius' mouth had fallen open at this betrayal, but he'd shut it quickly when he saw The Thing pointing at him and whispering to the king. "I'm still, ah, recovering from my trials," he'd said, when he recovered his power of speech. "I shall slow everyone down, so—"

Nerva had silenced him with a dismissive wave of his hand. "All of us are still recovering. Some have severe injuries, broken legs and arms."

"I'm sure they—"

"Roman!" Nerva had shouted, pointing at a solider whose arm was in a sling. "Would *you* go, if asked?"

"Sir yes sir! I live only to serve Rome through my general's orders!" the soldier in question had cried, having stood the instant Nerva's eyes alighted on him. "Were my leg broken I would crawl to serve you, sir! Hail Caesar!"

"A bit wordy, but admirable nonetheless," Nerva had said wryly. "Now, Petronius, do you still think yourself unable?"

"I …" Petronius could find nary a sympathetic eye. The barbarians had looked amused; they might not speak Latin but they clearly knew a call-out when they saw one. The Thing's eyes in particular had been glued to his face; she openly laughed at him, snorting like a horse. "I shall go. Hail—hail Caesar."

"Horsemaster Bronius has already informed me that none of our surviving steeds are strong enough to bear riders," Nerva had said, and for a moment Petronius had a mad impulse to ask if the horses were not Roman enough to serve their Caesar, but decided it would be best to keep his mouth shut, "so you shall have to go on foot. Light armor and weapons only. Now, Manlius—tell them to elect a representative to guide you."

"Barbarbar," the king had replied, gesturing to The Thing. To

Petronius' deep surprise, she did not protest. Instead, she looked very sober indeed, and nodded once in assent.

"A *woman*?" Nerva's tone oozed incredulity.

"He says she is the best scout among his people," Manlius had said.

And now, of course, they were lost—or going to the wrong place—or something, thought Petronius, gazing out over the mist-wreathed, heathered hills.

"I just don't understand how we can be heading towards Dubris if we're going north," insisted Manlius in low tones when Spurius trotted off on an urgent natural errand. "We could be taking a short cut, I suppose."

"Or heading towards our deaths," said Petronius. "That seems far more likely."

Manlius did not reply, but shouldered his pack when he saw Spurius returning. Then the soldier doubled back and disappeared again.

"I wonder if their food disagrees with him," remarked Manlius.

"Surely not," said Petronius. "It's just that tortoises always lay two eggs."

Manlius laughed. "You're nasty. Is that true?"

"Of course. Everybody knows that." Petronius glanced up and groaned. "But here he comes again. Godsdamn it, that means back on our feet. I'm already tired of this adventure."

"Cheer up!" said Spurius, trotting back into camp. "You look glum as a hooked fish, Petronius. Let us sally forth—exercise is the best thing to chase away the blues, you know."

Petronius sighed.

***

Late in the day they left the hills behind them and entered a beech-wood. The dim light and rustling branches were spooky—even The Thing seemed nervous. She had made it very clear before they set foot in the forest they should make their way through the slender, parchment-barked trees as quickly as possible, though Manlius had not been able to ascertain why she felt so strongly about it. Not for lack of trying, to their mutual frustration: The conversation became heated after a time, and ended with The Thing cawing like a crow and then throwing up her hands in disgust when the Romans stared at her without an inkling of what she might be trying to tell them.

As it turned out, the forest was thick with ravens. They perched everywhere, on branches, upon fallen logs and stones; flapped through the treetops and hopped through the underbrush. They saw no other creatures.

"She was worried about the *birds?*" whispered Petronius.

"Bar," said The Thing, holding a finger to her lips as she trod lightly upon the loamy forest floor, her pace quick, her expression grim. She relaxed somewhat after they reached the other side, but would not let them make camp until they were some distance from the treeline. Even then she would not let them light a fire.

"I wish we could talk with her more," said Spurius, as they shivered in their cloaks, eating cold rations. At the sound of his voice The Thing looked up at them, but when he smiled and waved at her a little she scowled. "She must have had an amazing life."

"Do wild animals have amazing lives?" asked Petronius skeptically. "She rises with the sun, hunts, eats, shits, mates, and goes to bed when it's dark."

"Why, Petronius! She is a woman of strength and courage; a human with a culture! Look at her! Even just her jewelry, the inlaid sheath for her dagger—"

"I have heard it said that magpies bring back shining objects to decorate their nests," interrupted Petronius. "That doesn't mean they have a culture."

"She let me hold her sword earlier, it's well-balanced and the blade is keen. You do not give these people enough credit." Spurius shook his head. "If only we could understand one another, I wonder what she could tell us."

Petronius drew his cloak tighter about his shoulders. A chill wind ruffled his hair. "You are a soldier, which means you've killed for Rome," he said, "so you know that one day Romans will conquer this whole land. Like everyone else, her people will either die in battle, unremembered and unlamented by history ... or they will yield to the standard of Rome and become civilized Latin-speakers." He looked up at Spurius, who looked disturbed, smaller, perhaps, after this description of his career. "*Then*, maybe—if you yet live—you can find out what cradle-songs her mother sang her, and what she likes best for breakfast."

"By Jove," said Manlius, "you're a cynic."

"You're not married," countered Petronius. "Take her to wife, if you think her such a treasure! Or are you a hypocrite, who in his heart sees these savages as the very worms of the earth, as I—"

"Ssst," said The Thing.

The Romans fell silent, and then they heard it too—a crunching sound, as of leaves trampled by feet.

Something was coming.

Spurius' dagger was in his fist before Petronius had time to feel afraid. Manlius had his hand on the hilt of his borrowed *gladius*—had the translator ever undergone any martial training? Not even pretending to valor, Petronius elected to pull on his sandals, all the better to make a break for it if things got ugly.

It was less dark than the night before: A thin crescent moon shone through the scudding clouds, as did the myriad stars. Still, in the shadows of these strange hills, the light did little to help them see, and the small group was tense with anticipation.

Another crunch, then a whining that did not sound human.

Petronius' blood pounded in his ears. He was terrified, and began to slink away from the direction in which The Thing and Spurius squinted.

The Thing stepped forward, sword in hand. Spurius tried to step in front of her, indicating he would go first, but she shoved him so hard he was caught off balance and almost fell.

"Bar-bar!" she cried in the blackness, taking a step forward. "Bar!"

The sound of quickened footfalls on the earth, and then something bounded out of the blackness and struck her in the chest. With a cry she fell backwards and hit the ground, and Spurius, steady on his feet again, rushed over—and then began to laugh.

"It's all right!" he cried. "It's—come and see!"

Petronius, nonplussed, cautiously returned to camp, and found The Thing laughing as the mongrel that had sat at her feet during the council licked her face raw. She seemed to have mixed feelings about his presence: While she cooed at and petted the dog, jabbering at him fondly, she kept looking worriedly into the darkness around them.

"Barbar," she said with a nod to Spurius, when he made motions as if he, too, would like to pet the animal. He reached out his hand and the dog snapped at him. The Thing laughed—but so did Spurius, which brought a ghastly smile to her face.

"Spurius," said Spurius, pointing at his chest. He pointed at her and said the name Petroinius couldn't even begin to puzzle out, and she nodded. Then he pointed at the dog.

She said something. Spurius repeated it, and she nodded at him, smiling.

Petronius shook his head. "Gods," he muttered to Manlius. "And now a menagerie."

"What is *wrong* with you?" said Manlius.

"Hey, *you* volunteered *me*. If you didn't want my company ..."

"You were talking the other night about wanting to do an ethnography of these people!" he snapped. "I thought you'd jump at the chance."

"I don't even have anything to write on!"

"You can do it later, though it escapes me why you would memorialize them at all if you hate them so much? What will your description be of these 'wild animals' with their culture you think no more of than a magpie's hoard?"

This took Petronius slightly aback. Manlius' accusation wounded him. "I will tell the truth—that they have rudimentary language skills, little architecture or agriculture, some barely-domesticated animals, vicious weaponry for war-waging, women who have no sense of their place—"

"Ugh," said Manlius. "I don't think so much of them as Spurius over there, but you're being a real asshole, you know that?"

"Whatever," said Petronius. "I'm going to get some sleep."

"Good."

"Good then." And, still feeling hateful, Petronius called into the darkness, "Just remember, Spurius—lie down with dogs, wake up with fleas!"

"You know, I've always admired dogs," replied Spurius. "Just think how nice it must be to have big teeth and strong paws! And their pack culture! Why, once I—"

Petronius pulled his cloak over his ears in disgust.

***

The next morning they broke camp at first light and continued to head due north. The countryside became increasingly hostile, steep knolls of flinty earth with fewer stands of trees and more scrubby bushes, and shocks of brown grasses that cut the skin if the travelers happened to brush up against them.

The Thing had seemed ill at ease when she woke them, and during the day quickened her pace, increasingly edgy. She allowed fewer breaks, and when Manlius tried to talk to her, she hushed him with a glance at the grey, featureless sky. Petronius wondered if she was disturbed by the ravens that circled overhead, the way they seemed to be following the party, and how they would all caw riotously for a time and then fall silent for hours.

Around mid-day they finally took a rest in the shade of a trough between two great hummocks. One of the coal-black birds landed on a nearby boulder. Petronius was surprised to see how large it was, it would have dwarfed the sea-hawks that he had used to shy rocks at when he was a boy. It was nasty, too—when The Thing's mongrel frisked up to the bird playfully, it screamed like a woman and winged upwards only to dive at the dog's eyes, beak snapping. The dog turned away just in time, slinking back to The Thing's side as the raven winged away from them.

"I was wrong," said Petronius to Manlius.

"Come around a bit, have you?" said Manlius coldly.

"No. It's just that I was wrong when I said that where we wrecked was the worst place in the world," said Petronius, through a mouthful of biscuit. "This is *far* worse."

"I think it has its own natural beauty," said Spurius, looking around at the jagged, colorless boulders that sat stark and foreboding against the washed-out sky. He gestured to The Thing. "Diana among the rocks. Catchy, eh?"

"Bar," said The Thing, getting to her feet. She stuck out her hand to Petronius, and he realized she was offering to help him stand. He swatted her away. Her face darkened, her hand went to her belt knife—the one she had thrown at him—but then she laughed at him mockingly and donned her pack. Clicking to her dog she began to trot away from them.

In silence they walked on, for they needed all their breath as they switchbacked up and back down the steepest ridges yet, yammered at all the while by murders of ravens. Petronius idly thought the birds might be laughing at them, but then checked himself. That way lay madness.

Then, when the sun had sunk halfway down the sky, they crested a high butte—Petronius and Manlius were gasping, and even Spurius looked weary—and The Thing gestured at what lay directly in front of them. Her dog barked and wagged his tail.

"Barbar," she said.

"We're ... here?" said Manlius, brow furrowed. "What the—oh, *shit*."

The place was no Roman stockade, but a great wasteland of strange black monoliths that were indeed surrounded by primitive fortifications. These looked immemorially ancient, and in places had collapsed, but where the ruins survived the stones were indeed piled high upon one another, and the shattered weaponry and human skeletons littering the earth certainly showed many battles had been fought there. A charnel stench emanated from the place, nauseating them whenever the wind kicked up—Petronius saw through a break in the rudimentary wall that a large carcass of some enormous creature decomposing among the menhirs.

"*Bar*-bar," said The Thing, and trotted inside the wall. Her dog whined, but she *bar*-ed at him sternly and he sat, whimpering, as his mistress proceeded alone.

"Jupiter's bunions," swore Petronius, as they followed her. The place looked even worse from the inside, and the odor of the nearby dead scaly thing was overpowering. Petronius pulled his cloak over his nose. "Motherfucker. I can't believe this, we came all this way and for *what*? Some sort of spooky Britannic boneyard! I'd bet ten *denarii* that these godsdamned skeletons come to life and kill us so we can join their undead ranks."

"You have a very fine imagination," said Spurius admiringly, "but that seems unlikely. Clearly," he said her name, "just misunderstood, but I think Manlius and I have really gotten some good insights into her language during our trip, so—"

"Shut the fuck up, Spurius," hissed Manlius, to Spurius' and Petronius' great surprise. His eyes were glued to the sky. "We need to get out of here, *now*."

A great shadow fell over them, and, looking up, Petronius went weak in the knees. An enormous raven, a raven that could have been the grandmother of all ravens, glided silently over them and landed on the closest monolith, right above where they stood beside the corpse. It perched there, peering at them. Then it hopped down, landing on the other side of the dead monster. It set to pulling at the rotting meat clinging to the carcass.

Petronius was horrified to note it had *teeth*. Two rows of them, like a shark.

"Manlius is right," he whispered, "we should—"
Welcome to the feast.

Petronius screamed and slapped his hand to his eyes; they felt like they were going to burst from sudden, painful pressure. He heard noises from the rest of his party, shouts, and even howls from the stupid dog beyond the perimeter. Apparently they had all heard the monster speak. It occurred to Petronius that it hadn't talked with its mouth. It also occurred to him that it had spoken in the Latin dialect used in Syracuse. Petronius wondered if The Thing understood its speech—if they all heard the language most familiar to them ...

The monster spoke again, and Petronius fell to his knees from the pain of it.

We thought it was this you sought. Well, eat! Make merry! You are our guests. Fewer and fewer of your kind come here, to worship at these stones. Let us be friends!

Something wet and hot was trickling over his lips, and Petronius, removing his palms, saw blood was flowing from some part of his face. His vision cleared, but he wished it hadn't—looking at the creepy giant raven gobbling the putrid corpse of a red reptilian horror with its awful bird-teeth was more than he could bear.

Relax. Eat. Rest.

The monster's advice suddenly seemed reasonable. He *was* hungry, after all ...

The enormous bird looked right at him. *Yes. You sense it, the power of the dreigiau's flesh! You seek the power of wishes, do you not? That is why you have come—so, eat!*

Not exactly, but whatever, thought Petronius, as he bent down and tore a strip of flesh from the carcass. He idly chewed the tough, rancid meat, feeling deeply at peace.

Why do you resist me?

Petronius was confused. How was he resisting? Looking at Spurius and Manlius, he saw they had also relaxed somewhat, though neither had tucked in, as he had.

But then he saw The Thing.

She yet stood, the corners of her eyes and both nostrils bleeding freely; sword out, she was brandishing her weapon valiantly.

"Barbarbarbar*bar*bar!" she screamed, and then, with a cry, she launched herself at the giant raven.

It was as surprised as Petronius, apparently, for it wasn't until The Thing got close that it began to flap away from the dead creature. Its hesitation cost it badly: with a single heavy, precise stroke she lopped off one of the claws on its right foot, which spurted viscous black blood all over her. It swiped at her with the other foot and caught her across the face, opening a diagonal wound from her right forehead down her nose onto her left cheek. Gore dripped into her already bloody eyes as it launched itself atop the tallest menhir.

Undeterred by its retreat, she dropped her sword, wiped her eyes, dried her hands on her wool tunic, and got out her bow; in the blink of an eye she braced the string, nocked an arrow, and aimed. The string twanged as she loosed it. The arrow hit the creature square in the right eye.

It screamed—not aloud, but in their minds. Overwhelmed, they all collapsed, even The Thing.

How dare *you!*

The Thing shouted something back at it, still on her knees, struggled to once again lift her bow.

Serpents! Vile worms! You shall be crushed, ground into dust, and the dust shall blow over this unremembered place! Your souls will—

Another of The Thing's arrows winged into the monster, this time embedding in its right nostril and spreading a bloody spider web of fissures across its beak. With an audible shriek, it launched off of the monolith and dove at her, but it could not open its maw wide enough to bite due to the lodged arrow. Instead it tried to drop on her like a falcon, claws outstretched, but she was too quick. Her sword seemed to jump into her hand, and she struck with the edge; the blade hit the creature in its left ankle—and stuck there.

Petronius watched, somewhat impressed, as she held onto the grip with both hands as the monster tried to flap away from her. The enormous muscles in her arms bulged and rippled as she tried to wrest her blade from its bone—or whatever—and Petronius didn't need a grasp of her language to tell she was swearing at it.

"To her, Romans!" cried Spurius, staggering dizzily to his feet and unsheathing his *spatha*. His eyes were crimson with blood but he rushed at their adversary and shaved off the tips of some of the feathers of its left wing with his first strike, but this just seemed to make the bird that much more furious. It kicked at him with its wounded but unencumbered right foot, opening a jagged gash along Spurius' left arm.

Manlius, apparently inspired, picked up his borrowed *gladius* and screamed "Come *on*, Petronius!" before charging into the fray, swinging so widely he endangered The Thing and Spurius more than the monster, in Petronius' opinion.

"Fuck that," the historian muttered, instead slinking behind an adjacent monolith—he might yet be able to escape if things turned dire for his party. Peeking around the side, it seemed the battle could go either way. The Thing had gotten her blade free of the monster and had managed to break its leg in the doing; its foot hung at a grotesque angle as it flapped in the air. Hovering over them, it struck only with its right foot now. It knocked Manlius in the forehead; he dropped like a stone and Spurius tried to draw the creature away from his body so he would not be trampled.

The Thing did not seem much to care for her fallen comrade's welfare. Holding her sword in both hands, she swung it over her head and chopped at the wound in the creature's left foot. This time she severed it, and it flopped to the ground on top of Manlius, oozing all over him.

The monster was bleeding badly now, and squawking like a fussy chicken. Spurius, arms trembling, struck it in the body with his sword. The bird crashed down on top of the soldier, pinning him. He cried out—the writhing creature was massive—but The Thing jumped away in time and, screeching something that sounded like the wailing of Furies, hacked at the bird's thick, feathered neck. The monster stilled after the first blow, but it took many swipes to chop through its spine, Spurius grunting with each impact. Eventually she severed its head, and then spat on the body.

It was very quiet for a moment, and then she began to sing a low, spooky song over the dead monster, which brought her dog to her side. It frisked beside her, jumping up and licking whatever patches of her skin he could reach. She either finished her song or broke off mid-stream, who knew, and sternly said something that calmed the mongrel—*bar*, probably—but she could not keep the grin from her bloody face as she turned back to the body of the monster.

It was then that it occurred to Petronius, as he watched The Thing try to rock the heavy corpse off of Spurius, that he was in deep shit. First he had succumbed to the creature's seductive magics, then he had failed to aid his companions. Manlius' abortive attempt to help had still been exactly that; he knew his cowardice would not go over well with this crew. Maybe ... maybe he should pretend to have fainted? No, too late for that, The Thing had seen him crouching behind the monolith, conscious and whole. Lip curling, she spat at him, then gave a tremendous push on the corpse that finally freed Spurius. Gasping, he sat up, and looked deep into her eyes.

She smiled down at him.

"Unngh," came a feeble cry from beside the monster's body. Manlius sat up, shoving aside the monster's severed foot with one hand as he held his bleeding forehead with the other. "Oh, you're both alive, too! But where's Petronius? Did he survive?"

***

Petronius tried to tell himself he didn't care that he was in disgrace as the battered party made their way slowly back to the Roman camp. Fuck them, fuck them all—the happy couple, who set to making out every time they thought themselves unobserved, the dog, who now loved Spurius, and Manlius, who acted like he'd saved the fucking day even though in reality he'd been even less helpful than Petronius if you really thought about it. He hadn't landed a single blow, and his unconscious body had hindered the warriors' assault. But whatever. They'd be back soon enough, and maybe, Petronius thought, he'd actually done well as far as his future welfare was concerned. Surely now he would not be asked to attend the next expedition in search of the other Romans stationed here in Britannia.

Due to the various injuries and general exhaustion—and the occasional petty assault by flocks of angry crows—it took them twice as long to cover the same ground. On the fourth morning of the return trip they saw smoke on the horizon, and when they stumbled out of the forest onto the riverbank that afternoon, Petronius was all smiles like the rest of them. He'd never been so happy to see a Roman encampment, and he basked in the shared glory of a successful return … until the story came out. Spurius, that goody two-sandals, told the general everything. Well, everything except for Petronius' carrion-eating, but Petronius sensed that was less a desire to shield his fellow man from shame and more that Spurius had simply failed to observe the incident.

"You should be crucified," said General Nerva, "but I shall spare your life, for you are useful in your way. As long as you make a record of the adventure, that is—with all the details of your part in it. I want all of Rome to know you for what you are."

"Sir, I—"

"Don't you dare call me sir. Were you under my command I *would* crucify you," said Nerva. "Just … be quiet and keep to yourself until we decide what next to do. I wouldn't even give you leave to come to the celebratory feast, but King," he said a name that sounded like 'Barbarbar' to Petronius, "wants you there." Nerva looked thoughtful. "Maybe *he* wants to crucify you. I'd allow that."

"You are generosity itself," said Petronius sourly, but that incensed the general to such a degree that the scholar fled to the lean-to by the cesspit that was to be his shelter, and sat there until nightfall, brooding.

He sat alone at the feast, too. Manlius, Spurius, and The Thing sat with the King, getting all the choicest cuts of venison and wild boar, and enjoying the bouquets of wildflowers, jewelry, and fine weapons given to them by other members of the clan. The tale of the adventure was told simultaneously by Manlius and The Thing, to everyone's delight but Petronius', for he found his only mentions in the tale were as the sniveling comic relief.

After they'd finished their retelling, the king stood. Holding up his hands, he called for silence.

"Barbarbar," he said. "Bar."

"Ah, the King would like to … announce? Make an announcement," supplied Manlius.

"Barbarbar-bar, bar," said the king. The Thing stood. Petronius saw she was *blushing*. Gross!

"A …" Manlius said something in quiet tones, and the king nodded. "Betrothal! He's announcing that his daughter—what?" More discussion. "She's his daughter, everyone! Well, she's engaged to …"

"Barbar," said the king, pointing straight at Petronius.

The silence was absolute.

"Bar?!" cried The Thing.

"What?" even the unflappable Spurius appeared bothered by the news.

"I'm already married!" protested Petronius.

Manlius was deep in conversation with the king, who was looking increasingly annoyed at having his decision questioned. The Thing was cawing like the terrible ravens that had bothered them on the way to and from the boneyard, and Spurius had gotten to his feet.

"He says he has heard much of Patronius' cowardice," explained Manlius to the confused Romans. "And he says having a coward for a husband will enable his daughter to have a family but still live the life she wants, for he can cook and clean and raise the babies while she hunts and goes to war," said Manlius, looking rather entertained as he turned to address Petronius directly.

"Bar!" cried the king, extending his hand to the bewildered Petronius. "Bar!" he said to his daughter, who reluctantly put her hand in his, looking helplessly at Spurius. When Petronius joined them, the king pushed them together and said some words.

"Congratulations," said Manlius, after the celebration began anew—more soberly on the part of the barbarians, more hilariously on the Roman side, who jeered as they drank deeply of the savages' liquor. "Best wishes on a happy marriage, may Vesta bless, and all that."

"Really?" said Petronius, looking at where his bride spoke animatedly to Spurius just inside the treeline. "Yes, it's very amusing, but what am I to *do*?"

"Looks like get cuckolded," said Manlius, as The Thing pulled Spurius behind a tree, and then he ambled off.

Petronius' guts tightened. "Like hell I am," he mumbled to himself, and strode over to where the lovers giggled in a shadowy glade. They were talking quickly in hushed voices, and exchanging loving touches. Petronius was having none of it.

"Hi Spurius," he said brightly, stepping out from behind a tree. "How's my wife?"

"Oh—Petronius," said Spurius, looking up. "No hard feelings? I mean, she doesn't want to, and you don't want to, so we'll just pretend. She'll come with us, and when we get back to Rome we'll—"

"What are you babbling about?" said Petronius. He was so fucking sick of Spurius, his smug kindness, his handsome face, his stupidity. "I'm here to make sure you don't take what's mine—it's my wedding night, you know."

"Petronius." Spurius' voice was taught as a bowstring. "You can't be serious."

"Serious as a heart attack."

The Thing hadn't said a word, but was looking back and forth between the two men with keen interest. Petronius gazed at her without fear, and was pleased to see she clearly resented this.

"It's outrageous. It's, it's—" Spurius was sweating, Petronius saw it glistening on his forehead. "I'll kill you before I let you touch her!"

"No, I don't think you will," said Petronius. He felt drunk, he was so happy to be in control of the situation for once. "Not in front of these people—think of what her father would do. He'd probably blame his daughter—and what would that mean for her?"

"Bar?" said The Thing, looking at Spurius. Spurius answered her, and her face darkened the more he spoke. "Bar!" she cried. "Bar!" Her hand went to the knife at her belt, and she looked right at Petronius. "Bar-bar!"

"You'd better tell her the way the wind's blowing," said Petronius smugly. "She'll need to shape up if she wants to better herself by becoming a good Roman woma—*urghhh*!"

The thin-bladed dagger stuck out of his chest, just slightly to the left of his sternum. Petronius could feel his heart struggling to beat around it.

"You!" he managed, looking into The Thing's eyes.

"Bar bar," she said, and spat in his face.

Petronius fell to his knees.

"Take her life! Avenge me!" he cried, looking up at Spurius. "A savage has killed your countryman, Roman! To arms!"

Spurius said something to The Thing in urgent tones. She nodded, and they both fled away from the camp and into the blackness of the forest.

Petronius, shocked, began to laugh. Spurius Calipash had to be the biggest hypocrite in the world, to enthuse so constantly over Roman this and Roman that, only to side with and then nip off with some savage slattern when it came down to it.

Oh, how he hated Spurius! He hated him too much to wish him misery in this life alone—he wanted with all his heart for the Calipash name to become disgraceful in every way that would be offensive to the soldier: Infamous among respectable citizens, associated with nefarious rather than for honorable deeds, and eventually deemed too worthless to hold a place in the historical record, excised rather than celebrated by future generations. To have his name and his heirs relegated to dark whispering and nefarious marginalia—yes, that would be a fitting memorial in every way.

Petronius' mouth tasted strange—at first he was reminded of the flesh of the putrid monster he'd snacked on, but then he realized it was just that a bubble of his own blood had pushed up his throat and popped between his teeth. Then a curious wind began to blow, sweeping past Petronius and deep into the wood as he laughed at the notion of anyone associating the Calipash name with iniquity.

No, if he wanted to punish Spurius, he would have to do it himself. Though he felt his life ebbing away, Petronius staggered to his feet and lurched back towards the shore, where campfires blazed and the smell of roasted meats perfumed the night air.

"Romans!" he cried, breaking from the treeline. "We are betrayed!"

Those closest to him paused, and Petronius smiled as he wrested the dagger from his own chest. The wound spurted black blood; the firelight was dimming to his eyes though he knew it burned just as bright as it had a moment ago.

"A barbarian dagger to the heart!" he shouted, holding it aloft with the last of his strength. "An ambush! They come for us, to kill us while we make merry! To arms, Romans! To arms!"

"To arms!" cried someone.

And then Petronius died, the last sound he heard that of myriad Roman swords being drawn from their sheaths.

Author's Note
—and—
Acknowledgements

Of how I came into possession of the original documents chronicling the long history of the Calipash family I can say only that they were bequeathed to me by Oliver Hubert Sandys, my lover in the early days of my college career, just before his researches into the mutability of human flesh when subjected to strange extracts from specimens of the order Cucurbitales, gathered on certain far-flung plateaus, turned him permanently into a begonia. At the time, I had to comfort myself knowing that the transformation was at least apropos; dearest Oliver could never stand full sun, and the delicate peach-colored blossoms that he still produces year-round yet recall to my mind his clear skin and winsome smile.

For some years, my grief over Oliver's untimely transmutation was too near to pay any heed to his strange collection of folios, church records, legal documents, diaries, journal publications, newspapers, and other sundry archives. I knew that he was a distant relation of an extinct, notorious family of once-impressive property and wealth; I never suspected that years later, in the course of my researches for my Master's degree, I would discover a reference to that same family in the marginalia penned by Samuel Clemens into his personal copy of Sarah Grand's *The Heavenly Twins* (1893), a photocopy of which the archivists of the Berg Collection at the New York Public Library were kind enough to send to me. While I do not wholly agree with Mr. Clemens' remark that "a cat could do better literature than [*The Heavenly Twins*],"[1] I was fascinated by this comment I found later in the text: "Between the first stanza of Holmes' poem "Truths" that opens this farce, and the characters of the mischievous twins Angelica and Diavolo, I wonder if Madam Grand was acquainted with those queer Calipashes, who never terrorized England as much as she has done with this work of fiction."

Upon reading those words, I felt myself aflame with new passion,

---

1 Well, a cat could probably do better than the ending of that novel, but parts in the middle are really quite good.

new purpose! At long last I had discovered a real contribution I could make to academia, and one which I was in a unique position to present. Turning to my Oliver, who was blooming prettily on my desk, in that moment I resolved to change the focus of my career. Instead of continuing with my work on how the ideas of amelioration versus abolition of slavery were represented in popular British literature of the 18th and 19th centuries, I would dedicate myself to researching and recording the strange history of the Calipash family. Even a brief perusal of what I possessed showed me a deep treasure-trove of unrecorded, unknown incidents that fascinated me. I hoped my advisor and major professors would feel the same.

Little did I know that I would be cast out of my program for my resolve to bring to light the lost saga of this debauched, unlamented clan of aristocrats, but that is what happened. My advisor knew too well the whispered rumors of the Calipash family, and told me in no uncertain terms that if I was truly determined to dedicate myself to this effort, he would move to withdraw my funding immediately. But I would not allow myself to be bullied by those without vision, and thus the work you have just read is entirely an amateur effort. I have endeavored to make it scholarly and accessible in equal measure; you, dear reader, must be the judge of whether I was successful.

The first piece in this collection, "A Spotted Trouble at Dolor-on-the-Downs," I transcribed after discovering that Oliver's documents contained several pages torn from the Junior Ganymede Club for Gentlemen's Personal Gentleman's "Club Book." (NB: I have since returned those pages to that club for re-inclusion.) The Junior Ganymede Club is, of course, best known for its most celebrated member: Reginald Jeeves, valet to Wodehouse's beloved subject, Bertram Wilberforce "Bertie" Wooster, Lord Yaxley. The only addition to Jeeves' record of those strange events at the Marine Vivarium is the title, which I hope would please both Mr. Wodehouse and Jeeves himself. I know the content of this piece may disturb Jeeves fans, for he fails to liberate those unfortunate victims of Cirrina's diabolic schemes. I, too, was surprised by his actions; I can only conclude that despite his powerful brain, there is only so much even that paragon of English virtue could do when faced with some of the stranger realities of this world. Yet his legacy is not a small one: He did singlehandedly end the Calipash family's legacy of petty horrors, and that is no mean feat.

The second piece, "The Hour of the Tortoise," was compiled largely from the diaries of the unfortunate Chelone Burchell, though I have modernized Chelone's spellings and included some exposition explaining the conclusion of that young woman's sad fate. I have also expanded the sections of her aborted pornographic novella based on her own writings in surviving editions of *Milady's Ruby Vase*. I believe my passion for the excellent, unusual—and sometimes unusually disturbing—pornography produced by writers in the late 19th century put me in a unique position of doing her some justice in this regard, and I hope readers who enjoy her passion and voice will investigate the delights, disturbing and titillating alike, of her contemporaries. Titles published by William Lazenby, including the magazine *The Pearl*, are a good start, as they contain excellent work by Algernon Charles Swinburne, "Jack Saul," and other fine authors.

Regarding "The Infernal History of the Ivybridge Twins," several errors have been corrected in this revised second edition. The original piece was my first effort at recording the Calipash family's sordid past, and when I submitted it to the editors at Innsmouth Free Press for their anthology *Historical Lovecraft* (2011), I never expected them to take it, much less for it to be reprinted in Night Shade Book's *The Book of Cthulhu* (2011), much less inspire my dear editor Cameron Pierce to request an entire collection of the family's history be brought to the public's attention by this humble scholar. For that reason, I felt free, for the purposes of storytelling, to bend, or tinker with, certain details, such as Rosemary's use of her foremother Honor's alchemical texts to switch bodies with her mother. Additionally, to the father Calipash I originally gave the name St John, as it is a Calipash family favorite. His actual Christian appellation appears in only one surviving document, and it is smudged. The name on the register may well be St John, but to keep things clear in this manuscript I have reassigned him as Clement, another popular family name.

A Pretty Mouth is one of the two pieces in this collection I had to do the most outside research for, and thus it consists of mostly my own extrapolation, collation, and, if I may, writerly voice. I had at my disposal only Honor's treatise on soul-exchange via blood transfusion—written, I should mention, entirely in ancient Greek, so I must here thank Dr. John Marincola, department chair and Leon Golden Professor of Classics at Florida State University, for his exemplary instruction in the fundamentals of that wonderful language—and a bundle of Henry's letters, all of which had been returned to Calipash Manor by their recipients due to their perceived insanity. That it is recorded by later Calipashes that "Mrs. Godfrey Vincent" was sent to live out her days "away from any potentially exciting influences" (a delicate way of, I suspect, conveying that she was sent to Bedlam or a similar institution) after producing two female children, and, finally, one male heir, is indeed sobering.

Henry's letters provided the backbone of *A Pretty Mouth*, but his bombastic style and poor grammar forced me to choose a different way of presenting his story. I also had to fill in the cracks, as it were, with such books as *Blood Work* by Holly Tucker and *A Profane Wit: The Life of John Wilmot, Earl of Rochester* by James William Johnson. Details of student life at Wadham, during the Restoration, were supplied by the latter of those two, as well as *Wadham College* by Jane Garnett and C.S.L. Davies.

The final piece of the Calipash puzzle, "Damnatio Memoriae," is also largely extrapolated, though hints as to what really happened during that blighted mission to build a lighthouse across the channel from Portus Itius appear in *Unaussprechlichen Kulten*, or *Nameless Cults*. In particular, there is mention of a "Queen Barbara," of whom it was said bravely slew some sort of winged horror, and of her consort, a once-famous warrior by the name of Spurius Calipash, who became outcast for abandoning Rome and living as a barbarian. Additionally, comparisons between the Germanic peoples and a tribe of rather unusual Britons that seem to have died out during Caligula's reign exist in a variant copy of Tacitus' *Germania* I was able to obtain via interlibrary loan from Colorado State University (many thanks to a certain good friend and scholar at CU who facilitated this, and several other research-related *coup d'états*). This helped flesh out The Thing's tribe; Petronius' character I have extrapolated from the tone of his only work, *The History of Sicily*, which was part of Oliver's collection. The rest is my own.

There are, of course, other generations of Calipash twins who do not appear in this collection; thoroughly researching this family will be the work of a lifetime. Despite its omissions, inaccuracies, and depravity, I hope *A Pretty Mouth* is as enjoyable to read as it was to research and write. It is truly a pleasure to be able to finally present this work to the general public.

***

I would like to thank the following people for their help with *A Pretty Mouth*, be it encouraging me during the writing process, reading or editing the manuscript, advising or believing in me, or inspiring various

Gove, my personal cheerleading squad (and hunky dreamboat friend) Jesse Bullington, my tolerant, brilliant BFF Raechel Dumas, Cameron Pierce, Nick Mamatas, Cameron McClure, Livia Llewellyn, J.T. Glover, Brooke Ehrlich, Alan M. Clark and Gina Guadagnino, Silvia Moreno-Garcia and Ross E. Lockhart, Michael Nyman, Sarah Grand, the fine folk at Folsom Street Coffee, H. P. Lovecraft, Candace Ward, P. G. Wodehouse, Kirsten Alene Pierce, and, of course, my parents.

About the Author

Molly Tanzer lives in Boulder, Colorado along the front range of the Mountains of Madness, or maybe just the Flatirons. She is a freelance writer and editor by trade, and also works as the administrative overlord for Clockpunk Studios, and as the assistant to the publisher at Prime Books. Her work has appeared in, among other venues, *The Book of Cthulhu* (Volumes 1 and 2), *Future Lovecraft*, and *Running with the Pack*, and is forthcoming in *Fungi* and *The Starry Wisdom Library*. She blogs—infrequently—about hiking, vegan cooking, movies, and other stuff at http://mollytanzer.com, and tweets as @molly_the_tanz.

LAZY FACIST 2012

The Obese by Nick Antosca
Anatomy Courses by Blake Butler and Sean Kilpatrick
A Parliament of Crows by Alan M. Clark
The Last Final Girl by Stephen Graham Jones
Zombie Bake-Off by Stephen Graham Jones
Chick Bassist by Ross E. Lockhart
The Collected Works of Scott McClanahan Vol. I by Scott McClanahan
The Devil in Kansas by David Ohle
Frowns Need Friends Too by Sam Pink
I Am Going to Clone Myself Then Kill the Clone and Eat It by Sam Pink
No One Can Do Anything Worse to You than You Can by Sam Pink
Rontel by Sam Pink
Broken Piano for President by Patrick Wensink
Everything Was Great Until It Sucked by Patrick Wensink

COMING IN 2013

Moon Babes of Bicycle City by Mike Daily
Zombie Sharks with Metal Teeth by Stephen Graham Jones
The Doom That Came to Lolcats by Douglas Lain
The Humble Assessment by Kris Saknussemm
Dyldoe: A Novel by Molly Tanzer
Colony Collapse by J.A. Tyler
Expletive Deleted by Patrick Wensink

Plus many more!